ALL POWERFUL:
THE HUNTED

Sarah J. Simon

For Grandpa Don and Grammy Joy, I hope you've found peace.

Chapter I: Orphan

Some things in life are inevitable.

A man receiving an eviction notice from the landlord after refusing to pay rent for three months—inevitable. A weeping mother newly informed of her son's death, a family pet being released from its misery after suffering from a cancerous tumor in its leg—inevitable. A mother dove abandoning her nest upon discovering a reckless human knocked it out of a tree; a broken collarbone when a drunk driver rear-ends a businessman on his way home from work in the city—all inevitable.

As Fate would have it, the pain my abilities were going to cause me was inexorable; inescapable, unavoidable, predestined, or whatever other synonym you can think of.

I never saw it coming; in more ways than one, my powers are both a gift and a curse. I never wanted them, nor asked for this burden to be put on my shoulders. They are something that I alone will always have to control, whether that means I live or die. It was on that fateful night, when the stars seemed to twinkle too bright in the dark sky, and the moon too full, when Fate would prove to be an unstoppable force— when my parents were murdered.

It was on that night, the fourteenth of October, that I realized that nothing was ever going to be the same.

☾

"Earth to Nekoda... *hellooo*? The bell rang five minutes ago! C'mon, it's time for lunch!" There was a flash of pale skin in my peripheral vision, and then the quick sound of snapping fingers in my ear.

3

"What the—? Oh, *crap!*" I jerked up from the rickety desk, a sheet of blank paper stuck to my cheek from where drool had dried. I rubbed the sleep out of my eyes and shoved the unfinished math packet into my binder.

"*Girl*, this is the third time you've fallen asleep in Mr. Brannan's class! What's up with you?" Logan Hendrix, my best friend at Weedsport High School, stood in front of my desk with her arms crossed, an annoyed look plastered on her usually cheerful complexion.

"I know, I know, and if I get another C in Algebra this year, my parents will literally kill me! Or worse, turn off the WiFi after 8 o'clock!" I huffed.

"Yeah, and you promised me we would have a Studio Ghibli marathon this weekend!"

"Ack, we will, we will. Hand me my orange folder."

"Oh, relax, you two. Kody, you can study during lunch. And besides, I can always give you the test answers after I take it." Maggie Landrus, my other best friend, was a math whiz. She bore tumbling locks and piercing eyes behind the frames of her glasses. Maggie is comedically tall for her age. She towers over half the students in our school. It's quite entertaining to watch her participate in P.E., particularly when the jocks all run for cover during dodgeball.

Logan and I resemble each other in many ways: the same light blonde hair, stormy grey-blue eyes and small stature. The only difference was that Logan stood at 5'2, and I was a humiliating 4'11.

I slung the strap of my backpack over one shoulder and made for the door. Together, Maggie and Logan grabbed my wrists and hauled me through the swarm of bustling students.

We speed-walked down the green and white- painted hallway, took a left, turned right, and then sauntered into the

4

cafeteria. Our school's lunchroom was like a literal zoo, as expected of most high schools. A cacophony of voices greeted us as we entered the spacious room full of crowded tables and teenagers who, just like myself, deal with matters pertaining to the repetitious daily struggle of school. Or Hell, as I deemed it.

The junior high and high school students mingled together within the same room, stereotypical kids sticking to their group of friends. Everyone knew who they belonged with, or were just trying to fit in. Our table was set between the jocks and computer nerds; we're not too popular, yet not too despised. I am fifteen and in tenth grade, but will be turning sixteen on February 5th. But that didn't stop naïve middle schoolers from mistaking me as one of their own from time to time.

Maggie and I inched our way through the lunch line and went to find the old textbook Logan had chucked on the corner table to claim our spot on the popularized side of the cafeteria. We sat down to eat our semi-cooked meals.

"So, do you gals want to go to the movies with my boyfriend and I on Saturday?" I asked my friends in between bites of hot lunch, ignoring the side eyes from other high schoolers as I shoveled the prepackaged food into my mouth. Most kids thought school lunches to be disgusting, but to a teenage girl with an appetite larger than herself, I wasn't one to complain, especially since I couldn't yet drive myself home for lunch.

"You mean your *imaginary* boyfriend. And no, not if Jared hogs all the popcorn again." Logan said, with a sly wink. It made me feel much better about my pathetic love life when she played along.

"Yes, of course we will." Maggie said, rolling her eyes at the two of us. We burst out laughing, if only to hide the fact that not once had the three of us hung out on the weekend with somebody other than each other. After we finished eating, I spent the last ten minutes fretting over the complicated equations written on the rumpled math packet. I dumped my trash and trudged over to room 156—Algebra.

I groaned, catching a few odd stares from passing students. "I'd rather run three miles in the freezing rain right now than fail yet *another* test."

"Shush. Trust me, you'll do fine," Maggie reassured. There was a piercing ring as the bell tolled for next period, and Logan sent a thumbs up in my direction before walking off to History.

I sighed. If only.

☾

"Excuse me, Mr. Baker? Mister? Erm, is there any way that I could get extra credit to change this test grade?" I asked my Algebra 2 teacher, shuffling from foot to foot in front of his chair. He was short and squat with greasy black hair and a fuzzy mustache, and was sporting a Green Bay Packers belt buckle that made him look even more robust than he was. He fought the urge to roll his eyes; Mr. Baker was constantly annoyed with everyone, or constipated.

He grunted, "No, Nekoda, you can't. It's your final test score until the end of the second quarter. Sorry, but you missed your chance three weeks ago. Good day." Then he went back to scrolling through Facebook, turning away from me. Welp, that was my que to leave.

I hadn't been doing so hot this semester, grade *or* life-like. I had suffered a series of emotional pitfalls since I first started my sophomore year of high school. It had not been a good beginning to the start of my life that would determine my future.

I turned and walked out the door, crumpling the piece of paper into a ball, and tossed it in the trash bin outside the office.

6

☾

"Mom, Dad, I'm home!" I announced, entering through the front door.

"We're in the living room!" Dad yelled back, his voice echoing off the high ceiling.

"Remember to take off your shoes, Kody." I heard my mom call from somewhere within the house. I kicked off my Converse, hung up my jacket and backpack, and walked down the hallway that veered off from the staircase and into the living room. My dad was lounging back in his leather recliner, TV remote in one hand and a Coors Lite in the other. He was watching Sports Center, per usual. My mom was on the floor holding my eight-year-old Toy Poodle.

Buddy, the adorable little furball that he is, wanted to play. He was nipping at my mom's chin, biting her fingers and scratching her arms, just like any over-hyperactive senior dog.

"Here's that book you wanted, *Gods, Myths, and Monsters* by Jeanne Frankfurst, sweetie." Mom handed me a thick hardback book. I squealed at the sight of the beautiful, shiny cover and kissed my mom on the cheek before walking over to where my dad was seated.

"Hey, uh, I was wondering," I said timidly. "Could me, Logan, and Maggie go to the movies on Saturday?" I was expecting an answer I didn't want.

"I believe it's 'could Logan, Maggie, *and I*'. But sure, tell them your mother is dropping you girls off," he corrected, glancing at mom.

"Sweet!" I pumped my fist in the air and ran into the kitchen with Buddy on my heels.

I snatched a pudding cup out of the fridge and ran down to the dubbed game and workout room. I plopped down in my beanbag chair and turned my Xbox on, adjusting the headset over my hair. Logan's voice crackled through the earpiece first and was soon joined by Maggie's. "Locked and loaded, girls?" My character peered through a rifle scope, targeting my first enemy on the game, colorful pixels loading.

"Let's goo!" Maggie whooped.

"Oo-ooh, I call targeting the campers!" came Logan's reply.

The match began.

Hours later, the numbers 12:34 a.m. blinked back from the screen on my phone. I was sprawled on my bedroom floor reading from my *Gods, Myths, and Monsters* novel. Countless other bound works were stacked on top of my dresser and in the closet.

At 12:35 a.m. I heard something come from downstairs. A clamor of thuds and stomping arose from the floor below me. The sounds of furniture being carelessly overturned or pushed came from farther away, but close to the second-floor staircase. I looked over at my dog. Buddy was curled up beside me, fast asleep. He was too lost in dreamland to be woken up. Buddy didn't hear a thing; he was deaf in one ear, after all.

I carefully set my book on the bedside table and went to my closet to change out of my pajamas. If it was past eleven o'clock, why were my parents still up? I don't recall my dad having mentioned anything about a late-night business call to me today, unless I just forgot. Scowling, I made to turn back to my bed and finally sleep, but another crash sounded from below.

Oh, goodie, the paranoia just kicked in.

I picked up my Swiss Army knife my parents had given me for my twelfth birthday from under my pillow and crept to the door, clutching a flashlight.

8

I took a deep breath in and opened the door. In that moment, I was thankful that all the doors in the house had been oiled a few days prior. I took a hesitant step out into the dark hallway before quickly retracting my foot.

Mixed feelings churned about in my gut; the uncertainty of what I was going to face was daunting. I didn't want to leave the safety of my room, but if no one was else was going to investigate then I might as well take charge. Maybe a very large raccoon had somehow slipped inside the house? Or perhaps it was some random burglar searching for cash? That would explain all the commotion coming from the living room. But what if it was someone dangerous? Surely, they wouldn't bother with me. But what if they hurt my parents? Or Buddy got injured in the process? What if this was all just an illusion and I was going crazy? I mean, it wasn't that far-fetched. After all, it *was* past midnight on a school night.

Yesterday, I put the milk carton inside the dishwasher instead of the fridge because of how exhausted I was, so perhaps lack of sleep was getting to me.

I shook my head, my thoughts scattering around in my brain like a marble in a pinball machine. At long last I crept into the gloomy hall, a heavy cloud of dread hanging over me. The old saying, 'curiosity killed the cat', crept into my thoughts.

Faint moonlight streamed in through the windows, illuminating the path before me in patches of yellow and white light, dog fur and dust particles floating in the air after each step. I gripped my knife tighter, tracing a finger down the engraved name on the blade.

Much to my annoyance, whomever was downstairs didn't seem to care how loud of a commotion they were making. I didn't understand how hard it was for people to grasp that your sleep-deprived, internet-addicted teen still needs her beauty sleep.

Chaotic banging and stomping came from the game room, kitchen, and living room now.

Here's a quick fact: my parents are extraordinarily heavy sleepers. Emphasis on heavy. They snore through hailstorms, severe thunderstorms, everything. They're the type of people you see on the news with the wild hair and bloodshot eyes who were passed out cold when a tornado ripped through the house. Just because someone was overturning a few pieces of furniture downstairs didn't mean that my parents were to wake from their peaceful slumber, especially if my dad had popped some Nyquil earlier.

I walked past my dad's office and the exercise room, taking a long, steadying breath. Silently, I climbed down the stairs and into the main hallway. I peeked around the corner, then pulled my head back. All I saw was darkness, but the noises continued, and I couldn't make out jack squat. Having a panic attack at this moment wouldn't do me any good, so I waited and listened, shrinking behind the corner.

Soon, various voices drifted down the corridor, giving the blobs of humanoid shadows that blurred in and out of the few rays of moonlight personification. Voices, harsh and gruff, echoed down the hall. Male.

"Sir, are you sure this is the right place?" said the first person, a deep, husky voice from the kitchen. "Do you really think she's here, in this house?" I froze, straining to hear more.

Was I *really* going to do this? Fight? I had a plan. Well, not exactly a real, practical plan, but a plan nonetheless. I mean, I don't exactly know *how* to fight. Usually I just go with my instincts. I normally wouldn't dare pick a fight with any one person unless they made fun of my friends, and only then would I not hesitate to slap the stupid out of you. Funny thing is, my anxiety is sort of two-sided: I would freeze up at the sight of a murderous clown running towards me, but if it went after my friends, I

10

wouldn't think of anything else but to stop it. I guess you could say my mother hen instincts kick in.

"Of course, you idiot! Have I ever been wrong?" A second voice spoke up, this one an octave lower.

"No, no, sir. Bruce just isn't thinking straight. This is the correct location, I'm sure of it, and this girl, uhm, Nerissa—"

"Nekoda," the second voice interjected.

"—is the person we're looking for. Your intellect never ceases to amaze me."

My heart leapt in my throat. They knew my name? Great, a couple of high school druggies broke into my house. And it wasn't even Saturday night.

"Yes, like I said, this is the right place. I'm *always* right," snapped the second voice again, with a steel edge to his voice.

Bruce spoke aloud. "Luke and Ezekial were informed of the plan, yes?"

"Yes, Luke is out back with the car, ready to be called in if need be. Ezekial is off scouting the area in case a neighbor spots us." the third voice replied. Ugh, both his voice and his attitude were irritating me already.

"I was! Ask me to relay every single detail of how this night is supposed to go down, go ahead, ask. I'll recite to you every line of dialogue Nath—"

"Alright, alright, *shut up*! Tony, get moving. Bruce, put those bulging muscles to use and try to at least look helpful. Remember, you can use force if need be. If the parents wake up, disarm them. If one or the other tries to fight, stun them, shoot them in the leg, hinder them unconscious, do whatever you can. But don't kill them. We need information, and they're the only remaining members who can tell us where the Camp is. Got it?"

11

I choked back a scream, pushing myself up farther against the solid foundation behind me. My heart seemed to slow, and suddenly I found it hard to think straight. I slumped against the wall, my legs shaking. Shit. Shit. Shoot my parents? Do these men actually mean to cause harm, or would they change their minds and end up killing? Were they planning on holding hostages as well, to get whatever it was they're searching for? Unwanted tears sprung to my eyes, but I hastily wiped them away with the edge of my sleeve. What was I going to do?

The voices continued to ramble on, their words their sentences their speech turning into incoherent garbling.

I needed it to stop.

All of it.

For the men to stop talking.

For them to stop disorganizing my fucking living room.

One moment I'm on the verge of a mental breakdown, and the next I can't help control my actions. At the very last second, I panicked, as one does when faced with the reality of their stupid decisions, and made to run back up to the second floor. But due to my carelessness, the figurine perched on the table next to the clothes rack at the bottom of the stairs shattered into a sharp mess when my foot bumped into it. All sound ceased entirely. Footsteps started in my direction.

Shit. *Fuck*.

Without thinking, I ran around the living room and towards the kitchen. Curse my irrational thinking. Fudge nuggets, this was *not* going to end well.

I flipped the light switches on as I slid into the kitchen, leaping on top of the nearest person I ran into and sending us both toppling to the ground. A wave of pain struck me in the side when the person's shoulder jammed into my stomach. I felt like I had

12

just attempted to tackle the star quarterback on my WHS's football team.

Instincts automatically took over as I threw punch after punch at the man's face, my knuckles sore after the second wild strike. From the quick glimpse I had gotten when the lights flickered, the man was bald and appeared to be in his late twenties or early thirties. The man was huge and built like a professional wrestler, but he clearly didn't know the element of surprise. I guess I had jumped the bronze with my flying squirrel attack. To my dismay, I was only able to bloody his nose before I was yanked from behind and thrown off the guy.

For a second, I was airborne, but all too soon landed a few feet away by the fridge, cracking my head on the tiled floor as I slid backwards. Tears burned my eyes. I was just struggling to my knees when someone grabbed the front of my sweatshirt and hoisted me up into the air, feet dangling.

I now peered into the face of a young man who appeared to be in his early twenties with smooth, tan skin peeking out from the collar of his black button up. His short gold hair was swept back, apart from a section that hung about his eyes. And his eyes... his eyes were so grey they were almost black.

No...wait, they *were* black. What the hell?!

I did a quick scan, willing my own vision to clear. Aside from his black pool-like orbs, there was something strangely *different* about the man, and I couldn't quite put my finger on it.

I struggled against the man's hold, but he had a grip like a steel claw. My knife had gone soaring after I had staged my attack; it was now lying a few feet away on the ground next to the man with the bloodied nose.

Keeping his gaze fixated on my face, the man holding me barked an order to his companions. "Bruce, get cleaned up and tell the others to get ready. Tony, get the parents. Tie them up,

13

securely, and bring them to me. Understand?" Bruce, the man whose blood now dried on my hands, nodded and walked to the bathroom outside the kitchen hallway. The other man, Tony, also nodded. He had shaggy, greasy hair and menacing brown eyes. A thin white scar ran from the corner of his left eye to his ear. He had a rifle of some sort slung over his back and what looked to be boxes of ammunition strapped to his leather belt.

"Yes, Nathaniel." Tony sneered and walked past us before vanishing up the stairs.

Nathaniel, the assumed head honcho, looked at me. A small, devilish smile touched the corners of his lips. "As for you, girlie, you're coming with us." It was then that I noticed that all the men wore dark clothing and were armed with various weapons, and not the flimsy water guns or a boy scouts' whittling knife type. Not a limb was bare of weaponry.

The man named Bruce had a pistol on his belt. A strap going across his chest held a mini Taser, walkie-talkie, pocketknife, lighters, and a roll of duct tape. Nathaniel, on the other hand, had nothing more than a leather sheath strapped to his waist. I did a double-take to make sure I wasn't hallucinating.

I'm no expert, but unless you're some sort of auctioneer or antique owner keeping one in a glass display, no one in this day and age carried a sword at their side. Aside from those British guards who stood outside Buckingham Palace day and night, or my dorkish cousin LARPing with a foam sword. Or a ninja... which clearly Nathaniel wasn't either of those. He was someone else. A someone else that I couldn't identify.

A deep sense of panic and unease welled up inside me like a tidal wave, crashing and rolling. I did the only insanely stupid thing I could think of.

"MOOOM! DAAAD! Help! Call the—" Before another word tumbled off my tongue, I felt the prick of something sharp

14

pressed against my neck. Nathaniel had a knife against my throat. A goddamned *knife*.

He gripped the front of my sweatshirt tighter as the cold blade dug into my skin. I felt a quick sting, like the kind of pain you feel when you cut the back of your ankles shaving, and I silently cursed myself. Dammit, how the hell was this happening? I couldn't move. I couldn't move. Couldn't...

"Don't you *dare* try calling for a savior." He leered in a low, threatening voice, his breath tickling my ear. I fought the urge to retch.

Bruce came out of the bathroom, face bare of blood, as Tony came stumbling down the stairs, forcing my parents to shuffle behind him and to the kitchen where Nathaniel and I were located. My dad was breathing hard and sweating. He had fought back; a black eye and a swollen lip proved as much. My mom's tears slid down her rosy cheeks and over a purpling spot on her lower jaw. Both my parents' hands were tied together behind their backs with zip ties, a plastic strip that can be threaded through its end and tightened.

Their eyes grew wide at the sight of me. My vision grew blurry, and their faces morphed into dizzying shapes. My dad tried to speak, only to break off when he saw Nathaniel with his blade to my windpipe. My mom started crying, shoulder-shaking sobs racking her small frame.

Tony snickered and shoved my parents forward where they fell at Nathaniel's feet. Shoving his weapon into one of the belt loops of his black jeans, Nathaniel set me down and knocked me forward.

"Watch her, and don't let her do anything reckless." he commanded, black eyes zeroing in on me.

"Understood, sir." replied Bruce.

15

With Bruce's hold on my arm and one hand holding the back of my neck, I watched, motionless, as the cold, clammy tendrils of anxiety crept up my spine. With bated breath, I quietly anticipated what was going to occur next. Fear was now wrapped around my chest, my throat, my lungs, squeezing and squeezing so that I couldn't breathe.

Nathaniel, scarred hands clasped behind his back, paced back and forth between my parents like they were a pair of criminals on trial waiting for the verdict. "So," he started. The house seemed to still at the sound of his voice. "Which one of you has the book?"

My parents stared at the floor in response, refusing to meet his deadly gaze. Wait, *what*? A-a book? A freaking book? Was that really what he had just asked about!

"A *book*?" I guffawed, swallowing my tongue. "If you're looking for a good read—do you read fantasy fiction?" Nathaniel looked like that gothic boy in the back of the classroom who liked dragons, so I'm going to assume he liked fiction. "Check out *The Lord of The Rings* by J.R.R Tolkien. I-it's a good book." I sputtered, forcing a fake smile to my face. Nathaniel scowled.

"Zip it!" hissed Tony, hand resting on the pistol at his belt.

"Why should I, freak?!" The black tendrils had now relinquished their hold on my neck and allowed me to breathe. Goddammit. I should've kept my big mouth shut.

Tony stomped across the room just as I scrambled backwards out of Bruce's grasp—

—and was met with a stinging sensation across my cheek.

I yelped in pain and surprise, desperately wanting to claw Tony's eyes out in that moment. From the center of the kitchen, my mom made a strangled sound in the back of her throat.

16

I bit my tongue to keep from crying out once more, throwing a hand up to cover my face. When Tony backed away a step, only then did I lower my arms and turn to see Nathaniel approaching my parents. "You wretched monster," I snarled, cupping my cheek. "Get away from them!" Nathaniel did not bother to acknowledge me.

Tony raised his hand again, making as if to strike. I couldn't help it—my cowardly self flinched. "That's what I thought." he sniggered under his breath.

"Don't you dare touch my daughter, you damn bastard! You sick son of a no good bastard! No wonder you were dis—" I stared, stunned. I had never heard my mom curse someone outwardly, save from the time she was clipped by a distracted driver on the road. Her outburst was interrupted when Nathaniel bent down on one knee and grabbed her chin.

"Look at me, Clara. Clara, look at me!" he roared, forcing her glistening blue eyes, the carbon copy of my own, to meet his. "Now, I'm only going to ask you once. Where is the book?" he spoke the last words as if addressing a toddler, slowly and meticulously.

"I'm not going to tell you, not on my life!" My mother said, visibly trembling. In that moment, I had never seen my mom look so vulnerable.

It was horrifying.

Nathaniel shook his head, whether in disappointment or annoyance, I could not tell. He snapped his fingers and the cold barrel of a 22 Caliber pistol was suddenly pressed against my mom's temple. I hadn't noticed Tony passing the gun to him.

"Hmph," he adjusted his finger on the trigger. "It's a shame you'll have to die without telling your daughter what she really is. Isn't that right, Clare?" Nathaniel shoved the pistol against her skull.

17

"Clara!" Dad gasped, his eyes shining with fresh tears, struggling against his bonds like a spasming mad man.

"Mom, no!" I shrieked between gulps of air. Now the black snakes had latched on to me completely; my chest ached with each shuddering breath I attempted to suck in. The blood pounded in my ears.

Goddammit. Goddammit. Goddammit!

My parents might be dead on the floor in five minutes time, and it was going to be all my fault. If only I had stayed upstairs, away from the scene. It would have been so much better if I had allowed a panic attack to consume my body and mind, instead of rushing to the rescue like some idiotic wannabe hero.

I choked back another sob when, to my utmost surprise, a loud *thump thump* came from upstairs. The noise didn't seem to be coming from anyone that was already in the kitchen. Every one of us, even Nathaniel, froze. His hand wavered for a millisecond; the gun pulled back from my mom's head as he whirled around. The thumping sound traveled down the stairs and through the dark hallway. Time seemed to slow as the mysterious noise grew closer and closer.

I half expected Buddy to appear in the doorway, only it wasn't him. Rather, it was something else that revealed itself in the dim lights of the kitchen. This beast didn't look anything like Buddy. It resembled an oversized wolf with floppy ears, blood-red eyes, and paws the size of dinner plates. For some reason, an itch began to form at the back of my mind. Something, the smallest of voices, was telling me that this animal was very familiar. Yet this wasn't any random escapee all the way from the New York City zoo, so what—?

As quick as the hamster running on the wheel in Mrs. Hook's classroom, the sudden realization of what stood before us hit me in the face.

18

But there was *no way*…there was no way a Hellhound from the depictions in my Greek mythology novels now lingered in the doorway. It wasn't possible. Nathaniel and his goons and his wicked looking sword don't exist. None of this was real. It was all just part of a very, very realistic nightmare. I would wake up by a soft knocking on my door before my mom barged in to throw open the curtains, and then I would go to school like usual and tell my friends about my insanely weird dream that my messed-up brain had concocted while I slept.

Yet why did I have a gut feeling that I wasn't going to be waking up from this nightmare anytime soon?

This thing, whatever it was, *did* seem oddly familiar. That something, that voice, pulled at the back of my mind, and it wasn't going away. What on earth was it?

"Buddy! Is that—is it you?" I asked the beast in trepidation. The Hellhound looked me dead in the eyes, and I fought the urge to look away. After all, most animals saw it as a challenge if you stared them in the eye for too long. To my greatest shock, the Hellhound stood up on its hind legs and spun around once, twice, three times. My dad's shoulders drooped, and I couldn't tell if it was from dismay or exhaustion.

A weight seemed to lift from my chest in that instant.

The triple spin was a trick I had taught Buddy a few years back so he could 'dance' at my aunt's wedding. I had also taught him how to open the fridge, roll over, shake, and play dead. He may be old, but he had more brain cells than half of the boys at my school combined.

"Oh, no, Buddy. Buddy, it *is* you! But how? I mean, how…what did—what?"

I glanced at my mom, the barrel of the gun still pressed to her bruised temple; then to Tony, standing with his arms crossed and face scrunched up in an ugly scowl; and up at Bruce, who bore an emotionless expression on his face like he'd rather be doing anything else in the world. I turned my head to stare daggers at Nathaniel's stupid face, a knot working its way on the spot between my neck and shoulder.

The gun was now tightly clenched in the black-eyed man's hand, the whites of his knuckles showing. I saw a spark of anger in his eyes, and…was I imagining it? I squinted. A flash of sorrow or grief passed over his face but was soon masked with a flicker of disgust.

I took a deep breath. I knew what I had to do, but it was up to me to time it right.

"Now, I'll give you one last chance. You get ten seconds to answer or I blow you and your husband's brains out. I don't want to, Clara, I really don't, but I will. Go!" Nathaniel said in a seemingly bored tone.

"It's…I'm forbidden to tell." Mom whispered.

"One." Nathaniel counted.

"I swore a sacred oath! Please don't make me—!"

"Two."

"I won't tell you. I can't." She bit her swollen lip.

"Three, four, five…"

"No, no. You won't get it. You know you won't." Defiant.

"Six, seven, eight…"

Buddy, the dog-turned-Hellhound, was crouched low to the ground, teeth bared in a silent, vicious snarl. Not a soul noticed. One, two, three—

"Buddy, attack!" I shouted, wrenching free from my captor's hands with all the strength I could muster.

They never saw it coming.

20

Buddy 2.0 soared through the air, knocking over Tony with his claws extended, slashing and scratching apart his shirt. He bit at Tony's ankles, wrists, and any bare patch of skin in a frenzied blur, teeth connecting with flesh. Buddy leapt for Tony's face but was knocked aside. He lunged again and again, forcing the man into a corner of the kitchen.

"Oi! Help me! Stupid mutt, get off!" Bruce's attention slipped as he ran to help his compatriot. When he drew near, Buddy snapped his jaws, and Bruce nearly lost his left hand.

"Get 'em, boy!" I cheered.

There was a glint of silver as Tony reached down and yanked something from his coat pocket, and down Buddy went.

I screamed as my furry companion's body hit the tiled floor. "NO!" A pool of blood now drenched Tony's black t-shirt and the area around him. I could not distinguish whose blood it was. Tony hastily shoved Buddy away and climbed to his feet, leaving the knife in Buddy's side.

Squatting beside Buddy, I inspected the wound as he let out a heart-wrenching whine. "Shh, shh, it will be okay. It's okay, sweetheart, you're all right," I whispered before rushing towards the sink.

I yanked off the towel and pressed it against Buddy's heaving chest, careful to avoid jostling the knife. My dog would only bleed out faster if the weapon was removed. I was no certified veterinarian, and there was nothing I could do but wait as the white towel soon turned a dark shade of crimson. My eyes burned, and more tears threatened to spill. "C'mon, c'mon..." the blood was never ending.

I could hear my parents' struggling going on behind me, and the rapidly increasing footsteps as one of the burglars approached. Tony was still nursing his well-deserved wound, swearing all the while Bruce mumbled something to the one of the other men nearby.

Wham! Someone's cold hand grabbed me from behind and slammed me back against the wooden cabinets. My head hit the surface with a crack that resonated all the way down my body. Nathaniel's cruel face greeted me after my vision returned. His black eyes, black as the night sky, met mine. I gazed behind him to where Tony had taken hold of the pistol and was aiming it back and forth between my parents. Bruce stood behind them, blocking our only exit out of the kitchen. Tears, snot, and blood flowed freely down my face.

It all came crashing down on me at once. This plan of mine, to fend off and possibly scare the burglars into retreating, had turned out rotten, as it should have. *Of course,* I couldn't stop these men, any more than I could drive a car and parallel park without causing some kind of catastrophe in the student lot. Buddy, my poor little dog, was slowly losing his own fight, as the last ounces of his life's blood drained out. Tony was probably going to shoot my parents anyway, book or no book, whatever the frick-fracking hell that meant. And I was going with Nathaniel either way, with little choice in the matter so long as I still drew breath.

"These stunts you're pulling must end! If I so much as hear another word out of you, I'll cut out your tongue. Gods, *stop talking*. Got it?" The tip of his blade, sharp like a rusty razor, pressed against my skin. I felt the cold kiss of the metal as he turned to glare at Bruce and Tony. "Lock these traitors in the closet. Search the premises for any signs. I don't want a single inch of this house left untouched." Bruce started wandering around the living room like an obedient child afraid of discipline, looking under the coffee table, behind the TV, inside couch cushions and the like. Meanwhile, Tony roughly yanked my parents to their feet and dragged them down the hall. I watched them drag their feet, writhing.

I averted my gaze down to where Buddy was dying on the floor, or rather, *was*. I blinked twice and looked away, then looked back. Buddy wasn't there. No trace of him ever bleeding on the tiled floor, just a peculiar smell in the air and a dark cloud of smoke.

Buddy was gone.

☾

"Ah, yes, your little dog friend, he's gone. You know where he went? To the Land of The Dead, the Underworld, where all monsters rot and mortals suffer in vain." Nathaniel chuckled, noting my expression. "Now he can play with that stupid over-sized mutt of Hades, Cerberus. Maybe one day you could join him there and engage in the human's suffering. Wouldn't that be lovely?" he went on as sarcastically as possible.

Despite myself, I rolled my eyes. What kind of drugs was this dude sniffing? Buddy suddenly disappears in a cloud of smoke, dead, and Nathaniel starts going on about the Underworld and Greek mythology like it actually…well, exists.

Here's the thing, I'm not religious, and I believe what I want to. My mom comes from a family of hardcore Christians and my dad is from a family of faithful Catholics, but I don't think I've ever actually attended church because I willingly wanted to. I've never thought much about religion, yet even for me this was a tad bit over the top.

"So," I managed to get out. "What—what are you going to do with me?"

"Oh, don't worry, you're coming with us. You will be of great use to me, and Shadarr will love to have a new playmate. But be careful, if you're not cautious he might burn you to a crisp, and

23

that won't be good for either of us. Especially you." Nathaniel sneered, jabbing me hard in the forehead.

"Wow, that's impressive. Maybe your heart isn't as cold and black as I thought it was," I said, putting on a fake smile, trying my best not to stare at the floor where the ghost of Buddy Jones might lay. "Mhm?"

"You little brat! How dare you—!" He began, stopping when someone came through the creaky backdoor. The new stranger was tall and stout with dark green eyes framed by wild red hair, a large firearm adorning his back.

"Luke, grab this girl while I deal with her pesky parents. Put her in the back of the truck. Make sure her legs are secure, too." Nathaniel told the red-haired dude. He nodded and grabbed my wrists, proceeding to half carry and half drag me out the back door. I spotted a short sword hanging around his waist in a decorated scabbard and thought better than to try and snatch it.

The air was brisk and chilly as we quickly walked to a creepy black campervan hidden a distance behind my house in the woods. Pulling the back door of the vehicle open, Luke hustled me inside.

I gracefully fell on my face attempting to catch my balance. The redhead, who I assumed to be the Luke Bruce had mentioned earlier, wrestled me to the ground as I struggled to rise, putting all of his weight on top of me. I tried unsuccessfully to kick him, elbow him in the ribs, anything to throw him off. When Luke pulled out zip ties from his back pocket to bind my legs and hands together, I fought him still, trying to afflict bodily harm, but it was of no avail.

Once I heard the click of the locked door, I slumped back against the wall of the vehicle, and cried.

☾

Minutes or an eternity after my mental breakdown, a light bulb popped up above my head. My phone! It was in the back pocket of my jeans! If I could reach behind my back to grab it, then I may be able to contact the police, depending if I had any cell service out here. Unfortunately, Luke had tied my hands so tightly together that I could hardly move them. On the bright side, it was a thin zip-tie-thingy he had used. When my mouth grew sore from gnashing on the thing around my wrists, I gave up and looked around the vehicle in vain. Who knew zip ties were so damn hard to break?

There was nothing but a box of ammunition, a stack of duct tape rolls, a sealed box, one moldy apple, and a small rusted pocket knife stabbed into the packaging of a water bottle pack in the back of the truck. It would have to do. I scooted towards it on my butt, laying down belly up and maneuvering my body to reach and pick up the item between my fingers.

I turned the blade on myself, pointing it down at the ground. Slowly and deliberately, I sawed at the wire. At last, with a loud snap and a flick of the wrists, it broke. I cut the other zip tie off and freed my ankles.

Soon I was up on my sore feet and free. *Almost* free. I had to call the police first, and then escape from the inconspicuous van. I dialed 9-1-1 and listened to the ominous hooting of owls as I waited for someone to pick up on the other line.

Much to my relief, a man's voice soon answered. "9-1-1, what's your emergency?"

I swallowed, bracing myself against the side of the interior. "Sir, you have to help me, a gang of crazy people broke into my house and are threatening to kill my parents unless they give them some—I don't know—very important book or whatever? A-and they've taken me hostage sir, and please—"

25

"Ma'am, this is Officer Wells, please calm down and explain what the situation is. Where are y—" The back door opened with a squeal, and there, frightening real, stood Nathaniel, Luke, Bruce, Tony, and some other guy who I could only assume to be Ezekial. With lightning speed, Luke yanked the phone out of my hand, threw it on the ground, and smashed it to pieces with his shoe. My heart pounded so fast I was afraid they could hear it.

I crossed my arms and pouted, summoning up what courage I had left, despite the tear tracks running down my face.

"Well, that was rude."

"Silence," Nathaniel hissed, his temper flaring. A tick started in his jaw. I felt a sharp pain in my arm, almost like I'd been stung, before the world turned dizzy and dark.

Chapter II: I Meet a Dragon

The warrior was fighting his way through a crowd of bodies, all kicking and shoving and writhing beings spattered with blood, mud, and sweat.

An intricately designed sword was brandished in one hand, and a heavy metal shield with the inscription 'Camp Wolf' adorned on his back. He bore no helmet or headgear of any kind, and his golden hair and bicolored eyes stood out like a beacon in the midst of bodies. His right iris was a dark blue, and his left was a bright blue merged with a shade of gold, like sunlight reflecting off water. A pink scar ran across the warrior's right cheek and down to the tip of his mouth.

His face was set in grim determination as he expertly fought his way through the mass of limbs, struggling to get to where three wolves stood their ground. One Grey wolf, one black wolf, and one white wolf, each the size of a motorcycle with piercing, glowing eyes. It was a strange sight to bear witness to.

The wolves lunged and snapped at anyone who dare get too close to one another and the person they were protecting—a girl stood in the middle of them, her eyes closed in concentration. In one small hand that she held out from her body, palm up, was a blue sphere of magic power. She was muttering in a language my dream self didn't understand. Each time an incantation was spoken, a bright fireball was shot out at an attacker. With each strike, an enemy was slain or thrown up into the air, flailing.

I felt a chill suddenly run down my spine, and the girl's eyes flew open. Unexpectedly, she was wearing no armor, just a regular day-to-day outfit paired with a long, double-edged sword with a crescent moon emblazoned on the hilt, across her back. Pure, raw power seemed to seep from the girl's aura, from the sense of energy emanating from her. With long, tangled blonde hair and bright eyes, the girl looked a lot like someone I knew. An itch formed at the back of mind, and then I realized why.

I was looking at a mirror image of myself.

It was me, but instead of blue eyes, they were now shining a bright golden color. Power surged from my hands and continued to crackle in the air around me. War cries sounded in the distance, and the ferocious sounds of wolves was not far off. It was then that I got the hint. It was something I've never imagined before, if naught only heard of.

The name speared through my mind like a ghostly whisper—Skin-changer. *Skin-changer. Skin-changer. Skinchanger*—*I was a fearsome creature with a human complexion, the soul of a wolf, and the blood of the gods…*

☾

I bolted up so fast I feared the bile racing up my throat went back down. My hands shook with the force of the adrenaline rushing through my body. It felt like pots had been relentlessly banging against my throbbing head for the past hour, and no matter how hard I grasped my head or pinched myself, the pain wouldn't stop. My right arm was throbbing, and it was probably due to the red bump on the underside of my wrist. I touched it cautiously, not daring to think about what Nathaniel may have injected me with.

What the hell was that? *Who* was that? If I hadn't known better, I'd say that a pack of mutant wolves were ripping out the throats of scary-looking guys in order to protect my doppelganger. What had been going on there, anyway? And that whisper at the end…a ghost? A ghost spinning the word 'Skin-changer' in my ear over and over again.

28

The loud murmur of voices coming from…somewhere around me shook me out of my trance, my headache only mitigating slightly when I stood. I seemed to be in a small room with peeling white paint on the walls and concrete floor. There was only a cot in one corner and a small table and a splintering chest occupying the rest of the space. A single, dim light bulb hung from the ceiling and did little to help the eerie mood. At the front of the small room was a barred door, like the kind you would see at a prison.

Cold, sudden dread squeezed my heart when memories of the previous ordeal all came rushing back to me in a flood of memories. My parents, oh God, were they alive? Hurt? Dare I even think of that? Did Nathaniel and his lunatic friends get that bloody book he so badly yearned for? And what was he saying about the Underworld, and Buddy being a Hellhound? Why was he going on about Greek mythology, and more frustratingly, about my mom not telling me who I really am? What the shit did that even mean? I am Nekoda Alessandra Jones, not a goddamn secret princess from a foreign country.

A wave of thirty different emotions hit me all at once, like a sucker punch to the gut. Pain, guilt, grief, anger, frustration, fear. Fear. Ice-cold fear.

I loved…*love* my parents and Buddy so much. They were—*are* my family, my life. Buddy, my play mate and the one who cheered me up with his doggy kisses when I was feeling sad.

My dad, who always took me to the doctor when I was sick and told me stories before bed to help me sleep. He always found time to help me with my math homework, which I still struggle with. My mom, who's my idol and best friend. She would take time out of her day to make me breakfast every morning before school, and never hesitated for a girl's day out. We would spend hours gossiping and chatting about the juicy events of one another's day while perusing around the mall.

The most recent memory I had of my family is one I will forever keep dear to my heart. It was the day of my grandpa's funeral, and I was to help my mom give a speech. She was nervous as all get out, and no matter what my dad or I said to her, she refused to give up her paper for one of my uncles to read in her place. "I can't do this. I can't do this," she cried. My aunt was trying to comfort her as best she could, but my mom didn't take notice.

Fifteen minutes before the memorial was supposed to start, my dad drove us up to the spot where my both my parents and grandparents had been engaged. We climbed out of the car and stood up on the hill, looking out above the town. My dad sighed and turned to my mom. "Do you remember this place? This was where we came to have a picnic with the Jones and Harrison families. Do you know what your dad said to me right before I was going to propose?"

My mom met his eyes and smiled softly. "Yes," she said.

"He said, 'Kyle, you're a good man. I want to tell you something that my dad told me many years ago. It's never too late to take a step back and look around at what you've done. But it's always too soon to step forward and see what you *could* have done. No matter what happens in the future, I want you to remember that you should make this moment something you'll never regret. It doesn't matter if you stumble over words or trip over your own feet, as long as you find the perfect in all the little imperfections.' I don't want you to regret not speaking at your father's funeral, Clara. I want you to take a little bit of good out of this and remember all the happy times you had with him. If you don't speak up now, there won't be a second chance."

Mom sniffled and leaned into her husband's open arms. "Okay," she whispered, "I'll do it. I'll stand up there and talk. But first—" I watched in awe as my mother reached into her jacket pocket and pulled out a folded piece of paper, and promptly rip it

30

in half. "There. Now let's take another step forward. If grandma can move past this, so can we." Minutes later, we were back at the church, and my mom was proudly reminiscing about her father up on the stage. Her hands were clasped firmly in front of her when she spoke, and she held her hand high, smiling when she recalled a happy memory and pausing to wipe her tears away.

I love my family with all my heart and soul, and right now it ached more than anything to think about. I leaned over, hands on my knees, and sucked in a lungful of air—

they're not here they're okay they're hurt they're not here they're dead—

I was going to shatter into a million pieces at any second, or crumble away into dust and nothingness like sand against a crashing wave...my mom...my dad...they couldn't be *gone*-gone. They couldn't. They just couldn't.

The loud voices I heard a moment ago grew louder and closer. I quickly scanned my surroundings, wiping my face with the edge of my snotty sleeve, forcing my legs to move.

With wobbly legs, I stood up on my feet, my head feeling like it was going to explode at any minute. The familiar voices I'd been hearing stopped at my door. Dumb and Dumber appeared through the bars like ominous shadows. Luke and Bruce were both dressed in dark clothing, and as expected, also laddered down with some kind of painful toy. Luke had a leather bandolier around his chest and Bruce bore some kind of firearm at his belt.

I crawled my way backwards on hands and feet toward the wall furthest. Perhaps when they opened the door I could run out and shut them in... no, that wouldn't work. My stomach twisted, and I worried that this time I couldn't keep my dinner down. I needed to think, think!

31

Bruce noticed me pathetically crab-walking away and said, "The boss wants to see you. He has a few things in mind he would, er, like to discuss with you."

I did not like the way he said that. Bruce pulled out a key from his pocket and unlocked the door, stepping through with Luke on his heels.

I glowered at him, prepared to claw out his eyes if they so much as touched me, sudden rage fueling my actions.

They killed my parents. They killed my family.

"Yeah, well if you think *that's* going to happen, think again, because you've got another thing coming."

Bruce's face flushed with anger. "Oh, shut up! You speak only when told, and don't talk to nobody unless the boss says otherwise!"

"I'm not the one harassing a minor, so I think I'm entitled to say whatever I want."

"Like hell you are, brat!"

I charged Bruce, ready to launch myself at him when he kicked out, striking me hard in the chest. Stumbling, I gasped for breath, now extremely winded. Before I had the chance to regain my balance, Luke laughed dryly and approached me, hands raised. I thrust my hands up to cover my face. Before I could react, Luke had lunged forward and picked me up, slinging me over one broad shoulder.

"Hey, put me down! Lemme go! Stupid jerk, put me down!" I punched his back and kicked my legs out. He kept his leisurely pace with Bruce leading the way.

We walked down a short corridor lit with torches on brick walls next to rooms that resembled the 'prison cell' I was just in. Which I was beginning to think it was just that.

32

I didn't know where we were. On a boat? Possibly. On a deserted island in the middle of the ocean? Likely. In a secret base for psychopaths? Sure, why not! I willed myself to focus, and began to map out every turn, hallway, and door we passed or went down in my aching head, in case of an escape route. There *had* to be a way out of this place.

We turned right down a longer corridor and stopped at a big oak door with the letter *N* carved into the front. N as in Nutcase? Bruce knocked three times before a deep, familiar voice spoke from the other side. "You may enter. Did you bring the girl?" Nathaniel asked.

"No, it's John C—" I replied sarcastically under my breath, loud enough for the two goons to hear. Before I could finish a classic zinger, Luke whacked me on the back, hard, before entering the room. Maybe I could annoy Nathaniel with my dumb jokes and he'd let me go free, or maybe I could stab him in the neck. Cracking jokes was just one of the many, varied ways I distracted myself when nervous, or faced with a sword-wielding psychopath.

They killed my parents. They killed my family.

Nathaniel was pacing back and forth in front of an old leather chair, like the kind you would see an evil villain spin around in. Assortments of bows, axes, knives, guns, shiny swords and any dangerous and crazy weapon you could think of in all types and sizes lined the wall behind him. I even spotted a few maces and an old-fashioned flamethrower from World War I that looked like it had been stolen from a museum.

Over yonder, Tony and Ezekial were standing off to one side of the room, blatantly bored.

"Lock the door behind you." Nathaniel ordered Bruce. He went to do as he was told while Luke dumped me on the ground at Nathaniel's boots.

I scrambled to my feet only to have Luke slam me back down in an iron hold while Nathaniel went to work strapping me into bindings on the old chair, just how the protagonist in spy movies would be tied to. I flailed around in the seat, trying to wriggle out of the bonds, but my feeble kicks did nothing to stop him.

No.

I bit my lip hard enough to draw blood; the pain would help distract me from going into panic mode. Panicking would only make things worse than they were.

"Now, let's get down to business."

I thought better of than to murmur, "To defeat the Huns!"

"I want to ask you a series of questions," Nathaniel the Nutcase continued. "and if you attempt to lie, I will be sure to exact consequences. First question, do you know why you're here?"

"No, I haven't the faintest idea." I muttered, staring down at my muddy shoes.

Nathaniel snorted. "The answer as to why you are here, with us, is because I need you. You don't know it yet, because your damn parents were so busy trying to hide your powers from you. Ah, but let's get to the point. You see, you have powers that are beyond measure, that only a few have been gifted with in a very, very long time. You are quite possibly one of the most powerful beings in centuries, as far as I'm aware. Once you master your powers, you would be strong enough to destroy the gods themselves! You are what I call a very valuable weapon. You could use your powers to take over this pesky world and destroy it to rebuild a new one all over again. Do you understand what I'm trying to say?"

I stared at him, dumbstruck. "I think that you were dropped on your head too many times as a baby, that's what."

34

Nearby, Tony chortled before stifling his laugh with a loud cough.

That's right, laugh it up.

SHMACK! With snake-like reflexes, Nathaniel had reached out his hand and cupped me in the jaw. The stinging sensation that followed doubled from the throbbing welt that had already formed on my cheekbone from Tony's slap. I chewed my lip, resisting the comment that was ready to escape my lips. I tried to reach up and touch my face, but the restraints were tight.

"I didn't ask for your opinion, girl. You better get that attitude in check, or I'll mess up your pretty little face." growled Nathaniel.

Through my blurred vision and the thundering headache that still lingered, I managed to choke out a retort. "How sweet. You think I'm pret—!" WHACK! Another slap, this time on the other side of my face. I slumped back in the smelly chair, stunned and throbbing as salty tears fell.

"This is all on you. If you're done interrupting me, I need to ask you more questions. And I *will* make you talk, one way or another, so there's no point in being a smartass."

I balled my hands into fists to stop them from shaking.

"Okay, I've tried to explain your powers, assuming you actually *are* the girl foretold in the Three Fates prophecy. Were you ever aware of having powers in the first place? Or have you ever just felt…different from others, like there's a sense of wrongness in the air?"

"Uh, just in case you haven't noticed, I don't have any kinds of wacky magic or powers. Are you talking about Superman's inhuman abilities? What am I, immortal or something? Am I gonna shoot lasers out of my eyeballs?"

35

They all looked at me with puzzled expressions. Finally, the dark-haired boy with the light hazel eyes spoke up. "Hi, um, who is this Superman that you speak of? Does he happen to know Thanatos?"

I made a big show of rolling my eyes before answering, ignoring the fact that he just mentioned the Greek personification of death as if he were a family friend. "Oh yes, Ezekial. You must be Luke's partner in crime. You aren't very bright, are you? Like angsty Bruce over there," I jerked my chin to where the balding brute was standing, arms crossed in front of the door. "Yes, I'm afraid Superman is a threat. Best be careful, or he'll use his laser vision on you in your sleep, and when you wake up—oops, I guess you won't wake up." I smiled slyly.

Ezekial, seemingly shocked, stepped back a few feet from the table. "Oh, for the love of Olympus—!" Tony started. Nathaniel held up his hand in silence. He whipped out a knife from his belt and walked toward me. *Oh no oh no oh no oh no oh no no*

My thoughts were interrupted as Nathaniel placed a hand not so gently against my red cheek. I froze, and I swear my heart did too. Out of the corner of my eye, Nathaniel had a shark-like grin on his face.

I felt the blade of his knife press against the smooth skin of cheek near the corner of my lip. All I could think of was the traumatizing scene where the Joker asks, "You want to know how I got these scars?" A shiver ran down my spine. I was practically staring death in the face.

"Each time you give a snide remark in place of an appropriate answer, I'll add a new scar or two to your adorable face. You either talk or you don't, it is all up to you, Jones. Luckily for me, your stupid mutt isn't here to protect you." He spat, eyes narrowing as his cold fingers gripped my chin.

36

I didn't dare say anything; I was rooted to the spot in pure fear, and Nathaniel could sense it. The black tendrils were knocking at my door once more.

He started back up with the meaningless questions, assuming I wasn't going to open my big mouth again. "Okay, so you don't know about your powers, that much is obvious. But at the very least, have you ever heard of such a thing as a Skin-changer?" I nodded my head as best I could, too emotionally drained to speak. "No? Or yes? Very well, I'll explain nonetheless. A Skin-changer is a half- mortal, but with the ability to shape shift, or Change, into any creature of their blood descendants. So, if one of your ancestors was a Skin-changer that had the ability and blood of, say, a lion, you would have the power to change into that animal at any given place, any time. Skin-changers are basically hybrid demigods."

"What in the hell is a hybrid demigod? You?" I spat. With a quick snap of Nathaniel's wrist, he dragged the blade upward. I first, I expected to feel nothing. Next, I sucked in a breath as something wet and warm slid down my face. Blood. Nathaniel had *cut* me. *Cut me.* I now felt a sharp, burning sensation zing across my cheekbone.

Son of a bitch.

He continued. "A Skin-changer may get Claimed on the night of the full moon on the year of their fourteenth birthday, which we call the Claiming Moon. That Skin-changer gets 'claimed' by a certain god or goddess. Thus meaning, their magical instincts kind of snap to life, and they're exposed to the raw magic of the world, the things that regular mortals cannot see. There is a rare case, however, once in a few thousand years, where one special Skin-changer turns out more powerful than the rest." At this, Nathaniel lowered the knife and cocked his head at me.

"This Skin-changer gains an essence of magic flowing through their blood from each god, not just the one birth god or goddess—although the baby Skin-changer is always birthed with the agreement of their mundane parents. When the baby of the Three Fates' prophecy was born, the prophecy was set in motion. That chosen Skin-changer is now destined to fulfill whatever prophecy the Fates destined them to, no matter how much they deny it. Once, there were more than one all-powerful Skin-changers alive in the world at a point in time, but that is no longer. The gods grow weak, even today, while their children grow even weaker, except for the ones that are strong enough to fulfill their destinies."

"But I-I don't have any other parents. I'm not adopted." I whispered, puzzled.

"There is a rare occurrence when two very powerful demigods have a child together, that they will have the pure blood of all twelve Olympians running through their veins. But that kid isn't always the demigod foretold in the Fates' prophecy. Although you, Jones, are the exception we've been seeking."

So, the all-powerful demigod is either an accident, or someone that was meant to be a pawn in the prophet's game.

And I was one of them.

"But if werewolves—"

"We're Skin-changers, not werewolves. They don't exist. The Werewolf tale is just a hoax that a bunch of moronic mortals created to scare children." Nathaniel corrected. I tried to ignore the fact that he said 'we're' as in 'we' (me included), and not 'I'.

"Whatever. So, if *Skin-changers* exist, does that mean all the stories, the old myths, are true?" I asked, trying to sound casual, when really I was screaming internally.

I was a Skin-changer with magical powers; therefore, let them believe that for the time being, if only to stall for a while longer until they figured out that I was just an abnormally short high schooler. I couldn't help but wonder, if what these men were saying was true, could they Change too?

"If you're referring to vampires, the Frankenstein monster, or witches: no, not exactly. Those particular myths aren't true. Okay, allow me to rephrase that. Salem witches are an entirely different story, but never mind that." He gave a dismissive wave of his hand. "If you're referring to the common Greek myths, yes. The Greek gods are still very much alive, as annoying and petulant as they are." He scoffed, the pressure of the blade diminishing.

I nodded, trying to absorb the information that was being passed on. "What you're saying is that demigods and Skin-changers are two different things, and more than one god exists? And that the Olympians, the Greek gods and goddesses, are real?"

"A demigod is a child who is also a half-god, meaning only one of their birth parents has to be a god. The deities of Olympus still rule the earth today. But now that you've got a faint grasp on that, there is someone who we would like you to meet. His name is Shadarr, and he won't harm you in any way unless I tell him to." Nathaniel replied, slowly losing his threatening composure, a giddy look now in his black eyes at the mention of Shadarr.

"But what were you talking about just a minute ago, y'know, about me being a very powerful, uh-hum, weapon? You're saying that I am one of these Skin-changers, and supposedly have a Greek god as a mom or dad or whatever, *and* mortal parents too? It doesn't make sense, that's not the way science, and the world, works. I can't be born from *two* sets of parents."

Nathaniel only shook his head. "I'll explain more later, but it's almost dawn, which is Shadarr's feeding time. He gets very grumpy without his morning meal. Once, my old soldier-in-training forgot to feed the Dragon, which was one of his daily routines to help get accustomed to working for me, and sadly, it

39

didn't end well for him. Fortunately for us, Shadarr did get to eat that day."

I cringed. Well, that was a gruesome story, whether or not it was actually true. "Tony, release her from the straps, but keep her hands secured behind her." Nathaniel ordered.

Luke held me still while Tony undid the bonds. I didn't bother to fight when we trudged out of Nathaniel's weapons room and down a different hall. With Nathaniel in lead, Bruce behind him, Luke, Tony, and I in the middle and Ezekial following in the rear, we trekked down a flight of stairs and into a dark corridor made of mossy stone.

The hallway ceiling grew taller the farther down we went, up to twenty feet tall and ten feet wide. I wondered what animal would be so large as to need this much space just to walk. Both the logical and illogical answer to that thought was Shadarr. This was the way to wherever they were keeping a supposed Dragon locked up. Damn, I hoped there wasn't going to be a pet lizard dressed up in a Dragon costume sitting in the center of the room. That would be the biggest joke of the century. And once the joke's over, I get to go home.

I couldn't shut out the daunting voice that whispered in my ear every passing second.

Don't be stupid. They killed your dog. They murdered your mom. Murdered your dad.

I've seen paintings and read books all about how big they were said to be, but up until five minutes ago, Dragons didn't exist. I guess since they do now, I should try my best not to piss it off. And if Shadarr was young, one would only assume he would still be awfully large compared to the average human.

We soon arrived at an eerie, spiked metal gate with a thick log of wood covering the entrance as a barricade. There was a wooden sign nailed next to the gate:

40

Shadarr the Dragon- Only open gate at feeding time & during emergencies. No weapons beyond this gate, as they make Shadarr very nervous. With all due respect, Payton Hilles the dragon trainer.

(P.S. Shadarr doesn't like trespassers and won't hesitate to attack).

Nathaniel flashed a devilish smile in my direction when Bruce and Ezekial moved the log out of the way. They pushed the door open and stepped over the threshold, pulling me along.

I almost forgot to breathe when I gazed upon Shadarr's pen. Or at least, I thought that's what it was. The room resembled an old, poorly treated farm estate. It was as long and wide as two football fields, and the ceiling I estimated to be as tall as a twenty-story building, about the same height as the Riverside Church building in downtown NYC from the time I visited a summer ago. The floor was hard packed soil covered with dead grass and a few rotting Bradford pear trees. Hidden behind a partially felled tree was a mossy pond, bustling with the activity of frogs, noisy amphibians, and groups of small fish.

Yet that wasn't anywhere near impressive as the enormous figure flying above our heads. The flying animal looked like a giant, black pterodactyl with a long-pointed tail and really, *really* sharp claws from down below. I gulped. It was Shadarr.

"Shadarr, *descende hinc!*" Nathaniel shouted.

I jumped in surprise when a gruff, deep voice reverberated in the back of my skull, like a drumbeat.

"I am Shadarr, *unus de natus est in dracones in saecula.*" The unfamiliar voice seemed to echo around me. Two

41

years of German did not get me very far when it came to translating weird languages.

I gawked at the creature, when, with powerful strokes of his wings, it flew down to our level and landed with a ground shaking thud before us.

Shadarr was as long as a school bus from snout to the tip of his tail, which appeared to have tiny spikes, and a wingspan close to that length. His narrowed eyes, red as the sun, held a fiery spirit. His scales were an array of colors ranging from dark sapphire to the color of coal, light from the flimsy light bulbs strung about the area reflecting off of Shadarr's hide in shoots of dark black and blue ombres. I couldn't believe it...although this massive beast was standing before me, I thought for a moment that this thing could all have been a result from whatever drugs Nathaniel had injected me with, but I could *feel* how real Shadarr was. From the warm air of his breath beating on our faces, to the miniature tremors that threw me off balance when he moved, and the gouges in the earth from his claws marking the soil.

I spotted Luke and Bruce throwing broken tree branches to the side of the pond, seemingly annoyed, and Tony still stood silently behind Nathaniel. Ezekial was busy dragging something that looked like a deer carcass to be dumped in a deep ditch to the right of a mound of feces, covering his mouth with his arm. Everyone seemed to be completely unfazed of the beast that was before them.

Shadarr couldn't be a trick of the mind, or a super realistic robot. The thought that Shadarr could not be anything but alive and breathing threw me off kilter. Shadarr stretched out his legs and neck, shaking his head like a dog. Small flakes of dust and dirt rained down. He flapped his translucent wings, buffeting the humans before him with a strong wind. The ground rumbled like an old building's foundation in an earthquake with each step the creature took.

42

"You're…magnificent!" I breathed. I could do nothing but stare at the massive beast in awe. The Dragon cocked his head in my direction as if he were listening to the secrets that floated on the wind, and his slit eyes zeroed in on me. This time when he spoke, he communicated in English.

"Nekoda, soon to be one of the most powerful demigods in centuries. I am honored to meet you. Nathaniel has spoken greatly of your powers, but I must admit, he has bad plans for you and your powers. Do not succumb to his tricks for a second." He sounded bitterly sad in my mind. Did Shadarr have only Nathaniel and his dogs for company here? I didn't know exactly how I was supposed to respond to that, so I voiced my question out loud to no one in particular. "Can anyone else hear the talking Dragon? Or is it just me?"

It was Bruce who answered. "If you are who you seem to be, then only you and Nathaniel, amongst a few others, can talk directly with Dragons. That is, communicating with your minds and sending thoughts to each other, sort of like an internal email. It's a rare gift not many Skin-changers are born with. That's also another reason why you're so different, I guess."

"Oh. Is that bad thing or a good thing?" I asked.

"Depends on who or what you're speaking to," Nathaniel replied. "Alright, enough gawking. Dragon, Jones. Jones, Dragon. This is important information you need to listen to. Since we've already introduced each other, we need to go over your feeding routine. As long as you are permitted, you're to be in charge of making sure the beast gets fed every day."

Heck, I was going to be taking care of an actual Dragon. A real, live, carnivorous predator! Was this why they decided to kidnap me and threaten my family? To take care of a mythical, fire-breathing specimen as well as hand over some fake book? Seemed a tad bit absurd to go through all that trouble just to find a Dragon nanny.

"From this day onward, every morning and afternoon you will be led down to Shadarr's pen with a guard to feed and accompany Shadarr. If you miss his feeding time, he tends to get a little hangry, as I've mentioned before. And since it seems he's taking a liking to you already, he just may not eat you. Anywho, Shadarr eats about one-hundred twenty-five pounds of processed meat per day. Which means for each meal, he needs to consume around seventy-five pounds. The portions of food will be brought out from the freezer at night to thaw so it's ready for the next day, every night. You get a half hour of free time to talk. Otherwise, it's safer for everyone if Shadarr eats alone, and you don't want to have to clean his mess afterward. You start in one day, with Luke as your guard. Got it? Good." Nathaniel explained, not bothering to listen to my unwanted protests.

First, Nathaniel wants me for some magical book, then he wants me as a weapon, and now he's wanting me to act as a dragon-sitter, too? I would be fine dealing with just one problem, but not all three. All of this was just...well, crazy. Was Shadarr a way for me to be more involved with what Nathaniel had planned?

With Ezekial and Bruce tugging me forward, we exited the pen, leaving Shadarr alone. On my way out, I glanced back at, and I couldn't help but feel a twinge of sympathy for the captive animal.

"*One day, you will see the sky again.*" I echoed the words in my head, hoping Shadarr could hear.

"*Good luck, Nekoda,*" Shadarr rumbled back. And like a speeding fighter jet, he took off into the open air of his pen, dark wings flapping up and up and up.

Chapter III: Man Gone Rogue

I don't remember falling asleep in my cot, but I was awakened by two large, cold hands grabbing me off of it. I didn't know if it was day or night, or how long I'd been sleeping as there seemed to be no clocks or windows in this place. I shrieked, trying to get away by running out the cell door, only to have Luke pull the back of my sweatshirt and wrestle me to the ground in a one-armed grip before dragging me down the hall. He turned left down a new hallway and entered an unfamiliar room.

The room we stepped into resembled a training facility. Ezekial, Bruce, Tony and Nathaniel were milling around the area, talking amongst themselves and fidgeting with pointy objects. There was another wall of weapons as previously set up in the Nutcase room that extended around to another section of wall. Along one side hung rows of various firearms and artillery up on large pieces of pegboard. I saw a few types of guns that I recognized, such as the common sniper rifle and submachine gun, AK-47's, pistols, and others used in military services.

But what amazed me the most was the enormous collections of blades and swords. Half of their weapon stock was common day artillery, and the other half was stuff you would see sold at an auction. I spotted throwing daggers, a couple ballistae knives and wicked looking hunting knives. Of the swords, I recognized some from my medieval history novels and History channel shows—Medieval Rapiers, ancient gladiuses, Roman short swords, Hoplites swords, Chokutōs, Katzbelgers, Khopesh blades from early Egypt, east-Roman falcatas, Spathas, some odd-looking ceremonial daggers, a few Kukris and traditional Japanese Katanas, swords made of steel, and—

"Is that dried blood on the mace? And is that a *gold* sword?" I couldn't help but ask.

A young man seemed to appear out of nowhere. He looked around the same age as the other men, with a trimmed beard and warm copper colored eyes above a slightly hooked nose. He looked like my dad's brother, my Uncle Travis, except for his brown arms were inked in strange tattoos and his face was adorned with multiple red scars running down the length of his jawline; I suspected he wasn't nearly as nice as my uncle.

"Err, yes, it appears to be. And no, to be precise, it's celestial bronze. It may look and shine like gold, but it's not. Celestial Bronze is a very strong metal, but quite rare nowadays. The Greeks, Romans, Trojans and Spartans all used this material for weapons and protection back in A.D. It's not a very malleable metal, though. Only an explosion from a bazooka, RPG, or another weapon made of Celestial bronze can conflict damage to it. Or you toss it into a volcano. There's another strong ore called Imperial gold, although it's used more to show off the dazzling shine of the material and flaunt your wealth." he informed, his voice a soft British accent.

Cautious, I went along with whatever this man was rambling on about, if only to delay my time spent with the five other psychos.

"Here we go again," Tony griped, rolling his eyes.

"Shh, I like his lessons!" said Bruce.

"Is celestial bronze stronger than normal bronze? What does the RPG do? I have an uncle in the military and he recently had an opportunity to use weapons such as those you have," I pointed towards the weapon wall. "But he never taught me too much about them, as he never had the time."

"Really? Well, I'd be glad to teach you the inner workings of—" the man started.

Nathaniel growled from his spot at the glass-topped table. "David, she's just trying to waste time. Get over here." He pushed out of his chair and stood up.

David nodded sheepishly and joined Nathaniel. I guess David wasn't as much as brute as I expected him to be. Everyone around here seemed to be afraid of Nathaniel, except for Tony, who followed him around like a lost puppy dog.

"Nekoda, meet David. He will be your trainer, you, his trainee. You and David will practice the art of offense and defense, and hopefully help you to summon your powers before the Claiming Moon." Nathaniel said.

"Is that possible?" I asked, trying not to sound too terribly interested.

"Yes, but it is hard to achieve." said Nathaniel.

"What Skin-Changer are you? A weasel?" *A stupid, ugly weasel.*

Nathaniel muttered, "That's classified."

"I bet you're a weasel, you're totally a weasel. Have you been through your Claiming Moon then, Mr. Macho?"

"That's classified as well," he grunted.

"Well, what *isn't* classified information?"

"Mhmph, no comment."

"Fine. When does practice start?"

"Now."

"Alrighty then."

Luke released his hand from my shoulder and pushed me towards Nathaniel and David. I stumbled, pathetically attempting to right myself. Without a word, David grabbed my upper arm and pulled me to the weapons wall.

47

"First session we will begin with is self-defense. Shooting firearms, knife throwing, and how to throw a punch. Sword fighting will be the last event in self-defense, and it's also the best. Offense is the second session. We'll practice more hand-to-hand combat, and you will learn to use your powers and control them, once gained. These lessons should be able to fuel your ability to call upon your magic. Is that clear?" David asked.

"Wait, what exactly does any of this have to do with the prophecy? Is there a real rhyme or reason as to why I really need to be doing this, aside from unlocking my so-called potential?" I inquired.

David sighed and rubbed the back of his neck. "No, it's not as simple as you might think. The Fates' prophecy says that 'A child of the gods shall be reborn to stop the war of worlds. With the creatures of the moon and powers of the mighty—'"

"What's the point in rambling off the prophecy if she doesn't even know who the Three Fates are? Not to mention, everything we say probably goes in one ear and out the other." Nathaniel scoffed, visibly irritated.

I crossed my arms. "Uh, yes, I do. They're the trio of goddesses who spin mortals' destinies."

Luke turned to David. "See? She knows."

"Look, you are already aware that the Olympians are very much alive and thriving. Our two worlds coexist every single day, albeit not for all the right reasons. You of all people should know this. I'm sure you've seen a thing or two in your lifetime that you can't possibly explain. There are monsters that need to be slain, gods that need to be reasoned with, and prophecies that need fulfilling. The mortals are to be reckoned with or ignored," Nathaniel grumbled. "They don't fit in with us, and we do not fit in with them. What you believe or don't agree with momentarily isn't a concern to us. What does is why and how you're the child chosen by Fate, and if you can prove it."

Bruce yawned. "Wake me up when that day comes."

"Clara and Kyle sure didn't have much hope in that happening." Luke snickered under his breath.

They killed my family. They killed my family.

I froze. "Wake me up when my dad has you arrested!" I seethed, curling my hands into fists to prevent more tears from falling.

"How about you wake up before you realize that the future will be far crueler to you than I will ever be?" Nathaniel snapped, slamming a hand down on the table. I glanced up. His eyes brimmed with anger, and unspoken questions balanced at the tip of my tongue. There was a lot Nathaniel wasn't telling me and wasn't going to. "David, prepare Nekoda for our first session. All of you, quit your fussing. *Now!*"

David, momentarily confused, grabbed a small pistol, a polished hunting rifle, and another gun from the pegboard I didn't recognize. Bruce came up and dropped half the stock of throwing daggers into a box and picked up two bullet-proof vests from the glass table.

We walked over to a section of the widespread target room where a red X was painted on the concrete floor. The cracked stone foundation behind it was peppered with bullet holes. "Stand here," David ordered, shoving the pistol into my hands. Bruce strapped on the bullet-proof vest and stood against the wall in front, a good eighty-five yards away, he informed me.

The next few minutes were spent by David demonstrating how to turn the safety on and off, reload, and hold the weapon correctly. I pulled on my own vest and put in the orange ear plugs he had given me and positioned the gun against my body, hands on the stock, finger on the trigger. "Look down the barrel of the gun with one eye, no, squint the other, and— no, lower the gun a tad

49

bit. Good, now aim carefully. When you're ready, pull the trigger." David instructed.

"Wait, you want me to *shoot* Bruce? What if I hurt him?" Actually, that wasn't sounding like such a bad idea at the moment.

"You won't hurt him; you'll be aiming for the vest," I was momentarily confused. Even for them, this was a reckless thing for me to be doing. They either thought that I was completely incapable of turning a gun on them, or they knew that if I tried, someone else would have stopped me. "And it's not a choice, aim *only* for the vest and nowhere else, or you'll find yourself standing up there in no time." Nathaniel threatened, standing ominously behind me.

"Yeah, yeah, understood. Everyone might want take a step back before I shoot someone's eye out." I forewarned. David stepped up to adjust the gun placement on my shoulder before giving his approval, positioning his hands atop of mine to help with the first shot.

I glanced over the instructor's head. No one had budged. I rolled my eyes, exasperated by their stupidity. Well, they can't say I didn't warn them.

Taking a deep, steadying breath, I squinted one eye closed and peered down the barrel of the gun, face up to the little scope. After a few minutes of adjusting, the two glass scopes aligned and focused, and Bruce came into sight. I aimed the tip of the firearm level with Bruce's ribcage—and fired. There was a loud CRACK! as the bullet whizzed out and struck Bruce in the side. "Oof!" I was rewarded with a painful jolt to the shoulder; the kick the rifle had surprised me. I also was the worst, most inexperienced person to currently be firing a gun. I grunted in pain, rubbing the sore spot on my shoulder blade.

Yards away, Bruce was assessing the damage to his vest. The bullet had lodged itself in the thick material of the vest, while the force knocked him back a couple inches. Otherwise, Bruce had stood his ground. I half-expected for him to be on his knees, bleeding, instead of bruised and dazed. I wasn't aware that bullet-proof vests could stop a bullet from a rifle without inflicting some extremely painful, er, pain.

"Not bad for a first shot. But if you really want to cause some serious damage, aim for the heart or liver." Nathaniel said, rubbing his chin thoughtfully.

I cocked the gun, whispering, "I'll aim for your liver."

"What was that?" barked Nathaniel.

"Nothing."

"We'll practice with that a few more times before switching to the other handguns." informed David.

I perched the rifle against my shoulder and took aim. This time I prepared myself for the weapon's kickback without David's support. The bullet hit Bruce square in the stomach, and he doubled over in pain. He wheezed from afar, flashing a quick thumbs-up.

"Uh..." If only Logan and Maggie could see me now, learning how to shoot a firearm while a bunch of lunatics praised me on my half-ass attempts.

"Nicely done! You're taking on faster than I expected." David complimented, clapping me on the back. I shifted away from his touch and took a few more shots with the rifle and went on to practice with the other guns. The 9-millimeter pistol I fired next had a lot less kick than the Rifle and a 0.40 caliber handgun. Although I did okay for the most part, there were a couple times I misfired, as shown by multiple new bullet holes decorating the walls.

"If only she could stand up there herself, see what it's like," Tony *tsk*ed, now speaking up from his quiet spot in the corner. "I think it'd be a mighty fine learning experience."

I lowered the gun, adamant on participating as a moving target. "Huh. Y'know what else might be a learning experience? My foot up your a—"

"Ah-ha, I was just thinking that, Tony. Good idea." Nathaniel agreed, his voice floating over mine own. I shot him (pun intended) one of my *are-you-serious?!* faces. David snatched the rifle out of my hands and laid it gently on a portable rack.

"Go on, get over there. And put this on." Luke handed me a pair of protective glasses. I reluctantly did so before trudging over to the wall, palms slick with sweat. *God, I'm actually doing this, I'm actually doing* this*!*

David stood on the X and picked up the pistol, which he explained was called a Desert Eagle, and was not the same as the caliber pistol I had handled. It felt like years had passed until he lifted the weapon and stared down the barrel of the gun. Sweat popped out on my forehead and began gliding down my forehead. His finger tightened on the trigger and—CRACK! He fired.

I braced myself for the impact—but nothing came. I didn't feel…dead. I peeled my eyes open and glanced around me, unclenching my blistered fists. Shards of stone and dust now decorated my vest and shoulders, but there was no bullet protruding from my gear. There was only a small hole in the stone directly above my head. If David had really intended to put a bullet in my brain…

Oh, God, I was going to puke.

"Are we done here?" I gasped, bent over, hands on shaking knees.

To my relief, Nathaniel said yes and we made our way over to the equipment area. Bruce and I took off the vests while Tony and David carried the guns back to the pegboards.

Tony motioned for me to stand behind a black painted line before a red target stand and Bruce placed the box of knives and daggers at my feet.

"Luke is your bladesman teacher. He's an expert at knife throwing and blade work and possesses excellent craftsmanship. He's also my right-hand man. If I can't get something accomplished, I send Luke out to do my dirty work. He's quite good at it, I might add."

Ah, I thought. *Exposed at last; he's your personal hitman.*

"It would not be wise to try and escape when he's around; Luke is always armed, and he's not afraid to carve you a new design or two." at that, Luke flashed a cocky grin. "You may demonstrate now, Lukas." Nathaniel ordered.

Luke walked up to the target beside mine and produced three throwing-knives from his leather jacket. He grabbed the handle of a sharp-edged dagger, cocked back his arm, and threw. THUNK! The knife hit dead center in the middle, a perfect bullseye. Then he proceeded to throw the other two knives, and unsurprisingly, Luke hit three bullseyes in a row.

The ginger-haired man turned to face me, seemingly unperturbed by his feat. "Now, you try." Nathaniel snapped his fingers, and Bruce handed me a throwing-knife, one of the many he held in his massive hands. Luke adjusted the angle of my arm as I prepared to launch the small blade at the target, knuckles white as icecaps against the tough leather grip of the handle.

CLANK! The knife soared through the air— and missed the red circle by a few feet, clattering off the stone wall. "Oops," I said.

53

"Try again," Luke said, and Bruce passed another dagger over. "This time, aim for the target, and not the wall."

With the next attempt, I managed to hit the target with the blade sticking to the very edge of the outer line. I tried a third time. No luck— it landed a couple inches left of the target next to mine.

"Uh-huh, I see what's wrong, you're not focusing enough. Concentrate on the target, and only the target. Nothing else. It's like baseball, you have to keep your eye on the ball in order to hit it with the bat. Except for you're going to bend back your arm, your thumb and forefinger should cross at a perfect ninety-degree angle, and the dagger should hit its target." Luke pointed out, expertly spinning one of the knives in his hand.

I wanted to scream. I wanted to punch someone's lights out. *How could* you *possibly know what's wrong?* I *know what's wrong! My parents are probably in the ground, my dog is dead, and I'm stuck with you freaks!* But I didn't. I wouldn't explode, and not was not the time, not if I wanted to get out of here alive. Instead, I grabbed a fourth and fifth knife from Bruce, sucked in a lungful of stale air, and stomped over to my target. The knife I was holding had a razor-sharp serrated edge, sharp enough to cut skin if grazed.

I cocked my arm back and threw. CA-THUNK!—the knife soared through the air, end over end, embedding itself a few inches closer in the outer ring, barely holding on. I made to hurl the last dagger, but my hand wavered, and my heart suddenly sank. I swallowed the bile that was crawling up my throat. Shouldn't these people be torturing me about whatever 'Book' it is they're wanting instead of teaching me self-defense, or revealing a live Dragon? Screw what Nathaniel had to say about my powers, the more I thought about, the more it occurred to me that what I had spent the last couple hours doing still didn't add up. I turned to David, the quiet one of the bunch.

54

"W-why," I cleared my throat. "Why am I learning how to shoot guns, throw sharp objects, and play nanny to a giant lizard? An actual Dragon…God, that's nuts. Saying it out loud, God, you are all insane. Frankly, I-I don't care who you are, but I don't want to go along with this. If I'm to be okay with being taught this stuff, shouldn't I know the real reason why you're training me? And I don't want some bullshit answer about how some old goddesses chose me."

David opened and closed his mouth like a fish out of water. I looked at the mysterious men around me. They all stood silent, arms crossed, lips sealed.

"Anyone care to speak up? What, you're all scared of this freakshow breaking open a can of whup-ass on you?" I hissed, pointing a finger at Nathaniel.

Shit. I was going to explode too soon. Too. Soon. But who the hell gave one lick about what I did?

The head boss gave me a cold, menacing look, which I stupidly ignored. What, did it take too much time and effort out of their day to give me a legitimate answer? My head pounded, and I released all the anger I'd been bottling since coming back to consciousness.

I shouldn't have snapped, oh, I told myself I wouldn't, but I did.

He killed them. He killed them and no one cares.

"Go to hell!" I yelled and chucked the other knife straight at Nathaniel's figure.

He stood ramrod still, calm, and held up his hand, palm out.

For one horrifying split second, I feared the knife was going to soar clean through his hand and I was really going to lose my head, but it didn't. The knife ceased rotation mid-air, a mere centimeter away from his palm. If Nathaniel hadn't stopped the knife, it

55

would have pierced through flesh and bone and embedded itself in the concrete pillar behind him, narrowly missing his shoulder. Instead, the blade floated as if suspended by a wire. It was like the scene from a movie where the main actor dodges bullets in slow-motion. Nathaniel grinned, a wild look now in his eyes.

I really fucked up this time.

His laugh held no emotion. He walked forward to where I stood, and fear consumed my body. With each step Nathaniel took, a shiver spider-walked down my back.

"You, girl, think you can *hurt* me? Take my life, without it resulting in your own untimely death? If I were you, I would not even think about trying that again. *Ever*," he raged. "Not unless you pay the price. Since you insist on me spilling all my plans, I will. But first—"

In one fluid movement Nathaniel had managed to sweep my feet out from underneath me. I was staring up at the ceiling, lying flat on my back. Tony and Luke pinned my arms, holding me firmly in place. Bruce, Ezekial and David stood nearby, unfazed.

"As I was saying before, I was going to reveal why we're training with you in the first place. And that being said, the obvious reason is because of your powers. But if you don't really have them, at least you'll be of some use in the upcoming war. A trained soldier is better than none. You have the blood of the *gods*, for Gaia's sake! You're a damn powerful Skin-changer! We don't know what specific breed of Skin-changer yet, but we'll find out on the night of the Claiming Moon," he pinched the bridge of his nose. "In order to master your powers, you need to master the art of mortal powers first. How can one possibly defend themself with skills otherworldly if they cannot defend themselves physically, without relying on magic? It is imperative that you learn how to defend yourself both physically and mentally, and to know how to make any of your surrounding objects a plausible weapon. It will help in learning how to yield to your abilities." Nathaniel crouched to be level with me.

"Since you're a Skin-changer with the blood of every powerful Olympian running in your veins, it makes you a hundred times more dangerous. A very powerful, and very dangerous hybrid demigod. If it wasn't for me, you'd have the highest bounty on your head right now. You have *no* idea what others will do to have you in their hands. I've prevented you from worse suffering at the hands of other demigods, assassins, and creatures who caught your scent in the wind." He stepped closer until his face was, terrible enough, inches from mine. "You are the key to saving, or destroying, both worlds. *You* are the weapon, Nekoda."

When he was through talking, I expected him to say that this was all some big joke that we would laugh about later. But he didn't. I was truly and utterly speechless.

"Why me, in particular? Why couldn't it have been somebody else?" I whispered in response.

"Your family's past and inheritance play a big role in that. It's more complicated than you think. It is not something that your parents may have revealed to you." he sighed, waited a beat. "Now, may we get back to training? There's been enough commotion for the day, and frankly I'm beginning to lose my temper." Nathaniel answered brusquely.

I was tempted to say no, then thought better of it. I simply nodded, and Luke and Tony released their grip. I trudged over to another section of the training room, a large mat covering the hard floor. Beside it lay swords and pointy things of all types and sizes, old and new. Ezekial and David carried over two sets of shiny, glittering metal shirts. The metal shirts resembled something from the knight statue on display in my town's museum. It was chainmail armor, or, in this case, practice suits. It was just a perfect day (or night?) to stab someone in the eye with a foot-long sword.

Ezekial also carried over two wooden circles with steel rims. Goodie. Practice shields.

For the next hour, give or take, David taught a clumsy teenager how to wield a sword, which actually turned out to be pretty cool, although I certainly wasn't going to admit it. I learned the basic sword tactics like parry, thrust, block, etcetera. We also did a bit of work on shield defense. At first it was hard to maintain a steady pace when attempting to listen to David spit out sequences of sword maneuvers, but pretty soon I got used to the sound of blade against blade, and the feel of the faux leather hilt in my hand.

☾

The next morning, (I assume), Nathaniel announced that I was ready for a practice fight, and I was to be David's opponent.

I had spent the rest of my time after our practice dozing on and off on my cot, after Ezekial had escorted me back. I was given no food, no water, nothing, for the first night. I was left alone to the emptiness of my cell. At first, I thought it was because they didn't care, but I realized later that it was most likely to weaken me so I wouldn't have the strength to fight back.

David and I both wore the chainmail shirt on over our clothes. I took off my sweatshirt and tennis shoes so I was left wearing my blue shirt and jeans, even though it was chilly in the training facility and humid throughout the rest of the building. The slight wind coming from one of the small electrical fans on the floor kissed against my skin, and the cut on my cheek stung in response. It felt like I had inflicted a deep razor cut on the soft skin behind my knee, and the pain would flare up every now and then. Luckily, the bleeding had stopped and dried on my face overnight, but the throbbing hadn't gone away. The lack of food in my stomach made me feel even more sickly, the nausea continuously hitting me in waves.

I got situated into my battle stance, knees slightly bent, sword grasped in my right hand, and feet spread out hip width apart, one foot slightly forward. The movement felt almost normal. Like I had done this a thousand times before, with all the hacking and slashing and stabby-stabbing. Yet it was different than that one time I attempted fencing lessons in second grade. It was a weird feeling, but nonetheless I was ready for this to be done and over with.

"When I give the signal, you may begin!" Bruce conducted, standing beside Nathaniel, Tony, and Ezekial who stood on David's side of the mat. Luke had wandered off to the other side of the mat where extra equipment was laid out.

"Adjust your battle positions, get ready... and... fight!" Bruce threw down his arm, like the girl who tossed a handkerchief into the air at a drag race. I could feel eyes at the back of my head, and I knew it was Tony judging my every move, praying I'd slip up and make a mistake. When I glanced back, he was making rude gestures at me, much like an immature toddler. Nathaniel stood, silent, watching us intensely. Ezekial was hovering by Luke.

"C'mon, Davey! Let's go, let's go! I want to see some arse kicking!" Tony spoke out, mimicking in a sore British accent.

"Shut up, will you? This will be over soon, and I sure don't want to be hearing your sorry ass shouting in my ear all day." Luke snapped, rolling his eyes.

Ezekial grumbled and rubbed the back of his neck. "Oi, the both of you are of no help whatsoever." Tony flipped him off and continued to entertain himself.

"Don't worry, I'll go easy on you." David whispered as we circled one another. He appeared to be a decent young man, as long as I've been around him so far. It seemed rather odd that

59

someone such as him was working for a monster such as Nathaniel.

I narrowed my eyes, not in the least bit fooled. I didn't—*shouldn't*—trust Mr. Nice Guy, or anyone here for that matter. He had yet to show any reason to earn my trust, aside from that fact that he hasn't slapped me.

"Oh, how sweet." I murmured, a line of sweat already dripping its way down my neck. Something flickered across his face, some emotion I couldn't read. He blinked.

And then I thrust my blade forward.

I lunged at him, aiming for a blow to the ribs. David blocked the move with his shield and jabbed at my side. I leapt away just in time, like a jackrabbit jolting away from a snake. I stepped back to gain more fighting room, my nerves already getting the best of me. A flimsy overhead cut was made, and I brought the sword down on David's shoulder blade, forcing him to take a step back. I thrust out again, and he parried the move before coming at me with a flurry of tricks and movements, which most of the hits I took. I could already tell just how stiff I was going to be in the morning. Ouch.

David paused to shift the sword from one hand to the other, and that quick window of time gave me a chance to try a disarming maneuver, which he shield-blocked (again) before pushing me backwards, toward the edge of the mat. As the minutes ticked on, we sparred, trying to knock each other off balance, him not letting up. Me not being knocked out on the floor within the first five seconds of the match was a dead giveaway that David was hardly putting any effort into this, and the fact that a sheen of sweat already covered my face, arms, and neck. David could fight a hundred times better than what we were doing right now, and that thought only infuriated me more.

At last, Bruce told us to stop and rest for the next session. David plopped down beside me and feebly attempted to praise me on my new skill.

"I admit, for a few moments there you almost had me beat! You're a natural, Nekoda. I never knew someone learned as fast as you could, and with such a different styled weapon. Man, I know this may sound corny, but it's like you were born to fight!"

"She was, David." Nathaniel explained curtly, as if that summed up everything.

"So, who should she fight next? Nekoda needs a challenge; I feel like she should know what it's like to be matched against a stronger, more powerful opponent. Just a fun little exercise." Ezekial spoke up, popping his head out from around one of the pillars. Luke, standing next to him, nodded his head in agreement.

"Yeah, I think so too. And I know who her next opponent should be." Nathaniel answered, eyes glittering.

Oh, I was so hoping the Man of Steel would beat Ezekial's face in in his sleep.

I looked back at Nathaniel, wondering if he saw the fear in my eyes or could hear the rapid thundering of my heart. Luke shoved me forward, back onto the slick mat. I picked up the sword and practice shield and got ready for a beating. This was so unfair; I was about to be turned into a punching bag.

"Alright, I'm good to go." I said, my throat more parched than it was before.

"Nathaniel, sir, go easy on her for this round." David whispered when he stepped away from the mats.

"If I must," Nathaniel smirked, unsheathing his weapon. The sword was the same one he had with him when he broke into my house in the middle of the night. It was a dark, emerald green sword with a black hilt wrapped in a shiny leather, the blade as

61

long as his arm. The weapon was remarkably pristine. There was something odd about seeing Nathaniel, graceful with his sword and threatening with his composure, that seemed so…right. To me, it was a beautiful and dangerous sight.

Bruce waited until the both of us were situated in our fighting stances, weapons at the ready. He looked to Nathaniel, fiddling with the collar of his shirt, one scarred hand gripping his sword. Bruce ran a hand over his bald top, and blew out a breath. I saw the edge of a curling tattoo peeking out from his shirt sleeve. "Fight!" he called out as Tony, Luke, and Ezekial cheered Nathaniel on. David, looking around shyly, mouthed words of encouragement for me to attack first. Again, I wondered how such a nice lad ended up working for someone like Nathaniel. I hoped he wasn't in some kind of trouble.

Honestly, the fight was over in a matter of minutes, but it would have ended twenty seconds before Bruce had even started the match if Nathaniel had actually tried. If David had given even ten percent during our battle, then Nathaniel was giving zero percent in this challenge.

Nathaniel thrust out and I deflected the strike, swinging randomly at his sword hand. He dodged it and came at me in a flurry of attacks and hits that I could not defend myself against, no matter how wildly I wielded my weapon. I inadvertently dropped my practice sword when tripping over my own foot, the dull silver sword clattering to the blue mat. That earned a few sniggers from the onlookers, and my cheeks reddened even more. We danced around for a while, stabbing and clashing, wolf versus pup. My arms felt like I was giving five-hundred percent in this fight, whilst Nathaniel did not appear to be out of breath.

He swung his blade in an overhead arc, and I ungraciously jumped and fell to the side, and in doing so miscalculated his next move by misinterpreting his motive. In mid-swing, Nathaniel had switched maneuvers, and with a flick of his wrist, my sword was now lying a few feet away on the cold floor.

Weaponless, I threw the shield at Nutcase Nathaniel's head only for him to duck and deftly move out of range. With a sweeping kick that knocked my legs out from under me, I was left sprawled-eagle on my back, wheezing and sore.

"OW!" In one swift movement, the tip of Nathaniel's sword was pressed into my throat. I held my breath, feeling a pricking sensation when he nudged the bottom of my chin with the emerald-green sword.

"There are three easy rules to remember when versing an opponent. Rule number one," Nathaniel held up one finger for me to see. "expect anything. Likewise, there are many tactics and sequences when fighting. Sometimes people take the easy way out and use trickery. Rule number two," he held up a second finger. "learn your opponent's strengths and weaknesses. When they fight, study them, learn their every move, how they're most likely to react. It will help to know how to defeat your opponent without a struggle. Rule number three: take every chance you are given to take down your opponent. Because someday soon you could be facing someone that's not so merciless nor clumsy. If you are to prevail over your greatest enemy, you need not only strength and speed, but intelligence too." scoffed Nathaniel.

Lately I've been thinking that *Nathaniel* is my worst, and greatest, enemy. Funny how things go.

He took a step back, raising his immaculate blade. Luke came over and grasped me by the arm, yanking me up off my feet once more.

"So, what now, we go again?" I asked sheepishly, wincing at the bruise I felt forming on my thigh.

"Actually, I think we've had enough sword practice for now. Perhaps it's time for some *real* fighting. Y'know, skin to skin." Tony piped up, glancing at Nathaniel.

"Oh, of course, we can get started—*right now.*" Nathaniel replied, gesturing towards the makeshift ring. He sheathed his sword and handed the practice equipment to his minions to dispose of. Right then and there, in a blur of movement so fast I didn't recognize who it was until he was face to face, hands clenched into fists, racing for me.

"Wait, what are—?" the rest of my words were choked off when Tony rammed into my side, knocking us both to the mat in a tangle of limbs, like a two-hundred-pound quarterback sacking a scrawny linebacker. "*Oof!*" I was knocked backwards a few feet, my hand stuck underneath my stomach. It took us a tantalizing long second to extricate ourselves and get off the ground.

"Come on, get up! Take a swing at me, girlie." Tony teased, hopping back and forth like one of those old school Rock 'em Sock 'em Robots. I stood, knees slightly bent, hands raised. Tony gave me a mischievous smile, anticipating my next move. I threw a punch at him, but he sidestepped my fist and lashed out. His own fist clipped me in the jaw, my head jerking back. I cried out and dodged another attack, falling to the mat, hand cupping my face. Crawling backwards to escape his next clip, I kicked out feebly when he drew near.

Cackling sounded from the sidelines when a swift kick connected with his groin. Tony fell to his knees and moaned, and I made no time to relish in his suffering, advancing on him, ready to retaliate. Tony recovered too soon for me to inflict any more pain.

One second, I was standing above him, and the next I was under Tony's booted foot, the air being pushed out of my chest. "Urgh!" he picked me up by the front of my shirt with one hand. I writhed, trying to loosen his hold on my shirtfront, but he was in a furious state of crazy now.

64

"Ezekial, come here and help me take care of this brat!" Tony urged. The obedient scamp ran over from the side and onto the mat, taking me from Tony. He held my hands behind my back. I was outnumbered one to two and the other men weren't making any motion to stop them.

Tony prowled toward me and grabbed my shoulders, clamping down with strong hands. He brought up his leg, kneeing me in the gut. As all the air escaped my lungs in one painful breath, I was cuffed above the eye and cheek with exceptional strength. I pulled backwards, desperate to hide myself, but Ezekial was a rock wall behind me.

Unwanted, watery tears ran down my cheeks as a fresh wave of pain rolled over me. The entirety of my face felt like it had been bashed in with a frying pan, and the cut on my cheek was on fire. Tony leaned in, his reeking breath causing more salty tears to drop.

"You think you're safe, eh? You think the SWAT is on our tail and plans to save your ass? Your parents are dead; I shot them and burned the house down with their corpses inside. There's nothing left but ashes. Nathaniel loved every second of it. *I* loved every second of it. You couldn't win, Jones, and you *can't!*" he seethed, a growl in the back of his throat.

He was right, and we both knew it.

"Bastard!" I snarled.

"You can't win," he opened his mouth, baring his teeth.

Ezekial laughed, a smug expression on his face. Tony leaned in so his cheek brushed mine, his breath tickling my ear as he whispered.

I watched in agonizing horror, Tony's front canines elongating, and his eyes changing to a bright yellow, the color almost a glowing neon. Or maybe they've always been yellow?

"*What* are you?!"

He didn't answer, and instead brought his mouth closer to my face.

I was frozen. It was like a beast slowly sucking the life out its prey.

"Dude, Tony! Don't do it! Let her go, that's enough!" Ezekial abruptly intervened, trying to push him away. I regained my senses and tried to wriggle out of his grasp. Bruce and Luke came over, followed lastly by Nathaniel.

"What in Hades' name do you think you're doing, Tony? Back off, it's not time! When she's strong enough to use her powers and Change, she will. It's not her Claiming Moon yet. And besides, you don't want Hades to come back and imprison you again for harming a minor demigod. Much less a Skin-changer." Nathaniel shouted, now infuriated.

He's going to bite me he's going to rip out my throat he's going to kill me—

Tony seemed oblivious to his leader. Bruce's hand came down and grabbed the back of Tony's shirt collar and yanked with such force that the material tore. Ezekial grabbed one of Tony's arm while Bruce grabbed the other, shoving him back. I gasped and lurched to the side, despising the way his breath had felt on my bare skin.

"Tony, I think you need to get some rest. You two, take him to his quarters. Gods, where's David with those syringes and tubes I need?" Nathaniel said, ignoring me. I lay on the floor, trembling, sucking in a lungful of air. Now that he mentioned David, I hadn't noticed him walk away during the fist fight, although I had been too busy trying to defend myself to care. Once I felt like the world had righted itself and my heart rate slowed, I hefted myself up on my elbows and looked around.

Luke and Nathaniel were talking quietly in the corner. Ezekial, Tony, and Bruce were nowhere to be seen.

66

"Nekoda, are you alright? I'd felt your pain and didn't know what happened. I'm so sorry…" Shadarr's voice rumbled in my mind. It was such a relief to hear him, albeit still weird. I almost cried with joy.

"Shadarr? How are you doing—ack, never mind. No, no, I'm not alright. In fact, I think I'm having the worst day ever. I just had my training sessions. When Tony and I had an impromptu hand-to-hand combat, Tony went kinda nuts." I paused, hoping Shadarr could hear the fear in my voice. *"I think he was going to bite me, or suck the blood out of my neck because he's a druggie vampire and—"*

"Ah, yes, that. In the instances when a Skin-changer loses control of his or her emotions, instincts take over. He was a wild animal that you saw, not a vampire." Shadarr said grimly. *"An out of control beast of nature. Since he isn't as strong as the others, if it was Luke or even Nathaniel, the odds of you surviving would have been very slim."*

"Wow, that would have been nice to know five minutes ago! Agh, Shadarr, I gotta go. They're coming back." I replied as Nathaniel and Luke strolled in my direction. Behind them trudged David, holding a metal tray with two small vials, a syringe and needle, gauze, and a towel. For some reason, David was trying his best to avoid eye contact with me. *What are you up to, you sly Brit?* Shadarr didn't respond. He was already gone.

I backed away as the guys approached, trying to place myself as far from them as possible, not caring if I was leaving trails of blood and sweat on the hard floor. I stumbled to my feet, one hand pressed against my swollen forehead, scanning my surroundings. The only exit that was visible was the door we had entered through earlier. Just maybe…

When Nathaniel got within a foot from me, I broke off in a dead run and sprinted across the training room towards the door, head pounding. Twenty feet away, fifteen feet, ten feet, five…

"Wooaah!" Luke appeared in front of the door, seemingly out of nowhere. I came to an abrupt halt and tripped, falling right into Luke's arms. And not in the romantic way.

He wrapped his arms around my waist, my hands stuck against his stomach, his hold tight. Nathaniel and David were waiting at the blue practice mat. I refused to cause any more trouble when Luke pinned me to the floor, all energy draining from my body in that instant.

I suppressed a groan as Nathaniel held my arms in place for David to draw blood from a vein in my left arm into a small vial. He passed the vial to Nathaniel who slipped the vial inside his coat pocket.

"Hey, why do you need my blood anyway? You're not from Grey's An-Anatomy, are you?" I questioned, suddenly feeling queasy.

"Of course not." Luke scowled, climbing to his feet.

Nathaniel escorted me out the door, Luke in front and David in back, and we exited the training facility. Our footsteps bounced off the damp walls as we trod down the corridor and past the Nutcase room. I was ushered inside my cold cell.

On my cot lay a tray of food. I hadn't realized how hungry I was until then, my stomach gurgling. The nausea told me I probably have not eaten in over 24 hours, perhaps even a day and a half, who knew. Nathaniel locked the door and I fumbled for the cot, that sensation of puking if I didn't get something in my stomach soon although there was nothing to throw up.

On the tray was one red apple, a glass of water, and a ham sandwich. No cheese or mayonnaise, just two slices of ham, or something that looked like pork. I crunched into the apple, the sticky juices leaking from the corners of my mouth and onto my fingers. I switched between bites of sandwich and apple in a meticulous manner. After chugging the glass of water and chowing down on the rest of sandwich I leaned back on the bed, my head aching, wounds throbbing.

"Tomorrow is your first day with Shadarr. Remember, Luke will take you in the morning. From there two of my men will lead you to the training room. After, you and I are going to meet up with Tony and the others. Since you've discovered a tiny sliver of what I can do, I think I could help you gain your powers faster." Nathaniel informed me, a shadow in the cell door. Luke and David sauntered away down the hall.

"Whatever," I mumbled, easing myself onto my side, face to the wall. With food in my stomach, the loss of blood and bouts of drowsiness, it was easy to drift into an uncomfortable sleep.

Four teenage boys trampled through the trees, weapons at their sides. They ran and ran, seeming to know where they were going. One dark-skinned boy sported a crew-cut hairstyle and a small earring to accentuate his round, chocolate eyes.

A boy's voice floated on the wind. He had messy, snow-white hair and bright green eyes that stood out against his pale skin.

"Hey, Jacob, how much you wanna bet that I can beat Alex in PE tomorrow, huh?"

Jacob, the black teen, shook his head. "William, I'm done making any type of bet with you. Last time, I lost ten bucks! Besides, we all know I could beat your rear end all the way back to Camp!" he chuckled.

A black-haired boy with sharp hazel eyes framed by strong brows cut in, running in front of the other two. "As if! Sure, you can climb trees like a wild cat, you're one of our best spies, and sure as hell kick-ass at American football but..." He paused. "Wow, this sounds really degrading to my ego." The boy, Alex, sighed. "But James is top dog! Ha...get it...top dog..."

The fourth teen, James, ran farther ahead of them all. With golden hair, bicolored eyes and tanned skin, he looked like your average Californian fresh off the beach.

All four boys looked like they could be anywhere from fifteen to twenty years old. They were strong combatants, clearly shown by the ease in which they ran the trail in the woods, pushing themselves to move faster. Each teenager stood well above 5'5.

Jacob bore a short sword at his belt and a war hammer in his pocket. Will mindfully carried a Sniper Rifle in his hands, like a military trainee loaded down while running through his courses. Something that resembled a Roman Gladius up on Nathaniel's wall bounced against his side.

Alex, with a quiver of arrows and a camouflaged longbow slung over his back could pass as the present-day Robin Hood. James wore a golden sword with weird lettering engraved in the metal, and a sheath on his belt. A heavy-looking, uniquely designed shield was strapped across his broad back, circular like Captain America's.

"So, uh, James. Had any more dreams about that girl? Nikki? Natalie? Nicole?" asked Alex.

James slowed to a halt and faced his friends, mouth pressed into a thin line, nose pink from the cold.

"Nekoda. And that fool, Tony, almost bit her on the neck, though fortunately one of Nathaniel's lackies stopped him. Nathaniel, he's pretty unpredictable. I still can't figure out what they want with that girl. It's confusing."

The others looked grim. "Well, can't she escape? But, you know, at nighttime. Unseen. With the Dragon." Will suggested.

"Wait—Dragon? I haven't seen any Dragons yet. How do you know there is one?" James' eyes bulged, a puzzled look now on his face.

70

"I-I can sense him. He's lonely and afraid. Afraid for Nekoda. Afraid for his race dying out and afraid of the future. I can just tell." Will said, solemn, wiping the sweat off his brow.

Jacob stepped forward. "Wait, what? I don't get it. How does Nathaniel own a Dragon, one of the most dangerous and rarest species alive? Not to mention they're practically extinct, or well, were. *It doesn't add up. Why can't we just go and rescue them? I haven't seen any action since... Vincent went missing seven weeks ago."*

"Because Halt prohibited any more rescue missions. We have to lay low until we're sure Nathaniel doesn't show any signs of actually hurting her." James frowned, running a hand through his blonde locks.

"What!? But Tony just attempted to Change her! How is that not *hurting her?" Alex rebuked.*

"Nathaniel is a bigger threat than all of his soldiers combined! Tony is not much of a problem, but as of right now they all are, simply because she hasn't unlocked her powers yet. Nor does she know how to defend herself properly," explained James.

"But they're teaching her how to fight, and that's only because Nathaniel wants her as his secret weapon. Am I right? The farther away she is from Nathaniel, the safer." Will said thoughtfully.

"Dude, they aren't teaching her how to fight properly. *The only way she knows how to defend herself is through sheer anger and fear. She has the blood of all twelve Olympians running through her veins; everyone wants her to side with them. Plus, if she really is part of the prophecy, that makes her, Nekoda, a special case." Jacob put in. All heads turned toward James.*

71

"What do you think, should we try and save her?" Will asked.

James sighed, picking at the dead leaves and grass stuck to his shirt. "I have a weird feeling. Like I'm supposed to find her, save her. Only problem is, I don't know how. We don't know where Nathaniel is. And there's only the four of us, and Halt, who wouldn't want us to get more involved. No one else at Camp would risk their lives for some mortal girl, especially since Nathaniel hasn't specifically said that he's going to kill her."

*"But she's **not** mortal! Maybe if we convince everybody else that you're not crazy, we could try and invade Nathaniel's base!" Jacob suggested.*

"Look guys, I know that. Don't you think I've already thought about it? No one is in the mood for a search and rescue mission, not since Vincent disappeared. But I think we should give it a go, try to talk to Halt about it. What do you say? Are you with me?" James asked them.

The others were silent for a moment.

"Where you go, I will follow," Will smiled.

"You're the man with the plan," said Alex.

"I can't wait to bash some heads in! Whoo-hoo, whoo-hoo!" Jacob crowed, pumping his fists in the air as he jumped around in a circle.

"Okay then, it's settled. Even if Halt says no, the mission is still on. Okay?" James smiled.

"Hey, I don't know 'bout you all, but I'm starving! Let's head back to Camp and get some grub, eh?" Alex said, patting his stomach. Jacob shook his head, and Will playfully punched Alex in the arm.

"Man, you're always hungry! C'mon, let's go." And with James leading the way, they circled around and ran back the way

they'd come, whispering through the forest like leaves on the wind.

I woke with a start. Whoever this guy was, *James*, had dreamed about me? Why? How do they know about Nathaniel? Who's Vincent and Halt, and the other four dudes? And was this Camp the same Camp Wolf that was inscribed on the one warrior's shield in my previous vision? And more importantly, who the hell goes for a run in the middle of a forest in fifty-degree weather? Some crazy ass kids, that's who.

I sat up, stifling a moan. My body felt like I'd been run over by a bus. Every muscle was sore, and the areas where Tony had socked me ached with every little movement. But then reliving the fact that my parents actually were…gone, hurt even more. With gritted teeth, I hurled the dumb metal tray at the wall.

I *hated* Tony! I hated everyone in this wretched place! They haven't even given me an accurate answer on how long I have been here for and what had happened in the last forty-eight hours. Was it too much to ask for to be permitted to crawl into a hole and never come out?

With the butter knife left on the tray from last night, I scratched two lines into the old wall of the cell, marking that I've been here for two days, maybe more, depending on how long I had been unconscious. And if necessary, the butter knife could be used as a weapon, despite the fact that the edge was dull. I've had enough pain to last for days. Nevertheless, I put the knife inside the small drawer of the table beside the cot.

Seconds later, Luke was at the door. He was twirling a small dagger between his fingers, a stupid smirk on his freckled face.

"Good, I see you're up. How are you feeling?" Luke asked. Instead of ignoring him, I whirled, an answer spewing from my lips.

73

"SCREW OFF! Don't pretend that you care, because you don't, jerk!" Luke smirked and unlocked the door with a key he pulled out from his pants pocket.

"You're right, brat. I don't care. C'mon, Shadarr is waiting. It's his feeding time." Luke snapped.

I stared at him before promptly dropping back down onto the cot.

"Fine, make me. I'm not moving from this spot!" I spat, hoping there was more venom to my voice than what came out.

"If you wish, be difficult. Why can't someone else do this?" Luke sighed, rolling his eyes. He stepped inside the dingy cell, hands outstretched.

Chapter IV: Breaking News

Logan Hendrix sighed and powered off her phone. "Why isn't she picking up? Nekoda *always* answers her phone! I don't get it." She grumbled, taking a seat at the dining table across from her older brother, Anthony, where she sat eating a bowl of steaming ramen noodles.

"Nekoda's phone could be dead. Or she's just busy. Have you tried calling and checking with her parents?" Anthony asked.

"Yes, multiple times. No one's answered yet. Perhaps Nekoda is actually outside and *socializing* for once." Logan put her hands up to her face. "Ew. People. I mean they might just be having a family outing or something. But she hasn't been at school for almost two days! Two! Maggie might know." she shrugged, forking a glop of noodles.

"That does seem a little strange. But I wouldn't dwell on it for too long. Besides, she'll probably pop up at school tomorrow. Kody could just be dealing with private family issues right now. Anyway, what time are mom and dad getting home tonight?" Anthony replied, refilling his cup of caffeine out of the fridge.

"Mom has to work the night shift again at the hospital, and dad won't be home until seven this afternoon. Hey, could you turn on the TV? Channel 3, I want to watch the news for any interesting reports. I have an assignment for school that I have to work on,"

"Sure. And try giving your other friend, Maggie, a call." Anthony said, walking over to the living room where he grabbed the TV remote and plopped down on the couch. He put his feet up on the coffee table and stretched.

Click. The TV screen came alive with pictures, playing an episode of *SpongeBob*. Anthony scrolled through the channels until he came to channel three, pressing the play button on the remote.

A news reporter with glossy hair and bright lipstick appeared on the television, looking directly into the camera. At the bottom of the screen the reporter's name flashed. *Julia Anderson— Live At 5.* Julia was speaking to a firefighter in a red and yellow suit, his gas mask pulled low under his chin, his mouth visible. Behind them was the town's fire department, trucks and ambulances unloading, while men milled around behind them. A dalmatian barked as two burly men wound up a long water hose onto a truck, lights flashing red and orange.

"We're here tonight with Cooper Wallace, one of the first on the scene of the fire. Cooper, would you mind telling us what happened?" Julia asked Cooper, holding the microphone out in his direction.

"Sure, Ms. Anderson. A day ago, around three a.m. sharp, we received a frantic call from the victim's neighbor. She reported that her neighbor's house was on fire, the flames consuming the trees around the area in a massive fireball. Her neighbors, Clara and Kyle Jones with their only child, lived in that house. My team and I arrived too late to put the fire out. The house was burned to ashes. We had discovered the remains of two adults. However, it is not clear that the parents were involved in a homicide or got trapped in the fire. The incident is still under investigation. It..." Cooper paused, brows furrowed, and then continued.

It's a very gruesome sight and we're urged not to show the scenes captured on camera; therefore, viewer discretion is advised. The NYPD arrived not long ago, and Officer Wells sent out a search team for the girl. As there is no third body found we assumed she had escaped. Wells got a call two hours before from a young girl saying a group of men broke into her house, threatening the parents. We can only assume that the suspects took her off the premises. The police department believe she was kidnapped by this

76

group that may have caused the house fire, but they have not been able to confirm anything yet; there was a loud crackling and a beeping noise heard on the other end of Wells' line before the call abruptly ended. Either or, we've got a real case on our hands. The police and fire department are sending out more search parties for the girl and the suspects. If there are no signs of them within another twenty-four hours, we will assume Nekoda Jones has been abducted and will notify the rest of surrounding area if they don't know already, alerting the people and nearby towns of a missing child." Cooper Wallace replied, a bead of sweat dripping down his face despite the cool autumn weather.

One of the other firefighters standing nearby called Cooper over, and the interviewee walked away.

Julia Anderson turned toward the camera, looking on with a grim expression. "And that was Cooper Wallace, head of the Weedsport fire department. Very sad and disturbing news this evening, indeed. The NYPD will be placing security guards around the scene until further notice. We will have more coverage of this story when we return tomorrow night. And now back to you at the studio, Brian." She finished.

By then Anthony was looking on in stunned silence, the remote having dropped to the ground with a clatter. His mouth wide open, he looked at his younger sister, Logan. She sniffled, tears welling up in her eyes.

"No, no, no… that couldn't have happened. I talked to her not long ago…" Logan muttered, a horrified look on her face. She powered on her phone and dialed a number.

☾

A few blocks away in a secluded house at the end of a street, a redheaded girl was in her bedroom listening to pop music when her phone rang. Maggie looked at the number that flashed back and pressed the answer button. A voice came on the other end, talking a mile a minute.

"Maggie! You will *not* believe what I just saw on the news! Where are you? Do you know what happened to Kody? Her parents—there was a fire—some people, news reporter said—I don't know, and just, just come to my house *now!* And quickly!" Logan ended the call before she could utter a response. Maggie stared back at her screen, mouth agape.

"What the—!" Regaining her senses, she ran out of her room and down the hall to the living room where her family sat watching TV and her younger siblings playing board games. She slipped on her shoes and coat and ran over to her mother, giving her a quick peck on the cheek. "Going to Logan's—be back in a while. See you later!"

She went on her phone and searched contacts, finding Logan's name, sending a quick text: **ON MY WAY. BE THERE IN FIVE!**

Maggie sprinted out to the garage without another word, jumped on her bike, and raced off in the direction of Logan's house.

☾

"Come on, you twit! Walk faster or I'll carry you down the hall again. Shadarr doesn't have all day, and I don't want to lose a limb anytime soon." Luke pulled me along down the hallway, footsteps echoing off the floor.

I huffed and rubbed my wrist, trying to ease the pain from Luke's tight grip. "Why do *you* have to be my guard? Why couldn't David do it? At least he's nicer! Unlike *somebody* here."

"Yeah, well, if it was a choice, I would've been the first to decline! I don't know why Nathaniel thinks you're still so special. It is quite aggravating. I would rather clean up Dragon dung than babysit a whiny bitch like you anytime." Luke growled, the lights overheard turning his hair an even redder hue like that of a burning fire.

"At least you don't have to deal with morons like yourself! You think you're such a goddamn badass. You're freaking wack. You guys are just a bunch of creeps working for the big bad wolf. Get a life! Quit this lousy job and become the world's greatest ballerina for all I care! And all you have to do is let me g—!" I didn't get to finish. Luke stopped and shoved me against the wall, his hand balling up the front of my already wrinkled shirt.

He pulled his face close. "How many times do I have to tell you? *SHUT UP!* Would you rather me hand you over to Tony to annoy, or stick with someone less ruthless? I've said it before, keep your mouth shut if you know what's good for you!" He snapped, shaking me like a child would a ragdoll.

I clamped my mouth closed and pulled away from him. In one smooth movement, Luke had slung me back over his shoulder. I hung limp on his back, not even bothering to kick and scream or hit.

I mind-messaged Shadarr. *"Hey, I'm coming with Luke. Please don't eat us; we're going to feed you. But if you can't help it, eat Luke as an entrée. I don't like him or any of the others, except David. Maybe spare David. I like him better. I'm on my way!"*

I waited a few seconds. No response.

☾

79

The gate shut closed behind us with a clang and Luke fiddled with the key to lock the door. Shadarr's so-called 'pen' reminded me of a small forest. Perhaps I could try to hide in here when I get the chance. Nothing like a good game of hide and seek with a fire-breathing dinosaur.

Luke walked over to a set of four wooden crates. Lying next to it was a crowbar. He had me pry open the top to reveal a package of raw, bloody meat. I gagged and put a hand up to cover my nose. Luke beckoned for me to pull out the slabs of dead animal and approach the Dragon.

"This is what the food is stored in when it's inside the freezer. In each labeled crate is twenty-five pounds of goat and beef. He gets fed one hundred pounds a day. Exactly fifty pounds in the morning and late evening. He's still young, well, young for a Dragon at least, but he's going to get a lot bigger as he grows into an adult. He'll have to eat more then. But for now he consumes a strict number of calories a day. Understood?" Luke informed.

"Yes." I muttered, shuffling away from the boxes, watching Shadarr lumber toward us. There was a small, cold freezer room off by the entrance on the inside of Shadarr's pen. Inside were more boxes of processed meat, frozen until his next meal.

Gloveless, I carefully pulled out the chunks of meat and laid one on the ground in front of me. Shadarr came over and cautiously sniffed the food before opening his mouth, showing rows of razor-sharp teeth. Each tooth was thicker than my thumb and roughly six inches in length. Shadarr snatched the meat and swallowed it down in a matter of seconds, just like the velociraptors from *Jurassic Park.*

It took me a good fifteen minutes to feed Shadarr, piece by piece, crate by crate. By the time I was finished, animal blood and grease covered my hands. The smell was horrid. I tried not to puke on myself, holding my sweatshirt over my nose.

"Hey, umm, is there a ladies' room around here. 'Cause I, uh, gotta go. And I could also use a shower. Quite *badly,* I must add." I asked Luke, my cheeks flushing as I realized that the smell that lingered around us wasn't coming from Shadarr, but from me.

He stared, a dumbfounded expression on his face.

"Err, right. Since Nathaniel wanted to jump into interrogating and training when you first got here, we didn't get to cover the daily routine properly. After you feed Shadarr, you get a short bathroom and snack break in the mornings before training. And lunchtime is after your training sessions. In the evenings following Shadarr's last feeding of the day, you get an hour to wash up in the bathroom, talk to Shadarr, eat, whatever it is girls do to entertain themselves," Ah, yes, just what every teenage girl does in her spare time, shovel food into her mouth. "We may be the bad guys, but we care about personal hygiene. Besides, this place is already full of mold and cobwebs anyway," Lukas snorted, wiping his hands on his pants.

"Ok-ayyy," I replied.

"I'm going to bring out the next meal to thaw. Meanwhile, you can sit and chat with your buddy for a bit. And just in case you try any funny business, that gate is locked, and I am armed. I really don't feel like using you as target practice today, so I'll spare you." Luke mocked, turning away.

"Gee, thanks." I stuck my tongue out at Luke's back and trudged over, sitting down in front of Shadarr. The creature lay with his head down on his front feet, head tilted. If you stared at him for a while, Shadarr was kind of cute in his own way. Cute for a big, dangerous lizard. We watched Luke carry some crates out of the freezer and place them by the gate. After a moment's silence, I started talking.

"So, how long have you been here?" I asked Shadarr, trying to make small talk with a Dragon.

He studied his six-inch long claws before answering, gazing at me with his blood red eyes. He let out a deep breath, his breath reeking of dead goat. "*I do not know. For as long as I can remember I've been with Nathaniel; presumably ever since I was a hatchling. They care for me, so it's okay. But if you're wondering why I haven't escaped yet, it's because I can't.*"

"Y-you can't?" Shadarr was built like a flipping tank. He could trample Nathaniel and his loons as easily as an elephant could squash a field mouse. How in the seven hells could a *Dragon* not escape?

"*I belong to him. And since he put me in Nathaniel's care, I'm forbidden to harm my master.*" Shadarr let out a long yawn, the energy seeming to be sucked out of his body.

"Who is this person, and how does he own you? By all means, if anyone around here could overpower Nathaniel, it'd be you. Couldn't you just break a few universal rules to save yourself?" I asked, scratching my head.

Shadarr sighed, a deep rumble like the purring of a car engine resonating in his chest. "*Alas, I cannot. We Dragons don't have control, as we are so few in numbers. They own us, and we owe a debt to them which can never be repaid. Nathaniel knew this and that's why he took full advantage of me. But trust me when I say this Nekoda, when you leave here don't come back for me. It's not worth your life. It wasn't worth Payton's, either. I belong here, and you don't.*"

"Shadarr, when I make a promise, I intend to keep it. I don't know how, but I *will* free you, whatever it takes. And I-I *will* get revenge for what Nathaniel did to my parents." I felt my throat close up. "You can fight me all you want, but I won't give up. No one, not any creature no matter how big or small, deserves to be locked up."

82

"Yes, because that's exactly what Nathaniel wants. You're a pawn, the secret weapon in the war. If you defy them, no good can come from it."

"But who's *them?* And who's *he?"* I whispered back.

Shadarr stood up and stretched, flapping his wings as he did so. *"All will be explained in due time, Kody. I have one thing left to say to you, though. The gods are cruel, Nekoda, let that be a lesson to you. Good day. You must go. It's time for your training, is it not?"* With that being said, Shadarr jumped into the air and took off, spiraling into the darkness of his cage above. Luke walked up behind me, brushing his hands on his jeans.

"Enjoyed your chat with Shadarr? Real mysterious, that Dragon. I don't understand why Nathaniel keeps him." he shook his head. "Alright, come on. David's really looking forward to training with you again," Luke rolled his eyes. "Let's go." He walked over and grabbed my arm, pulling me up. Luke threw me over his shoulder without hesitation. Again. Gods damn him. Apparently, this was how I'd get around the place during my stay.

We exited through a side door, Luke stomping down the hall toward the training room. I was deep in thought, my mind whirling, thinking about what Shadarr had told me when we arrived at the practice room entrance.

☾

"Keep your guard up, Kody! No, no. Block like this, yes, excellent! Ow! If your opponent surrenders, you don't continue jabbing him in the side. Let me up. Okay, come at me with all you got. Nice parry, you're doing well! Again, it is no time for a rest, Nekoda."

I slumped on the ground, sweat trickling down my neck and face. My practice sword clattered to the side, David lecturing

83

me as it did so. I stood back up, trying to keep a straight face. I feigned towards David, catching him off guard. He swung at me, bringing his sword down above his head in a wide arc, and I jumped aside just in time to avoid a fake shattered collarbone. If the swords were real, then I would have already suffered multiple injuries. Instead, bruises were beginning to purple on my arms and legs.

David rolled to the side and I attacked him in frenzy. Over to the left, Nathaniel was watching us, a smug smile plastered on his face. Bruce and Luke were getting the equipment ready for the next course, talking quietly. There was no sign of Ezekial and Tony, whom I didn't care for in the least.

"David, why don't you and Nekoda take a break for a minute. I need to talk to Bruce. And keep an eye on her, too. With you around, she'd take the chance and run for it like last time." Nathaniel advised and walked away.

David and I sat down on the mat, sipping from cool water bottles and relishing in the small break we had been given.

I cleared my throat. "Soo, do you perhaps know anything about why Nathaniel wanted a sample of my blood? And what did he mean by 'the Changing' after Tony tried to bite me? Surely you would know. Please David, look, I'm sorry about what I said earlier. I could really use an ally here."

David fingered his sword, tracing the pattern on the blade before turning to face me. "I'm not supposed to tell you why he wanted your blood, nor do I really even know. The boss keeps all sorts of secrets. But I guess it's okay to give you an early lecture about our—I mean, *your* kind. Skin-changers."

I held out my hands in front of me, palms up. I studied them. Nope, not changing into big furry paws. "I'm a Skin-changer, yeah? And supposedly with *magical godly powers, too*." I couldn't help but scoff.

David replied in a flat voice, exhausted with my unwillingness to accept my 'true nature' bullshit. "Yes. Will you please let me talk? When a mortal or anyone that's not a Skin-changer is bit, it changes them. Quite literally. Makes them one of us. But if you were already born with animal blood, it will make the process of Changing a lot faster. If you're too young, it can make you go crazy, mess with your head.

You see, we only develop our Changing abilities by the ripe age of fourteen, even younger in some rare instances. If our parents don't educate us, then they send us away where we can learn all our training and history, and better fit into the modern world. We stay there, at a big facility for Skin-changers only until the age of nineteen and twenty. After that, some demigods choose to stay behind at Camp and become trainers or teachers at the facility. Others join the United States Military, Navy, the Marines and so on, or become famous and find a life career and start a family. However, most of us were born to fight; we were created to protect and defend."

David finished his bottle of water and chucked it behind him. He crossed his legs and rested his chin on his knees.

"Our race has been dying out though over the past few centuries," he continued. "In the past, humans misread our intentions and thought of us as monsters, making up fairy tales to scare children. You know, what humans are best at. Making monsters out of people who aren't. There are many species within our race. There's the Hunter species, which are wolf, big cat, or predatory Skin-changers. They are our fighters. Then you have the more formal Skin-changers that fit in with the humans, like a giant hawk or forest animal or a pet dog; and they're also the predictable kind. That group is called Darkshadow, meaning you blend in with human life.

Lastly, there are the Outcast Skin-changers. An ex Skin-changer who defies the way our world works, and our Laws;

85

someone who doesn't belong. They want to change everything. Like us." He looked around, pointing at Luke, Bruce, Nathaniel, and himself. I'm sure he would have pointed at Tony and Ezekial if they were here too.

"What do you mean? You don't seem like an Outcast to me. What are you guys, then? What, uh, animal, I should say?" I said.

David grunted, putting his head in his hands. "Nathaniel would have my head for this if he found out that I'm telling you anything at all. Alas, I think you have a right to know, since it seems you'll be here for a long time to come. Tony is a black panther, Ezekial is a bear, Bruce a hyena, Luke an African lion, I, a Bengal tiger, and Nathaniel is...a Dire Wolf."

Dang it. It would make me feel much better if Nathaniel actually turned out to be a weasel instead of some mutant wolf thing.

"What do you think I'm going to be? That is, if I actually go through this whole Claiming Moon thing."

"Hmph, not a clue. Not until you experience the Changing and your Claiming Moon for the first time. You are feisty, so I reckon a Hunter." David responded.

"Huh," I stood up, stretched, and helped David up.

Nathaniel hurried in our direction, Bruce and Luke menacingly in tow behind him.

"Chit-chat is over. It's time for target practice." Nathaniel ordered. Bruce grabbed my arm and David went to put the practice swords and equipment away. We walked to the shooting area and I stood on the X, same as last time. Bruce strapped on a vest while I prepared. David came back with the same guns I had used earlier and the 22 Caliber Rifle strapped to his back, and an Assault Rifle in hand. David bent down and placed the guns on the floor in a single line.

"You will only practice with each weapon for ten minutes, just so you can get a feel of it and know how to handle them. For today we will do an extended training period with long ranged guns. After this set, we'll use other weaponry to fire at Bruce." David chuckled half-heartedly. Bruce whipped around at the sound of his name, annoyance written across his pockmarked face.

BANG! BANG! BANG! Bullets sprayed with all the various guns I was told to fire, the stone wall peppered from the bullets pelting the walls. My shoulder grew sore after a while, so I propped the gun against the wall for Luke to take away. We had been practicing—and failing— for so long that my arms now screamed for a break, but I knew I wasn't allowed to rest yet. I dreaded what was coming next— hand-to-hand combat. I didn't know whom I'd be facing off with.

I shuffled over to the fighting mat, Bruce pushing me from behind as I dragged my feet. I wanted desperately to practice with my sword, pretending to hack into my imaginary enemies (in this case, Tony) more than get my brains beaten out.

I took off my dirty socks and shoes that I've been wearing since I was last in New York. I smelled worse than what Tony looked. I prayed there was a laundry machine around here that I could convince someone to let me use. If I could just sneak out of my room once, I could learn the whole interior of the place, wherever I'm at, and then plot an easy escape. It would be tricky, unless I'm somehow able to convince Luke to show me around when we next see Shadarr.

"Since your first fist fight didn't start off very well, I would like to show you a demonstration. Luke, Bruce, come forward." Nathaniel said dryly, shrugging off his trench coat.

David was standing alone, leaning against a pole while he polished his sword. Grim faced, Bruce and Luke came over to the mat where we stood. I was still dressed in my purple Nike sweatshirt, short-sleeved blue t-shirt, and holey jeans. I shucked my sweatshirt and shoes off and stretched my arms above my head.

Luke and Bruce got into their fighting positions, a few feet apart from one another. I stood off to the side by Nathaniel.

"On my say, you may wrestle until someone is knocked to the floor, off the mat. If either of you aren't down in five minutes, I'll stop the match and Kody can have a go." I bristled at Nathaniel's prohibited use of calling me Kody. "Ready...set...fight!" he barked.

Immediately, Luke took a swing and Bruce ducked. Luke snarled when his fist hit open air. He growled and spun around, and they both lashed out at each other. Bruce caught Luke in the shoulder, and he staggered back before swiping his leg in an arc, aiming for Bruce's shin. His foot made contact and Bruce howled, clutching at his knee. He returned with an elbow to the ribs and took a shot, tackling Luke to the ground and throwing a punch that Luke blocked before rolling to his feet.

Luke grabbed Bruce's arm, twisted his body around, and effortlessly threw him over his shoulder where he landed on the ground with a loud *oompfh*. He stood on Bruce's chest where he raised a hand in the air and counted. "One, two, three, four, five, six..." but on the count of seven, Bruce shoved Luke off with a strength I didn't know he had. Jumping up, Bruce caught Luke in a headlock and started roaring with laughter, a deep throaty laugh.

"Silly, stupid Luke. You can't take me down that easily!" and with that he pushed Luke down and pinned him to the mat, a knee digging into his back. The match was over quicker than I anticipated. Nathaniel called for time, and the two fighters brushed themselves off and went over to stand next to David who was done polishing his already shining sword. They earned a few sneers from me.

"So, who's up next? Oh, right. Nekoda, it's time to test your skills. Boys, who shall be seen to fight a little, innocent girl?" David narrowed his eyes in his boss's direction while the other men smirked. I felt someone flick the back of my head.

"No takers? Alrighty then, I shall fight her. Besides, children need to get some sense knocked into them once in a while."

"Screw you!" I muttered.

"What was that?"

"Nothing." I said.

"Wait, wait, wait! Why must she fight you, out of all of us, first? Shouldn't we take this slow? We need to help with her training, not use her as a punching bag! I think she needs to be taught properly. After all, she's only been here for two days!" David exploded, pounding his fist into his hand.

Ugh, my thoughts exactly.

"Why not? You soft-hearted fool, remember your duty! You take my side, not hers. I don't want any pity or empathy for this girl. If she really is who I think she is, then we can't afford to have a vulnerable soldier! We must train her like a strong soldier she's supposed to become. David, if you're going to try and stop me then I'll have no choice but to silence you for good. Understand?" Nathaniel threatened, his voice sharper than a razor. His knuckles turned white as he gripped the hilt of his sword.

"Understood, sir. Sorry, sir." David bowed his head. I could visibly feel the tension grow and swell as he walked out of the training room to wherever it is he goes outside of this room.

Nathaniel turned toward me, and that familiar shark smile made an appearance. "Nekoda, you and I will face off in hand to hand combat. Three rounds. Two minutes before we start. Get ready." He grabbed a bottle of water from Bruce, threw one at me,

89

and got in the center of the mat. I took a sip, the cool drink soothing my parched throat. I gulped.

I was going to be fighting Nathaniel! *Nathaniel*, of all people! For once, why couldn't David have kept his big mouth shut?

☾

DING-DONG. The bell rang, Maggie pacing outside on Logan's front porch.

"It's open!" Someone from inside called out. In a rush, she pushed open the door and stepped into Logan's house. She saw Logan's older brother, Anthony, looking shell-shocked and staring out the window. He didn't look at Maggie, but merely whispered aloud, "L is in her room. You know where."

"Thanks,"

She bolted through the kitchen and past the neat living room where the flat-screen TV was turned off. Her heart raced as she walked down the yellow painted hall, glancing at old photographs hanging on the wall. Maggie sped past the bathroom and laundry room, coming to a door at the end of the corridor. She walked in to find her friend Logan going in circles around her bedroom. The lights were on, revealing movie and band posters taped to the purple walls, things scattered about on her bed, and a fish tank set on an oak table next to a wooden drawer. Magazines and clothes lay on the fuzzy, carpeted floor.

"Umm, hey. You called me." Maggie said.

Logan turned at the sound of her voice, tear streaks running down her face.

"It's Nekoda. S-something happened! You didn't see the news?"

90

Maggie shook her head slowly, almost too afraid to say anything. "No, I was up in my bedroom. My parents were watching the sports channel. What's up with Kody?"

"Ah, here, we can use my tablet. I'll just go onto the Channel 3 website..." Logan turned on her device and went online. A few taps and flashing screens later, Maggie was looking at the face of Julia Anderson. She clicked the play button.

Logan watched Maggie's reaction when the image of the burned house popped up on the screen. She gasped and put a hand up to her mouth.

"Wait—you mean Kody is gone? She just up and left in the middle of the night?" asked Maggie.

"No, the Weedsport Police Department have reasons to suspect she was kidnapped. The police department got a call from her cell, saying men had broken into her house early in the morning. The call abruptly ended when she was mid-sentence. I-I think...I think she really is gone."

"But that's not possible! Who would have broken into her house? And why?" Maggie was astounded.

"I've no idea. There hasn't been a robbery in town for years. But there's a—" Logan choked up. "There's already a funeral in the works for next Sunday, for her parents. Mrs. Sims sent Anthony a message. We ought to attend and pay our respects. Half the town and the whole school will be there. Clara and Kyle Jones were good people." Logan informed, giving her friend a weak pat on the back.

"Yeah, of course." Maggie nodded. "But there's one question remaining."

Logan powered off her tablet and set it aside.

"And what is that?"

91

"Why *Kody*?" She scowled.

Chapter V: A Small Taste of Revenge

"Breathe in, breathe out. In and out…" I slowly inhaled then exhaled. David, being the only one whose soul was somewhat pure, was trying to calm me whilst I pushed down a manifesting panic attack. In approximately two minutes I was going to be fighting Nathaniel, the badass on Psycho Street. A few feet away, Nathaniel slid off his sword belt and leather boots, handing them to Luke. I stared daggers at the back of his stupid head.

"Trust me, you'll do fine." David whispered into my ear. I bristled. *Trust me, you'll do fine*; that was the last time I saw my friends, the day of that absurd Algebra test. It seemed like months ago. Maggie had said those exact five words to me. "Are you okay?" David asked, catching my arm.

"Don't touch me," I hissed, yanking my arm away from his grip. Backing up onto the blue wrestling match, muscles tensed, I shouted at Nathaniel. "Over here, I'm ready!"

Nathaniel whipped around and stalked over to the mat in all his horrifying glory. He stood three feet in front of me, crouched like cat about to pounce on its prey. We shifted into our fighting stances as Luke, Bruce, and David lined up on the sidelines as impromptu referees.

"I have one thing to say, Nathaniel—don't break her. I know I shouldn't be the one telling you this, but you know what would happen if anything bad purposefully happened to her. They wouldn't be too happy about that." Luke grinned, a toothy sneer on his face. Again, I wondered who *they* were. Bruce pushed Luke aside and spoke.

"You can shove off now, Luke. You two may begin when you're ready. So let's get to it." I swallowed the bile that was

93

slowly rising up my throat and took my first cautious steps forward.

Nathaniel and I circled each other for a bit, the cat and the mouse, neither one of us not daring to move. Nathaniel was a foot away, his black eyes seeming to look right through me. He was a good two heads taller than me, about or over six feet in height, lean and muscled like a professional athlete. All I could think about was how screwed I was going to be in point five seconds...

In a blur of movement, I swung a blow at the side of his head, but Nathaniel only jumped aside with ease. I sideswiped him, hoping to get him from afar, but my foot only hit open air.

An instant later, Nathaniel was behind me. My brain didn't even register movement until I ducked right before two large hands grasped empty space. I jumped, shouting in surprise. I took the opportunity to punch him in the gut. He moved not even an inch; he snarled and spun, lashing out with an uppercut to the chest that sent me flying a few feet away.

The impact left me breathless. I struggled to sit upright as Nathaniel advanced. As he got closer, I rolled backwards and landed lightly on my feet. Deciding to take a risk, I ran up to meet him and kicked the back of his shin as quickly as I could. Before Nathaniel had even a sliver of a chance to react, I launched myself at him. We landed on the ground in a tangle of limbs, me trying to push him off and away. He caught the back of my arm and twisted it, deftly maneuvering himself over my back. I yelped when he shoved me face down on the mat, tightening his grip so hard that tears sprung to my eyes. I was pinned, and Nathaniel was kneeling above me like a predator that overthrew its prey.

David's voice rang out, loud and clear. "C'mon Nekoda! You got this!" With what little strength I had left (and Nathaniel's loosened grip), I yanked my arm away and flipped onto my back, bringing my knee up to his pelvis area in a quick thrust. Like Tony, he crumpled to the floor in pain and I took the advantage to punch him in the cheekbone. My knuckles stung with the impact, and my hands and wrists throbbed from the many strikes I had endured and delivered.

Off on the sidelines, Luke and Bruce were hollering like madmen.

With a roar, Nathaniel lunged forward and struck me in the collarbone and shoulder before he landed on his feet again. I stumbled, grasping my shoulder in one hand and pushing myself up with the other. Nathaniel grabbed my shirtfront and lifted me up only to push me back down. The air left my lungs in a painful gasp, and I could do nothing as he positioned himself above me, digging an elbow into my stomach.

In a voice so low only I could hear, Nathaniel brought his mouth next to my ear and whispered, "I've been wondering why the gods picked you. Your filthy bloodline. Your parents were weak; they wanted to protect you from the real world, from your own kind, because they were scared. Clara and Kyle loved you too much to make the same mistake with you as your great ancestors had a long, long time ago," he stopped, catching his breath. "My father would've killed your parents himself if he could. But alas, father always makes me do the dirty work for him. A powerful Skin-changer like you should not be stupid and weak. But you are, and here you are thinking you can overcome us, overthrow *me*." he scoffed, jabbing me in the side with one hand for emphasis. "You can't and won't. There is a war brewing and sides to be chosen. Powers like yours are meant to be used to destroy things. And that's exactly what you will do. This is why you are training, why you must unlock your powers. For you will be fighting for one thing only, and that is your life."

I flinched. Tried to block his voice out. Failed.

"Don't," he hissed, "think any second I wouldn't hesitate to kill you, just like we did your mother and father. They died with

95

ALL POWERFUL: THE HUNTED

the weight of the past in their hearts, and the false hope that you could save them…"

I couldn't take it anymore.

It was like a raging storm was brewing inside of me and needed to be released. I felt everything and nothing at the same time. Hot tears streamed down my face, blurring my vision. My blood boiled and my hands shook with the iciness that burned through my veins, my mind, and my heart. How dare he provoke me, cause me this pain of which I did not bare to suffer? I growled and thrust out my hands, palms up, and I felt the anger and strength of a thousand warriors.

My heart was now pounding in my ears, a frantic drum beat. All the inky blackness that had been coiling up inside of me yearned to be free. I felt it bubbling up and up and up and let loose…

KA-BOOSH! Nathaniel was thrown backwards across the room, crashing into the far wall like a crash dummy thrown from a test car. Head throbbing, I climbed to my feet and sprint towards him. I didn't care if he was still standing, if he could shake himself off and knock me unconscious. I was burning hot, like a fever running through me, and I—

I gasped, and for a moment, bright, red flames flickered and then grew as a ball of white-hot energy burst from my hand and launched at Nathaniel's fallen body. He somehow absorbed the impact and lurched to the side, struggling to get back up. From behind a mask of dust and ash, Nathaniel's eyes widened so much that I could clearly see the black pools sunk into his head.

I glanced down. And screamed.

I was literally on *fire!*

Flames, real *flames* covered my entire body. For a split second I thought I was being burned alive, and I half-expected to shockingly feel my skin blistering. But I felt nothing, absolutely nothing.

I turned around to face the direction from which others were watching. Luke was even paler than before, his skin as white as paper. Bruce's eyes were full of terror. And David—David was gone.

I hung my head, losing all intention of hurting Nathaniel. The thought of being a disappointment to David racked my brain. I dropped my hands and curled them into fists, and the flames flickered and died out. Not a single inch of my body was bloody or burned.

I shook my head. *Why did I care what David thought? He was the enemy here, not a friend. Right?*

I heard footsteps shuffle behind me and a gruff, raspy voice boomed, "Congratulations. You unlocked the first stage of your powers. Fire burns in your heart for revenge of what pain we caused you. Fire may be the thing that fuels your soul. Now, Luke and Bruce will finish up your training for today. I will go see to Tony and Ezekial as soon as I change." I whirled and saw Nathaniel on his feet, a burnt smell in the air and small sparks dying off on his black skull shirt.

"Oh-okay." I gulped. I braced myself for what might come next, but there was no punishment from him. No punches or threats nor insults. He had a blank, unreadable expression on his face. Gathering up his sword and boots, Nathaniel ambled out of the training room without a word to the two remaining men, slamming the heavy wooden door behind him. The faint smell of campfire smoke clung to the air when he was gone.

Luke and Bruce looked to each other and then started toward me. Shaken out of their trance, they stalked over. "Alright, I guess we move on. Bruce, grab the throwing knives, will you? And I'll take the girl—" I was gone in seconds. Before he had time to finish I had shot past him and Bruce and pulled the door open to slide into the hallway. I heard swearing and the clanking of metal on stone.

Was it possible that I could find my way out of here? Which way to go, which way to go? I zoomed in the opposite direction of the 'Nutcase' room and my little cell. I ran down the stone halls, my feet pitter-pattering on the cold floor as I bolted past doors of mysteries and turned right. Next, I took a sharp left and up another flight of stairs. Luke and Bruce were thundering after me; I could hear them cursing yards behind, but I sped up, my short legs pushing me further as the blood pounded in my ears.

The looming stairs I had bounded up were covered with long burgundy flooring. Bright lamps hung on the walls, casting long, ugly shadows from the three people storming up the steps. I started to slow my pace as I caught a whiff of something delicious, something that smells vaguely like fresh baked bread.

Could it be? Maybe, just maybe I had found the main chambers! I took another step forward, perhaps one step closer to freedom, before a creaky door burst open and I came face to face with Ezekial.

☾

"—And then she threw a ball of fire right at my chest. Damn her!" Nathaniel growled, pacing the bedroom.

"What do you mean she *threw* a ball of fire at you? Isn't it too soon?" Tony repeated the statement, exasperated. After his deliberate attack on Nekoda, he had been ordered to be locked in his chambers until he cooled down.

Tony brushed a strand of dark hair out of his eyes and took another sip of his wine. Sitting at the birch wood table by his bed, he had a collection of knives laid out, all waiting to be cleaned and

98

polished. In a chest lined up on the wall of his bedroom was a small stash of alcoholic beverages beside his dresser he kept to calm himself down in one of his freak-out moments. A small dash of magic powder was mixed in to each drink to help keep him from Changing and going off on people. It was really just a concoction of vodka and ambrosia. It helped control his anger issues.

"You heard what I said, Tony. Nekoda has a very strong will, and one can only assume that through her emotions she can gain her powers easier while channeling them in a certain state of manner. Gods, she's at the age where she is old enough to develop her powers. Let's just hope her Claiming Moon won't affect her in ways I think it would."

There was a brief silence, then: "So... let's just not piss her off? Nathaniel, when I started the fire at her house, what were you thinking when you decided to bring her *here* of all places, instead of straight to your father?" Tony asked.

The rough leader blanched and glared at his comrade. "My father, he gave me orders first. To take her here. But only when she's become a strong enough warrior must I bring her to see him. He has plans of his own. I can't let him have her just yet, not until he meets his end of the bargain."

"Well, he is a bastard of a god if I say so myself." The black-haired Skin-changer spat before taking another long sip of his drink.

"Yes, but best not let him hear that or he'll have your pelt hanging above his bed. I just wish we knew where the damn Book was! If only the brat wasn't as clueless as she looks!" Nathaniel tapped the pommel of his sword in thought. If he could get his hands on the Book, he could destroy the Olympians as easily as crushing a wilted flower between his fingers.

He could take his rightful place back on Zeus's filthy throne on Mt. Olympus and hammer in the last nail of the Camps'

99

coffin, subsequently sending both worlds into ruination once and for all.

℃

A few weeks ago…

Hundreds of miles away through the snowcapped mountains deep in the wilderness walked a man with a small backpack on his shoulders and a scruffy canine at his side. A pony sized Dire-wolf named Taz, his coat a dark grey with streaks of silver, was the stranger's only companion.

The sky was growing dark as the setting sun sunk behind the clouds, casting gold and orange hues around the mountainside. The only source of aid to help him navigate the rough path ahead of him came from an old and ancient amulet worn around his neck on a leather cord, which glowed with a soft blue light. The moon, shrouded by the puffy clouds, did little to illuminate the area. "Don't worry Taz, we're almost there. Just a little further…"

The man climbed over a log and jumped over rocks, nearly twisting his foot on a gnarled tree root jutting out of the ground, almost falling to his death when his wolf playfully pushed him towards the edge of the narrow pathway up the mountain. Not far from his location lay ruins thousands of years old, and so mysterious that not even the mortal climbers have stumbled upon them.

A glamour, or a sort of strong spell, shielded the ruins from view and any afflicted damage that could be inferred upon them. The ruin was called the *Sepulchrum Of Ignis,* or translated, Tomb of Fire. It was supposedly built under sacred battleground where the Dragons once ruled the land of men. After the final war between mortal and Dragon, monsters and demigods, the site was

100

designated a secret tomb for all Dragon kings and riders to lay in death.

But there were also tales of Krane de Royce, the last Dragon king and first Skin-changer of his kind, son to Lycaon, the first werewolf and king of ancient Arcadia, hiding his gifts from the gods farther below the Tomb, farther belowground, whence no Skin-changer dared venture. His Dragon, Balios, also lay entombed with the treasures where storytellers say he guards it still.

Of the gifts were Krane de Royce's enchanted fire-sword called Death, his shield *Aegis* that is to be from the god of the sky, Zeus, gifted prior to Athena. The Book that contains the secrets of the Titans, the gateway to the Underworld, and dangerous knowledge of dark magic from Skin-changers past—*The Book of Spells.*

Lastly, the Amulet of Twelve, which hung from around the stranger's neck. The Amulet of Twelve had been created from Hephaestus's forge millennia ago, having been dipped in the Olympian's own blood after the god or goddess cut themselves on Kronos' scythe to bind their powers into one. The Fates decided that a hero would arise someday with a prophecy of perpetual doom for the child of the Dragon and saviors of the Skin-changers.

The man's wolf, Taz, pricked up his ears and crouched low to the earth, fangs bared. This was it, he was here. If Taz could sense the spirits of the Dragon Riders, then the Tomb of Fire was close…

"V*incent, true-born son of Camrice Lockwood, protector of the Amulet of Twelve, fellow Warrior of Camp Wolf, we command you go no further…*" a voice, barely more than a whisper, caught Vincent's attention. It drifted through the wind, growing louder with each step. A misty white figure appeared in front of Vincent, blocking his path with his hazy body. Vincent kept walking, one foot in front of the other, but Taz refused to move.

101

"C'mon boy, we have to do this. The spirits can't hurt you. C'mon, we have to go. If what Halt said is true, then we have to fulfill this task. The prophecy is real. Get up, Taz!" Vincent nudged his wolf with his muddy boots, and still the young Dire-wolf did not get up.

Vincent sighed. "Fine, I'll just go alone then. No problem. But who would be there to tell my story if I get gobbled up by a monster or crushed under a rock? Surely not the great and adventurous Taz. Oh, no. Why, I think I just might even go into the ruins with my eyes closed, weaponless, unguarded from evil spirits and gods-know-what, while my loyal and friendly companion Taz is too chicken to get past a mindless and senile old ghost!" Vincent huffed, poking Taz's nose and play-acting his fatal death.

When Vincent continued to tease his wolf and brush past one of the spirits of the Tomb, Taz realized that he had no choice but to hop up and bound after his master.

"Good Taz, that's a goood dog!" Vincent scratched behind Taz's ears when the Dire-wolf rushed up to him. Both adventurers ran until the Skin-changer noticed the ground change from uneven, icy earth to dead grass and mossy stone underfoot.

Before them stood an enormous crumbling mass of stone, marble, and wood. Small piles of yellowing bones were half sunk into the ground, skeletons of the long-deceased rested together beside Dragon, men, and Skin-changers alike. If Vincent was correct, then the Tomb of Fire was located directly underneath. Vin, vision strained in the near darkness, rummaged around until he at last spotted a symbol carved into a broken pillar. He pressed his fingers to the symbol; a crescent moon with a howling wolf head jutting out from the center, and a sword pierced through both. A low rumbling noise sounded, like that of a distance train.

To Vincent's utmost surprise and wonder, dirt and rock slid aside like a panel, revealing an opening five feet in length and seven feet in height. He looked to Taz who stood still as a statue, unblinking, waiting to follow orders. Vincent unsheathed a bronze dagger and moved forward towards the mouth of the ruin and the Tomb of Fire, wolf and man side-by-side.

☾

Oof! I ran smack-dab into Ezekial. With his rumpled hair and stained t-shirt, he looked like he'd just woken up from a five-hour nap. The young man fixed his cold, hazel eyes on me.

"What are *you* doing here?" The lines on his forehead wrinkled in confusion. I didn't wait to answer; Luke and Bruce had bounded up the stairs, and their footsteps were closing in on us.

"Zeke! Don't just stand there like a fool, grab her!" shouted Luke. Quickly, I considered my options. Attempt to get past Ezekial, or go back the way I came from and straight into Luke's arms.

Brain too jumbled to make an appropriate decision, I kicked Ezekial in the shin as hard as I could, dashing by as he yelped and clutched his leg in pain. I sprinted past various doors, daring a glance over my shoulder. Luke and Bruce had abandoned Ezekial, who now regained his composure and followed suit. It was like an episode of *Tom and Jerry,* except much less comical.

Thinking fast, I threw open the heavy oak wood door that the mouth-watering aromas seemed to be coming from and slid into a small tiled room. I found the kitchen! Pots and pans hung up on a rack above the center island, baskets of fruit and pastries sat at a counter. I would have rifled through the fridge's contents, but I didn't have the time, much to my aching stomach protests. Nor, to my discovery, could the door lock.

I reached into a random drawer and pulled out a flimsy spatula. Nope, that wouldn't work. Spotting a frying pan, I yanked it off its hook and ducked under a metal table stained with old sauce and crumbs, anticipating the next person to walk into the room. Mere seconds later, Luke, Bruce, and Ezekial rushed into the kitchen, the door slamming open before them.

"I swear I saw her enter through here! There's no other way out. Nekoda, no harm will come to you if you show yourself now. Come out and we can do this the easy way, or don't, and we can do this the hard way." Luke grunted, an edge to his voice. I gripped the frying pan tighter as their footsteps drew near. There was a crash and then the clanking of kitchenware as someone slipped and fell into the table next to my hiding spot.

"Dammit! Bruce, how many times do I have to tell you? Make sure your trash goes in the garbage can, not on the floor!" Ezekial cursed. I spied Bruce's feet as he wandered around, inspecting every corner and checking every cabinet.

Abruptly, Luke reversed direction from the other side of the room and made for the direction of my table. A scarred hand roamed under the table cloth, feeling its way along the floor. I brought the pan down and smashed the poor soul's finger in one blow.

"OOWWW!" Luke screamed and retracted his hand. Bruce ran over with Ezekial, upturning the table together just as I scrambled to my feet. Bruce leapt for me, one hand out to close around my arm, but I swung around and lashed out with my transient weapon. There was a loud crunch as the pan connected with Bruce's face, nose shattered. He doubled over, holding his nose as blood gushed between his fingers.

I flung aside the frying pan and made my way towards the door, zooming in the opposite direction from which I had come from—WHACK! My shoe landed on something small and round, and my legs went out from under me. My shoulder, having taken the brunt of the impact, felt numb.

Great. My clumsy ass had tripped over my own two feet.

Cold, greasy hands wrapped around my shoulders and threw me up and over a broad shoulder. "Nice try," Zeke said brusquely.

I kicked and punched but gave up the effort when we exited the room. From behind us, Luke stepped through the kitchen door, cradling his purple hand. Bruce had a towel pressed to his face, eyes watering and blood trickling down his chin. I smirked.

They were in pain. Good.

Ezekial followed the other soldiers down a dark hallway and enter into a new room. The door this time had the letter 'T' carved into the wood. (T as in tool?) It was someone's sleeping quarters.

I didn't get the chance to soak in all the details of the tapestries hanging on the wall or the birchwood desk before I spotted him.

Seated at the table, wine glass in hand, was Tony. Next to Tony sat Nathaniel, casually leaning back in the chair like this was all just a perfectly normal situation. Apparently, they were in middle of an important conversation because their talk descended into silence upon noticing us.

Nathaniel straightened and clapped his hands together, rocking all four legs of the chair back onto the floor. "Ah, look who it is. Have a seat, everyone." Tony stood up from his spot and moved to stand by the door when we entered, avoiding any kind of eye contact. Bruce, Ezekial, Luke and I walked farther in.

"Sit." Nathaniel commanded, pointing to the bed. Ezekial awkwardly dropped me onto the large mattress. I sat, slouched against one of the bedposts, glaring at each of them in turn, despite their ugly faces meeting mine. Luke and Bruce took chairs at the table while Ezekial remained positioned in my proximity. Perfect.

Tony snatched one of the various knifes resting on the table and pulled a rag out of the chest. Grumbling, he ran the rag up and down the blade, the metal shining with the light.

105

"I believe we have something that needs to be discussed about the previous incident between you and Tony," Nathaniel queried, sounding bored. "What do you think happened, Jones?"

"Umm..." I shrugged my shoulders at a loss for words.

"That's not an answer, Nekoda."

"I guess, uhm, I don't know, Tony is struggling with addiction? Like with heroin or something? It seems how someone would act if they did heroin, but I'm unsure." I answered nonchalantly, not wanting to meet his empty gaze.

Nathaniel pinched the bridge of his nose, blowing out an exasperated breath of air. "Holy Hera! Do I have to explain everything?! Yes, yes, I do," He turned his chair around and straddled the seat, hands clasped over the back of it. "M'kay, so what did Tony do exactly? It's something all Skin-changers may experience from time to time. He was Changing. But not because he wanted to, just because it what's in his nature." He paused, shifted in his seat. "What Tony said and did was not entirely under his control, although you may think that. Some Skin-changers are Wild, meaning they can't Change at will, or at the very least don't have the strength to control when they do; their blood is tainted. They say things they don't entirely mean, and at times break out into bouts of rage. He is a Wild Outcast Skin-changer. When he's angry, he *will* try to hurt you, maybe even kill you, in order to satisfy that thirst for blood, vengeance, or guilt."

"Our species turn Wild whenever emotions from previous tragic events or self-inflicting pain rise up and choke the humanity out of us. Quite a few of our people cannot suppress our emotions. Much like humans, there are demigods who suffer from mental illnesses such as bipolar depression or other mood disorders. It's a bit like that, except for Skin-changers are much, much worse in the ways that they bear it. It's harder for us," Nathaniel sighed and ran a hand through his hair. "And to try and quench his thirst for some petty revenge, Tony tried to sought a way to cause you pain, or

106

indirectly cause your parent's harm for what your family did to his years ago. He was going to Change you, plain as that.

Since you're at a younger age than most Skin-changers, we can only expect for you to go through a very painful process before your Claiming Moon. You have the blood of the Olympians running through your veins, mingled with your hereditary Skin-changer DNA. We can only hope your Claiming Moon initiation doesn't kill you." Nathaniel unsheathed his precious possession and cradled it in his hands, peering down the edge of the blade at me. He seemed satisfied with the too-perfect gleam of the sword and shuffled it from hand to hand.

I cleared the bile that was slowly creeping its way up my throat, summoning up what little courage I had left to speak. "W-what did my family instill on Tony's?"

A tick started in Luke's jaw at that. Bruce eyed Tony from the corner, arms folded. Nathaniel only guffawed and sheathed his sword at his belt again.

"Years ago, before you were born, your parents were part of a group who called themselves Seekers. This little rag-tag group of mortals knew of the existence of our kind and made it their duty to seek out and destroy us, one by one. When on their last mission, searching in the small coastal town off the coast of Oregon, the Seekers and your parents discovered Tony's family in hiding, blending with the humans.

The Seekers sent two people, being Clara and Kyle, to go and dispose of him and his entire family of three sisters and one brother in the middle of the night. It was to help 'cleanse the Earth' as they exclaimed. Sort of like when a parade of Salem witch hunters went around slaughtering innocent girls back in the 1800's because they seemed to be 'in league with the devil', so to speak. At the time, Tony was eight years old," Nathaniel continued, noting the way my eyes widened.

107

While his family was sleeping, Clara and Kyle Jones snuck into his house and set it ablaze, but not without slitting the throats of all his siblings first. His mother sent him to hide in the cellar. When he smelt the smoke, he bolted back out to find his house burning to ashes, his family inside. There was nothing he could do but get the hell out of dodge; he was devastated, as you can imagine, for if he didn't flee then the Seekers would kill him as well. Just envision," Nathaniel spread his hands out, arcing them over his head in a rainbow. "an eight-year-old boy running for his life all because humans thought of him as a vile creature of Hell. Somehow, he had managed to find me six years later after living in a miserable orphanage."

It felt as if a hand was wrapped around my neck, squeezing and squeezing until I could hardly breathe.

"We traveled in a group after I took Tony under my wings; we fought and hunted together. One night, he had filled me in on the details of what had happened the night he lost his family. He vowed to cause the Seekers' families the same pain and torture just as they had bestowed upon him. Three years ago, I chose to make Tony my soldier and partner in my mission. We both had the same feelings for mortals and the Council's Laws. Spiteful and strong, we made our home here, far away from the outside worlds. Not soon after, the four other lads joined my crew and have been training and fighting ever since. Oh, how both the gods and humans alike have been cruel to us. And for Shadarr to have— hmph. Nevermind." Thankfully, he stopped his talking, dismissing the last comment with the wave of his hand.

Yeah…I think I know *exactly* how Shadarr came to be here; these bastards didn't deserve mercy or revenge nor power. They deserved a lifetime behind bars. If what Nathaniel was saying was true, then how have I never heard of that happening? Clara and Kyle Jones were good people; they would never think to hurt someone else, no matter the situation. My father could have chosen to shoot Tony with one of the hunting rifles he kept locked in his

ALL POWERFUL: THE HUNTED

safe when he had broken into my house, but had decided not to, although it didn't take much to walk into the other room, punch in the code and open the gun safe, and load a cartridge into any one of the firearms within.

"B-but why would my parents think of such things? How old were they when they joined the group? Did they really hurt Tony's family? And why? How many Wild Skin-changers are there? Outcasts? Darkshadows? Hunters? Where is *here*? What and who is the Council?" I blurted out, unable to stop the flow of questions coming out of my mouth, the buzzing in my head growing louder by the second.

And how come everything seemed so different now?

☾

They stared at him.

All seventy-two pairs of yellow, green, blue, black, copper, brown, purple, and grey eyes looked back at Will Orchild. James, Alex, and Jacob stood patiently by, watching. Will was walking up and down the lanes of their wolves' eight by eight kennels. About half were filled. After a brief discussion with his friends, they had all agreed on which wolves to choose to guide them on their journey.

The Skin-changers were in the Den, the ground level of *Camp Canis Lupis* where their animal friends stayed. Each specially constructed kennel consisted of heating and cooling systems, hay bedding, food and water feeders, and giant doggie doors leading out to the main twenty-five-acre courtyard where they were free to roam at any time of day. The wolves played and accompanied the Warriors, Camp Wolf's soldiers and combatants in training, while surrounded by a fifty-foot stone wall that was guarded day and night to keep the monsters that lurked in the darkness at bay.

The Skin-changers' sleeping chambers (made up into ten total sectors) and dining hall were also located on ground level. The rest of the building's rooms, including the training gyms, fighting arena, security control bases, garages, forges, ball courts and infirmary, storage units and classrooms were either located a level lower (underground) or outside. There was a west, east, north, and south gate to the outside. Gravel roads led to the outside world and connected to the highways and interstates miles away, off the paths that linked back to Camp.

Camp Wolf is a safe haven for Hunter Skin-changers ages thirteen to nineteen, and any adults who wanted to continue living and working at Camp. Only demigods born of wolf-blood and raised in a Hunter Skin-changer family (Darkshadows and Outcasts excluded) could be accepted into Camp Wolf, unless Halt Lockwood, Camp's Alpha, permitted them to stay. Mortals were forbidden to step foot inside his Camp, although it was highly unlikely for one to wander into the camouflaged base without repercussions from the sentries standing guard.

And if one were to take a peek inside the main foyers of Camp Wolf, they would see the many mosaics and murals depicting The Great Battle lining the walls.

Thousands of years ago, there were countless Hunter Skin-changers thriving in the world. The Were-Hunters, to be specific, were the first guardians of the gods. They served and protected the Olympians as was their duty. When Lycaon, the first werewolf, created a new species of human and animal, he sought out the city of Arcadia and crowned himself king. His Were-Hunters fought his wars, died for him, harassed the Arcadian people, and created new life so that one day mortals would see how incredible and powerful he really was.

King Lycaon had been greedy and selfish towards the Olympians, as they undermined him as a mere mortal. He didn't build temples nor offer sacrifices to be made in their honor, and he punished anyone that was caught publicly praying. Secretly, Lycaon had practiced dark magic and was willing to take Zeus's throne if and when he had the chance. After years of hellish reign, the people started attacking and murdering Lycaon's Were-Hunters, deeming them 'abominations worthy of death'.

Centuries later, the creatures were later dubbed Werewolves. King Lycaon's Were-Hunters were uncontrollable beasts on the full moon, never bothering to control when and how they Changed. His soldiers went about slaying livestock, destroying houses, and injuring citizens; thus began the war between human and beast, foe against foe, for survival of the realms.

Lycaon was furious and went to see Hades, the god of the Underworld and keeper of souls. He begged the god if he could hide his creations down in his territory so that way they could live in peace from others. A group of humans who called themselves Seekers had started moving from city to city, causing panic and fear as they captured and slaughtered all the Were-Hunters. Hades reluctantly agreed and hid the feeble king's people for over a century until all thoughts of them were erased from mortal minds.

Once it was safe enough to return to the surface, the last remaining Were-Hunters traveled to the far reaches of the Earth and bred a new species: Skin-changers. These creatures would protect the humans and their world, instead of raining hell. There were three races of Skin-changers established—Hunters, Darkshadows, and Outcasts.

It was a new start. The Olympians gave Lycaon one last chance to redeem himself as king and a god. From there he granted the Skin-changers be blessed with the blood of the Olympian's immortal power. From then on, secret bases, much like future Area

51, were made as places for their kind to live and train in quiet from the outside world.

But the peace wasn't going to last forever.

A new threat emerged.

Dragons.

For land, power, and love, a great battle initiated that changed the course of men, Dragons, monsters, gods and all creatures of the universe. The battle dwindled on for six hundred long years, with small wars over land and skirmishes being fought every century or so when the mass fighting ended for a short while. At least until one side had gathered enough resources and grew in population, or one race turned measly affronts into something bigger.

Each side, each creature, and each family held a grudge. After years had passed, one would still resent another for something that happened long, long ago, neither wanting to forget or forgive. Then the mass fighting and slaughter would begin again when the species saw new generations born and raised. And even long after the war was won, tension between the groups still simmered. The humans had victory, and so few Skin-changers still walked the Earth with even fewer Dragons to be seen for.

The students of Camp Wolf's race were and still are slowly decreasing as the elders die out and the young are slain by monsters of Tartarus; however, with a new generation came a new hope that Skin-changers will once again thrive in the world.

To keep that sliver of peace in place, the twelve major Olympians fixed their supreme ruling over *every* living being on earth, excluding some monsters. For gifting them their life's blood and inherited powers, the demigods swore to guard the gods' children with their lives, giving the people security.

Left in existence were only ten functioning Camps when before a hundred. The Camps were located in London, England,

112

Seattle, Washington, New York, New York, in the southern ranges of the Rocky Mountains, Mt. Everest, Berlin, Germany, Cairo, Egypt, Rome, Italy, Athens, Greece, and middle-of-nowhere, Antarctica.

The warriors of this world, the strong-willed trainees, and the ruthless cut of a blade was no match for any monster. The beasts could not endanger any mere human without facing the wrath of a Hunter's blades in return.

The Skin-changers have a job to do.

Protect and serve.

Chapter VI: Mission Impossible

One week ago...

James Dawn, Jacob Vendéen, William Orchild, and Alex Rayn were hunched over a list of names. "Hmm, so Cherise and Joffrey will come with me, and we'll go east. Will, you'll take Jaz and Izzy south. Johnathen and Aaron will go north with Pearl and Greyback. Jacob will go west with Nike and Orpha." Alex thought aloud. "And that will leave James here to have our backs. He can help guide us, right? Oh, don't look at me like that, Jay." He glanced over at James who was glaring at him from up above, hanging from a tree branch. The teens were huddled under a massive oak tree, discussing plans and sharing ideas.

"You know it's better for you to stay at Camp. If one of us finds a lead or you have another of your recurring visions, it will be easier for us to find the girl." Alex explained. "Besides, Will's already talked it out with our pack and they agreed to the plan, but they have certain conditions that *we* have to follow since they're coming with us." The eight wolves that would be traveling with them glanced around at their human companions, ears pricked.

James sighed. "I know, but it doesn't seem right that I'm the one *not* going."

"Yes, we've already established that. But Vincent is still out there, Taz is missing, and Halt has been occupied with negotiating the peace treaty between Rome and Athens. Meanwhile, we have all been going about our daily lives whilst an unknown evil by the name of Nathaniel has been planning to take over the world! Not to mention we're still sitting here complaining about who stays and who goes on this very important mission!" Jacob exclaimed.

114

"C'mon James, if we don't return within a month or so—" Will started.

"A month!? Nekoda will be a mindless fifteen-year-old demigod slave by then!" James sputtered and jumped off of the branch, landing with a soft *thud* on the ground.

"As I was saying, you are free to come and save our arses before it's too late. However, you'll also need to help keep order here at Camp Wolf. If Damon is still gossiping and spreading lies about the Council, it could go terribly wrong for all of us. Apparently, he seems to think his father is the rightful heir to High Council instead of Halt. He also claims to know where Krane de Royce's talismans are. Obviously, I think he's just bluffing about that last bit. Yet it is still a bit fishy, considering his half-brother presumably has a Dragon egg in his possession. But since Michael fled, we have no idea where they'd be. Even worse, we don't how soon Nekoda's powers will unleash and if Nathaniel has a super army of Outcasts to help with this master plan of his. So, we five need to go and scout across the country while one of us stays here and Johnathen and Aaron deliver this," Will unfolded a piece of crinkled parchment paper and handed it to James. "Here."

He skimmed the page and asked, "How are we so sure that this will get to her?"

"Oh, Johnathen knows this Hellhound that used to live and watch over Nekoda long before we even knew who she was. His name's Buddy. I'm sure you've seen him wandering around near the Den? But he was, uh, recently killed and sent back to the Underworld by Nathaniel. We need only find him. Buddy can Portal, so he can assist in finding where Nathaniel's holding Nekoda captive. But he can only carry objects, not people, when he Portals. And since he isn't loyal to anyone but Nekoda, he'll willingly obey to help her. That's the second part of the plan. We just have to hope that the gods are willing to help, too, for their sakes and ours," he replied solemnly.

"Okay, but do you even know what it is you're looking for exactly?" James crossed his arms, huffing.

"Yes, sorta... well, I have an idea. Our Camp is shielded from mortals up here in the Rockies, correct? And since Nathaniel would want to stay hidden as well, our best bet is he is anywhere secluded, like a forest, or maybe by the ocean. That's why we're traveling in the four cardinal directions." Will fingered the cord on his satchel bag that was slung over one shoulder.

"Okay," the boy harrumphed. "Supplies, then. What about those? Halt hasn't agreed to this plan, I know that. But I don't care if he's happy about it or not, since now I'm not going. How are you going to get past him with a pack full of necessities?" James argued, determined to get every little twist and turn of the plan known.

"Aaron and Johnathen are raiding the kitchens as we speak. As for the weapons and clothing, I doubt Timothy or yourself will miss a few sharp swords. Jacob can just bring his war-hammer, Alex his bow, and I my Sniper rifle. We can pack our own items of clothing."

No one spoke for a solid minute.

"And if anyone discovers we're missing?" Alex questioned.

"Then James can make something up." grumbled Jacob. "When should we head out?"

"By noon, on the sixth. I reckon if all four of us split up and leave at separate times we'd appear less suspicious." Will answered. Alex rubbed his forehead, deep in thought. Jacob muttered under bated breath. James looked at the letter again and handed it back to Will.

"Fine! But if Halt does find out, he'll come straight to me and I'll have to tell him everything. I would love to stay and chat but I've got a sword-fighting lesson to attend. I don't think my new students would appreciate their instructor being late for class."

116

With that he turned and jogged off in the direction of the courtyard and the sword-fighting arena.

Jacob straightened. "Well, I've got to forge a new steel rim for my shield. Alex, I suggest you come with me. I need you to look at a new helm that's cooling. I think it'll suit you nicely."

The demigods left, leaving Will to ponder alone in his thoughts. *The plan's not perfect,* he thought. *But it's the only plan we've got.*

☾

Alex whistled. "Whoa, baby! Look at that! How long did it take to craft this?" he examined the bronze helm adorned with a dragon inscription. The tail and body wrapped around the left backside of the helmet to meet up with the head on the right side, its maw opened in a roar. There was an M shaped cut out in the front for the wearer to see. Rays of sunlight reflected off the metal, rainbow light bouncing around the forge.

"Well, it took quite a bit of time. I worked on the design all day and then crafted, melted, and heated the shape of the structure for forty hours straight. That's why I benched out on the floor during Brayden's lecture over Rome's greatest general, Scipio, and the battle of Zama. Still surprised that dude fought Hannibal, the brilliant military commander of the Carthaginians during the Second Punic War." Jacob answered casually, unawares he was rambling.

"Oh, I thought you just died of boredom and flopped lifelessly to the ground. Wait, didn't you say you fell *asleep* during class?"

"Thanks for your sympathy. I'll be glad to know you'll be at my funeral when I die," Jacob rolled his eyes. "And yes, I did doze off. But I felt bad for interrupting Brayden's lesson so I studied up afterwards."

Alex snorted and clapped his friend's back. "Jacob, always so sentimental! C'mon, I'll smell like wet dog if I stand in here any longer. No pun intended." He wiped the sweat off his brow. Together they left the Camp's forge, a large open room with anvils, crates of minerals and building materials, cooling weapons and pieces of metal. Safety gear was lined up on the side of the back wall. A few wood-burning ovens, fire pits, and cooling stations were set up around the area.

The two marched out the door and up the stairs to the main level, heading for their bedchambers. Each room had a single bath and full-sized bed or two sets of bunks, depending on how many students roomed together. When the young Skin-changers start their new life at Camp Wolf, they get to decorate their sleeping spaces with pictures and book shelves and buy flat screens, game systems, speakers and other electronic systems to make their bedroom feel as homely as possible.

Alex remembered when he was first brought here. He had been a scruffy child of thirteen, face purpled and swollen with bruises from where he would fight with the other mundane students at his old school. That was back when he thought he was human, and boy, did things change for him. A few days after his arrival, he had first met Jacob and Will when they played a game of football on the wet grass. Some of the other students were being too rough and the boys stepped in to help. James had been nearby practicing swordplay when he saw what was happening and summoned Halt, the director and Alpha of their new home and Vincent Lockwood's father.

Johnathen and Aaron have trained at Camp for many years, and the teens all met by chance during an archery session. They were mission operatives, instructors, and managers for the center of security and control for Camp Wolf's defense. Their rooms may have been in different sectors since the dorms were assigned by age, but the boys still messed around and trained together whenever they had the chance to in their leisure time. Ever since, they've been a team.

Alex was currently the youngest of the group at fifteen, Jacob and Will were the second and third youngest at sixteen, James was nearing seventeen, Aaron was twenty-three years old, and Johnathen twenty-four.

"Hey, let's go see how James' class is going." Alex said, shoveling a packet of skittles into his mouth.

"Good idea, we can try to humiliate him in front of his own students. We can go meet up with William, J-Dog, and Aaron in the dining hall next." said Jacob.

"Sounds like a plan, man." chuckled Alex. The two pals fist bumped and made their way in the direction of the east gate.

☾

Crack! Thwack! Crack! The sounds of blade matched against blade echoed throughout the courtyard. James was helping a younger student, Kaleb, learn to keep his balance while handling a sword. Every time Kaleb swung, he would either lean back too much to gain more force with the blow or falling on his butt when he brought the blade down on James, henceforth missing his opponent.

"Ow!" Kaleb cried as he pushed his shoulder forward and spun his sword to hit James' gauntlet, tripping over his own feet. "Y'know, I think this sword is just too heavy for me. Let's go back to the armory and pick out a new one. I don't think I can do this." The young boy started to turn when James' reached out and placed a chain-mailed hand on his arm.

119

"It's not the weapon, it's he who wields the sword that can't accomplish it. But you can, Kaleb. I've seen how you fight. It all comes with practice. A few more minutes, okay?"

He nodded and raised his sword level with James'. "Okay, ten more minutes. I want to brag to all my friends I beat my sword instructor in a duel." Kaleb laughed half-heartedly. James saw the determination in the kid's eyes and continued their lesson.

As each student sent a last parry or thrust or jab at their partner, soldiers, instructors and friends dwindled inside to clean up before feast. James sighed. Of recently he hasn't been feeling his usual self; he and his friends were all worried about this mission. If it failed or was achieved, only time would tell. And time was one thing they didn't have. Nor did *she*. His friends— gods, he loved them so much, they were his own family—were putting their own lives at risk for someone they, and himself, hardly knew.

Halt was too busy and too tired to even care or listen to a word they had to say, but if the Fates' prophecy was true then they would need her to raze or save Olympus. It was her choice and her path, yet nonetheless her decisions would set their destinies in motion…

'**A child of the gods shall be reborn**

To stop the war of worlds.

With the creatures of the moon and the

Powers of the mighty whose strength

Not even Gaia's monsters can subdue,

She shall live to see the world's fate to

Stop an evil yet no one's faced and destroy

An enemy whose name is smeared in

Blood and chaos to find the Tomb, where fire

Slumbers and where dark secrets and even darker

Creatures dwell, to retrieve thy four talismans,

Unlock the spells and in the end, save Olympus

Before its fall, binding both worlds once

And for all.'

The words still rang through his ears. As James pulled up a chair at the head table, he mulled the prophecy over in his head. What did it mean? The child born of the gods was clearly Nekoda Jones, he knew that much. But a tomb where fire sleeps? What's a bunch of dead guy's burial ground got to do with anything? Both worlds meant to bind the mortal and the immortal. Is Nathaniel really this great evil being hiding behind a mask? And what of the four talismans?

Supposedly long gone, lost after the battle between men and beast, legend states that they were Earth's strongest weapons and were given to the last Dragon king and first Skin-changer of his kind, Krane de Royce and his Dragon, Balios, by the Olympians themselves.

After they were killed at war, his most loyal soldiers buried him and his precious items underground. Nothing was recorded of where or what happened to his Dragon. And that was centuries ago, so not much is recorded in the history books either.

Alas the tricky Three Fates, being followers of the gods themselves, came up with a prophecy for each of the talismans to help reveal them. No one has yet to discover them, and many who do go off in search are never heard from again. It sounded like an

121

old ghost story to James, but to his missing friend Vincent, it all seemed like a leap of faith.

'Death, an ultimate weapon for man's enemies. Its veil
Like no other, shaded in bronze with an edge that can
Bring another to power.
Once rested in a king's hand, thou rest alone in
The fire-lizard's claws and seeks refuge in the belly
Of a chamber deep within the valleys of a long forgotten
Tyme.'

      The prophecy for Death, Krane's sword, was quite mysterious.

'Passed down from generation to
Generation, an ancient piece of divine power
Shall one day reveal itself to the world and save
The throne, for better or for worse. Made from dust
And enchanted with magic,
Now lost to the treacherous confines of earth.'

      The historic prophecy for the *Book of Spells*, James now knew by heart after spending his early years memorizing the prophecies, as did every young Skin-changer growing up with tales of the next big war.

'Blood made life, and it can end it.

Forged down, down

Under the mountains the talisman was crafted, as one

The Olympians put themselves to the Scythe and watched

As the beginning of a new era began. When it is time, the

Keeper shall set free what was meant to be.

Bestowed upon thy who carries with them the past and

The future, must continue their journey to find what was

Forgotten.

The Amulet of Twelve prophecy was too puzzling for James to figure out.

'Bringer of storms, lord of the skies.

The upholder of men and gods who wielded the shield

Of the Gorgon queen's head. It shall be bestowed upon he

Who tamed the beast, for he was the one whom gave the

Command and in the end, failed to make amends.

Once returned to its rightful place, piece by piece,

All may finally be restored.'

And the last prophecy, for Aegis, the mythical talisman that Zeus once possessed.

"Urgh, why does everything have to be so complicated!" James muttered, silently wishing he were somewhere else tonight as he picked at his half-eaten plate of food.

His friend and former teammate on the Camp's local soccer team (as part of their other activities), Kai Chen, nudged his side. "Hey, you going to eat that?" Shaking his head at his friend's usual large appetite, James scooped his steak and mashed potatoes onto Kai's platter. "So, are you going to Sunday night's bonfire? Some of the guys and I are going to celebrate Paul's promotion to Sergeant in the U.S. Military. It'll be fun."

Even though he doubted he would show up, James replied, "Sure."

The double oak doors of the dining hall opened and in walked Johnathen and Aaron. They wore giddy expressions as they rushed over to James' side and took a seat beside him.

"Dude, we packed a butt load of snacks in our bags! Meredith even managed to slip me a small slice of chocolate fudge cheesecake while I charmed her with my flirtatious personality before heading back out." Aaron flashed a toothy grin.

BelAnne Tarly, Elizabeth Fey, Arya Ronsin, Natasha Lee, Meredith Noble and Zoey Stark were Camp Wolf's cooks, nurses, and trading management crew as well as the only females at Camp Wolf. Following the world's sexist history and the traditional Greek way of life, the woman only played a few minor roles at camp. But each had been born with the Sight, so Halt had inclined they come and learn at Camp Wolf, after their parents, half-human and half-demigod, begged him to take them in. Male Skin-changers were more common than females. The Seekers have been killing most females of the Skin-changer species so the race could no longer procreate. There was a bigger chance of finding a four-leaf clover in a field of sunflowers than running into a female Skin-changer over the age of forty.

Normal demigods were a different story as they blended in easiest with human life than animal-creatures.

Most adult Hunters, Darkshadow, and Outcast Skin-changers got married or were in relationships with a significant other who didn't know their true side until after they finished their training. For the most part, it was prohibited to fall in love with another student at Camp Wolf, as it caused problems and was considered a distraction. Kind of like if someone's girlfriend or boyfriend were to work in the same office or shop and continue to draw you away from your job. Over the years, a few students opened up about their sexuality, which wasn't strictly against any camp rules, but having a boyfriend or girlfriend was still a no-no within the walls of Camp Wolf. No one really cared but now, in this time and century, more citizens seem to dislike the idea of the same gender loving each other. James knew a few classmates like that, and a few classmates who had secret boyfriends, like Tanner and Po, having been together for almost a year now. And James' good friend, Kai Chen, came out as bisexual not too long ago. As long as you're happy, what does it matter what anybody else thought? If you love a person, you love them for them.

"Ah, nice. But aren't you kind of taking advantage of her when you're about to leave on a top *secret* and *dangerous* mission?" James scoffed.

"True, she does have a huge crush on you. Don't want to break her heart. I hope you haven't told her yet." Johnathen spoke, finger-combing his dirty-blonde hair. Stormy grey eyes glanced at Aaron, then flicked across the hall to the kitchen's entrance.

"Relax, bud. No, I haven't and I know if I do break her heart, BelAnne will judo-flip me," Aaron responded.

"Good boy." James cooed. "Have you guys seen Will, Alex, or Jacob recently? They should've been here—" he was cut off when the three stepped up to the table and sat. "Never mind. Where have y'all been? You're late."

Jacob sipped his glass of Coca-Cola and looked at the others. "Sorry, Alex and I were at the forge and Will was, well, where were you, bud?"

"Thinking," Will said.

"Thinking." Jacob repeated.

"Oh, that's never good. About what, exactly?" Alex asked.

Will sighed. "Everything, mainly, but mostly about the Dragon. The Dragon who's trapped like Nekoda. I can't explain it but...I feel I can sense him. Like I have some, uh, sort of connection with him. It's weird, I know." Five sets of eyes gazed back at Will.

"I think I've figured out the Dragon's name— Shadarr, and he's young. Not a baby, but young for a Dragon." replied James.

"Hmm. Let's think about this for a moment. Why and how, if possible, could we save both Nekoda *and* Shadarr?" Johnathen questioned, receiving a few scowls and wrinkled noses in return.

"First off, we're not even sure if our plan to save Nekoda will go well. I think our first priority is saving the girl, not the Dragon. It'll be hard enough enough trying to find their location, deliver the message, and hopefully free Nekoda. So, if we can pull off all that, then maybe, just maybe, we can escape with Shadarr too."

Will looked glum. No one spoke for a moment.

"Aaron, Johnathen, can I see that note?" Alex asked.

"Yeah," Johnathen pulled it out of his back pocket and set it on the table.

"Tell me, just how do you plan to call upon a Hellhound and command him to sniff out Nekoda?" He fidgeted with the piece of paper.

"I can contact Leo and his pack who can travel down to Hell's Gate with the letter and seek out Cerberus. That mutt can

126

locate Buddy for us. Once they tell Buddy our plan and he agrees to go, we can send Buddy on his way." Johnathen replied.

"Yes, but we—I mean, y'all—are leaving soon. How long will it take?" asked James, growing weary.

"Uhm, three to six hours, tops. Buddy should be back by late in the morning." The other teenagers looked round the table, double-checking to see if anybody was eavesdropping.

Jacob nodded. "Sounds like a plan, man. James, you okay over there? You look as if you're going to puke."

The sixteen-year-old stared at his plate before whispering, "I just don't want anything to happen to you, or to *her*. I may not know Nekoda, but she's important, and like it or not I'm also the one who's sending you off and you may not even come back…just like Vincent. I'm responsible for all this, so I'll be responsible if you live or die…" he stopped, choking on his words.

Aaron stood up and walked around the table to pat his friend on the back. "Look dude, I think you are worrying to much about the gravity of the situation. Nathaniel, in the upcoming future, is apparently going to start a war and dominate the world. We know *who* his secret weapon is, but not the *what*…besides, Vincent is a different story. He probably just wanted to get some fresh air and go live off on his own for a while. We don't know for sure though, do we? No, but there's always hope. We're a team guys, blood brothers. That's good enough for me." Aaron gave two thumbs-up and ruffled James' hair.

A light went off in James' head. "Hey! After dinner, meet me by the gnarled old oak tree, the one directly by the pond. I need to tell you all something very important, but it's private. I have an idea, or at least a clue to how this will help us solve what Nathaniel is looking for and why Vincent went missing. Stay here and finish your supper, I'm going back to my room to collect a few items!"

Leaping to his feet, James ran out the double-doors and into the bustling alleyway.

☾

Frogs croaked. Crickets chirped. Stars shone. "Ugh, I wonder when James will get here." Aaron sighed. Johnathen checked his watch: 12:47 a.m.

Alex yawned, stretching out his legs. "It's getting late, and if that boy doesn't get here in two minutes then I'm going to hit the hay."

"Same here, bro." Jacob adjusted the lantern that hung from a low branch above their heads. He was anxious to find out what his friend was going to share with them. Anything about Vincent and Jacob was all ears; Vincent was his best friend. A foot away, Will sat cross-legged on the ground, meditating. One breath in, one breath out. Slow and steady, cool and calm.

Aaron nudged him. "Yo, what's going on in that head of yours? You've been at it for half an hour now, William." Will opened an eye and blew out a deep breath. He mumbled a quiet "Whatever" under his breath and focused once more.

For the past few days, Will had been trying to see if he could come into contact with Shadarr, being the only person at Camp Wolf to be able to 'talk' and understand animals, so he figured it would be worth a shot. Communicating with another creature was easy, at least for him. You had to become one with nature, listen, smell, see, grab hold of that small sliver of essence and expand the mind. He could *feel* an animal's aura as he searched for the connection. One moment he was alone—the next there was a SNAP—and he was a part of another being—and then SNIP—the sense vanished.

128

There were perks to being a unique son of Athena sometimes, the Greek goddess of wisdom and sister to Artemis, the nature goddess.

From nearby, branches rustled and the sounds of leaves crunching underfoot greeted the boys as James came stumbling into view, carrying a leather satchel bag. "About time!" Aaron complained.

"Hush. Let me show you what I've got." He rolled his eyes.

Unlatching the clips, James flipped over the bag and pulled out each content. The first item was an old, thin paged journal. The next item was a sketchbook belonging to Vincent Lockwood, a faded map, and a golden compass.

"Where did you get these things?" Jacob flipped through Vincent's journal, tracing over his friend's writing with a finger.

"The record was stolen from the Archives, the sketchbook from Vincent's bedroom, and the compass was hidden in a small box that, coincidentally, also happened to be in Vincent's room." James answered nonchalantly. Johnathen scratched his head at a loss for words.

"So, why?" Aaron pushed. Blowing dust from the leather cover, James flipped open the journal and skimmed through it, stopped, and showed his buddies a diagram of four objects.

"Apparently, Nathaniel needs these ancient relics to find more important ancient relics and the Lockwoods, aka Vincent's family, is in possession of one of these such talismans. It's just been hidden in plain sight for so long. Each is designed of its own purpose and craftsmanship in order to, how would you put it? Gain immortal power." Blank faces stared back.

"How would these objects help us find Nekoda or lead us to Vincent? Elaborate please." Johnathen frowned.

James recited the Fates' prophecies to them first. "With these talismans, you basically have ultimate godly power and can dominate the world and perform necromancy because of the powerful black magic contained in the *Book of Spells*. But you'd have to uncover a lost tomb first and find the burial grounds of the last Dragon King. And oh, yeah, if you wanted you could pretty much *destroy flippin' Olympus itself!* Yup, that about covers everything."

The hooting of an owl echoed. Something crashed through the trees in the distance. Silence greeted the boys. Then: "Day-am!" Jacob whistled. "That sounds totally depressing yet wicked at the same time."

"Agreed." Said Alex.

"If you've ever snuck down to the Archives," James scoffed. "Then you surely would have come across something about the prophecies or discovered family history books. The Lockwood's are the most popular in historical events, by the way. It explains in one of the Keeper's old diaries, like what I have here, that centuries ago after the outcome of the Titan war, a civilized family was brought a talisman to protect from evil until the end of time."

"Yes, we all know that story," Johnathen Dogo interjected. "That talisman would be passed down from father to son, mother to daughter, and one of the first families were the Lockwoods. In recent events, our dear Halt Lockwood passed down this specific talisman to his son, Vincent."

"Wait, but what exactly are these special talismans?" Alex questioned, curious.

"There's one called the Amulet of Twelve, and the talisman, Death, the blade of Krane de Royce, Zeus' shield, Aegis, and the *Book of Spells*. And this compass-thingy could probably be accounted for as one."

"And you believe Vincent owns one of these magical items?" Worried gazes.

"Yes, I do, and that item is the Amulet of Twelve. Like all Lockwoods before him he also possessed this compass, which is believed to be enchanted with magic from the goddess Hecate to guide people to the hiding spots of the other objects. Only problem is it will only work if it is in the hands of a Lockwood. I don't know if he intended to leave this stuff behind, but certainly the Amulet is gone with him. And this compass—" James held up the golden compass with the letter 'L' engraved on the outside. "Goes along with this map. If you know how to read it correctly it can lead you to the other talismans, too."

"Okay, but how did you come to find it was the Lockwood's and get a lead on *all this* in the first place?" asked Jacob, spreading his hands out at the objects resting before them.

"Ha, that's a long tale. But long story short, I searched up the names of the Council members and dug up their history books. Add in Vincent and Taz's strange disappearances, my crazy visions, and the odd legendary prophecies, and there's lots you can try to piece together." When it came down to it, James would do whatever it took to get something done.

"Camrice Lockwood is Vincent's true-blood father, while Halt is his adoptive father, so shouldn't Halt know anything about this?" said Aaron.

"Technically, he shouldn't know, but he may since Camrice and him were so close. It's a dangerous secret to tell and only if you are immediate family can you ever know about such things. But I think Camrice gave the Amulet of Twelve, the compass, and the map to Halt to give to Vincent when he was old enough. Camrice was forbidden to. Perhaps Halt didn't ask any questions and just locked it all up for safekeeping." James informed them all, picking at a blade of grass.

Eighteen and a half years ago, Halt Jackson and Camrice Lockwood were best friends, two peas in a pod. Later, at the ripe age of thirty, Camrice married his new mortal fiancée, Laura. Laura knew about Camrice's real identity and nature, but that didn't stop her from marrying him and starting a family together. Nine months after their son's birth, both parents died tragically in a car crash. They were hit head-on by a drunken driver whom also died in the accident.

Overwhelmed by the families' loss and the reality of a newborn orphaned infant, Halt took up the surname Lockwood in honor of his friend and took care of Vincent, taking up the responsibility of a second father. Vincent is now nineteen.

"Okay, and nobody has ever tried to locate the talismans and fulfill the prophecies of possible perpetual doom before now?" Alex took a turn at inspecting the compass and the journal, admiring the peculiar things.

"Actually, yes, most people who have ever owned another talisman or heard the prophecies have tried, but it leads them nowhere. Many have died horribly, without so much as a trace apart from a smashed in skull or a severed limb. But anyone outside of the Keeper's families believes theses prophecies aren't true. Obviously, there's not much said about the legends. Minimal evidence is left of their existence besides the knowledge passed down from generation to generation, along with the journals and documents in the Archives which, by the way, are over hundreds of years old. Every so often one member of the Council and or the Keeper's family goes out searching. I think Vin decided it was his turn to go."

"But why go searching if he knows *all* this information and how it could cause the end of the world!?" Johnathen exclaimed. "Un-unless he *didn't* know…"

"Can you read through the journal? Maybe it will say something in there or in the sketchbook." Aaron leaned over Alex's shoulder, peering at pages.

James shook his head. "The writing is in ancient Greek, and my language skills aren't very apt. I haven't even passed class Latin 1 yet with Mr. Keegan. And I know none of you can read it fluently either."

"We certainly can't ask anybody else or they'll get suspicious. If we get the chance to talk to Halt though..." Will began, twiddling his thumbs now.

"If we mention anything or drop so much as a hint to what we're trying to figure out, he'll know that we're up to something and will make us abort our mission." Johnathen added.

"Halt already knows we're up to something! He's just too busy to even contemplate it," Aaron countered.

"Right. Does anyone know somebody who can help? It has to be somebody trustworthy, very wise, and knows a lot about the Council and the secrets of the Archives." Will stated. A slow, devious smile crept across Aaron and Johnathen's faces. Jacob, Alex, and Will looked around at each other and sighed. James looked at them in confusion.

Finally, James cleared his throat, daring to ask. "Uh, who are we thinking about here? Honestly, I lost my mind reading abilities the last time I fell out of a tree, and I really have no idea as to who you're thinking of."

"Not a *who*, but a *them*. Mitchell Garner and Cole Burnett!" Jacob responded sprightly.

☾

Down below ground-level and located next to the forges and security control rooms lay the underground parking garage. Parked and ready to cruise sat many types of vehicles all in good condition. There were back roads through the mountains that only the Skin-changers of Camp Wolf knew about. It was quicker to travel in cars through the area than on two or four legs. It was also the trade routes used for trucks to pass through to get to the base.

To earn money in order to buy sustained goods, the warriors at Camp Wolf help fought for the country by fighting in the world-wide wars, the forgers and armories made modern weaponry used in national security companies like the FBI and S.W.A.T., and the countries' other problems. In return for their help, a very top-secret governmental department kept the Skin-changer's world a secret and gave money to the High Council to help their people's survival. Technically it was a government within a government, or a trade for a trade. As long as there was peace between the two races, Mr. President and his crew were happy to be of service.

Tinkering underneath a blue Jeep, Cole stuck his hand out to his friend, Mitchell, who sat by a tool kit. "Wrench, please, I need to fix this leak." Cole, a dark-haired, athletic boy of fourteen worked in the garage almost all day long with his best friend, Mitchell. Both students knew just about everything there was to know about cars; henceforth they were the Camp's youngest engineers and most brilliant tinkers.

Cole's phone beeped from the bench. "Hey, it's Johnathen. Want me to answer?" Mitchell asked.

"Sure." Came the muffled reply.

Mitchell tapped open the newest text message: **We need to talk. I need ur help. Me and the guys are heading down to the garage. Be there soon!**

134

Mitchell typed back: **OK, see u.** He turned off the phone and grabbed Cole's foot, abruptly dragging him out from under the car. "What, dude?!" Cole yelped, wiping grease off his cheek.

"Johnathen and the squad are all coming down here in a few minutes. I guess it's important, because they want to talk. Evidently, they need our help. You done fixing the leak now?"

Cole grumbled, shoving a tool into the pocket of his overalls. "Yeah, yeah. I finished two seconds before you yanked me out from under the Jeep. Could've just said so. I can hear perfectly fine, thank you very much."

Mitchell shrugged. "Sorry. I'll help pick up." As the boys gathered the tools and went to put up their equipment, all six friends trudged down the flights of stairs.

At the bottom, Aaron cupped his hands to his mouth and shouted, "ECHO!" His voice carried around the large room.

"Over here!" Cole waved. They managed to slip in between the vehicles without setting off the car alarms and into the back workspace. "Why the texts? It's late." Cole questioned.

"I should be asking why *you're* still up, but that'd be stupid. Listen, my buddies and I, we need you to decipher something for us. You two know Greek well enough, considering your lineage, unlike the rest of us uneducated fools. We can't read it, and it's very important for you to help us. But you cannot tell anyone. Ever. Can I trust you?" Johnathen pleaded.

Mitchell looked at Cole. Cole looked at Mitchell. In unison, they confirmed their answer. "Yes,"

"Alrighty. We know you know a lot about the Council and its secrets. More importantly, about the prophecies. Just skim through these real fast and inform us if you come across anything unusual." He produced the journal and sketchbook from behind his back and handed one to each boy.

135

Cole sat on a stool while Mitchell sat cross-legged on the dusty cement floor. James watched them squint and concentrate as their eyes skipped over each page.

A couple pages into the journal, Cole jumped. "Got something! It says here, according to the journal's entries from 1980, that this was first written by a man named Camrice A. Lockwood. He goes about explaining how his father today gave him some sort of," he struggled to make out the next word. "talisman and a-a really old compass? And that it is also very important he keep it with him at all times. Also, he writes about how his human dad told him about the 'real world'." Cole makes air quotes with his fingers before continuing. "Camrice says, 'I always knew there was something odd about my family. I just wish I didn't have to inherit my family's past. This dumb Amulet has been putting me at risk and I can't shake the feeling that I'm being watched.' That's all I've made out in the past couple minutes now."

Jacob responded first. "Very good, keep reading. Maybe skip some dates and find the entry for 1996, the year Vincent Lockwood was born."

Mitchell, startled, looked up from the sketchbook. "Wait, are you investigating Vincent's disappearance? Halt said—"

"It doesn't matter what Halt says! And yes, we are, sort of." Jacob swallowed.

Mitchell narrowed his eyes at Jacob. "What do you mean *sort of?* I want to know why we should help you. About any other topic I wouldn't question, but this I will. It mentions stuff about one of the talismans from the prophecies. Why?"

"If you trust us like we trust you, then please tell us exactly the reason why we have to read through these. I don't even know what I'm looking for!" Cole exclaimed, eyebrows raised. Aaron groaned. Will faced James.

136

"Well, it's your decision. Shall we tell 'em or not?" Will eyed the two younger boys. James thought for a moment. He plopped down on one of the metal stools, defeated.

"Fine. But to be clear, it is imperative to swear that you won't tell a soul here aside from us five." He pointed to himself, Johnathen, Aaron, Jacob, Alex, and Will. "Got that?"

Cole nodded and placed his fist over his heart without a second thought. "I, Cole Burnett, swear on the blood of my blood that I shall never tell a soul about anything that James and his friends forbids us to, or I shall suffer for all eternity when I die." Mitchell repeated the same silly vow.

James gave them a brief summary on everything they missed. The visions, Nekoda, Nathaniel and his gang, Shadarr and the four talismans, Vincent's disappearance, the clues he left behind. When he finished, both fourteen-year-olds were left standing, mouths hung open and eyes as wide as saucers.

"That's, uh, wow guys, that's some plan. Jeez." Mitchell mumbled, fiddling with a drill bit.

"Sooo, this may take at least a few days to translate this whole entire journal. Hopefully I can find some type of Greek dictionary lying around my room for y'all to use if you want it done faster. But there's gotta be something in here that will tell you more about the talisman's, right? And I'm just the guy to find it. Mitchell can study the drawings overnight, see if any of the descriptions mean anything." Cole said after a few seconds.

Alex scratched the back of his neck. "Well, you see, we need that journal to be translated by the day after tomorrow morning. It's... " he trailed off.

"It's very important! Top-tippity-top secret. Sorry, we'll have to rule you two out of this one." Will bumped in.

"Again, there is no point in lying. Look, Jacob is already sweating." Mitchell pointed out. Sure enough, thin tracks of perspiration of ran down Jacob's forehead.

"What!" he croaked, "It's, like, really hot down here!"

Aaron pinched the bridge of his nose, eyes closed. James and Johnathen rolled their eyes simultaneously.

"Tell." Cole began.

"Us." Mitchell said next.

"Now." Cole commanded, exasperated.

"All right, okay. Just chill. But this is seriously and literally one of the most dangerous things we're about to tell you. And I swear to the gods, if you tell anybody at all, I will hunt you down and murder you both." James growled, frustrated.

"He's not kidding, just FYI." Johnathen mumbled. James was starting to think coming here to these boys was a bad idea. Now, everything was at stake if they went blabbing off about this to Halt like a bunch of tattle-tale little sissies. James moved until he was directly in front of Mitchell and Cole, his full height towering over them both. With a piercing gaze, he waited until they finally answered.

"W-we believe you, dude." Cole gulped.

"Truth." Mitchell replied.

James snorted. "By Thursday night, the guys and I will head out on foot at separate times, with two wolves, packs of provisions, Vincent's items, and the whole of the country ahead of us. We will each head in a different direction until we come across something. I have been coming up with a plan to try and track down Nathaniel and lure him out of his hiding spot to free the girl. But it's very difficult because if Halt or anyone else finds out that four more men went missing just a few weeks after Vincent, it will be hell. I am not going since Will insists that I stay here and help them from home. In case I have another dream or something. I'm giving them a month to search and rescue Nekoda before Nathaniel turns her into an enslaved Hybrid demigod with scary powers." he paused, noted the look on the young boy's faces, and carried on. "The point is, our mission is our one hope of solving the whole end-of-the-world crazy prophecy come true issue. You see where I'm getting at? Great. Okay." Running a hand through his golden hair, James took a deep breath and stepped back.

"Look man, I've known Johnathen for a while now and I don't see any reason why Cole and I should betray him. We'll help you, and that's final," Mitchell exclaimed.

Will smiled a weak smile at everyone in the room. "I think we could wait one extra day. That alright, bud?" James nodded.

"It's settled. Now I'm going to get some shut-eye. See you all in the morn'." Alex yawned and walked towards the garage stairs leading back up to the main level, Jacob and Will following sleepily behind. Aaron patted Cole and Mitchell on the back before those three left. Johnathen and James were the last to go, striding abreast in the dim lighting. Back up the stairs they climbed before turning in for the night.

As James lay in his bed, he kept thinking to himself. He repeated the same words over and over in his head until his eyelids drooped closed. *"If there is something I'm doing right in the world, it's this. No matter what they all say. If Nekoda can't be saved, then no one can."*

Chapter VII: The Messenger's Arrival

Nathaniel stared at me, his foot tap-tap-tapping on the floor.

"What?" I snapped. No one had spoken since my burst of questions came out of my mouth like popping popcorn. Of course, they wouldn't answer me. They don't give a damn about anything I've got to say. Leave it to me to sugarcoat everything with sprinkles and cherries on top to make them blab. I pouted, and as best as I could, stood up straight and crossed my arms. Defiant.

Ezekial made a move to shove me back down on the bed but thought better of it. I put on my best winning smile, and batted my lashes at the table, where Bruce and Luke and Tony were sitting. Nathaniel was now leaning against the wall to my right. David was still nowhere to be seen. Yippee.

"Will one of you fine gentleman help a gal out here and actually talk to me, huh? Oh, how I just *adore* absolute silence." I mocked. A low rumbling sound came from the birch wood table. I recognized it.

Laughing. Tony.

He was out of a state of moodiness and was now clutching his sides, huffing. I glared at him. "Listen, mister—" I began.

"You really think Nathaniel will tell you anything? You now know my whole damn backstory and yet you think it's a good idea for Nathaniel to tell your parent's secrets now? I guess it wouldn't matter because they're dead. As for my family, they're all in the ground, too. The Council—" Now it was Nathaniel's turn to laugh. It was weird to hear such a human emotion being produced by these monsters of men.

"The Council doesn't give a crap about us, either. You'll be better off with us than with those people in the dark robes and high standards. They all are just a bunch of snobby-nosed founders with major egos. Basically, they control the way we live. They're the reason we're stuck here and why Tony's siblings are dead."

"But I thought that the Seekers was a secret organized group formed outside of the Council's laws—" I started again.

"Exactly. But a few of the supposed loyal Council members helped create that group in the first place. Some thought it necessary to reduce the stain in our population. Meaning, Skin-changers like us were meant to go. Be exterminated," Nathaniel motioned around the bedchamber at his soldiers and himself.

"Technically, the Council folk don't like douchebags like you going around breaking their laws." Yeah, that sounds like the most civilized answer to a civilized explanation. Smirking, I sat back down on the bed as far away from Ezekial as possible.

"For a supposed legendary child, you sure are bitchy." Bruce said. I almost lunged across the table to throttle him. Holy crap, what did he just say? Turning towards him, I went full-blown war elephant on his ass.

"ME!? I HAVE EVERY DAMN RIGHT TO BE! You freaking punks make me like this! Ooo, look at me I kidnapped a fifteen-year-old girl because we mistook her for a wizard! YOU KILLED MY PARENTS, DESTROYED MY HOME, AND RIPPED APART MY DIGNITY! I mean, for God's sake, what's next? You're gonna sacrifice me to a boiling volcano!" I stamped my foot, realizing tears were spilling down my face like raindrops. My chest heaved as I sucked in a lungful of air. No one spoke. No one moved. I think I had made my point well enough.

Then, a quiet "I'm so sorry." I gazed at the door. Standing ominously in the entryway was David.

☾

I hadn't heard him come in.

"It's about time you got here. What happened to you?" Nathaniel finally spoke, eyeing me still but directing the question to David.

"I wasn't speaking to you," David spat. "I was speaking to her." He pointed at me.

"It's okay." I answered numbly. It was then that I noticed a dark patch of red covering David's left side. I gasped, "You're bleeding!" but he didn't seem to notice. David lumbered into the room and came face-to-face with his boss.

"For once, the little brat is right. You are bleeding," said Nathaniel.

David glanced down. "I...had a run-in with a grumpy Dragon. H-he...wasn't too happy to hear what had happened."

"What? Do you mean Shadarr?" I cut in.

"Yes." A soft response from David.

"And what exactly was it that you were you trying to accomplish by telling the beast about my teaching? I assume that's what you were complaining about." Nathaniel asked his soldier.

"Your teaching? Blasphemy! All you're trying to do is turn her into a reckless slave to do your bidding! See how well that's been working out for you? Nekoda is not cut out for this!" he turned to the side and violently coughed. "She isn't Alessandra, okay? Why can't you see that! What do you even expect from her? By what you call 'unlocking' her powers, will only put her in more danger! Nobody is ready for what's to come! Nobody knows where the talismans are! She's not going to let you get away with—"

Suddenly, he stopped. Coughing again, a bright bubble of red spewed from his mouth and dripped down his chin.

Blood.

Gripping his side, David dropped to his knees, hacking up dark blood on the rug. Luke jumped up from the table. Tony's hand jerked and his wine cup shattered against the wall. Bruce cursed. Ezekial made a sound much like a dying cat. I flinched, shrieking.

142

Nathaniel grunted and pulled out his knife, now stained red with David's blood.

"Wha-what the hell did you do? Ohmygod, ohmygod, DAVID!" I screamed, clambering down beside him on the floor. *Shit, shit, shit...*

"No!" Nathaniel growled, and for a brief second his eyes flashed gold. He grabbed the back of my shirt and flung me backwards where I crashed against the wall by the door. A wave of air, or energy of sorts, came from Nathaniel. I struggled, but it was like a giant invisible hand covered in superglue had pinned me to the wall. I felt frozen. "He brought this upon himself, Nekoda. This is what happens to traitors like David, and now you're going to watch him suffer for it."

"He didn't do anything! He was only doing his job and making things right!" I shouted at the men around me. "Are you cowards just going to stand there? Help him!"

Ezekial shook his head, pale-faced. "David—he's...gone." I turned my head and stared at David. The shortages of breath, a pool of blood around his body. He was crumpled on the ground, motionless. My head pounded as I absorbed the shock of the last few minutes.

"He's..." I whispered.

"Dead." Nathaniel slipped his knife into his back pocket, voice ice-cold. "Out, all of you. Now! Ezekial and Bruce, move the body someplace else. Tony, go downstairs and check on Shadarr. Luke, you'll stay here with me. I need your help."

In a deafening silence, Bruce and Ezekial grabbed David's arms and legs and hauled him up, carrying him out of the room. "Goodbye." I whispered. Tony walked out and slammed the door behind him. The magic air seemed to dissipate and I began to feel lighter. I could move freely. Shaking, I got to my feet.

"C'mon, let us see it. Bring out the inner beast and turn us into human torches. Go on, do it!" Nathaniel taunted, pacing around the room. I tried. All I could manage was a small spark on my fingertips before it faded.

143

"So, what do you want me to do, boss?" Luke asked. Nathaniel glared at me before responding to Luke by whispering something incomprehensible into his ear.

Luke stepped toward me and I put my hands up to cover my face. As soon as I felt his cold hands make contact with my skin on my wrists, I began to squirm. All he had to do was drag me towards him and yank me up off my feet. I managed to try and kick him in the ankle, but I ended up toeing the wall. He caught my fist in his hand when I attempted to punch his jaw. Luke pushed me into Nathaniel's awaiting arms. He grabbed my hands and held them together behind his back. With the other hand, he motioned for Luke to pull something out of the nearby chest. Luke rummaged through until he produced a bagged needle and syringe into Nathaniel's free hand. I gasped and flailed, trying to break free. Nothing I did loosened his grip on me.

"No! No! No! I hate you all, go away, go away, I don't want you here!" I cried. My hair was brushed back from my neck by Luke. Nathaniel put the needle to my neck and I felt a small, stinging pinch before going limp. I gave up and sagged to the ground with Nathaniel holding my head.

Luke stood up and wiped his hands on his pants. "I'll meet you there in a bit." he said, and walked out the door.

"In about one minute you'll start to feel the results of the serum I injected into your system. It will make you feel groggy and weak. After, you'll be asleep for several hours. When you awake, I have some things more to discuss with you alone, without any distractions from the others. You'll skip the rest of today's training too. In the meantime," Nathaniel bent his head down low and whispered in my ear. "Try to get some rest..." My eyelids started drooping shut and I fought to keep them open.

"Why," I croaked. "Why are you doing this?" it was all I could manage to get out before I met the darkness.

☾

Carrying her limp body was like carrying a rag doll. She was so small; it was hard to believe she would be capable of so much in the future.

Nathaniel trudged down the damp halls, an unconscious Nekoda in his arms. He didn't want to kill David, that much he knew. But it had to be done, he talked too much. And she knew too much already. Maybe Tony was right—they probably should have given her up to his father. But no, he wanted to prove himself capable and took charge. It wasn't easy tracking Nekoda Alessandra Jones and her family down. But with a lot of research and patience, he and his crew were able to track her down to the cozy town of Weedsport, New York.

The plan was supposed to be simple. Well, as simple as it should have been. But how was he supposed to know that she had a vicious Hellhound as a playmate? The *Book of Spells* should've been there. It should have been a quick in-and-out. Grab the girl, grab the Book, and go. The parents should not have interfered, otherwise they *might* still be alive. The Jones' were one of the founding families and Keeper of the talisman.

Neither Clara nor Kyle Jones knew that their daughter was going to be a mutant Skin-changer, or a Hybrid demigod. They had expected their child to be born a normal demigod, despite her being *the* prophecy child. And neither knew the chain of events to come would happen so swiftly.

Walking past many, many doors Nathaniel reflected back on what his father told him before he left. Well, Hades wasn't really allowed to see his son anyway, but still. Nathaniel didn't like thinking about his dad a whole lot since the last time he had visited Hades had said something quite scarring.

Nathaniel had Portaled down to his father's throne room and knelt before him on the obsidian dais, a few months earlier, awaiting his next objective.

"Son, it is time. The Titans are stirring, and Nyx and Gaea are summoning their armies. My foolish brothers and sisters are prepping for battle and scouting the far reaches of the earth. They think their precious talismans are being stolen from them by one another. They are starting to turn on each other. War is coming and we will be at the center of it; time is the most precious resource we could need to become victorious, but we have so little of it." Hades' black crown glittered atop his head as he pounded one fist into the arm of his throne seat.

"You must find the girl before the others do while my subjects and I distract my siblings to coming any closer of finding the talismans. We will have the upper hand if you get to the girl before *them*. I've already alerted Kronos and Nyx, whom is gathering her Empousa together. And she sent Thanatos to deliver the message to Hecate. Meanwhile, the Cyclops are rallying.

I expect you'll turn the prophecy child over to me. As long as those burdensome demigods don't come searching for me, they won't be a problem. It is hard to choose sides when I have the ability to birth or kill anyone, anytime. I'm not going to make the mistake of joining those mutant children of my brethren again."

Nathaniel scowled and met the god's eyes. "Father, I can do this. Spare me your words of spite and grant me the task of finding the girl *and* the four talismans. You said so yourself, the parents might have a talisman in their possession since their ancestor was a Keeper."

The God of the Underworld considered it for a moment. "Fine. You may. But if you fail me, you'll end up like Alessandra."

Like Alessandra.

That struck Nathaniel deep. Too deep.

"It was not Alessandra's fault! You tricked her into doing your dirty work! And now she's eternally damned, stuck in the pit of hell by the Furies. If you hadn't gone and told them of her true identity, she would still be alive!" Nathaniel hissed.

"You know very well what would have happened to her sooner or later! One such as Alessandra is a dangerous beauty of sorts; Alessandra is bad news for both sides of the family. My Olympian siblings would've killed her off eons ago if they hadn't

146

known. Technically, she was your responsibility. It was *your* fault!" Hades roared back.

"It was *my fault* for loving her? Is it going to be *my* fault when the Olympians find out who really has hold of the talismans? You, father, have no power over me. Not anymore!" he yelled, fists clenched, teeth gritted and eyes flashing.

"I do, because I am your father! If you disobey me once more, then it's the depths of Tartarus you'll be speaking to next! Understood? The fate of both the mortal and immortal world now rests on your shoulders until you can find that girl! And I want those talismans hand delivered, too. Now be off with you, and do not fail me!" Hades commanded, dark magic crackling off and around him in sparks of lightning. With that last warning, Nathaniel Portaled away in a whirlwind of darkness.

Stopping at a painted door with a 'N' carved into the front, Nathaniel kicked the door lightly three times. Luke opened the door and Nathaniel entered his own bedroom. It was designed much like Tony's room, except for one wall was stacked with books and scrollwork floor to ceiling, and various maps were spread out on his desk. His green bladed sword hung on a hook above his bed, sheathed and ready to use.

Nathaniel gently lay Nekoda down on his bed. Luke went to work tying her wrists together and her feet at the ankles until they were sure she wouldn't be able to move. He knew she'd be freaking out when she awoke a few hours from now.

"Okay, I'm only asking once. Are you positively sure that this will work? Because this is our last hope of finding the *Book of Spells*. If not, we move to Plan B. Am I correct?" Luke questioned.

Nathaniel sighed, rubbing his eyes. Hundreds of years of stress rested on his broad shoulders. "Chances are this will work; chances are it won't. If not, we move on to Plan B and continue training the girl until further notice."

"Okay, well...I really hope you're right." He replied attentively.

147

"Come, let's get ready before she wakes. Go check on the others and report back to me."

"Yes, sir." Luke set up five candles around a pentagram and lit one for earth, water, fire, air and spirit. Luscious fragrances wafted around the room. Luke went out the door to follow orders. That left just Nathaniel and a sleeping Kody in the room.

"Oh, what am I to do with you now?" Nathaniel muttered, brushing aside Nekoda's hair from her forehead. He sat there on the bed, watching and waiting.

☾

I woke drowsy and panicked in another bedroom. I groaned and looked around, spotting a five-pointed star painted on the hardwood floor. A candle was aflame at each point. Rolling around on my back, I slowly sat up and— "Shit! What?" Nathaniel was sitting at the foot of the bed, staring back at me.

"Good, you're up," I didn't respond, only leveled him with a look of pure hatred. "Let's get straight to business. I haven't much time. Have your parents ever—?" Nathaniel asked, finally speaking.

"No."

"Mentioned anything about—" he tried again.

"No."

"The Book of—"

"For the last gosh forsaken time, NO! I don't know anything about some stupid book you want!" I growled.

Nathaniel scooted over and cupped a hand over my mouth. I jerked my head and bit his finger. "Gah, dammit!" He stood up, shaking his hand. I smiled in satisfaction.

"Have your parents ever spoken of something called the *Book of Spells* and do you know what it looks like?" Nathaniel glowered at me, getting the sentence out in one breath.

"No, they have not and no, I don't." I spoke through gritted teeth.

148

"Hmph. Ack, you leave me no choice now. We are going to have to do this the hard way." He picked me up and set me down in the middle of the star. "Know what this is? A pentagram. Used for summoning monsters mostly, and delivering messages to other worlds. But I've figured out another purpose for it, though." Nathaniel clapped his hands together and pulled out a solid goblet from the chest, placing it in front of me. He took out his knife and loosened the cord around my wrist to pull one hand free. Baring my left palm, Nathaniel ran the knife down my hand. I cringed and shut my eyes tight, blocking out the pain. He closed my hand into a fist and made me squeeze, letting the blood run through my fingers and drip into the goblet. *Plop plop. Plop.*

I shivered and yanked my hand back. Sitting crisscross applesauce a foot from me, Nathaniel set down the goblet in front of himself and raised his hands over it. Then, chanting again in the same language he spoke to Shadarr in, he moved his hands in circles over the ring of the goblet, almost like a voodoo witch and her magic ball. I stared in horror as I watched my blood start to swirl and bubble and rise up. The red liquid created a sort of blood wall, almost like a window. It was translucent, and I could see Nathaniel straight through it. As I continued watching, I noticed images start to form in the blood.

And for the umpteenth time today, I passed out yet again.

☾

A little blonde toddler ran barefoot through the flowers, giggling. Her mother and father, in their early thirties, stood aside watching their only child wrestle with a little Hellhound in disguise.

A change of scenery and there was Nekoda at her first day of grade school and a class bully had pushed her down on the playground. Nekoda stood back up and socked the guy right in the lip. She went to the principal's office with mud-stained pants.

There was a flash of lightning and the cacophonous booming of thunder that lit up her bedroom window. Intrigued yet

149

frightened, Kody crept up to the windowsill and looked out through the storm. Another blast of light lit up the room and illuminated the front yard where she caught a glimpse of a man all in black watching her from below. The shy seven-year-old backed away from the window and ran into her parent's room. Her dad said it was just a figment of her imagination and she should go back to sleep. But when she did go back to her room, the figure was still there, standing and watching.

Hiking through the woods with not a care in the world, splashing in the creek with her friends, Nekoda looked about, a smile on her face. Turning, she told her friends that they should play hide-and-go-seek-tag. The big rock marked with their names on it was base. As her friend counted, she and her look-alike classmate dashed behind a fallen log and waited. When she spotted her tall red-haired friend getting closer to their hidey-hole, Nekoda took off like a shot, running through the trees. Laughing, she rushed to base and began to hear pounding footsteps racing behind her.

Kody glanced behind and saw that it was not her friends that were chasing her, but a large golden wolf.

Shrieking, she clambered up a tree and sat on the low branch, clinging for dear life. The wolf sat on its haunches and stared up at her, cocking his head when it heard voices coming from the distance. Before Maggie and Logan could see the wolf when they both came into view, the wolf vanished.

Tossing and turning, she mumbled in her sleep. A few times she cried out and pushed her pillow to the floor. Kicking the blankets off, Nekoda lay talking in her sleep. Suddenly, she screamed. Her parents came running into the bedroom and flicked on the light switch. Shuddering, mom came and hugged Kody to her chest.

Now fifteen, Nekoda was helping her mother clean out the attic. Dusting off shelves and searching through old cardboard boxes, Nekoda pulled out a small and delicate wooden box. Opening the lid, an ancient looking leather-bound book lay on a piece of silk, safely tucked. She turned to her mom. "What is this? I've never seen it before now."

"Oh, that is your great-times-ten-grandmother's journal. It's been passed down in your dad's family for generations. I've been meaning to bury it as a time capsule to the next generation of Jones's us so they can uncover it." Clara Jones laughed nervously, lying through her teeth.

"But it's so well preserved after all this time! Can't I read through it?" Kody asked, curious.

"No dear, I'm afraid anyone else who touches it will make the pages fade away to dust. It's really old. I'd rather it stays whole." Nekoda was disappointed, but she understood.

A few nights later, Kody was inside looking out the window watching her mom carry a small chest down from the attic and outside. Her dad had dug a hole to place it in. Nekoda watched closely as her mom buried it, shoveling in dirt and patting it in place. To mark the spot, she planted a white rose.

Skipping through and digging deeper into her memories, Nathaniel saw the night he took her away. It was still so fresh in her mind. After that, Nathaniel stopped chanting and dropped his hands. The blood trickled back into the goblet and with a gasp, the young teen awoke once more.

☾

My head was throbbing even worse than before, and now my palm was slick with blood. Nathaniel shook his head as if there was water in his ears and rubbed his eyes. He reached forward and cut the rope that bound my hands and feet and blew out the candles. What happened next surprised me. He started laughing, laughing like he knew a secret I didn't.

"What? What is so funny? You think it's cool digging around in other's minds, huh? Well, that's just low." I stretched and crossed my arms, unsure of what to do or how to get out from the pentagram lest something blew up or burned me alive.

151

"Oh, nothing you need worry about, Nekodal. Just that I'm one more step ahead than the rest." He grabbed my arm and pulled me out the door.

"Hey! Where are we going?" I pinched his elbow.

"First off, you are going to bathe and change into something else besides those rags you're wearing. You smell." Nathaniel snorted.

Dick, I thought.

"Gee, thanks. I noticed. But I didn't have enough time to shower before you took me from my home!" I spat back. We walked down the hallway and down the flight of stairs where the flooring changed from wood and carpet to cement and concrete again. Ah, memories. He dragged me past the kitchen where the table was still flipped on its side and the dented pan I used on Bruce earlier was lying on the tiled floor.

The place really was confusing. I had no idea on what island we were on, or what country, state and continent we were in or if it was an underground prison or log cabin or a strange house in the middle of nowhere. There were a lot of options. For the most part, I knew which way to Shadarr's pen, the kitchen, the actual bedrooms, 'training' rooms, Nutcase's weapon room, and soon the bathroom. But I just needed to figure out where the entrances and exits were here. Any other door or secret hatch that leads to the outside would be just fine. Heck, I'd go to Narnia and live with the talking beavers and lions if there was a wardrobe I could hide in!

Nathaniel and I trudged down the halls in silence until we passed my cell and the 'N' room and farther down to a new door. He grabbed the handle and pushed me inside. I looked around the small space and sighed. There was nothing fancy or even remotely pristine about the small shower, rusty sink, and toilet in the room. Laid on the sink counter were a towel and two bars of soap, a pair of oversized pants, a black T-shirt, and a pair of socks. Hmm, homely. I frowned.

"Hey, when you're done grooming yourself and such, knock three times and Bruce will let you out. He'll be standing outside the door the whole time, so don't even think about doing anything stupid. He's a lot faster and stronger than you are." I heard footsteps coming from the opposite direction we came in.

"Bruce, take her back to her room afterwards. We're done with training for the time being."

"Sir." Bruce's deep voice rumbled. Nathaniel's footsteps receded.

Making sure there weren't any peepholes, I undressed and folded the clothes before gingerly stepping into the tub and turning on the showerhead. I bite back a yelp—the water was freezing! I quickly grabbed one of the bars of soap and scrubbed myself good. I gathered as much soap bubbles onto my hands and tried rinsing my dirty, tangled hair as best I could. My fingers got caught in tangles and knots and I managed to actually yank strands of my hair out.

Shivering, I turned the water off and stepped out to dry myself off with the scratchy towel. At least now I was a little cleaner than before. Standing in front of the cracked mirror, I feebly tried combing my hair with my fingers since I wasn't supplied a brush. I wrapped the towel around my head and filled the sink up with water before rubbing some soap off into the sink. I grabbed my sweatshirt and jeans and tried scrubbing the dirt and sweat out of the fabric as much as possible, hanging the clothes up over the curtain rod to air dry.

I tried on the spare clothes someone had loaned me and walked around the bathroom in circles, seeing how they fit. I decided to ditch my old jeans and keep the pants, as my previous outfit was trashed. Soon as it was rinsed, I put my sweatshirt and shoes back on, the sole items of clothing that reminded me of home.

"Hey, are you done in there yet? It's been, like, an hour!" Bruce whined.

"Yeah, yeah, whatever. I'm almost done," There was a small drawer under the sink. I opened it up and spotted a little automatic clock inside. I squinted at the clock face: **10-19, 4:49**

PM, FRI. What?! I've only been here for five days, when it really seemed like weeks. I huffed and stuffed the little clock inside my sweatshirt pocket.

"Okay, open up! I'm fresh." I shouted through the door. Click, the door unlocked. Prodding me forward, Bruce and I made the short trip back to my cell. I allowed him to open the door so I could glumly sit down on the bed. After Bruce left, I took out the butter knife from the chest and marked more faint scratches into the wall.

I hid the clock and extra clothes in the chest and slumped down on my cot, suddenly exhausted. As much as I wanted to sleep, I couldn't. I stared up at the dim light bulb swinging above the cot until my mind settled.

Swish. Bump.

I shot up. Did I have a Peeping Tom?

I held my breath and looked through the bars. Left, nothing. Right, nothing. Whew. Perhaps it was Tony or somebody else walking around. Actually, no, I'd much prefer if it was a ghost.

Whooosh—

I spun around, a full 360 circle. You ever get that feeling when something is right behind you and the hairs stand up on the back of your neck?

Yeah, I got that feeling.

I turned around veerryyyy slowly, letting my eyes wander, trying to make things out in the near dark…annddd bingo! A shadow behind the light, just out of view. *Something* was near. "I know you're out there! Come out wherever you are!" I whisper-shouted. A chill caught up my spine. Then, *it* walked into the light and I— it *was Buddy!* Buddy! BUDDY!

I almost cried. I almost screamed. I almost broke into my happy dance. Buddy was alive and well! How on earth was he still living? I had watched Tony stab my dog in the chest, bleed to death, and magically disappear in a puff of smoke! Okay, the smoke part was really whacked, but still!

154

Instead of Buddy being in his normal fluffy Toy Poodle form, he had transformed into the Hellhound I had last seen him as back in Weedsport. This time he was carrying something in his mouth. When he trotted up to me through the bars of the cell, I leaned forward and wrapped my arms around his neck. He licked my cheek and whined, head-butting me.

"I missed you so, so much bud! Where have you been? Whatever happened?" I spoke softly, rubbing his ears. He gently set the object by my feet. Buddy, of course, didn't say anything; he simply laid down on his belly and rested his head on gigantic paws. I glanced down. It was a rolled-up piece of parchment paper with a piece of twine tied around it. "What's this?" Unfolding the paper, I saw that it was a handwritten letter addressed to me. ME! I was even more baffled by just *how* Buddy had gotten here, but obviously that would have to wait.

I started reading.

Nekoda—
We all know the first question you are going ask. Buddy is a Hellhound, as you may know, and Hellhounds are immortal. So technically, even if he did 'die', he really didn't. He just got sent back to his homeland, that is, the Underworld.

I stopped and glanced at Buddy, raising an eyebrow.

He can also Portal, so that's why we sent him to deliver this message to you. My friend, James, has been having visions about you, Miss Legendary Child. And I presume, you, him? (This is William, FYI, James just told me what to write). We've known about Nathaniel and his gang for a while now (and by 'we' I mean me, James, Alex, Jacob, Johnathen, and Aaron) and how he is searching for the talismans and wants to take over the world and blah blah blah. Also, we've recently discovered that you've developed one of your powers. Nice going barbequing Nathaniel! I laughed so hard when I heard about that.

But for the past few days we all have been revising a plan to rescue you and take you back with us to Camp Wolf, a.k.a. our isolated home for Skin-changers here in the Rockies. Don't worry, we aren't evil :) Well, you will have to live with those bad guys for at least one month, perhaps a little longer because frankly, we have no idea where in the world you are. Literally. You could be in Switzerland for crying out loud! Hopefully, Buddy will be able to tell us something about location when he gets back to us.

The five of us will each be heading in the cardinal directions with our traveling companions, (the Camp's freeborn wolves), supplies, and weapons sometime after you receive this note. James is not permitted to go because we all agreed that it'd be better for him to stay here, just in case he has another dream and learns more about what's going on. That way he can contact us faster from base. Next time you go visit Shadarr, tell him I said "hi" and to burn this letter ASAP. We don't want anything to go wrong. When one of us reaches your destination or we figure out where you're at, Buddy will be sent back to you. Also, there is extra paper stapled to the back so we can keep in touch with you too.

Talk to you soon, please stay sane.

—Sincerely, a couple of students from Camp Wolf

Gods above and below, I can't believe what my eyes are seeing! Just to double check that I wasn't hallucinating, I re-read the letter back to front. So, they *were* real! James, and everybody else, *they're real!* But a whole month before they get to me? I get that the going's tough and all but I don't think I could last that much longer with these bastards. What if something happened to me before then? What if I died of salmonella? There were two really big problems, though. Shadarr is one of them; how is Will supposed to free me without Shadarr? I just can't leave him here; I'd be breaking my oath. And what if they can't ever find us? My best bet right now is to not have high such hopes, even though I felt a small fluttering in my heart every time I glanced at the scrawled handwriting.

Buddy nudged something else towards me: a chewed-up, slobbery pencil, but a writing utensil nonetheless. "Oh, thanks. Kinda need this to write with." I said, already brainstorming a response. I tore off the extra paper and started scribbling in my best handwriting. A couple minutes later and I was finished.

Dear students of Camp Wolf—

I can't believe it! You've no idea how much this changes things! And my utmost gratitude for bringing Buddy to me. Also, yes, these guys are complete douchebags. So, I get that Nathaniel wants something to do with me because I have these godly powers, I see that now, but Nathaniel knows that my parents have something called the Book of Spells. I assume it is also one of the talismans he's looking for. He kind of... got inside my head, I guess. And he also... well, I think my parents passed away.

I only have one problem about your plan. If you somehow free me, then you will have to free a captured Dragon, named Shadarr. He's my friend and I want to help him. I made a promise I cannot break, so it would help if you figured out a way how. Really, I think this place I'm at now is some sort of isolated/abandoned prison or building with lots of add-ons. Oh! It would help you to know who Nathaniel's soldiers are. There's Tony, Bruce, Luke, Ezekial, and David... who's now dead.

Also, I cannot stress enough that I really think they might kill me if I prove to be useless. There's something off about Nathaniel. Besides kidnapping a fifteen-year-old, I mean. I will definitely try to gather some more info. I hope you guys

know what you're doing, Nathaniel is... something else entirely.
And honestly, I'm scared.

-Kody

I rolled up the paper and set it down by Buddy's paws. I looked at him one last time before he left. "Love you, Bud." I whispered, giving him a pat on the head. He disappeared into the shadows, nothing but that same smoky substance in the air.

I stood up and put away the pencil, an important tool I'd need later. I climbed onto the cot, wrapping my arms around my torso to rub some warmth into my limbs. Soon, I fell asleep. That night I dreamt of a black wolf chasing a small, scared puppy through the woods...

"Lo and behold the sleeping beauty." A voice. I jerked upright, springing to my feet. I groaned when I saw him. It was Tony. Ugh, would it kill him to just leave me alone? I refused to acknowledge him.

"C'mon, get up. Don't you want to see Shadarr?" Tony inquired. I deigned to answer when I stepped aside and let him open the door. Our footsteps echoed off the walls as we made our way past the many doors and rooms until we reached a staircase, spiraling down to Shadarr's pen.

The heavy door shut with a loud clanking noise behind us. Ah, nature. I inhaled the freshness of the pond, the grass, and...chicken? Shadarr came lumbering into view, ready for his meal. "*Hi.*" I mind-messaged him.

The Dragon snorted in response, blowing light, billowy smoke through his nostrils as he approached Tony. "Back, stupid animal! You want to eat or not?" the Skin-changer snapped. Tony slid on gloves and yanked a piece of dairy cow meat from inside the storage freezer and chucked it on the ground.

In one gulp, Shadarr had downed a cow haunch, his knife-like teeth crunching through bone. "*That's better.*" he mumbled. I gagged at the smell, breathing through my mouth.

"C'mere and feed the rest to him. You're his favorite."
Tony implied, waving me over. For the next few minutes I messed
with bloody mammal body parts, hoping my face wasn't as green
as I thought it was. Twice, I resisted the urge to run off and throw
up in the nearest bush.

Wiping the grease off my hands on the grass, I went to go
sit by Shadarr. Double-checking to make sure Tony was far
enough away, I produced the letter to Shadarr and read it to him.
"So, what do you think?" Yawning in a way only Dragons can,
Shadarr opened his mouth and set fire to the paper. It was
incinerated to ashes in a second.

"They're going to get themselves killed. That's all I know."
Shadarr said.

*"What? Isn't there anything else you have to stay? I'm
going to be free! And you along with me."*

*"Impossible. Just how do they plan on secreting away a
two-ton beast? The halls are too narrow for me to walk through,
even with my wings folded."*

"Oh," I actually hadn't thought of that yet.
"Well, think back. Do you remember how you got here?" I asked
aloud.

Shadarr sat and thought, his eyes narrowed. *"I—I think I
was asleep. But all I remember seeing was rock and dirt. The last
thing I saw before I drifted asleep was the sun, and I felt myself
plummeting from the sky."*

"Nathaniel shot you down?" my stomach dropped.
*"No, no, not Nathaniel. I belong to him now but he wasn't the one
to bring me here."* Shadarr stood up and stretched his black wings,
sending a blast of hot air when he shook them out.

"Who did?" I asked.
*"I do not know, but my head hurts if I try to think about it too
much."*

That's wasn't a good sign. I would've presumed Shadarr
knew a way out. I glanced upwards, sighing. Something in the
back of my mind clicked into place. He had said the sun was the

159

last thing he saw before *falling* out of the sky. And if the sun is *up* in the sky...the ceiling! *"Shadarr! The roof! If you can gain enough speed and force to fly upwards, maybe you can break through the ceiling! If the last thing you saw was the sky then that means you must've landed here or—"* I stopped.

"Someone brought me to this location. Hmm, you might be onto something." Shadarr turned in circles. I beamed. At least we were getting somewhere. *"Oh, uh, Nekoda. Last night, a Hellhound came to visit, he said his name was Buford? Or Barry?"*

"Buddy!" I squealed, using my actual voice.

"Right, he Portaled down here. We were communicating and he said that when he had arrived, a little ways outside of this place, he saw a wall. A really tall wall with lots of water running through it. I think the building we are at is by the ocean, or some big body of water." Spoke Shadarr.

"Wait, that might mean we're by a dam! Which one, I have no clue, but if we're by a dam that means life. Water means people! And if there's people then there's help! Safety! If we can find any possible way to get to the outside, we can walk along the top of the dam and into the nearest city!" Oh, the possibilities! But there were a lot of *ifs*.

"I don't think that'll work very well, Kody. They could catch us and Nathaniel would surely punish you," Shadarr replied, unsure.

"Punish? Look what he's already done to me!" I cried, showing him the bruises on my arms and face.

"He'll do a lot worse than that, believe me, I've seen worse!"

"What they are doing is child abuse! And last time I checked, kidnapping is illegal, like, everywhere!" My chest heaved. "I promised you your freedom Shadarr, and I intend to do just that!" I got to my feet and brushed the dirt and dust off my pants.

"I know, child. I know." He sighed.

Tony called me over. "Time's up. Nathaniel called a gathering so I have to take you back to your room. Say goodbye." I moaned. I wanted something mildly entertaining to do aside from sitting and staring at a wall all day. With one last wave in Shadarr's direction, Tony ushered me out and closed the gate.

Chapter VIII: Free Falling

November 27th, 5:15 p.m.

I was so bored.
Ever get that feeling that you want to do something productive but there's nothing *to do?* Ack, forget rainy days. I would've gladly traded places with anyone in this moment. According to the small clock I'd kept since my first bathroom visit, I had been stuck inside this hellhole for three weeks. Every day, the same routine. Dry breakfast, bathroom break, Shadarr's breakfast, target practice, hand-to-hand combat, swordplay, cell, bathroom, dinner, Shadarr's dinner, bathroom, lights out. New change of clothes once a week to prevent me from being smelly. I was just glad a certain friend wasn't due to come visit for another two weeks.

Nathaniel's soldiers took turns walking me back and forth from my cell every morning, and they were never in a good mood. After the first three days that David was gone, Nathaniel toughened up. He went harder during practice, and I was on the receiving end of his fist, foot, or blade, every time. There were bruises on top of my bruises, and the cut on my cheek was now a white scar.

"Wwhhhrrroooouuuuuuu!" I cupped my hands around my mouth, howling like a wolf. Just for fun, I started mimicking animal noises.

"Hoo-hoooo!" Owl.

"Bork!" Dog.

Silence. What does the fox say? I don't know. What does a teenage girl say? Nothing. Bored. Bored. Bored. Bored! I took the butter knife out and scratched my initials into the wall along with a clever little doodle to Nathaniel in my best wall-art print, as there was nothing better to do.

I smiled. Who knew what fun it was to etch a little drawing of a Dragon chewing a man up? Funny, if this was to be the thing Nathaniel saw after I escaped. There were plenty more doodles etched into the wall, little things I had spent my time carving out when I was alone. Playing tic-tac-toe by yourself grew old after five rounds, and Shadarr couldn't grasp the concept of I Spy very well.

Shadarr *will* come with me when James comes, willingly or not, I'll make him. Somehow, I needed to get ahold of Buddy again. The last time he had Portaled to my cell was three nights ago, and there had been a bag of chips tied to his collar. If Buddy can search through the inside of the building, maybe he can find a way that leads to the outside. If there isn't an easy escape out of here, I hoped James is going to bring a hand grenade.

Grr, why does everything have to be so difficult! It'd be much easier if there was a door with a red glowing EXIT sign. Alas, there wasn't. I just needed a way to walk around the place without getting caught, and I could memorize a route for Shadarr to flawlessly sneak away and squeeze through the corridors. If I could slip through the cell bars and travel down to Shadarr's den, we could both bust out. Right now, my abductees were in some conference of sorts, probably chatting away about blades of death and reading *Ruining Nekoda's Life: For Dummies*.

I slipped the knife into my sweatshirt pocket along with the pencil. Sucking in a lungful of air, I stuck my arm between the gap of two bars. I squeezed my shoulder through next, and then my head. It hurt, but it wasn't like I hadn't gotten my head stuck someplace before. After all, it happened to me when I was four. The fire department came and sawed off the wooden railing of my grandmother's staircase to free me.

Pushing and pulling, I finally popped my head free, while the rest of my body was still inside the cell. I wriggled around and managed to pull my last foot out, tripping in the process. I speed-walked towards my destination as deftly and swiftly as possible.

The only problem was going to be getting back *in* the cell before someone returned to get me. That would take longer.

Left turn, sprint down the short hallway. Stairs, two at a time. Right turn, and I was at the door to Shadarr's den in record time. I pushed aside the log and creaked the door open.

"Shadarr! It's me, Kody!" I called, venturing around until I spotted a glistening black hill. Shadarr was sleeping. His huge chest rose and fell, and deep rumbling came from within him. Snoring. Laughing, I ran over and hugged the mass of Shadarr's snout. He blinked a few times, staring directly into my face.

"*Morning, already?*" He yawned, my head filling with the sound of his voice.

"No, probably midnight by now. But I had to come and see you. I couldn't wait. Nathaniel called a meeting, so everyone else was busy and no one came to get me. I slipped out of my cell." I said.

"*Really? What do you need to tell me?*" stretching, Shadarr nudged me.

"Well, I've been thinking about the escape attempt and I was wondering if, maybe, there was a way out through your den. But rather you bust out from the roof, I can find some secret switch or something."

"*Okay, good luck with that.*" he responded sleepily, turning to tuck his head back under one wing.

"What? You are helping me look! Fly me up to the ceiling," I demanded.

"*Fly? What do you think you'll find up there other than cobwebs?*" my Dragon chided.

"Just let me climb up on your back!" I waited until Shadarr was lying flat on his belly before clambering up his side, using his shoulder as a foothold. Grunting, I sat on the crook of his neck and straddled my legs on both sides. Standing, Shadarr stood and flapped his wings, a blast of air whipping my hair around. Soon we were hovering a few feet above the ground.

164

"Woaaah!" I clung on for dear life. Crap, this was going to be quite the challenge. "Hey, when you get to the top, tell me. I'm closing my eyes. I, um, I'm not a fan of heights." I told Shadarr. He didn't answer; instead, he aimed his wings back and soared upward. I squeezed my eyes closed, fingers digging into his scaly back, feeling my feet slip and slide. From floor to ceiling, the room was a little over a mile high in height, or appeared to be.

"We're up." Shadarr said. I opened my eyes and gasped. At the sight of the ground far, far below me, a new wave of nausea swept over me. "Oooh boy, oooh boy. Oh boy. We're high. We're really high!" I whispered-shouted, afraid of speaking too loud in case the ceiling fell. Rising inch by antagonizing inch, I slowly wobbled to my feet and placed my hands above my head, feeling along the cold ceiling.

Tapping lightly with my fists, I moved my hands across the slabs of stone, listening. Nothing sounded hollow. *Tap tap tap.* Slowly but surely, Shadarr began to glide along the ceiling as I knocked, nothing sounding out of the ordinary yet.

Frowning, I sat back down and instructed Shadarr to fly over to the nearest wall. I leaned against the wall and knocked again. *Tap tap bang.* Hmm, interesting. As I poked and prodded around the area, I realized that I was now hearing a different sound. *Thunk* noises ricocheted back to my ear over a few yards of brick and rock and stone. There had to be something behind the wall.

I wedged my fingers in between the rocks and pulled. A trickle of sweat rolled down my neck, and at last I pulled free a small hunk of wall. I peered through. To my surprise, there was a hole a foot in width dug out in the middle of the old wall. It was a clear, straight shot through and behind that, the blue, blue cast of the sky.

"Shadarr! Shadarr! I found something! Right here!" he turned his head up and glanced at the spot I pointed at.

"*What's inside the hole?*" he asked. On further examination, I noticed a strip of white passing through. I stuck my fingers in and poked something cold and long. Piping.

"I think we hit an old pipe line." Scowling, I went on my knees, half my weight on Shadarr's back and the other against the wall. In this area, the piping must have gone all around the perimeter. "I can't see anything else besides the sky. No spire of a building, no dam-like structure Buddy saw. If you can fly into the wall fast enough, then you could literally bust us out of here!" My mind was racing now.

"*Nekoda, I've already tried that. It won't work. Years, or maybe it was months ago, I created a big hole in the other side of the wall, and there was nothing behind it but an invisible barrier of sorts.*"

"Like a force field?" I questioned.

"*I do not know, but perhaps it was some spell Nathaniel put up. Unless it's broken, no one can pass through. At least I cannot.*" Glum, I sat back down and wrapped my arms around his neck. Shadarr flew to the ground and allowed me to hop off, back on solid ground. "*What are we going to do?*"

"I do not know." I twirled a strand of hair between my finger, willing my brain to think. "If you can smash a hole large enough for me to climb through, I can see if I'm able to get out of the area. But I'm wondering if we should wait and see when and if James comes up with an official plan."

Suddenly, Shadarr jumped to his feet, a growl sounding low in his throat. "*Kody, stand behind me. Now!*"

"What? What is it?" I scampered under Shadarr's wing. "*They're coming. Luke came to check on you, and when he discovered you weren't there, he must've notified Nathaniel.*"

"*How do you know?*"

"*I can hear them speaking.*"

"Hear *them? Like, you have heightened senses?*"

"*Yes, something like that. I am a* Dragon *for goodness sake.*"

166

I heard them too. Voices. Shadarr walked up to the edge of his pond, glaring at the door. With a squeal of hinges, the gate was forced open, and in came Nathaniel and his posse. "Where is she!" he roared up at Shadarr.

"*Who?*" Shadarr responded patiently. "*You woke me up from my nap! I was having the loveliest of dreams.*"

"I don't care! Don't play games with me. WHERE IS NEKODA?" Nathaniel stormed right up to us, his boots sinking and squelching in the mud. Shuffling backwards, I crouched behind Shadarr's back leg, which was thicker than a tree trunk.

"*How would I know? Have you tried searching around the place? She's probably in the kitchen for a quick snack. Don't bother me. After all, this is* your *problem.*" He huffed. Shadarr turned in a circle, bumping me behind him as he walked to shield me from Nathaniel. He promptly flopped down on his side, his wing over my body. I lay crunched between his chest and his front forearm. Breathing lightly, I listened to Nathaniel rage.

"I know she's in here! The first place she'd go to is you! Bruce, Ezekial, you two search the east and north sides of the den. Tony, Luke, and I will search the west and south walls. If you're hiding her, it's going to be harder on the both of you." He sneered and stomped away. I gulped.

"*Shadarr, if I run back to my cell now, they'd still know I was here and we'd be in even bigger trouble. But if you make the hole bigger, I think I can make a run for it.*" I thought.

"*Then what? You don't know what's out there. There is nowhere to go, and someone would catch you in a heartbeat. Either way, we're stuck.*" Shadarr groaned.

"*Not unless you stall them.*"

"*Like how?*"

"*I'll hide in the tree by the pond while you fly up and break the wall. Pretend you're scratching an itch or there was a giant spider you were trying to crush. Something stupid enough for them to believe.*"

"*This plan of yours is stupid.*" He sighed. Trudging over to his murky pond, he bent his head down low in front of a bushy tree and drank. With his body in front of the tree, I slipped out from his wing and clambered up onto the branches. I hid in the brush and watched as Shadarr flew upward. Angling his body, he bumped his tail into the wall, the cracking of stone resonated around the room. *Thump thump thump. Thump thump thump!*

"Hey, what's all that racket? Cut it out!" Luke shouted from afar. Shadarr kept pounding. *Thump thump thump. Thump thump thump.* "I said cut it out, you dim-witted lizard!" Luke was scouring through a bush from the far wall.

Shadarr roared back in response, teasing, "*Don't keep your panties in a knot! I have an itch and I can't quite reach back and scratch it myself, can I?*" Nathaniel snorted. Luke looked between the lizard and Nathaniel. He probably thought Shadarr insulted him, since he is one of many who can't communicate with a mythical creature.

"Good work, keep going." I whispered, watching Shadarr's progress.

Thump thump thump—crack! I could hear the stones give way, Shadarr baring his teeth in triumph. Leaning off the branch to get a closer look, we waited until the men were caught unawares, busy at their searching. Shadarr swooped down and brushed against the tree. I leapt up and scrambled atop Shadarr's back, my heart pounding. "*Now!*" I screamed in my head. Quick as a whip, Shadarr whirled around and practically crashed into the wall. Grappling for the sides of the rocky, two-foot diameter hole, I slid through belly first, hands scraping against the rough brick.

Shadarr proceeded to pretend to file his claws on the walls, mostly blocking the hole for me. Without much light, I couldn't see all too well in the dim hole. My head smacked against the rock. "Ack!" I grunted, inching forward. I didn't know how close or far away the ground was once I reached the end of the tunnel.

"What do you think you're doing!?" I could picture Tony sprinting across the den towards Shadarr.

Suddenly, my hand was clawing at empty air. I stopped and pulled myself to the edge. Thankfully, there was enough moonlight streaming down so I could make out what was in front of me.

Bracing myself, I glanced down—and almost choked on air.

Oh my… it was at least a thirty-foot drop. Beyond stood trees, stretching for miles and miles around. Just barely out of eyesight, I glimpsed a tawny brown structure looming in the distance. It *did* look like a giant wall as Buddy had described. Wager it was actually a dam, or some old abandoned fortress. *"Umm…Shadarr?"*

"Yes, Nekoda? I think you should hurry; they're growing suspicious!"

"I know but… I don't think I can jump down easily without breaking, like, every bone in my body."

"Uh-oh…" Shadarr warned.

From below, I heard pounding footsteps. The light from inside the den reappeared through the hole and I knew Shadarr had dropped down. Scuttling closer to the edge, I braced myself for the jump. There was no other way out except for the hole or to go back in the way I came. And I wasn't going back. Ever.

On the other side of the wall, Nathaniel was giving orders. "Shadarr! Move away! Ezekial, Bruce, get the grappling hooks from the weapons room, stat! Tony, Luke, give me a hand." I heard Shadarr roar in a frenzy. When I looked back, Nathaniel's form was hovering in front of the hole, and he shook his head, seemingly disappointed. I squeaked.

What the actual f—*!?*

"Redire! Non dolet se ire! Ego sum, nolite timere vos in medium, ut rip!" roared Shadarr.

"Hold up, hold up. All I hear is gibberish. What is he saying?" I froze.

"Latin." He paused upon hearing the click of a gun being loaded. In a millisecond, a loud boom echoed off the walls. I flinched and cupped my ears, my elbows scraping against the rough rock. The sound ricocheted around the room. Shadarr spun

169

out of the way, distancing himself from the hole, and gave an angry growl.

They were shooting at Shadarr! If anything, Shadarr wore a suit of armor unable to chip. Guns wouldn't have any effect on him, would they?

Oh, gods, I hoped they wouldn't.

"*Kody, get out of here, now!*" Shadarr commanded.

"*I can't leave you!*" I started.

"*I don't care! Leave!*" he answered. I had all of five seconds to make up my mind and take a deep breath before sliding the rest of my body out through the hole

—and fall thirty feet to the ground below.

Screaming, I flapped my arms like a bird trying to fly. I don't understand why people say that they see the rest of their lives flash by on the brink of death? Yeah, well, they're lying, because I sure as hell did not. All I saw was the ground rushing closer and closer. Flailing like my life depended on it, I twisted my body around so my feet would hit the ground first. I'd rather the legs in my bones shatter than my skull.

Chances are I'd come out of this fall paralyzed, broken, or dead. Grasping at thin air, I rocketed to the hard, green ground below.

Suddenly, a black blur came hurtling into my side out of the corner of my peripheral. It slammed into me, changing the path of my fall by a few feet when I was just a couple inches from becoming a stain on the earth.

Whoof! I came crashing down into a giant, thorny bush, a large weight struggling underneath me. The air was knocked out of my lungs and for a moment I lay still, struggling to move, thorns poking me from every angle. Pain flared up my right ankle. I hung, stuck in the bush, gasping for air.

My savior crawled to its feet. Buddy shook himself off, hacking up a glob of dead leaves.

"Bud!" I wheezed. "How did you know I needed help?" Buddy sat back on his hind legs and cocked his heads, ears pricked.

"Nevermind. But, my ankle, damn, that hurts." I winced. I picked my way out of the rosebush and stumbled to the ground, my left foot sinking into the soft soil. Rolling up my pant leg, I inspected my ankle. I could just make out the large, purple bruise that was beginning to form. I grimaced. I was no doctor, but I didn't think my ankle was broken. A fracture, perhaps, considering that my ankle was severely throbbing, but I could still somewhat move it.

I turned around and gazed up at the building in which I'd been held captive for the past few weeks. No wonder there were many more passages to discover—the place was huge! In fact, it was one big brick and stone building stuck out of the side of a steep mountainside. Only Shadarr's side of the building was actually protruding from the outside, while the rest of the handmade structure was built inside the mountain. Similar to a rock fortress, it blended in perfectly with the forest area. If you were to look at it from above, there was a 99.9% chance you wouldn't see it, as the mountain camouflaged it. But that's really all there was to it. There was no entrance or gates in which to get in or out except from the hole I created. Maybe it was an old secluded prison from the 1940's, or a secret underground mansion? I could not tell, since the inside appeared to have had a lot of remodeling done.

Rising up like a hawk descending on its prey, the moon hung in the night sky, bright and mysterious.

"Which way home my trusty steed?" Buddy perked up and pointed his nose in one direction as if to say 'Follow me!' "C'mon, we need to get out here before I change my mind!" With both my heart and head pounding a mile a minute, together we raced into the darkness beyond as fast as my swollen foot could carry me, wincing and cursing all the while.

I was finally going home, and soon I could see for myself if my parents were dead and my house was a pile of rubble and ashes. I could not and did not trust Tony's words, so I was going to travel to the nearest city and call my closest friends. Knowing them, I knew they knew that I was still alive somewhere in the world.

Combing my way through rushes, thorn clumps, and crossing a low stream, Buddy and I walked farther and farther from the fighting. Shadarr was still holding his ground, protecting me. His roar echoed back to me, miles and miles away; I could hear both man and beast fighting, left far, far behind us. I prayed Nathaniel wouldn't hurt him. And whether or not Shadarr was one of the last Dragons alive, Nathaniel probably didn't care.

Hisss. I reared back as a snake slithered around my foot. I heard a squeak when the creature found its victim. Trudging on, Buddy led the way, pushing through brambles and dodging trees. "Wait up, I can't see where I'm going!" I called after Buddy, now yards ahead.

I wasn't sure how long we'd been running and hobbling, for the building and everyone else was growing farther and farther behind us. Huffing and puffing, we stumbled on into the night. In the distance, the wall loomed before us. Once there we'd be safe, at least for a while.

Patting my pockets, the edge of the butter knife and the pencil sent a sigh of relief rushing through me. The items would bring some use to me if possible. When I was seven, I thought running away and living off alone in the wilderness would be awesome, but now that reality was a whole lot worse than what my childhood self had envisioned. If Buddy could survive being stabbed in the heart and not lose his immortality, he'd have no problem joining a pack of wolves and defending his own out here. "Slow—" I gasped, out of breath. "Down I—" *pant* "can't breathe." *pant* "Need. Rest. Gonna." *pant* "Pass out!"

I dug my heels into the dirt, slumping against a wide tree trunk. Buddy turned around and trotted over, licking the various cuts and scrapes I had from running through thistles, and shamefully, falling in the creek not long ago. Running my fingers through my tangled hair, I sat in silence. After two minutes, Buddy grew impatient and began tugging on my arm, anxious to leave. "No, I'm not ready yet."

That only made Buddy more eager to go. He sat down and howled. "Shhh! That's a good way of attracting unwanted attention, mister! Fine, I'm coming. Be quiet." I hushed him. Bud looked at me and showed his teeth, gleaming white. "What are you smiling about?" Pushing myself up, I swatted his rear as he leaped away.

I pushed myself forward to catch up so as to not lose Buddy, hobbling along, pain lancing up my leg with each step. "How much farther?" I groaned. Buddy only whined in response.

I wasn't a track star back at school, but I played main defense with my friends on the soccer team, so I guess I was a decent enough runner, but I'd never had to do physical exercise on a possibly fractured ankle. I felt myself slowing again but willed my legs to move faster, shifting most of my weight onto one leg. Buddy was racing along beside me, his ears flopping in the chill breeze.

When we drew close to the dam, I realized there was no easy way for us to cross. If it truly were a dam with a body of water on the other side, and not a bridge, we'd have to travel on the top walkway where tourists visit and take pictures by the edge. Climbing up to the top was going to be the tricky part. We would have to run up the steep slopes to the sidewalk and make our way without being unseen. At this early in the morning (or late at night) no one would be there except for the guards, and maybe a few workers.

But what would people think if they caught a missing child, dirty and wounded, with a shape-shifting dog on top of a dam in the middle of the night? I don't think I could go to the police first; they would ask too many questions that I did not have the answer to. Instead I'd have to pay a visit to my friends. Logan and Maggie

173

would understand, right? Maybe they'd believe my tale, but certainly not officers of the law.

Even from this distance, I could hear the thundering of rushing water. This close to it, and I almost couldn't hear my own thoughts. I laughed. We were correct, it was a dam! And a dam meant civilization. Once past the dam, Buddy and I would make our way through the nearest city and take a bus back to Weedsport. Or, since I didn't have money, I'd have to forage, beg, pickpocket or walk, depending on how close we were to home.

I saw a small gleam of light up ahead, either a light pole or a very bright flashlight. We came out into a clearing alongside a rushing river, which was ridiculously loud. Ahead rose the gigantic wall. Dam water flowed out from generators and large tunnels at the bottom, creating hydroelectricity for homes, if there were houses nearby.

I rubbed Buddy's head and walked the steep path up the sides of the dam, my legs screaming in protest at the exertion. Overhead, a bird circled. I smiled, breathing in the fresh air.

☾

Heat melted off Luke's shield as he blocked the burst of flames from Shadarr. The tunnel in which Nekoda escaped was situated high in the wall, and Shadarr was blocking it. Swiping the air with his claws, Shadarr battled against his foes one by one. Spinning, biting, roaring, slashing, Shadarr was in frenzy as tiny missiles bounced off his neck and legs. Tony tried flanking him from the left while Nathaniel fought him face-to-face. Luke ran up and back, seemingly trying to attack him, but Shadarr knew better. He was bigger, faster, wiser, and could fly. Ezekial and Bruce returned with metal machines with hooks attached to the front. Grappling hooks useful only to the flightless human.

Shadarr growled and snapped his jaws. Lunging forward, he swatted aside Tony as if he were batting a pesky fly. Nathaniel bounded up and attacked with his sword. There was a flash of

174

green as he sliced at Shadarr's thighs and slipped under his belly, sticking the blade through the inside of his leg. The blade found a small crack in his scales, and pierced through.

Shrieking in pain, Shadarr whipped his tail and stomped his feet. Blowing steam and smoke blew through his mouth and nostrils, he missed Nathaniel and Luke by a few centimeters. Thrusting his palm outwards, Nathaniel pushed Shadarr backwards with the same invisible force he'd used on Nekoda, stopping the flames with one hand. Sneering, his chain mail shirt glinted in the light.

"Back off!" Luke shouted as he charged the Dragon. Luke jumped and dodged around Shadarr, and a *whizzzz* sound passed his head. Shadarr saw the gleam of iron and heard a loud *thunk,* and he knew they had deployed one grappling hook. Slamming one paw down on the ground, Shadarr went after Luke as the man sprinted around him and ran for the far wall. Storming after him, Shadarr roared, flames licking the back of Luke's steel helm. He jerked right, ran back in the direction of the hole. Grasping the line, Luke hoisted himself up hand over hand. Bruce and Ezekial used the other two hooks to shoot out and wrap around Shadarr's front and back leg. Stumbling, Shadarr flapped his wings as the men pulled away. Tony raced over to assist.

Nathaniel paralyzed Shadarr on the ground. For the time being until he released the spell, the Dragon wouldn't move. Feebly, Shadarr cawed and attempted to burn the rope off of him, but to no avail. Hissing, Shadarr narrowed his deep red eyes at Nathaniel.

"Oh, rest assured old friend, we'll find the girl before anyone else does. And we'll get the *Book of Spells*. The parents hid it in the backyard of their house. Bah, shame we had to kill them anyway. If it wasn't so difficult to point it out…ah, well, there's nothing to be done for it now."

Dragons don't cry, but they can rage. Like a rabid animal, Shadarr roared and screamed, bucked and spit until his throat was raw and he was too weak to move. That he could, anyways. He watched as Luke scrambled back out of the hole, calling for Nathaniel. He watched as Nathaniel blew apart the hole with his bare hands, a whisper of a breath on his lips as the small tunnel expanded. He watched as Luke pushed himself out through the hole, followed by Ezekial, then Tony, Bruce, and Nathaniel.

Motionless, he watched, one by one, the demigods slip out into the night until Shadarr was alone with his thoughts, his mind, and his heart.

Chapter IX: Travel with Care!

November 9th, 7:33 a.m.

Cole was flipping through the pages of the journal, encoding the message within. There was a clue hidden inside these words, he just knew it. At the beginning of each entry for a new year, there was a mishap in the Greek literature. So far he could only make out a few words written above and crisscrossing the others: move, Helen, northeast, and maybe the word Ireland. Nothing was making much sense yet. He had a task he intended to finish.

After a few entries of Camrice Lockwood, he got to Vincent Lockwood. As told by the writing, he had inherited the journal as a young boy of seven in the year 2003. Camrice Lockwood was twelve when he started writing in the journal. What made Vincent so special? His blood. Both sides of Camrice and Halt's families were all Keepers themselves. And since Camrice's great grandfather, Vincent has been the only Keeper to venture out yet in search of the talismans. That, and Vincent was kind of a twentieth century prophet. At least that's what some of the other kids spoke about at *Camp Canis Lupis*.

When he came across something interesting, like the name of a city Vincent had visited, Cole was supposed to contact James so then he could tell the others who were heading in that direction. Mitchell hadn't really noted anything special either, except the descriptions of the four missing talismans. But without the location, their profiles were useless to the Skin-changers.

Frustrated, he went to go meet Mitchell and the gang for breakfast. Cole slipped the journal into an old shoebox under his bunk and walked down to the dining hall.

Smells of cinnamon, spice, and bacon greeted him when he grabbed the brass handle and stepped through the huge doors. At

7:45 a.m., the tables were already crowded with bodies. Soldiers, kennel masters, craftworkers, and instructors seated along wooden benches, gobbling down plates of food.

Cole found Mitchell talking to a fellow classmate, Trevor, and waved him over. Mitchell stood next in line besides Cole, trays in hand. The cooks (and nurses) of Camp Wolf, BelAnne, Arya, Zoey, Elizabeth, Natasha, and Meredith were behind the glass windows piling pancakes, strawberries and the like onto plates and bowls.

"Good morning, Cole. Mitchell," BelAnne acknowledged them. "How did you sleep? It's the weekend! You should be happy." She asked, noticing the circles under their eyes.

"Y'know, playing too much League of Legends last night. Darn those secret levels!" Mitchell nudged Cole, who let out a yawn. BelAnne *tsk*ed. "Well, you know what people say. Video games rot the mind and body." she replied.

"Uh-huh," Cole mumbled and moved forward, greeting the other girls. The boys made their way to a table in the back of the semi-organized hall, where it was easier to talk in secret. Instead of their usual spots at the high tables with the rest of the instructors and Alpha Halt, Cole's older friends were gathered at the table, much to their surprise. James and Johnathen were shoulder to shoulder with Will and Alex, Jacob and Aaron seated on the other side. Aaron waved the boys over when they saw them. "What's up, guys?" Aaron smiled.

"Did a little more work on the journal last night, and Mitchell couldn't find anything else on the sketchbook this morning. But I have four words, and I do believe that each is a clue to getting one step closer; move, Helen, northeast, and Ireland." Cole responded, nibbling on a pop-tart.

"Eh, it's a start. We got a name and a place, and a cardinal direction. Johnathen, Aaron, you guys remember that when you head off." James said.

"Sir, yes sir." Aaron executed a mock salute.

"How soon will each of you be leaving?" Mitchell asked, brushing crumbs off his chin.

"We decided that Johnathen will leave here at 10:30 a.m., and Aaron not long after at 11:15. At 1:00, Alex will go. Then at 1:30, Will. Next, Jacob is the last to leave at 3:00. Cole, I, and yourself will see them off when it's time."

"Okay. Seems simple enough." Mitchell shrugged. "Well, getting our little hunters outside the walls unnoticed will be trickier. The wolves aren't allowed outside of the Camp unless we have permission from Halt himself, or a permit from the Council." Will bristled, forking a strawberry.

"Can't we just say that we're going pack hunting? I'm sure the guards won't mind. Unless Marco Diego is on duty," suggested Jacob.

"Or Damon. But we can't act suspicious around anybody." Will added.

"I'll travel down to the creek with Cherise and Joffrey after Johnathen and Aaron. We'll just say that we are meeting them for a hunting spree, and the guards should let us go as there hasn't been many monster sightings since Louis ran into that manticore." Jacob said.

"Hmm, true, but what about the rest of us? I'm supposed to drive down with Thomas and Paul to pick up the delivery for a stock of iron, gold, and timber. We have to make thirty-five new chariots for the battalion in Athens. If we don't come through to them, Crispo Pansino won't be able to help form up the defense in Greece, and the Greek union won't be able to bring down the Romans." Jacob said, reminding his friends of the foreign battle that Camp Wolf decided to help aid their former allies in. For years ongoing, Athens and Rome had been secretly at war with each other. The two ancient cities have been rivals for centuries, and that rivalry between peoples still existed today.

There was a war brewing, a war that two of the North American Camps had agreed to aid, if only to prevent the fighting from spreading across the seas. Italy's Prime Minister, Sergio

Colombo, has an grudge against Greece's President of the Hellenic Republic, Caesar Alexopolous, and is waiting for Caesar to keel over and die so that he can rule over Greece. Both political ruling families inherited godly DNA, so both leaders are Skin-changers, unbeknownst to the rest of the world.

"Y'all will just have to come up with some excuse on your own; you should've known what would happen before you agreed to this mission. We can't waste time worrying about such other matters aside the problem at hand. And that's Nekoda. Any updates, James?" Alex spoke up, shoveling sausage patties into his mouth.

"Actually, yes. But y'all aren't going to like it," he told them all about Shadarr and Kody's escape attempt, Nathaniel knowing where the *Book of Spells* is and his plan to retrieve it, Buddy and Nekoda running off to some faraway dam somewhere in the states, and about Buddy's return letter. "Late last night at four o'clock, Buddy came back with a note from Nekoda." James unfolded the note and read the neat cursive print on the paper aloud.

"But Nathaniel can't kill Nekoda, right? He couldn't if she's too valuable a pawn in his game of chess." said Aaron, forehead wrinkled in concern.

"Maybe, but I believe there's something else going on with Nathaniel, and so does Nekoda. We will just have to figure it out first." Johnathen replied.

"Either way, one of us has to get the *Book of Spells* before the others do. I wished Nekoda would have explained where she lived in the letter." James cut in.

"Actually, if you watched the news the night Nekoda went missing, you'll know where. Here," Alex pulled out his phone and googled the news channel he had watched the video on. Will reached over and pressed the play button. Noises and voices were heard in the background as the reporter explained the situation.

"Between 1:30 and 2:30 a.m. this morning, a fire was started in a house of the small town of Weedsport, New York. A next-door neighbor called for the fire department when screaming awoke her from inside the house. Later, Officer Wells of the WPD explained he had gotten a frantic call from a young girl that was abruptly cut off. The Jones family who lived here was burned alive in what is believed to be a homicide, but mysteries still remain as to what happened to their fifteen-year-old daughter—" Alex paused the video and set his phone down.

"Why didn't you show us this sooner?" James asked, now irritated, playing the video back.

"Sorry, man, I forgot about it. I just thought it was some depressing news story before I found out it was tied to the prophecy child," Alex took a swig of strawberry milk. "Whatever we think now doesn't matter. We have clues, James who can't stop fan-girling about *her*, and a pretty good reasoning for Vincent's disappearance."

"Yeah, Will is right and— hey!" James sputtered.
Cole laughed. Mitchell almost choked on a blueberry.
As Aaron pounded Mitchell's back, Jacob, James, Alex and Cole threw out their trash and cleaned their plates off.

"WE WILL, WE WILL, ROCK YOU! STOMP YOU! THROW MUD ON YOUR FACE, YOU BIG DISGRACE! KICKIN' YOUR CA—!'" Over on the far side of the mess hall, a table of rowdy boys were stomping and banging their fists on the tables in unison, singing the infamous song.

"They sound like a bunch of dying cows. What are they doing?" Will asked once the others he sat back down on the bench. James smacked his forehead, clearly distressed.

"Oh, I forgot! Wednesday is the yearly NSL championship, and I'm playing defense for the first game. The second game Kai and I are supposed to switch out for goalie." NSL stood for National Soccer League. Twice a year in the fall and early spring, the Camp's soccer team split up in two and played for the championship at Camp Wolf. Team Blue versus Team Red.

"They all seem pretty pumped. What time will it start? Practically everyone will be watching the game. That gives us

181

some free time to do some preparation for the mission." Jacob asked, perking up.

"Around 5:00 p.m. But we'll be setting up and practicing almost all day until then." James' eyes lit up. He couldn't wait to get out on the field, but he was also eager to rescue Nekoda Jones.

Aaron glanced at his watch. "It's almost 8:45, I'm going to finish packing and feed Zoe and Greyback down at the Den. Johnathen, you coming?"

"Yeah, just give me a minute to finish, please." Johnathen stuffed the rest of his Belgian waffle into his mouth and left.

Will folded his arms over his chest and sighed. "Well, it is Saturday. I'm going to lay in bed for the rest of the day until three o'clock watching reruns of *Star Wars.*"

"And I shall join you!" Alex said promptly.

"I'll be smithing in the forges. See you later." Jacob got up and followed Alex and Will. That just left James, Mitchell, and Cole.

"You guys want to kick the ball around with me?" James asked.

"Sure!" Cole and Mitchell agreed. At Camp Wolf, there were two soccer leagues. One for boys ages 13-15, the other for ages 16-20. James was on the varsity team while Cole and Mitchell were on junior varsity. The three students walked outside to the equipment shed. They rummaged through their cubbies and pulled on shin guards, socks, and cleats. Rifling through the ball cage, James found a blue and green soccer ball and headed to the fields. James walked to the goalie box as he slid on his gloves, and Cole and Mitchell stood at the fifty-yard line.

"Ready?" James braced himself, bending his knees and putting his hands out in front of his body to catch the ball.

"On three! One, two, three!" Mitchell shouted, backing up a half-step, passing the ball to Cole who ran up towards the eighteenth line. Cole tapped the ball to Mitchell, zigzagging ahead of him. Mitchell closed in on the goal, bringing his right foot forward and kicking the ball with the inside of his foot, aiming for the left corner of the goal. *Whoosh!* The ball soared through the air just as James brought his arms up, barely catching the ball as it grazed his fingertips.

Falling to the side, James muttered, "So close! I could've had that!" Cole high-fived his friend. Getting into position again, Cole knocked the ball back and forth with his knees, and then dropped and hit it backwards with the heel of his shoe.

"Okay, try to block this shot!" Cole yelled. Raising his hand up and bringing it down, he motioned that the ball was now in play. Charging forward, he aimed for the top of the goal and rocketed the ball out. James jumped up and caught the ball before running out of the goalie box and cherry-bombing the ball towards the other side of the field.

James, with hands cupped around his mouth, boomed, "And bouncing the ball off the top of his head, Kai Chen crosses it over to Sam! Sam runs down the left side of the field and blocks the troubled opponent from getting the ball and—oh! Look! Francisco steals the ball from a troubled Sam and he shoots, he scores! Goaaaalllll!" he spoke in his best announcer's voice, eliciting a few laughs from his friends. Mitchell and Cole cheered, waving their arms like crazed fans.

"Mitchell, I want you to come in from the right before the goalie box and juke me into thinking you'll pass it back to Cole, got it? Cole, you will then take the shot and try to get open. Next, I want Mitch to pass to Cole, and he will shoot on me. Tonight, the other team will be playing dirty, like elbows-to-the-face dirty. You can't think, just do." James backed up.

On cue, Mitchell raced up and feigned to the left, James following his every move. Moving up and over the field, Cole pumped his arms, anticipating when Mitchell passed the ball to him. Eyeing the goal, Cole abruptly kicked the soccer ball. Flying towards James, the ball bounced skyward right as he blocked it with the mitt of his hand. Taking a few running steps forward, James blasted the soccer ball out of the goalie box.

"Nice one," Cole gave a thumbs up, wiping at the sweat dripping down his neck. Deciding on a keep-it-up competition, the boys made a small circle and tapped the ball back and forth in the air using only their heads.

"So. Are you ready for battle?" Cole blurted.

"Huh?" James was puzzled.

"You know, the war of today. Haven't you guys heard? If Athens doesn't win the battle against Rome, they'll start marching on the European and Asian Camps!"

"No, actually, I haven't. Who said that?" Mitchell looked at his friend.

"Damon Scott." Cole said sheepishly.

"Damon!" James sputtered, letting the ball fall to the ground with a *thump.* "Why would you believe anything that moron says?"

"Well, his half-brother, Michael, and I were classmates before he ran off like Vincent. Damon saw his Dragon egg with his own eyes. And that's apparently another reason why Italy and Greece are fighting. When they heard about the egg, the nations started arguing about who gets ownership of it. But there's also tales of more Dragon eggs in incubation somewhere else, yet that's most likely a lie. Plus, we're still trying to figure out how to stop the gods from warring because of Nekoda, right? It puts both the realms in danger and—"

"Woah, woah, woah! Hold up there." James put his hands up as Mitchell shook his head. "How would Damon know about these things?"

Cole shrugged. "His dad told him after a High Council meeting."

"And why would Damon tell you this info rather than Halt?" James asked.

"Because I was friends with his brother. After he disappeared, he asked if I knew where Vin went. I said no and asked him why, to which he explained about the situation. Basically, if one group can get ahold of the next Dragon egg, they control the next generation of Dragons. And that's a pretty big

184

deal." It was. But James wanted to learn more about how and why Rome would declare war with the rest of the globe, if they even would.

"The people believe that one of the remaining Camps is secretly raising the Dragons on their own. By marching against everyone else, they think that'll make the others back off into submission of the egg or egg*s.*" he paused. "I thought Johnathen and you guys ought to know. Maybe because it might affect your mission."

"We weren't sure of rescuing the Dragon along with Nekoda because frankly, it'd be hard enough to distract Nathaniel to get the girl from him in the first place. That's why Will has been trying to contact Shadarr. Shadarr could be the last living creature of his species. The egg Michael has could be a stillborn as well. But we obviously don't know that." James interpolated.

"There *is* a chance you're right about that, and a chance that you're wrong." A deep voice said from behind Mitchell. Spinning around, Mitchell backed away from the tall, intimidating man.

"Damon. Eavesdropping again?" James growled, casting him a loathsome look.

"Oh, how could I not? My little friend here was sure to spill the secret sometime." Damon sneered, poking Cole in the back.

Cole blanched and looked away. "Sorry." He mumbled, stepping toward James.

"Back off, it was *your* fault for telling Cole in the first place." James Dawn spat, bristling. He was not in the mood to deal with the notorious bastard, Damon Scott.

"Really? Because a little birdie told me all about your 'secret mission'." Damon threw up air quotes.

"Cole, Mitchell?" James averted his attention to the boys.

"It wasn't us, we swear! I went to bed after our conversation, just ask Jacob. Or William!" They pleaded.

"Fine, but I'm not going to let this go!" James poked Damon in the chest. "If you dare tell anybody about this at all I'll—"

Damon snorted. "You'll what, Mr. Macho? I don't recall having your permission about what I do or don't say around here. I think I can spread any little lie I want to, and I will continue to do so. It's fun watching you little pups squirm."

"You're a snitch." Mitchell piped up.

"Am I?" Damon bared his canine teeth, eyes glowing.

"Damon, you dick! Whatever, tell anyone you like! It's not as if they'll care one way or another." James snapped, hands balled into fists. If Damon Scott let this news of his friend's mission spread to Halt, they were screwed. Big time. And there was someone out there in the world who needed their help.

"You're sure about that? Because half of the Council members are thinking of replacing Halt with my father, Nickolas Scott, as Alpha and head of Camp Wolf. He'd make a *much* better Alpha." Damon crossed his arms, seemingly satisfied with the way he easily slipped under his enemy's skin.

"Shut up! Your father would be the *last* person the Council appoints as Alpha! And how dare you diss Halt like that. Have some respect, half-breed!" James snarled, shoving Damon in the chest.

"How about you remove that stick up your ass and quit acting like Halt Lockwood is better than anyone else! At least my dad didn't go apeshit and close off the gates after his son ditched Camp!" Damon rebuked, lunging for the other camper, eyes holding a fierce gleam. James dodged his arm and tackled him by the waist. They fell to the ground, and Damon managed to graze James' jaw with his fist. Grunting, James pushed Damon off himself and they rolled to their feet. The younger boys backed away, frightened.

"At least I'm not a disgrace to my parents!" James' eyes blazed from gold and blue to stoic gold. Grabbing Damon's wrist, he twisted him around into a headlock. With one hand, Damon clawed at James' arm and punched his opponent in the stomach. James didn't flinch. He merely pushed Damon to the ground and brushed himself off.

186

James started to turn and walk away with his younger friends when he felt something hard and jagged knock into the back of his skull. James cursed and put a hand up to head, warm blood coating his fingerprints. Damon was standing, teeth bared, rock in hand.

Things were about to get ugly.

Smearing the blood on his pants, James lunged forward and roundhouse kicked Damon in the side. Howling, he counter reacted and grabbed at James' throat, who batted him away.

James cuffed the side of Damon's cheek, and pulled back before Damon could swing his fist at him. His face turned red, and he pushed himself up, elbowing James in the face. Blood came gushing down his chin, and unwanted tears sprung to his eyes.

"Jackass!" James fired, dead-legging Damon. As he tumbled to the ground, James bent over and cupped his own face. Before Damon Scott could rise back up, a streak of grey and brown flashed by and landed on his chest. One of the Camp's wolves, Dior, sat on Damon's chest. She brought her snout up to his face and growled, digging her nails into his shirt front. "What the—!" he started. Dior barked and jumped up at James. Almost as tall as he was on hind legs, Dior snapped her jaws to get the boy's attention and eyed James.

"She wants us to stop fighting," James established, Dior resting her giant paws on his shoulders. At five years old, Dior was one of few female wolves who ran the show at Camp Wolf amongst the other canines.

"Yeah, I see that." Damon pushed himself to his feet, sneering. Dior saw him move and ran up to him, nipping at his heels. She watched as Damon left, growling all the while. With one last look at James and the others, Dior gave a warning bark and raced back to her playmates.

"Well, that was something." muttered Mitchell. James shot him the stink-eye.

"We're going to gather everyone else before they leave. You two have some explaining to do."

187

"Yes, sir." Cole stared at his shoes. Mitchell rocked back on the balls of his feet, also not daring to meet his eyes.

"Let's go." James stalked in the direction of the forges, his blood both running, and boiling.

☾

"He—what!?" Johnathen sputtered, chucking a t-shirt into his bag. "Explain again just how, exactly, Damon heard about our mission!?" he demanded, glaring in the tween's direction. James, Cole, Mitchell, Will and Aaron, Jacob and Alex were lounging around Johnathen Dogo's room.

Cole hunkered beside his friend on the couch. "I-I don't know who he heard it from. Reckon he has some sort of spies about the place, or-or something."

"*Or something?*" Johnathen zipped his small duffel bag closed. Crossing his arms, James went to put a hand on his friend's shoulder, comforting him.

"I know you're upset, we all are." He cast a glance at the two younger boys. "But we shouldn't be worrying about this now. Damon may not even tell Halt, not that he'd listen to him anyway. This is our own little thing, no one else's. And hopefully we can keep it like that."

"Are you kidding me?! Damon Scott is the biggest gossip in Camp, quite possibly the whole entire friggin' world! And here I am being the one freaking out about this, instead of you, James!" Johnathen brushed him away.

"What do you mean? Of course I'm freaking out about this! I got punched in the face!" James gingerly touched his new bruises, wincing at the throbbing pain in his head from the rock.

"You know what I mean, since *you* are the one who's been making goo-goo eyes at some strange girl that's in your head! If Damon tells anyone else, we're doomed! The Council will be on our asses about hiding some big prophetic secret from them, an

188

evil villain planning to overcome Olympus, clues about Vincent's whereabouts, and stealing items from the Archives! *Ahem*, James."

"Don't be getting all prickly at me! You all agreed to this; I would've kept this all to myself and gone off alone just like Vincent, because *I* thought it was a special calling from the gods!" He tapped his chest for emphasis. "Maybe I could've figured it out, who my real parents were. Maybe I thought I could figure it out on my own, just like Vincent did! *Maybe* I thought this was the beginning of something new! *She* is the beginning of something new! Because otherwise, I don't know why I'd be seeing these visions of mine, if the messenger weren't my true mother or father! If this is true destiny guys, this is it! Destiny came to us! *To us!*" James huffed, slamming his fist into his open palm.

"Dude, we don't know how much bigger this'll all get! With Nekoda, with the mystery of Vincent Lockwood, with the war against the other Camps, with anything! We are all as worried as the both of you, so let's just get through this first step together!" Jacob exclaimed, spreading his hands out.

"He's right, I don't know any other way around the situation. We gotta solve it together. It's all for one, or one for all." Alex added.

Cole spoke. "Look, if it makes you all feel any better, I've been working some more on the journal. At least that will get us some more feedback on what Vincent was doing."

"And Taz, don't forget about Taz. Poor Dior hasn't been the same since he left." Will cut in. Dior and Taz, two of the wolves who made their home at Camp Wolf were canine lovers. Doggie gf and bf.

"Yeah, poor pups," agreed Alex.
"Yep. There's nothing left to say. You're in or you're out." Aaron nodded at the others.

No one said anything until Mitchell put his hand out in the center of the room with Cole. Will and Aaron sighed, piling their hands on top of Cole's. Johnathen, Alex, and Jacob piled their hands on. They looked expectantly at James.

"Okay, fine." James smiled and laid his hand on top of all the others. "On three; one, two, three…"

"Camp Wolf!" Together, eight best friends shouted, throwing their hands in the air.

Once again, James smiled.

☾

It was nearing 10:30 a.m. Wednesday morning and Johnathen was consulting with Aaron after they finished feeding their companions, Pearl and Greyback, when they returned to Johnathen's dorm.

"I will meet you down on the left side of the river, about twenty yards from the paths. Okay? Just try to follow my tracks. Up until I reach the cave tunnel by the mouth of the river, you'll keep going straight."

"Noted. What color are you using to mark the trees?" "A sparkly pink spray paint. That way the Nymphs won't get pissed off and start throwing pine cones at us like last time." Nymphs are the nature spirits, animating flowers, and trees of the forest. During what was supposed to have been a small, harmless paintball game, one of the players shot a still tree six times with red, green, and yellow paint. Unbeknownst to him, it was actually the sleeping face of a wood nymph he had decorated. She had Changed into a green-skinned, hazel-eyed, angry, colorful girl. Dressed in a lace skirt and top with flowers braided into her flowing hair, she at first didn't seem so harmful. That is, until she picked up a pinecone and threw it straight at the face of Tom, the player who had hit her tree spirit. Mass chaos erupted. Some idiot had yelled, "Pinecone war!" and after that, a flurry of pinecones and acorns were flying through the air. Halt had banned all activities like that outside of the Camp's walls when multiple Skin-changers were left in the infirmary.

"Yeah, that's a good idea." Aaron said.

190

"We know that Nathaniel's base is by a dam or a big body of water, so we'll be heading north to Canada. One of the biggest waterfalls, Niagara Falls, is there. Maybe they're hanging around somewhere. I printed off a map so we can travel by the highways. It'd be easier that way, and quicker."

"True. But Niagara Falls isn't a dam, not really. I guess Nekoda could be hiding out in one of the water coves."

"I guess, but still, it's an option to go by." Johnathen reasoned with a shrug.

"But how are we going to get past the Canadian borders? We aren't driving and I'm almost positive you can't have a wild creature, such as a wolf, be smuggled across the border." Aaron asked, rubbing his brow in thought.

"No, we aren't driving, so that means we will just have to go around the stations without getting caught. And if we need extra money, I'm bringing some Canadian currency if we cross. But most businesses close to the border will accept U.S. cash, too."

"It sounds like you got this all figured out."

"I do." Dogo grinned.

"There's just one problem. If we run into any big monster, which we will, would us two be able to defend ourselves?"

"Dude, we're mutant demigods. And monsters fear demigods, last time I checked. As long as we don't encounter an angry Chimera, or a Hydra, we're golden." Johnathen shoved a dagger into the side pocket of his duffel.

"Hmm, I have my sword and shield, along with a light chain mail shirt I can wear underneath my clothes. You?" Aaron wondered, noting the extra set of switchblades his friend threw in.

"Packed in a few small bottles of Greek fire, got my longsword and switch-canister and arm braces. If I can't lift a sword, I'm dead." Johnathen responded. He was right; everybody had his or her strengths and weaknesses. A switch-canister is a small, portable silver cylinder about five inches long, with a button on each end. Once clicked, the cylinder expanded into a full-length double-sided spear.

191

"I'm just worried." Aaron said, rubbing the back of his neck.

"I know. We're all nervous about rescuing Nekoda." Johnathen said gruffly.

"Hold on, you didn't let me finish. I'm just worried if one of us doesn't come back...alive. Or we don't get back to Camp fast enough if anything were to happen." He sighed and flopped onto the couch. "I just hope we can figure this out."

"Me too, but whatever truth we uncover during this mission we cannot let it affect us. You get my meaning?"

"Yeah, I do."

"Good, cause it's about time we head out." Johnathen's watch beeped. He clicked a button on the watch surface and shouldered his bag. Aaron watched as his best friend walked out the door, knowing that he was starting a new journey.

"See you soon, bud." Aaron waved good-bye.

☾

Johnathen wandered down the halls, his feet smacking the pavement as he walked, his sword digging into his hip. Making his way to the outer north gate, Johnathen pretended to act like usual, happy-go-lucky self on a sunny Saturday morning. Most of the halls were deserted, as many students were inside their rooms playing video games or enjoying outdoor activities on their break from school.

As of today, everyone associated with the soccer league would be helping to set up for the tournament. Johnathen wasn't much of a soccer fan like James, Cole, or Mitchell. Mainly, he just liked to play basketball. Aaron enjoyed football and baseball, and Will didn't do any sports unless you counted reading all day and studying all night a physical education for your brain. Jacob just spent his time in the forges, crafting. Alex played basketball a lot and used to join in on paintball tournaments before it was banned.

192

Camp Wolf seemed like a somewhat normal school-like facility with its soccer and football fields, baseball diamond, and blacktop basketball court. But there were plenty of other things that made it seem different. Apart from the outside forges, the structure was made up of limestone, resting against the side of a mountain slope. The main structure had been built to blend into the mountainside of the large range in the Rockies, and the secret location shielded the school from mortal eyes.

All the classes were taught inside, above ground or below. Just like a regular school, there were a variety of different courses and electives a student could choose to take. Language courses like Latin I, Latin II, Greek I, Greek II, and Greek III were combined with Romanian I. The more basic language courses, Spanish I through IV and German I through IV could be chosen as electives, too. The varying levels of mathematics classes were offered as well: Math Concepts, Pre-Algebra, Algebra, Calculus, Honors Geometry, and Trigonometry.

Greek History 101 and Roman History 101 was the opposite of American social studies, but the Council had set up the school system so that students were required to learn American history before learning Greek history and culture. Of the few Camps left in the world, depending on what area the student lived in, they choose to follow both the Greek gods and their original religion, or one or the other.

The next available class was the most dreaded and exciting one—gym. It was an hour and a half of free time outside, and the Skin-changers went through a daily routine with their instructors to exercise both the mind and body. The demigods got to play standard games such as dodgeball and flag football, but there was always a dangerous twist. Last week, Johnathen had ran three miles in under twenty minutes on a worn dirt path.

It had seemed simple enough, but what the instructor didn't tell him was that tripwires, triggered nets, bear traps, and Burmese tiger pits were set up before the class was told to run. The Skin-changers were supposed to better practice how to follow their instincts and use their reflexes to navigate the path as quickly and safely as possible, all the while trying to outrace their opponents. That day he had almost lost his foot—three times.

Finally, there were the real training courses. Battle Tactics, Weapons of War, sword and archery lessons, crafting, and health safety were all required classes for every student. In total, students get to choose between twenty classes to take.

Demigods woke up five days a week before 7:00 a.m., washed up and ate breakfast in the dining hall, and had to be seated in their first period classroom before 8:15 a.m. The last class of the day ended at 3:30 p.m. The teachers were older students who had lived and trained at Camp Wolf before deciding to stay behind as a kind of 'forever home'. Most students went out to live and work in the mortal world after graduation. Instructors could be of any age sixteen and up (depending on the skill level), and their requirements were accounting only for intelligence, sportsmanship, and loyalty to others. James was one of them.

Johnathen reached the main entrance to the building and the guards shoved open the huge cherrywood doors. The sun shone down on the mountain, rays of sunshine warming his skin. There was not a cloud in sight. In fall, the surrounding area bloomed in hues of oranges, reds, yellows, and browns. Winter was the harshest season because students would have to train inside, the wolves had more difficulty hunting, and everyone would be stuck inside the campus by ten feet of snow piling at the doors.

Whistling, Johnathen shaded his eyes and searched for his traveling friends, Pearl and Greyback. He whistled a piercing high note, and two blurs plowed into him.

Greyback was named after his coat color. His fur was tawny, aside from the silvery grey color on his spine and ridge of his back. He was a handsome fellow with deep brown eyes. Pearl was a year younger, but was far more skilled at tracking. Her eyes were ice blue, almost translucent, and her fur was a creamy color with black specks.

Johnathen pushed himself up, nudging the wolves away from his saliva-slicked face. He gave them a pat on the head. As they walked past the playing fields, he saw students cleaning off the bleachers on the soccer fields and painting the lines on the mowed yard. He spotted Cole, Mitchell, and James passing a soccer ball back and forth. He grinned and waved.

"Hey! Wanna play?" Someone shouted. Johnathen turned around and saw his basketball teammates Cameron, Henry, George and Tom dribbling a ball between them. All four wore short sleeves and sweatpants, waiting for his answer.

"Nah, sorry guys, I can't. I'm going hunting." He shouted back, pointing at Pearl and Greyback. Greyback barked in response.

"Okay, have fun. Hope to see you at the game tonight!" Cameron shrugged. Johnathen gave a bleak smile and yelled, "Sure thing!" and walked off. His friends wouldn't be seeing him for a while.

Marching on, Johnathen made it to the fifty-foot wall. A massive iron-spiked, timbered gate stood before him. Four guards stood watch, two on the ground and two atop the wall on the parapet, their armor shining in the sunlight. When they saw him and his wolves, all three lowered their spears and swords, eyes hidden behind visors.

"What is your duty out beyond the north gate?" One guard demanded.

"Um, I was going hunting. This is Pearl and Greyback. May we pass? Please, we are trying to hurry so we can get back before the big game."

The guard, recognizing Johnathen Dogo, considered his plea for a moment. "Fine, but be back before sunset. You know the rules." Tossing a biscuit at Pearl and Greyback, he stood aside and cranked the handle. On the left side, another guard grabbed the hand, and they pulled in unison. As the gate opened, the hinges let out a horrible groaning sound. At last, the gate was up and the guard who had spoken to Johnathen motioned to let him through.

Gravel crunched underfoot as he took the first step of their long adventure. The trees on the path leaned into one another, creating a kind of canopy overhead to block the sun. When the small group was well away from the gate, Johnathen took off in a sprint as he produced a bronze-plated compass from his pockets, the needle flicking into position. Taking out the spray paint can, he dabbed a spot on a nearby tree, drawing pink arrows pointing toward the river. Luckily, no pinecone-throwing nymph rushed out at him.

Turning around until the needle pointed north, Johnathen stepped off the path and through the trees until he reached the river. Making his way through a brush-hidden tunnel, he emerged from out of the cave's mouth and onto the riverbank. The murky, cold water rushed by. Pearl and Greyback ran into the water, wrestling and splashing around. Johnathen laughed at the wolves as Pearl bit Greyback's tail and he whirled on her, snarling. Pearl batted at his face, rowling up her partner. Setting his bag on the rocks, Johnathen pulled out a granola bar and chewed. His wristwatch read 10:40 a.m. A little over a half hour until Aaron met him at 11:15.

Johnathen sighed.

Chapter X: Pass GO

Aaron's excuse was a little less believable. His palms were sweating as he fiddled with his backpack strap. The guards changed posts every hour and now four new guards were in position, weapons at the ready. Aaron knew their faces, but not their names. After passing by his younger friends, Cole and Mitchell, James had ran up and wished him luck. He had expected at least one of the sentries to go all Gandalf-style and break out their magical staff, shouting, "Yooouuu shall nooott paaasssss!" but to Aaron's dismay, it never did happen.

"What is your duty out beyond the north gate?" A grim-faced soldier eyed him up and down. "You've no wolves with you like the last boy that passed. What business?"

"*B-boy?!*" Aaron sputtered, quickly shutting his mouth. The guards standing watch now must be a few years older than Johnathen, if they were to address him as such. "Was he tall with sandy blonde hair? Had a white and peppered female wolf, named Pearl, and a grayish-brown male wolf named Greyback?" he asked them.

"Err, I believe that is what Don said." The guard glanced at his partner for confirmation. He bobbed his head yes.

"Well then, I am meeting—" Aaron looked at the first guard. "That *boy,* Johnathen. We're going pack hunting."

The first guard sighed. "You are free to go. But remember, you must return here at sunset. If you're not back by then we will be forced to lock you outside where the monsters lurk, no ifs and buts about it." he said, his voice a low warning.

Aaron shrugged. "Okay, sure."

He started to glide past the gate when Second guard spoke up. "Just double-checking, there are more of you boys coming, right? We were told by Alpha Lockwood not to let many people outside the walls."

Halt had made it perfectly clear that no one else would go missing since Vincent had disappeared a few months back, as Aaron kept reminding himself.

"Oh, yes actually. Three more *boys*." Aaron rolled his eyes.

"Three?" he asked.

"Three." Aaron repeated, irritated.

"Ralph, remember that." Second guard told Third guard. Third guard answered with a firm, "Yessir."

First guard cut in. "You may pass, but don't cause any trouble, you hear? Or we'll all be in deep shit."

Aaron agreed and at last, he was on his way.

☾

Brushing his fingers against the dried spray paint, Aaron wove through the trees toward his destination. He could hear the rushing river before he saw it. Coming out of the darkness of the tunnel, he found Johnathen skipping rocks across the water with Pearl and Greyback playing on the bank.

"Heyo! You ready?" Aaron called, waving to his long-time friend.

"Ah-ha, there you are!" his friend called back, and the two young wolves raced up to be coddled. Aaron's boots crunched on the gravel as he moved.

"Let's get started. We got a long way ahead of us." Aaron sighed. Pulling out a map, Johnathen pointed his finger on a small red dot.

"So, that's us, here up in the middle of the Rockies. And here…" He took out another map, a tour guide of the hiking paths of Yellowstone National Park, and pointed at a green line. "Is the way out." Trailing his finger down a line to a dot that read 'northeast entrance' and down a road to the town of Silver Gate, Montana. "From here we'll travel by compass, and we will be heading southeast until we reach Chicago," Johnathen produced two more maps from his bag and unfolded a map of the states.

198

"We'll keep going around the Great Lakes and through Indiana and Ohio. We can take a bus to Weedsport, New York from the border of Pennsylvania. After we search the area and the remnants of Nekoda's house, interview some of the citizens, we head northwest to Canada."

"But you know there's, like, a one out of one-hundred chance she, or Nathaniel, will be at Niagara Falls. There are hundreds upon thousands of dams and reservoirs in the U.S." Aaron groaned, flicking the map.

"Unless you know if Nekoda has a tracking chip implanted in her brain, I don't think it's going to be so easy to find her."

"But we're traveling hundreds of miles! On foot!"
"Oh, you're a big boy, you can do it. James said it'd be better to say on foot in case anything comes up and we have a change of direction." Johnathen folded the maps up.

"But will we be able to rest at hotels? These two—" Aaron pointed at the canines, "can take care of themselves, but I can't live on granola bars and juice boxes forever."

"Yes, that's why I brought American cash." Johnathen said, growing exasperated.

"Good, cause it's going to be a long walk down the yellow brick road." Aaron scratched Pearl's ears.

"Shall we?" Johnathen held out his hand, motioning in the direction of the river.

"We shall." Aaron strapped his shield to his wrist and followed suit.

☾

Alex Rayn was slouched on the beanbag chair in Will's room, a gaming controller in hand. *The Star Wars* season one CD was scratched up so they were playing a mission on Halo 4 instead. Alex's bag lay on the floor beside him, but he wasn't ready to leave yet.

Alex wanted to help. He wanted to help an innocent life no matter what it took, but now the matter was eating him up from the inside. They had no clue who Nathaniel really was. James only had a glimpse of how he really looked, but he didn't know *what* he was. And no one knew just how powerful he really is. It's one thing to see someone, and another to know them. How could they defeat an enemy they knew nothing about?

The gang only had ties with loose ends; no one could say where Nekoda was being held captive or where they were headed on this mission. Johnathen and Aaron were traveling to the remnants of the Jones's house as the seconds ticked by. Alex was going to be heading east, toward the coast. Looking for what, he had no idea. Maybe he'd just walk to the nearest police station and ask what they knew about the mystery murder of Clara and Kyle Jones and their missing daughter. Alex had no lead, no exact destination.

Although there *was* actually something to check out, it wasn't much.

The beaches along the east coasts were being battered by storms and hurricanes. Zeus, the Skin-changers knew, was growing angry and enacting his rage onto the eastern states. Maybe, just maybe, Alex could talk to Zeus's children, demigods of the sky. If they knew anything about the talismans, that would also be incredibly helpful. The Lockwood and Jones families were two of the four Keeper families of Krane de Royce's talismans. Researching online wasn't going to get Alex anywhere and he didn't want to get caught 'borrowing' from the Camp's Archives, so perhaps someone could help him. The bizarre tropical storms weren't much; nonetheless, it was something to look out for.

Alex knew of another phenomenon to check out, and it may be of more use than the crazy weather signs. Additionally, there was a legend called the Blair Witch, a popular dinner conversation in Maryland. The legend dates back from the Revolutionary War.

All the Blair Witch events have taken place around The Black Hills Forest in Maryland. One day, it was said that seven kids mysteriously disappeared into the woods and were found murdered days later. Locals say that each child was led to an old, crumbling house by an enticing woman who disguised herself as an old hag. The children were supposedly led inside the house and told to face the corner, paralyzed, while their friends were killed in turn behind their backs.

Nearby, in what was called Coffin Rock, seven graves marked the bodies of the victims. When searchers went out to investigate, they found bloodied handprints on the walls of the basement house and stick figures hanging from trees. This was the work of an ancient goddess, a deity who referred to herself as the Night Witch.

In the year 1994, three high school students had gotten lost in the woods, gathering footage for their 'Blair Witch Project.' But what Alex had figured out and struggled to connect was that the Blair Witch legend was just the work of the goddess, Hecate, and her shadow demons drawing innocent demigods to their deaths to strike back at the Olympians. There was word going around that was she was siding with Kronos in the upcoming wars.

Alex wanted to investigate the legend for himself, and speak to Hecate, if she could be summoned. Just maybe, he could convince her to help them with their mission. It was dangerous, yes, and Alex was making a slight dent in their mission, but the guys didn't have to know about it.

Yet.

William was wanting to travel down to the Grand Canyon in Arizona. Apparently, there had been strange sightings of what, he wasn't sure of, but it was a case the townsfolk didn't like to talk about. The case seemed interesting enough for him, as the national landmark was an all-around excellent hideout for breeding Dragons. They were all going in different directions, literally and metaphorically.

If the Camp's wolves could sniff Nekoda out, they had a sliver of hope. Jacob would be going west towards a dam in upstate Idaho—the Dworshak Reservoir. Nekoda could be hiding out anywhere since she escaped. Or maybe she was already caught.

Or dead.

Shooting an ugly, big-headed Grunt in the head, Alex moved his character around the biome and up a ramp into a Scorpion tank. Running over countless enemies, Alex's character drove through a ditch and squashed an Elite alien. Cursing, Will's screen turned a deep red as his character died. "Dammit, man! Base got overrun!"

Alex chuckled. "Maybe next time Tom Cruise will swoop in and save us."

"Whatever," Will stood up and opened his black mini-fridge to tear open a chilled pack of M&Ms. "Want some?" he asked through a mouthful.

"Sure." Will dumped some chocolates into Alex's palms. "Tried 'connecting with Shadarr' yet?" Alex asked, making air quotes with his fingers.

"Not recently. It's freaking impossible. My great-great-great-great-great-great uncle used to be able to communicate with animals," he counted off on his fingers, "before the Dragons almost died out hundreds of years ago. I just don't know how it was so easy for him!" grumbled Will.

"You'll get there. There's only a few living adult Dragons left in the world and anyhow, they probably haven't been in contact with humans most their lives."

"I know, but I'd really like it if my mother spoke to me more often."

"You do realize, as harsh as this sounds, Athena doesn't really *want* to speak to her children. No offense. Even so, the gods are preoccupied like the rest of the world."

"But what if we got everything all wrong? The mortals are not the ones who need assisting, it's them!" Will ran a chocolate-stained hand through his snow-white hair.

"What do you mean by that?" Alex asked, queer.

"Over the centuries, humans and demigods have been asking and praying to the gods for help. In war, in death, in love, in life. They gave *us* the talismans to keep instead of holding on to them themselves! When Lycaon created the very first line of Skin-changers, Hades gave *us* a last chance. During the war of man and beast, the gods stepped in to help *us* by gifting Krane the talismans in the first place." Will tapped his chest. "Afterwards, they let the Dragons live in peace and the humans did not. But when Rome fell, we rebuilt the nation ourselves. We are taking on our own tasks down on earth while the gods are suffering below and above. What I mean is that this time, instead of them helping us win our battles, we help them win theirs. It will affect both mortal and immortal alike, yes, but in this instance, humans can make a change."

Alex was silent for a brief moment. Then realization dawned on him. "Holy Hera! You're a freaking genius!" he exclaimed, slapping his forehead.

"I know," Will fluttered his lashes. "C'mon, help me write this letter to Halt. If he won't listen to me, he'll listen to our kin. Dior can help deliver this." he went to his desk and started scribbling on a notepad.

When he was finished, Alex wrapped the parchment in a blue ribbon. The pair walked down to the Den together and found Dior asleep in her kennel. Slipping the paper through the links of the fence, Will set it down by her head. If Dior awoke soon, she'd find the paper and deliver it to Halt herself; she was a smart girl. Alex reached Cherise's and Joffrey's kennels and let them loose. Wagging their tails, they nipped his hands affectionately.

Crouching down to their level, Alex scratched each canine on the head, right behind the ears. "Hey cuties, you ready for our own little adventure?" Will glanced up at Alex, eyebrows raised. "What? It calms dogs down if you speak in a baby voice. Everyone knows that."

"Uh-huh." Alex Rayn mumbled.

"Want to help me check my bag? I feel like I'm forgetting something."

"Sure," Will handed over Alex his duffel bag, which was currently being chewed on by Joffrey. Dumping out the items, Will laid them out in order. "Okay let's see...my wallet?" Alex asked.

"Check," Will popped it back into the bag.

"Walkie-talkies with extra batteries?"

"Yes,"

"First aid kit with athletic tape?"

"Yep,"

"Under Armor sweatshirt?"

"With the food stains? Got it; you're wearing it."

"Gloves, hat, dog booties?"

"All here...and seriously?"

"It's very easy to get frostbite!"

"You're impossible,"

"Deal with it. Pack of ramen noodles?"

"Sí,"

"Lighter and can-opener?"

"Uh-huh," Will chucked the items in the bag.

"Road maps?"

"Yup. You have quite a few,"

"Canteen?"

"With the smiley face sticker? Got it," Will rattled the container.

"Uhh...Greek fire and bottle of liquid poison?"

"What are you planning on doing? Murdering a hobo?" Orchild looked pointedly at his friend. Alex scribbled something down on his check list and sighed.

"Dog chews?"

"Yeppers."

Will flung Alex's stuffed bag over to his friend. Helping lead Cherise and Joffrey up to his bedchamber, Will whistled the *Star Wars* theme song. Heading to their joint room, Cherise and Joffrey decided to slip through the door at the same time.

Between Will's and Alex's legs.

Together.

All four tumbled to the ground, swearing and laughing. "Really?" Alex wrestled with Joffrey as Cherise started pulling on Will's shirt.

"Aah, cut it out! Cut it out! I already have to deal with seven other animals, I don't need two more!" Will snapped at Joff. Chuckling, Alex managed to pull the wolves off one another.

After saying his goodbyes to Will, Alex headed out toward the gate. As expected, the guards had changed posts. Johnathen had called ahead of time informing Alex that the best thing to do was say that he was meeting him and Aaron. Jacob and Will were to do the same.

As usual, James was waiting outside for them. Cole had left earlier with Mitchell to go into the city with a group of older men for supplies.

"You ready, Rayn?" asked James.

"I guess so," Alex fiddled with his bow that was slung over his chest. A quiver of arrows was flung over his shoulder and a wrist brace covered his right arm. James patted him on the back, eyes shining. "I wish you could come with."

"Yeah, I know. Just remember, if you run into a major problem—"

"Like an earthborn army storming L.A.?"

"Uh, I guess. You be sure to contact Camp Wolf immediately. Not the others knuckleheads, not me, but Halt. Cause that'd be such a disappointment to the world knowing the most notorious gambling city in the United States was ransacked by monsters."

"That would suck pretty bad. I haven't been to the bars or dance plazas yet; I've always wanted to try and outrun a club bouncer." Alex smirked.

James laughed. "Don't worry, you'll get the chance someday. Alright, see ya soon. I'll be in touch."

"Okay, bye!" Alex called after him. Cherise howled.

Anxiety eating away at his insides, Alex made his way past the guards and through the East gate without trouble. "Score!" Alex cheered when he was well away from watchful eyes. Alongside him, Joffrey and Cherise trotted. "What do you say, pups? I think it is time we take a nice vacay to Little America!" Alex sprinted ahead, finally leaving all his worries behind.

☾

If Will had a boat, he'd travel south to Antarctica. Maybe adopt a penguin or two. But why not investigate an ol' mystery down in the world's largest canyon ever, without a tour guide?

Will reached under the bed to pet his wolves, Jaz and Izzy. Female siblings, the middle-aged Lycanthropes looked identical with their reddish-brown coat and wide paws. The only difference was that Jaz's eyes were moss green, and Izzy's were golden. Will had faith in them; they were loyal partners forever and always.

Upon happenchance, Will had come across an article about neighbors in Phoenix, Arizona who reported seeing a big figure with glowing eyes flying around the neighborhood at night. Only a few people were witness, and most claimed it to be an alien. Someone had posted a video on Youtube, but that ended up being a bust. The footage itself was too grainy and dark to see anything. However, there were tales of a Dragon living under the earth far back in the Grand Canyon, deep in the desert. That was all there was to go by. No clear description of a creature, no actual tracks or DNA samples to prove much. Still, some people were getting pretty spooked and fewer tourists had showed up to the national landmark for the past couple months. It was autumn, but that didn't mean anyone ever stopped visiting something as spectacular as the Grand Canyon.

Sure, James was focused on finding Nekoda, they all were. But in the process, they had blocked out everything else. William wanted to solve a mystery for the discovery of a live Dragon, Alex wanted to check out a haunted forest in Maryland for who-knows-why, Johnathen and Aaron were going to examine the scene at Kody's house, and Jacob was going to visit the Dworshack dam in Idaho.

Scrolling through his contacts, Will sent an email to Jacob Vendéen. He probably wouldn't hear his phone go off even if he called; the banging of metal on metal down in the forges was deafening.

Will's quick fingers tapped out a message:

To: MetalMann@yahoo.com
From: WildDawg.net.org.
Sub: hey dude
Re:
Jacob, not sure if you'll get this before I leave. Do you think you and your boys could spare an extra helm? Or hand grenades? Johnathen and Aaron are packing some Greek fire, same as Alex. Knowing me, I'll engulf myself in flames on accident. I'm bringing loads of extra ammunition for my Sniper, and I'm packing my sword. But you know I tend to be a lightweight when for both monsters and mortals lol.
-W

Will sat patiently on his bed as he waited for a response from Jacob. Finally, his phone beeped.

To: WildDawg.net.org.
From: MetalMann@yahoo.com
Sub: hey dude
Re: hi
I think I can spare a few boom machines, ;) You'll have to come down to the forges and get them yourself. I still have to gather last minute equipment and I have a bronze and gold-rimmed helmet w/ visor cooling for you right now. And please leave Cherise and Joffrey in your room; my instructors really don't won't another wolf pooping diamonds! LMAO.

207

**Seriously, though, it sucks washing off dried dung from a
perfectly good stone. See ya!**

-Jacob

Laughing, Will commanded the twins to stay put and
headed out the door. Humming along with each stride, Will
counted down the minutes after Alex's departure. He wondered
how the others were doing. Were they already lost? What if they
found someone dead, floating down the endless river? How would
they find their way back to Camp if something terrible happened?
Were Vincent and Taz still out in the world, lost? What would
happen if they couldn't ever find the talismans? Or worse,
Nathaniel got to them first. All these thoughts and more jumbled
around in his aching head.

Growling low in his throat, Will smacked his forehead and
reminded himself that nothing was impossible. Everything was
possible, it had to be. If anyone had more faith in this mission, it
was James. James would help them get there. Yet it was sort of a
split mission now; each teenager had a different role and each one
of them a different goal in mind. James wanted to rescue Nekoda,
Will wanted to rescue both Nekoda *and* Shadarr, and check out a
place that could possibly lead to a Dragon nest. Johnathen and
Aaron wanted to help James and find the *Book of Spells*, Jacob
always wanted to do what was right, and Alex was going to check
out a mystery in Maryland and stop Nathaniel. Will thought about
the situation over and over again.

They were going to need all the help they could get to stop
Nathaniel and figure out his plot to overtake Olympus. It was a
nearly impossible goal, but not as impossible as discovering
Atlantis. Even though in all actuality, Atlantis was hidden from
sight from everyone except the gods. How little the mortals really
know...it's impressive.

As Will strode down the stairs that led underground, he
could hear the sounds of hammers striking against metal, swords

being sharpened, and chests heaving. A blast of humid air hit him as he entered the forges, his palms already slick with sweat because of the dense, humid air.

Slipping in between work spaces and dodging huge machinery, Will made his way to the back of the forge where Jacob was pounding away at a wicked looking blade inlaid with rubies. Bending the metal into place, sparks flew off the anvil as Jacob brought his arm up and down, up and down, up and down.

Cupping his hands around his mouth, Will leaned forward and shouted, "CAN YOU HEAR ME?" Startled, Jacob dropped the hammer and pulled out an earplug.

"YES, I CAN! BUT IT'S EASIER TO TALK OUTSIDE." he pointed towards the door. Jacob reached behind him and pulled out a box and a black briefcase. Carrying the box under his arm and the latched briefcase in hand, Jacob followed Will to the front of the room and stepped outside. Gently handing the items to Will, Jacob slammed shut the heavy iron door.

"This is it?" Will asked, eyes lighting up.

"Yup, and the hand grenades are covered with foam so they won't explode if you drop the briefcase on accident."

Eager, Will opened the case and removed a piece of thick packing foam to see eight hand grenades, half of them marked with the letter S.

"Dang, dude, this is great! Thanks!" Picking up a marked grenade, Will turned it around in his hands, inspecting it.

"Oh, that is a mega smoke-bomb. Like a regular smoke bomb but with ten times as much power. The smoke takes minutes longer to clear so it would blind your targets for an extended period of time."

Patting his friend's shoulder in gratitude, Will unboxed the second item. Whistling, Will held up the same helmet Jacob had described in his email. It was made of shiny bronze with a circlet of gold rimming the outer edges. A visor was attached to the front to guard his eyes. Will tried it on.

"I owe you one!" Will fist-bumped his best friend. "Boo-ya!"

"Eh, it's no problem. Anything to help a brother out." Jacob replied.

"Hey, should I keep a few of these grenades on my belt? 'Cause I'll be on the move a lot and I don't know if these things can handle being jostled around in a bag. I've already got enough packed." Will asked, worrying his lip.

"Actually, yes. You don't have to take all of them with you, but if you do, store them in a pouch and check to make sure the pins are secured every hour. Also, after throwing out the pin on the grenade, you have to *throw it immediately*. Otherwise…"

"I go boom."

"Pretty much."

Will shook his head, relieved that he had some extra help to keep him safe while traveling. "Okay, I think I should get going. We'll keep in touch."

"Yeah, good luck." Jacob said.

"You too,"

As Will started back up the stairs, Jacob whisper-shouted, "Wait! If you find the Dragon, I want you to fly home on its back and prove me wrong that there are still living, breathing Dragons. Prove *everyone* wrong! Got me?"

Will snorted. "Gotcha loud and clear."

☾

Izzy and Jaz padded alongside him, tongues lolling out. Will had passed through the south gate easily enough. Armed with his trusted firearm, helm on his head and extra supplies at hand, he was ready. Will knew where he was going. It was going to be a long walk through deserts and mountains, but he could make it to Arizona.

Skin-changers were bred to be stronger than the average demigod, more so than the average human. Skin-changers were almost immune to the cold—yet Idaho's weather sometimes got too cold for William's liking—and could complete laborious work hours without stopping, at least full grown. That's why his kind were built for war—Skin-changers made excellent fighters.

The fastest track star, champion Usain Bolt, owned the record for fastest man alive. He was fast as a Cheetah, running at a high of thirty-five miles per hour. Unbeknownst to the world, Usain was a hybrid demigod. His true form was, in fact, a Darkshadow Skin-changer, and his great-grandmother was a daughter to Poseidon, the creator of horses and god of the seas. His family came from a line of pure Thoroughbred racehorses. Usain's uncle was related to Secretariat, a famous Triple Crown winner of the Kentucky Derby. Obviously, the race officials kept quiet. Well, the non-human officials of the Olympics kept quiet, anyway.

Will hadn't seen James outside when he departed, so he assumed that he must have already contacted the others or was preparing for the tournament tonight. Either way, James would alert them all if anything peculiar came up. For now, the talismans would have to wait until after they saved Kody. Hopefully, Buddy would come back to Camp and lead Kody here.

If Nathaniel didn't get to her first.

If James dreamt again.

If Nekoda didn't go through her Changing Moon beforehand.

If there were an easier path.

If there weren't so many *if's*!

(

James Dawn adjusted the walkie-talkies by his bedside table, one for each of his traveling friends, five in total. Only Jacob was left, and he would be gone by 3:00 p.m. After icing his bruised face again, James had wandered back into his room to think. It was something he was really good at. Finally, the mission was a go. All that was left to do was wait and see.

Polishing his sword until it was spotless and shining, James set to work writing another letter addressed to Nekoda in case Buddy eventually Portaled back. Putting pen to paper, he wrote. Plucking a rubber band off his desk, James rolled up the letter and tried to connect with Johnathen via walkie-talkie. A static voice was soon heard and James put his mouth up to the device.

"Earth to Knucklehead number one and two. Johnathen and Aaron. Over." James pressed the button.

"What's up? Miss us already?" Aaron's voice came through the other end.

"Yeah, right. No, I need Johnathen to call Buddy back home. Over," James rolled his eyes.

"You don't have to say 'over' after each conversation. We're not up in a space shuttle." he heard Johnathen grumble.

"Ooh, that'd be so cool!" Aaron squealed.

"Guys, just call Buddy back home for a few. I have a letter for Nekoda. If Buddy is still with her, then he can deliver it."

"Okay, fine. Just give me a moment." Johnathen sighed. Buddy, like most trained Hellhounds, were able to be summoned by a special whistle Johnathen wore around his neck. From anywhere in the world, Buddy could hear it, and he would come.

James stared around his room. After a brief silence, he heard scratching coming from outside the door. Yanking it open, he found Buddy the Toypoodle. Carrying him into the room, James coddled him. "D'aww, look at the little puppy. You're so cute, yes you are—ouch!" James yelped. Buddy jumped out of his arms and triumphantly strutted to the desk.

"I was only teasing, Bud! You didn't have to bite me! Jeez, mutt." James sucked his finger and walked over to Buddy. He had Changed into his Hellhound form in the matter of a second. "Okay, go find Nekoda and make sure she gets this." James said, presenting the note. Instead of leaving, Buddy rolled onto his side, legs splayed in the air. Groaning, James reached down and gave him a long belly rub. When he was satisfied, Buddy picked up the paper and disappeared in a black cloud of smoke.

James breathed a sigh of relief.

☾

I didn't know how long we slept for. Instead of climbing up to the dam straight away, Buddy and I had stopped and slept in a tree. Well, I slept in the tree and Buddy stood guard at the trunk for a few hours. Exhausted, I didn't bother to worry about my purple ankle or the branches scratching at my clothes.

When we awoke, the sun was breaking the horizon, casting everything in hues of pink and orange. For a brief moment, I had forgotten where we were, and so startled was I that Buddy almost became a black pancake when I fell five feet to the forest floor. My stomach was rumbling so loud I feared I would attract unwanted attention. I picked around for some acorns and peeled out the inside of the shell. Inside was the softer nut that squirrels lived off of; I remembered that fact I had learned off a documentary. If animals could eat it, why couldn't people? I bit into the acorn. It was a different texture, dry, but crunchy like a peanut. To my surprise, not half bad. I definitely wasn't tempted to eat bark after that.

Lost mountain climbers said that if you didn't have any real food on hand if stranded, you could chew on tree bark. There were tiny bugs living inside the tree and if it tasted as rough and dry as it felt, I wasn't going to put that in my stomach. And I was not an expert to tell poisonous berries apart from the edible ones. But if Buddy and I could make it past the dam, there was a possibility that maintenance crews were on duty and they could give us a ride into the nearest town. Forget not talking to strangers, no one was as terrifyingly aggressive as Nathaniel.

Carved into the side of the slope was a steep staircase leading up to the top of the reservoir. From closer inspection, the dam itself looked pretty old. The wall was made from thick cement, rugged and cracked from years of erosion. Sighing, I pulled myself up, step by step. I only could hope there was something or someone at the top.

I was tiring after the fifth flight of stairs. My ankle was throbbing so bad now I had to shut my eyes to block out the pain; I needed to down an entire bottle of Advil.

Buddy moved behind and held me up as we moved, slowly but surely. Glancing upwards, I tried to calculate how high the tallest stair was. Keeping me on my foot (plural), Buddy helped me hop up one foot at a time after my arms began to tremble from dragging myself up the stairs. Pain lanced up my leg every time I attempted to put weight on it, and my knee began to feel a bit swollen At least I could wiggle my toes.

Even though it felt like the weather outside was below fifty degrees, sweat was trickling down my forehead from the effort. Growling in my throat, I pushed myself up and up and up.

After a total of two-hundred eighty frickin' steps, we were standing on the top of the dam. I hobbled along the walkway, checking the surroundings. Somewhere along the river and in front of the dam was the way we had come from. Nathaniel's base was hidden somewhere within the endless terrain. Behind us was a gigantic lake, moonlight casting a soft glow over the water. Around the lake were patches of sand and mud and more trees. To my right, meters ahead, was the other end of the dam. Same as on the left. But there were no security cabins, tourist shops, porta-potties, nothing.

Nothing.

An endless, vast terrain of nothingness! I clenched my hands into fists and stared at the bleak horizon.

With no phone, no GPS, no sign marking my location, and no people, I was stuck.

Absolutely stuck, absolutely afraid, absolutely pissed off!

With fresh tears streaming down my wind-bitten cheeks, I hit the closest thing to me. Crumbling stone ledge. Pounding my fists against the hard stone, my knuckles turned red and raw. Buddy bit my sleeve and yanked me backwards onto my butt.

Licking my face, he whined. "I'm sorry. I'm sorry. I'm sorry." Blubbering, I put my head in my shaking hands, squeezing my eyes shut. *"I'm sorry, I'm sorry, I'msorryI'msorrysorry..."*

When the burning in my chest ceased and my hands stopped bleeding, Buddy pushed me back onto my feet. I wiped at my face, the shaking in my hands ceased. I placed a hand on Buddy's back to hold myself up as we hopped along. I bit my lip, eyeing the path ahead. Surely there was something here. An old vending machine, a shed, anything that meant human life.

Suddenly, I was falling. My foot caught on something hard, and with a yelp, I caught myself before I face-planted into the ground. On closer inspection, I had not tripped over a speed bump of sorts, but a hatch. Bending down, I twisted the handle on top of the hatch until it creaked open, rust and paint peeling off. Below us was a rickety ladder that led down into darkness. Upon peering farther down into the hole, I noticed a very faint glow coming from the bottom. A light! Buddy crouched on his belly and looked down. In an instant, the old dog I knew and loved was back. In his little Toypoodle form, he waited.

"What?" I questioned, unsure of his proposal. Buddy smiled, baring his canine teeth and glancing down into the hole again.

"Wait, you want me to carry you down? Really?" I sputtered, sitting up. Yipping, he pawed at my hand. "Are you kidding me? How can I! I can barely walk in a straight line,"

Buddy placed his front paws on my knees and looked me in the eyes. He pawed me in the chest. "Oh my gosh, this is ridiculous!" muttering, I picked Buddy up in one hand and unzipped the front of my hoodie with the other, setting him against my chest. He wriggled his head up and out of the hole and licked my chin.

I tentatively felt for the first rung with my good foot, and stepped down. Buddy's small head bobbed up and down as I focused on the light, and together we made our way down beneath the surface.

215

Chapter XI: Lone Rangers

Thump! My feet finally hit solid ground, and my head swam. Every second I spent climbing the ladder, I had a sinking feeling that my feet would slip and I would fall to my death. The hole was only three feet wide, but still just large enough for a person to fall straight through and end up as smashed tomato below. Buddy was squished against the ladder the whole way down, burying his head in my chest. He now sat at my feet, and as soon as I blinked, immortal Buddy was back, tail wagging.

"That was fun for you, wasn't it?" I pouted. He threw his head back and barked. "Well, I guess there's no other option but forward." The hallway was made entirely of hardened earth and stone. Torches flickered in rows down the endless path as I leaned against the wall for support. Turning to Buddy, I motioned him ahead. Strutting down the hall, we walked right into who-knew-what. As time passed, I made a pros and cons list in my head.

Pros: I had Buddy. James and the gang were coming and I hadn't lost my mind yet. Cons: my mom and dad were most likely dead. Even I, much less than the others, knew where in the world I was. We both were hungry, tired, and dirty. Nathaniel could undoubtedly find me and take us back at any moment and another con just popped into my head—Buddy just disappeared. Spinning around, I called out to the emptiness.

"Bud, this is *not* funny! Come out and show yourself! I thought you were out of the hide-and-seek phase long before you were a year old!" Listening and waiting, Buddy still didn't show up. Then I smelled it. Smoke.

Squinting in the dim light, I could make out the same smoky haze that appeared when Buddy vanished after he had bled out.

Shit! He Portaled; where could he have gone to now? "Buddy!" I cried out. There was nothing beyond the darkness but possible death. Moving alone was not sounding like a very good idea at the moment.

Something cold and wet touched my hand.

I shrieked, raising my arms in defense. "Ah, *bad*! Very bad dog! Why'd you do that?" Buddy was back, this time with another letter. Tearing it from his mouth, I held the paper up to the light and read aloud.

"Dear Nekoda, in acknowledgement of your escape, my friends Johnathen, Aaron, William, Alex and Jacob are sent out around the states. As you and I both don't know your exact location, they are searching across the country. Assuming Buddy is still with you, safe and sound, he would have been sent back here to retrieve this letter. If you had panicked, don't worry, help is on the way. If you happen to fix your mind on our whereabouts, please try to find us. Camp Wolf. I promise you will be welcomed here, and no harm will come to you. It isn't safe for you to go back home, trust me on this. We are up in the Rocky Mountains, by Yellowstone National Park, in Idaho. Simply say to Buddy 'go home', and he'll lead you right to us. Hope to see you soon, legend child. From James."

Now that's what I called fast-paced delivery. Folding the paper up, I shoved it into my pocket and turned to my dog. "This is brilliant! Ahem, Buddy, go home!" I said, stern.

Perking up his floppy ears, Buddy spun and trotted down the hall. Catching up to him, I clutched the back of his neck where his collar had somehow appeared when it hadn't before. I paced myself as we walked along. The tunnel swerved left and down a short hallway, the passage growing so narrow we were now walking single-file. Eventually, my eyes adjusted to the dimness of the tunnels.

Hours later, and Buddy never stopped moving forward. I ran into a low beam as Buddy suddenly veered toward another route, this one seemingly endless. The tunnels must be from some sort of underground passageway from long ago. Who knew how far under the earth we were? If Shadarr wanted to be saved, we had

217

to keep moving; I had to get help first. I highly doubted I would be able to bulldoze my way back into that death trap by myself.

"Ah, hell!" I swiped at my face and arms, cobwebs clinging to my clothes. "Bud! Hold up!" He was gaining speed and was now full-out sprinting down the corridor, kicking up invisible dust. "Hey! Come back!" Yelling, I started off in a slow jog, gritting my teeth with each step I took. I barely missed Buddy as he snaked around a sharp corner and through a hole in the wall. "Oh, c'mon! While we're at it, just make me jump over a pit of vipers, huh?!" I whined.

Scrambling through the hole, I flopped to the floor and landed at Buddy's feet. He held a torch in mouth, the flames spitting upwards. "Woah, woah, careful!" Handling it away from him, I held the torch out from my body and scanned the room.

Fallen masonry was heaped on the ground, layers of dust and mold changing the original colors to a dull grey and brown. Against the walls stood human statues, like the kind you would see in a museum. They were all made of marble, limestone, obsidian, and smooth stone. I counted the statues of the beautiful men and woman, with twelve in total, six on each side.

The one closest was the image of a man in a toga holding a staff with two intertwined snakes, wings sprouting from the tip of the staff. The statue's feet bore carved sandals with tiny wings attached to the sides. Why would that be? What historical figure dressed like this?

In a flash, it clicked. A dusty lightbulb went off in my head. The staff the statue was carrying was called a caduceus, and the man was supposed to represent Hermes, the Greek god of travel.

"Wait a minute…" I moved to the next one, the statue of a young woman leaning over a fire. Her hands were clasped together, and a shawl was draped over her thin shoulders. I reckoned she was Hestia, another of the Olympians. Goddess of the hearth, family, and domestic life. Beside her was the statue of god Dionysus; the bundle of grapes he held in one hand and his disgruntled expression carved into stone gave it away. He was the god of wine, fertility, and was considered a patron of the arts in the myths.

Well, I suppose they weren't really myths anymore.

The next statue down the line depicted a female bending low to pick wheat from the ground as vines wrapped around her wrists, a small crown of twisted flowers adorned her head. Demeter, goddess of agriculture and harvest. She also had a daughter, Persephone, who was married to the god of death.

A carving of a man carrying a spear and dressed in a helmet and chest plate represented Ares, the god of war. In the other hand, Ares held a human head frozen with a scream on his lips, one eye gouged by an arrow. I walked away from the highly disturbing art and nearly bumped into the stature of a female warrior.

She had a sword on her back and a shield strapped to her arm. An owl was perched on her shoulder, and the likeliness of all the statues were so real, so carefully detailed, I thought the owl would fly out and attack me. It was Athena, goddess of wisdom and battle strategies.

Waving the torch around the other side of the room, I focused on the last six statues. Zeus, I recognized first with a bolt of lightning clutched in his fist and a halo of gold wrapped around his head. He was the bringer of storms and king of Olympus, husband to Hera. After him came Aphrodite, the Greek goddess of love and beauty. The statue showed her as a less appropriately attired lady, nothing but her bare, smooth skin was carved into the marble. A dove rested on her shoulder. Behind her came Hephaestus, a mighty beard covering the statue's round face and a war hammer at his side. Carved flames ran up and down a blade he held in his molded grip, eyes wide.

A halo crested his curly hair, and his hands gripped the reins on his sun chariot, carved from bedrock. Apollo stared back at me, pointing a figure in the direction of his sister's figure, Artemis, who was flanked by two carved dogs. Her bow and arrow were strapped to her back, and an image of the full moon was etched into the moon goddess' cloak. Artemis, or Diana, was the goddess of the hunt, wilderness, and chastity.

Poseidon, god of the sea, was portrayed rising out of a cresting wave, his torso bare, and a three-pronged staff in hand. Fish jumped out of the wave behind him, frozen in mid leap. A coral crown adorned his head. Soon came Hera, the goddess of marriage, birth, and queen of Olympus. Her statue was sitting atop a throne, a single rose grasped between her fingers. Her mouth was set in a scowl.

Last was Hades' image, a brooding being with a horned helmet placed on his head and a tall, wicked scythe in hand. He sat on a throne of human bones, which looked all too real to originally be a part of the statue. Cerberus stood guard beside him. He was the god of Death and ruler of the Underworld.

What puzzled me the most was how all these statues had gotten here, and how long they've stayed undiscovered. "Why do you show me these?" I asked Buddy, confused. He cocked his head, whimpering. "What is it?" the hairs on the back of my neck stood up. Instantly, I noticed a change in pressure, and I swear the temperature dropped by twenty degrees in the room. When I exhaled, my breath turned to icy coils of air in front of me.

There was something, or someone, in this room. "Bud…" I cautioned. He sniffed the air, fur bristling. "Who-who is it?" shaking, we backed up as far as the wall would allow. Holding the torch out as long as my arm could stretch, I peered into the distance beyond. Buddy growled. Oh, how I despised the dark. It played tricks on you, made you think you were seeing things that weren't actually there, and nothing was worse than fumbling around on the ground, blind and anticipating something to bump into.

A white, limp figure loomed into view as we took one step forward. It started off as a small, hazy blur in the distance, but continued to grow closer and clearer with every minute. I rubbed my eyes and blinked, hoping I was hallucinating. My heart dropped in my chest.

Oh, fuck. No no no no—
"Buddy—!"
The figure rushed forward, and a cold hand clamp down on my shoulder.

The torch blew out, and I screamed.

☾

Smoke and steam billowed through the door as Ken and Henry put out the fire. Holding his breath, Jacob raced inside with a pail of water sloshing in his hands. "Hurry, put it out! Henry, hand me another bucket!" Jacob coughed. Over at Thomas's workstation, his projects were being burnt to cinders. While putting a sword through the furnace to heat the metal into shape, Thomas's sleeve had caught fire when he leaned in too close. Flailing his arms, he had jerked his two-thousand eight-hundred-degree iron sword out of the furnace. It flew through the air and burned a hole through the wall.

Ripping his shirt off, much to Jacob's liking, Tommy slapped at the fire until Ken dumped a jug of water on his head. The blade melted into the wall almost instantly. The molten liquid dripped down onto the floor, lighting a tiny stray piece of dynamite afire. The crate next to it was engulfed in flames as Jacob pulled the nearest shield to his body—and jumped on top of the bomb.

The impact from the dynamite pushed Jacobs's body upwards with a puff of smoke, but he had managed to envelop the explosion with the inside of his celestial bronze shield.

"Ol' Betsy never lets me down." Jacob kissed the rim of his good luck shield and hung it back on the rack just as the rest of the dynamite crate fizzed and popped. Barging through the tables and people, Henry, Charlie, Isaac and Ethan threw the buckets of well water at the flames right when the nearest instructors took out their shields and jumped in front to guard Jacob's exposed back.

The explosion sent them flying backwards, but no one was seriously injured, and ninety-five percent of the crate was doused in water just before it had erupted. Flames licked the sides of the wall as on-goers rushed to put the stray fire out.

As the last of the soot-stained students exited the forges, Alpha Lockwood came storming down the stairs, panicked. "What happened? Is anyone hurt?" Halt asked, running his hands down Jacob's arms for any bumps or bruises.

"No, we're all fine. Just a rookie mistake. I think Ken forgot to take the crates down to the storage before class. And if it wasn't for one of my forgers, Jacob Vendéen, the back row would've been fried bacon." Kai Chen, an instructor and major player on the soccer squad, informed.

Halt smiled meekly. "Thank you for being quick and light on your feet, Jacob. Excellent thinking there."

Jacob replied, "Thank you, sir."

Halt turned to Ken next. "As for you, Kenneth, we have all reminded you a hundred times over to move the crates where they belong! It doesn't matter if they're a box of brownies or a pile of emeralds, I want them out and put away safely. We don't want any more accidents, is that clear?"

Ken gulped. "Crystal, sir."

"Good, because you will be on trash duty at the game tonight and I want every inch of that stadium garbage free after the tournament. Charlie and Kai, I need you to get your sections underway. Class is dismissed."

"Yes, Alpha." The teachers said in unison. Getting the leave to go, Jacob went back to his room after taking Thomas to the infirmary to get his burns checked. Glancing at the clock, Jacob dialed James on his cell.

"Hey, what's up?" James answered.

"I'm going to be a little over schedule, Jay. We had an accident in the forges. I'll leave within the next hour. And I was thinking, if I could scout along the coastline and up in Seattle, Washington, perhaps I can gather some info. I heard the President is up there for a conference meeting."

"Since we may or may not need all the help we can get, that's a considerable idea. I think you could verify your options and notify the government," There were many government organizations that knew of the other, magical world. Some government officials were also respected members of the High Council. "I can try to send a message through Halt's account later if need be to the Pentagon. Surely one of his connections can get in touch with the higher ups. Once we learn more about Nathaniel and how dangerous he is, national security could help us find him. I mean, they may not want to get involved in our business if it is going to hurt the mortal community, but we could try. Hey, do you remember your excuse?" James suggested.

"Sure do. And okay, but we should wait to involve the mortal head of state and their organization until we have Nekoda in our possession and a clear shot of what Nathaniel is planning. Um, James, if we actually do find Kody, how will she know to trust us?" There was a pause, then a flutter of static as James sighed into the phone.

"I hadn't thought about that until now. But in any circumstances, I think it's safe to say she'll follow suit. As long as she knows we aren't with Nathaniel, Nekoda ought to go. Besides, she lost her family, and what better place for her than at Camp Wolf?"

"But won't she'll be, I don't know…kind of lonely here?" Jacob questioned.

"BelAnne, Elizabeth, Meredith and Arya, Zoey and Natasha also live at Camp. They can help her adjust." James responded.

"I know, but I mean people her own age. Preferably girls. I mean, Cole and Mitch are great friends and all, but I think it'd be odd to be amongst so many boys, even with the older girls. What if she chooses not to stay?"

James laughed. "I'll persuade her, somehow. I will."

"Oh, James, always the charmer."

"Be quiet, shower up, and I'll talk to you later,"

"Bye." Jacob hung up and zipped open his small traveling bag. Sorting through the contents, he was pleased everything was in order. Changing out of his dirty clothes and throwing them in the hamper, Jacob washed off in the shower. Scrubbed fresh, he finished packing and went to gather his weapons down in the smoke-smelling forge.

He cleaned his shield and sawed out the edges of his well-loved war hammer. A solid crafted piece of mineral, Jacob's weapon of choice was studded with iron edges and a firm padded grip wrapped around the handle. Alex had once joked that if his father was Odin of Valhalla, Jacob could've been named Thor Junior.

Solemnly, he added, "I'd need to dye my hair bleach blonde and grow it out past my shoulders. And I don't think that style would fit me."

"Yeah, that style would not suit you at all. Me, on the other hand..." Alex chuckled, flipping his imaginary hair. Quietly exiting, Jacob made his way down to the storage room where a selection of gunpowder to food stocks to extra socks was piled high. Reaching the isle of explosives, Jacob counted the crates of quarry dynamite sticks. A total amount of twenty-three boxes with thirty sticks in each stood. So, Ken eventually *did* put the crate back.

While he was in storage, Jacob nabbed a packet of flares and an extra capsule of ambrosia—the drink of the gods. Or, to put it simply, the most powerful drug in the world. It healed you faster than any pharmaceutical medicine, and tasted sweeter than the warmest cup of cocoa. But too much down your throat at once and it made you all whack-a-doo. The nurses at Camp Wolf used it quite often to heal patients.

Since Skin-changers weren't exactly human, their senses were ten times stronger and physique twice as healthy. Shortest height for a full-grown Hybrid demigod was 5'7, and the tallest was about seven feet. An older student, Lucas Lopez, was 6'9 and was the tallest person at Camp yet. Jacob was only 5'9 and the rest of his friends were between 5'6 and 6'6. Compared to most mortals, that was pretty damn tall. If you were walking down the street in the middle of a crowded city, others would assume that you were on steroids or played for the NBA.

Shuffling out through the doors, Jacob slid the bolts across and locked the combination. Every supply agent at Camp Wolf, like Jacob and other smiths, were gained access to the storage room. If some idiot waltzed in and decided it'd be worthwhile to incinerate their friends with persay, a Nuke or other missiles, then Halt decided to keep the storage room locked up for safekeeping.

Slinging his pack over his shoulder, strapping shield to wrist, walkie-talkie and hammer to belt, Jacob went out in search of his furry friends.

The sun shone down across the courtyard as Jacob exited the main building. Scampering over, Nike and Orpha licked his face when he bent low. "Oh, yep. Slobber. Mhmph." Orpha was a laid back, gentle kind of gal. She was a pretty specimen, with her glossy black and brown fur. Her eyes were like melted chocolate, entirely mesmerizing. Nike was two years younger and rowdy as ever. He came to Orpha's shoulder. He was a dappled grey-coated wolf with a white streak across his chest, hence his name. Wiping off his cheek, the three made their way to the west gate. Only three guards were on charge instead of the usual four. Putting on his best winning smile, Jacob approached.

Hefting his spear, the closest guard asked the same question he did every time anyone wished to leave the premises. "What is your duty out beyond the west gate?"

Searching through his list of excuses in his head, Jacob answered. "I am meeting a small band of friends beyond the woods. We're going pack hunting."

"Pack hunting, eh?" the guard paused. "Marco, come here. Do you remember what Don or Ralph said over on the north gate?" Jacob's stomach flipped. No, *no*, not Marco! For some reason, Marco had a tendency to dislike people on and off. He was rather moody. And Jacob's gang was on his list of 'folks to annoy as much as possible'.

The guard to his right stirred and slipped off his helmet. Marco's shaggy hair hung in his face, briefly distracting Jacob from his cold eyes.

"Hmm, I can't recall. Besides, Halt said no one else is allowed to leave without his permission, remember? Or do you want to end up dead in a ditch, where Vincent's most likely at?"

Jacob stomped his foot, livid, refusing to ignore Marco's abrupt jab. "Don't you dare talk about Vin like that! He's not *dead*." Among the other campers, Vincent Lockwood had very few enemies. It just so happened one of them happened to be Marco Gomez, for reasons unknown.

Marco smirked, smacking his gum he was constantly chewing. "Really? How would you know?"

"I don't. But how would *you* know either? I don't see you doing anything to help the situation. All you're good for is sitting around on your ass all day. A parade of donkeys could've snuck past if you were on watch."

A tick started in Marco's jaw. "Actually, I *am* on watch, and I say you can't cross through the gate. So head back to your room and cry about it."

A second guard spoke up. "Hey, Gomez, not cool." he lowered his sword. "Why don't you turn around and head back, Vendéen."

Jacob snorted. Son of a— "Y'know what, fine." No point in trying to argue. Turning to his canine companions, Jacob urged them back to the fields. Crouching behind a huge spruce tree, he talked to Nike and Orpha. Every animal that has lived their lives at Camp Wolf could understand human speech and interactions. Since Jacob was part animal, he probably had about fifty distant cousins in the area.

"Nike, I need you to distract Marco. Go in on the left and rip his sword out of his grip if you can, or try and lead him away from his post. Orpha, sweetie, I need you to tackle the second

226

guard next to Marco. He's a bad man, he bullies. Got it? Just give me enough time so I can run a good half mile away. Meanwhile, I'll go in and wrestle the first guard. When I snap my fingers, run into position." They cocked their heads, tails wagging. For the next few minutes, everything was still. Waiting for the perfect moment, Jacob went up to bug the sentries again.

First guard raised his spear level with Jacob's chest. "I thought we said you couldn't pass."

"You did. But I'm asking once more. We *really* need to go through those gates. Do we have the right to leave?" Jacob tensed.

"No," Marco responded, raising his sword.

It was his fault for being an imbecile, Jacob thought. In the next moment, he snapped his fingers behind his back, and Nike pounced.

Growling at Marco, the young wolf placed his jaws over the victim's arm and yanked. Cursing, Marco dropped his gladius and tumbled to the ground. Nike grabbed the bejeweled weapon in his mouth and took off running. Marco held his arm at his side and chased after him. Orpha, being the bigger of the two wolves, knocked over the Second guard.

As the First guard stared in shock, Jacob took the chance and reared back to punch the guy in the jaw. He tripped the guard as he stumbled, cupping his face. "Sweet son of Poseidon! What the hell was that for?"

"Sorry, but we *really* need to pass through," he replied. Kicking off at full sprint, Jacob whistled. Snarling one last warning, Nike and Orpha rushed to his sides, panting. From behind, he heard the guards' shouting "Get Halt!" and "There should be a policy about being able to fend ourselves against these mutts!" and "I'll be damned, the grey one about ripped my hand off!"

Chuckling, Jacob veered off the rocky paths and through the trees. Halt was going to be furious when he hears about this, he was sure. James too. Jacob didn't know what else to do; the more time wasted here in Camp Wolf endangered Nekoda even more.

The guards would notify the Beta, Halt's second in command, and the Omegas to go in search.

Johnathen, Aaron, and Alex should be far from home by now, Jacob thought. They could still keep going if Jacob got caught, but the mission would still be compromised because of his insane idea. On foot, it would take a good many days to reach the Dworshack dam and at least a good to week to travel to Washington. The men would have driven or flown to their destinations, but that would have been too suspicious and too complicated. From the ground, they could check things upon closer inspection and not have to deal with checkpoints or traffic. Everything was hunky-dory.

It would definitely be easiest to have the whole nation on the lookout for Nekoda Alessandra Jones, and let every major police station know she's on the Unsolved Missing Children's list. Like everything else about their mission, it'd have to be kept secret for now. Her town, Weedsport, knew the tragedy that was bestowed upon her and her family. But nobody knew just who she really was, aside from an average high schooler.

Jacob would have to follow the river in order to find the dam, or travel along the highways to Ahsahka, Idaho up in Clearwater County. Either or, he and his traveling companions had some exploring to do.

Cinching the hood of his sweatshirt tighter, Jacob ran into the cold.

☾

Screaming louder than I thought possible, I spun around and stared into the eyes of someone very familiar. Too familiar. I was chilled to the bones. Something stirred within myself, and a little burst of flame spurted from my fingertips.

I kept screaming.

228

"Shush, child. No need for that yelling. But great job on summoning your power! Now, if you want to find your way home, follow me." I backed away from the ghost.

His figure still showed a patch of misty blood on his shirt, and a deep gash in his chest from his wounds he had sustained. It wasn't David, not exactly. But rather a see-through image of a former friend, a white and green haze surrounding himself.

"Okay, Buddy was immortal but you-you—*I saw you die!* How are you still here? Every person I thought dead seems to come back to life!" Shaking, I put a hand on Buddy's head, backing away a step.

"I am quite dead, Nekoda. In fact, I'm very dead. Merely a spirit of the old me. But I can't rest in peace without fulfilling my fate." He smiled. As weird as it seemed, I was genuinely happy and frightened of the return of David.

"Why did you come back for me? And what fate is that?" I clenched my hands into fists.

"Saving you, of course." Blunt.

"Saving me! What do you take me for, a moron? You and everyone else back with Nathaniel are pure evil, evil!" Sensing my frustration, Buddy barked at David, his fur standing on end.

"Listen, you don't understand. Just let me explain. I want to help, I *can* help." Sighing, David stood, or floated, before moving closer. "Back at our hideout, the night before you were brought here, I had a dream."

"So…?"

"So, it was about the Fates prophecy. The legend child. I knew what would happen before it ever did. You would meet Shadarr, begin training, and plan to escape. Nathaniel would learn where one of the talismans was at and seek more information. To this world, you are the most important and the most dangerous being there is. Many sacrifices will go towards helping the new era. People like myself would die for you, because of who you are. You are just starting to grasp a small sliver of who you're becoming and

229

what it brings. Nekoda, the gods gave me a task. It was a chance to redeem myself again and I took it."

"David—"

"In life, there is only a beginning, middle, and an end. Clara, Kyle, Buddy, and myself all gave our lives for you."

"No, no, no! My parents didn't die for me, they died because of Nathaniel and his loons! Buddy was just being a loyal, albeit dumb, friend, and—" I felt my throat close, and an aching started in my chest.

I paused. Clara and Kyle Jones died for me. For *me*. The *Book of Spells* was what Nathaniel wanted, so he could gather the other talismans. Because of myself, my whole entire existence, my parents were dead. They had to die to save their daughter, and maybe even the world.

"B-but you didn't have to follow through! You can change your fate!" Whimpering, I slumped to the floor, grasping my head in my hands.

"Kody, you can cheat death, but no one can ever change their destinies. Every single person was born for a reason, to live or die it makes no difference." David tried to reason.

"Yes, it does! Why couldn't you stay? At least tell me how you plan to save me!"

"By taking you where you were meant to be." He said it like I was supposed to know.

"And that's where?"

"Home."

"There's nothing left for me, my house was burned to the ground by Tony! There is no home for me anymore! What am I to do?" Buddy whined and nuzzled my hand.

"Camp Canis Lupis."

"Camp Wolf?"

"Right."

"Is that like a girl scout thing or something?"

David bit his white lip, thinking. I was now more confused than ever. After a brief silence, he answered.

"No, Camp Wolf is where all natural blood-born demigods stay. You know about Skin-changers and that you are one. Hybrid demigods such as yourself are considered myths, just like the gods." He glanced around at the statues. "That's where Hunter Skin-changers like James and many more have lived half their lives. We don't normally fit in well with humans, so we dwell where no mortals look. High up in mountains, deep underground, or even in the middle of the sea. Camp Wolf is your real home."

So that's what was inscripted on his shield in my dream of the battle: Camp Wolf. James and Will and Alex and the rest of those guys were from Camp Wolf!

"Wait, why's it called Camp Canis Lupis?" I asked.

"Simply because it is a Camp, or hideaway, for Hunters. Specifically, wolf Hybrid demigods or Were-Hunters. For thousands of years, wolves and other predators were sacred to the Olympians. It was decided that after the first race of what mortals call 'Werewolves', or Skin-changers, for any and all canine species be protected. Every student that trains at Camp Wolf is a Hunter of sorts when they Change, and can morph into their animal self. As Nathaniel would be a Hunter, he can Change into a special breed of wolf. Dire-wolf. The biggest and baddest of them all. Your other friends may change into other large predators, such as mountain wolves, lions, tigers, etcetera."

"Okay, okay, I think I'm getting it, but how is that my *home*?" Questioning everything was the best outcome.

"Your, hm, parents were supposed to have told you. But they had wanted to hide the real world from you. That is why they joined the Seekers a while back. They were young and naive, and they wanted to help make the world a safer place for *everyone*. Eventually they figured it was impossible to keep you hidden from everything else because around the age of twelve or fourteen, any human with immortal blood pumping through their veins are to be sent to one of the remaining global Camps until they complete their training. The process takes years to complete, and is kind of like going through college and becoming an adult, but twice as dangerous."

"Skin-changers, demigods, or whatever you want to call them. I'm one of you. But what makes me the prophecy child?" My head swam, and my brain felt like it was going to explode, whether from the massive headache or the slew of information I was struggling to process.

David chewed his ectoplasm fingernails. "Your parents were both demigods. Both had godly parents. Clara Keyes was the daughter of Poseidon, and Kyle Jones was the son of Athena. In reality, it's uncommon for demigods to have children together. Normally, a mortal would meet a Hybrid demigod and unbeknownst to them, they'd create another line of demigods. Very rarely do you see a full-blooded Skin-changer. That is where you come in, Kody."

Wow. Not something you hear every day. Then again, last time I checked, I wasn't the most wanted person by the most psychotic villain.

"How does that make me a child of fate?"

"Easy. Because you are the descendent of a great leader, and oh-so-powerful being by the name of Alessandra, daughter to Gaea."

"Woah, woah, woah, slow down here. You mean to say that a mythical earth goddess, the mother of Titans, is my great times a thousand grandmother?!" I gaped open mouthed at David."Are you sure?"

"Precisely. And her first daughter, Alessandra, was one of the most powerful demigods of all time. *She* controlled Fate, not the other way around."

From what I've known, Gaea was considered kind, caring, and an all-out nature-lover in some myths, (she was earth itself, after all), and in other tales a cruel, evil, overprotective literal dirt face. Yet it was always said that her twelve Titan babies and their twelve Olympian grandkids were her children. And before them, there was no live on earth until the first humans were created by Prometheus.

"I thought Pandora was one of the first female mortals placed on earth? Nor was it said that Gaea had a mortal daughter. You don't hear about Perseus or Helen of Troy being born human."

"It's, well, it is all too hard for words to explain, but in due time you'll come to understand." David replied.

"Riiiight," shaking the dust and specks of dirt off my clothes, I stood. "Well, if you should take me home, then do so. But my actual home first. I want to see what's left and figure out what this *Book of Spells* has to do with anything."

David fidgeted, refusing to meet my eyes. "No, you cannot go back home to New York. I'm sorry, but you must go to Camp Wolf before Nathaniel finds you."

"Nathaniel is after one of these talismans, correct? And my mother buried the *Book of Spells* in our backyard. That's what he was looking for when he invaded my house. So why don't we just get there first?" I concluded.

"Because many, many people are looking for you. There's a large bounty on your head in the Underworld and up on Olympus. Some of the gods want to kill or use you to win the present war, and others want to keep you safe from all harm. You are the balance between life and death for everyone."

"Hold up, before you get all 'I'm supposed to save the world' crap, tell me why and how these talismans are important?"

"There are Keepers, families who pass down the knowledge of the talismans for generations. The Jones' family is one of four Keepers in the world. If Clara didn't decide to hide it, you would've possessed the *Book of Spells*, which is exactly what it is. If in the wrong hands, the dead could be raised, the Titans could walk the earth again, or Olympus would be destroyed. Anything is possible." David glanced around and lowered his voice, as if expecting listening ears within the dank passageways.

"There are the other three remaining talismans: Krane de Royce's sword of Death, which was a gift from Zeus to help win The Great Battle of seven hundred years. The Amulet of Twelve, which grants to the wearer the power of all immortal elements. And Aegis, a special shield also gifted to Krane de Royce," he paused, running a hazy finger down one of the statue's arms. "There is one other special talisman, but it's considered more as a tool than a real object of power. The Lockwood compass is a magical object that guides a Keeper to the other talismans. Krane's Dragon, Balios, is said to guard the Tomb of Fire, a sacred battleground burial site where the talismans rest. Balios was believed to be one of the first Dragons alive, but that was many years ago. All this time passed, and no one can say where the Tomb of Fire is located. Maybe it's lost forever, but who knows?" he said.

History 101 with David sure was interestingly absurd.

"Yeahhh, I'm still not following. Repeat all that you just said, please. Whatever it was." I groaned, rubbing my dry eyes.

"Look, James can tell you all about it when you get to Camp Wolf. But we better get moving, and fast. We don't want Nathaniel getting hold of that Book!" Mumbling, David turned around and started to float away down the dark hallway. With nothing else to do, I scampered after him. My hand still ablaze, we focused on the light.

"Hey, I'm becoming a full-blown Avatar! I could join the Fire Nation!" I muttered to myself.

David must've overheard for he asked, "The what and the who?"

I shook my head. "Man, you need to get out more."

"I apologize, I haven't had much mortal experiences lately so I wouldn't know. Just follow me, please."

"Of course." I rolled my eyes and sniffed. "Buddy, home!" Pricking up his ears, he raced off again.

"I hope he knows what he's doing." David worried.

234

"Obviously, he's a Hellhound!" Laughing, we followed suit.

Chapter XII: Rivals, Mud, and Flying Balls

Halt Lockwood shuffled through files on his desk, thinking hard.

"Alpha, there has been a breach on the west gate. Three guards wounded, sir." A Beta stuck his head through the door after knocking.

"Report, Shane." Halt replied, eyebrows raised.

"Marco Sanchez is bleeding from various wounds to the hands and arms, Samuel Allen has a fractured collarbone and many claw marks, though none too fatal, and Frank Morris has one bruised rib and a swollen jaw."

"Interesting," he said tersely. "How did this happen?"

"A student by the name of Jacob Vendéen and his two wolves were trying to pass through the gate. Marco got in the way and apparently Jacob was really was desperate to leave." Shane said in a monotone. Halt scowled. He only saw Jacob but a few hours ago. A good student and a loyal friend to Vincent, but he wasn't one to start trouble.

"Did he perhaps say why?" Halt puzzled.

"Uh, yessir. Jacob was to meet Johnathen Dogo, Aaron Smith, Alex Rayn and Will Orchild outside to go pack hunting. Aaron had noted that after him, two more folks were to come along. Five demigods in total. They thought you knew."

"Johnathen, Jacob, Aaron and Alex…who else?"

"Will Orchid."

"And William. Unbelievable! I told the guards not to let anyone through, even if it were for a few hours. Any of the others pass that same gate?" He frowned.

"No, Alpha. Johnathen and Aaron both went to the north gate, Alex to the east gate, and Will down to the south gate."

"And Jacob to the west gate." Halt finished, frustrated. "If they were all supposed to go pack hunting, why'd they split up and go at separate times and to separate gates?"

"We don't know, Alpha." replied Shane.

"You better find out; those gates are officially closed at sundown and open at sunrise! I don't want to spend my Sunday searching for five corpses, understand?" Halt ordered, slamming a fist on his desktop. "Assign a small force of elite Warriors and get out there!"

Shane rushed out the door just as Dior entered. Gracefully, she dropped a thin, rolled-up document by his feet. Pawing at the note, Halt picked it up and unfolded the paper. It was a short but fairly formative note.

We as a species only have one hope left, and she will bring us together, for better or for worse. If we do not take action soon, our worlds will collide and Olympus will crumble. I urge you to help us by choosing sides and taking chances. They need us, as we called out to them in the most desperate of times so that we may flourish. Nothing will matter if we don't win these battles. Prayers and wisdom will not suffice, but the one person that matters most. She will lead all to victory, and only she can fight for us. Before the world falls, you must think but one thing; the end is only the beginning. And before you make a rash decision about cancelling future quests, think of the good your students can bring to the world.

"Bloody hell. Dior, what?" Halt was alarmed. "Who is this, and what do they mean? *She*, who's she?" he rubbed his forehead, flustered. "I—what battles?" Halt voiced out loud to the she-wolf.

"Are my kids not telling me something? Is this why they left?" His stomach dropped. "If something happens to them…" A moment later, a piercing pain ripped through his head. Crying out, he slumped back in his chair, trembling.

"Vin. Vincent. My son. Oh, the gods curse us all! Vincent went after the talismans! I should've known, Camrice was a Keeper and he was supposed to go in place of his son! Why now, why? Olympus is falling, and the Olympians are preparing for war. G-gathering f-forces." Halt sobbed hysterically. "I-I see what is coming…Gaea and Hades…w-working together…Vincent shouldn't have gone! Too dangerous, too dangerous, too dangerous. No, no, no, no what has he done!" Sweeping his files and utensils and books clattering to the floor, Halt grabbed his head in his hands and wept. Dior whined, flattening her ears.

A swelling emotion overcame him once again, and he knew what was coming. A wave of pain crested through him. Halt cried out, "I don't want to see, please, I can't take much more! Please, I can't." his voice grew hoarse. Moments before Halt Lockwood's eyes rolled up in his head and he blacked out, he whispered one last thing. Dior cocked her head, whining, pawing at her master's hand.

"Gods save us, every last one…"

☾

James hustled, tightening his straps and tying laces. In approximately twenty minutes and six seconds, the NSL tournament would begin. With nineteen players on the Blue team and seventeen players with two absent on the Red team, the game would be fascinating enough to watch.

James was glad that Coach Taylor had chosen him, Kai, Trevor, Lou, Curtis, and Richey to play for the Blue team. Some of the best players were on James' team, but Red team had Martin, Francisco, Lance, Dean, and Damon, who counted as three players for his size and strength. James was excited about Damon Scott

238

being on the other side, it gave him a chance to make a fool out of his enemy. James smiled to himself.

There were six different soccer teams for each age group. The team colors were the same for both the younger and older groups. Greeks are orange, red Romans, purple Spartans, and blue Trojans.

"Line up, kiddos! Get in position and give me twenty-five jumping jacks! Then I need you to do a few suicide runs from the six-yard line to the eighteenth yard line, six to mid-field, six to the opposite goalie box and back." Taylor blew his whistle.

Groans escaped from the soccer stars as James and Kai led stretches and counted with each jumping jack. "One two three four, two two three four, three two three four, four two three…" And so on. The teams paced themselves in conditioning and shook out their muscles, pumping up.

"How ya feeling man?" Trevor jogged over.

"Uh, honestly? Like I'm about to puke." James laughed.

"It's alright, just got pre-game jitters." He patted his friend's shoulder.

"Yeah, something like that." James sighed back.

Glancing over at the small stands of demigods, he looked for Cole and Mitchell. He spotted them up on the top step of a bleacher, waving and giving the thumbs-up. James waved back.

The referees signaled both teams over to line up. "Lift one foot up, front spikes are illegal, boys." Referee Wyatt insisted. "All clear, pat your shin guards." All players did as told. "Great, captains up here for the coin toss." James and Kai ran over just as Lance and Damon did. "Introduce one another."

Reluctantly, James shook hands with Damon, squeezing his hand a little too hard before letting go. "James," he said.

"Damon." They shook hands with the opposite partner.

"Lance."

"James."

Kai greeted them next.

"So, Trojans. Heads or tails?" asked Wyatt.

239

"Tails!" Kai decided. Wyatt flipped the quarter. Gazing down at the grass, he announced, "It's heads. Okay, Romans, which field do you want to start on?"

Lance nudged Damon, "We'd like to start the first half on the right side."

"Okay, you can run back and inform your coaches. Good luck, players." Wyatt walked off to join referee Kevin on the sidelines.

Coach Taylor blew the whistle. "Alright, everybody circle up! I'm going to start with line up for defense. James Dawn, you're right defense. Kai Chen, left defense. Freddy, you'll play right forward and Ryan will be left. Oh, I need a left and right mid, that's going to be Roger and Lucas, got it? Curtis Long will be sweeper," Taylor motioned around. "And Richey in the goal. Everyone else will sub in for starters, but I want you all to play long and hard. I won't sub as much for the first half than for the second. We have another game after this so don't sell yourself short. Okay, hands in!" All nineteen hands piled on top of each other. "Count of three, Thundering Trojans. One, two, three...THUNDERING TROJANS!" Nineteen Hybrid demigods and their coach shouted. Over on the opposite field, the red team yelled out equally loud, "RAVING ROMANS!"

The gathering of Camp Wolf cheered. "Play hard tonight!" Taylor slipped off his baseball cap. Taking a deep breath in, James jogged out to the right side of the field and stood a few feet in front of the eighteenth line.

"Trojans get the first ball!" The ref held up the soccer ball with one hand in the center circle of the field. In front of him, Freddy and Ryan took stance near the left and right outsides of the field, while Kai took the position opposite James on the left. Roger and Lucas went up into the half center circle, ready to take the ball once dropped. Richey went into the goal as Curtis paced in front of them, up in the middle section of their side. The other players on the Roman team took their places, and Kevin blew the whistle, tense as the ball thudded to the hard ground.

There was the thud of cleat on leather, and in a blur, Lucas had hold of the black and white ball between his feet. He veered left with Roger at his side. Freddy and Ryan, James, Kai and Curtis moved forward. Zigzagging across the field, Lucas passed to Roger, twisting around Dean to avoid getting shoved to the ground by Payton as Damon rushed up. "Come on boys! Muscle!" Roman's head coach, Billy, shouts. Freddy moves in from the half line and takes the ball from Roger. Roger gets in front of another player, blocking him as they ball chase. Freddy sprints towards the goal and smashes the ball past Fran, veering by Ryan's legs.

Dribbling the ball, Martin, defense on the red team, moves to kick the ball away from Ryan. He swings his foot forward to collide with Ryan's shin guard. Grunting, Ryan turns and skips the ball backwards. Kai runs up to the half-line just as Payton intercepts the roll. Gliding across the field towards Richey and the goal, Payton struggles past Curtis and slams the ball into the corner of the net.

"Go, you got this!" James yells. Richey leaps up and barely catches the ball. Rushing forward, he cherry-bombs the ball right to James. James gets into position and head butts the ball as it soars down. Freddy moves up field as Damon charges back. As James rushes up past Damon, he swings at his ankles and swishes the ball in between them, towards the middle. Cursing, Damon shoulders past him. Curtis and Kai both run up, and the other players are moving back to their goals.

"Ryan! Get open!" Curtis calls before smashing the ball to him. Sweat beading his neck, he runs to snatch the ball. Fran and Dean double-team him and all three come crashing down. As Fran falls, his arm lands on the ball and Kai sprints to help Ryan stand. Wyatt tweets the whistle, announcing, "Hand ball! Trojans get throw in!"

Lucas runs up to pick the ball from the ground. "I got this one. Roger and Ryan, be sure to get this." he says. Holding the ball above his head, Lucas waits for the call. Referee Kevin blows the whistle and Lucas leans his body forward, chucking the ball to where Roger is guarding Martin.

The students in the stands are shouting and making cat-calls, whistling and jumping in their seats. Martin lunges past Roger as he steals the soccer ball. Kai sees it and sprints at him, plowing through. They both roll to the ground and Curtis swoops in, running up to the center circle as he motions after James.

Shouldering Damon in the side, James rushes up with Damon on his heels. A red player, Cory, sneaks up and lunges for the ball. In a tangle of legs and arms, James manages to get the ball away from them. Cory growls and stands up only to get knocked down by James as he bunts the ball toward Freddy. Freddy and Ben grapple for it and he gets an elbow to the gut as Damon barrels past. Breathing hard, James resists the urge to tackle Damon. Payton and Dean come in from behind as does Lucas and Roger, Ryan standing at the ready. "Freddy, back to Curtis!" he shouts.

Grunting, Ben dribbles the ball and weaves around Roger and Lucas, almost taking out Ryan as he stops him in his path. Kai comes speeding and zooms past Ben, smashing the ball from his possession. Racing along with Ryan at his side, they make their way through Fran and Dean and then Payton interferes.

Practically tripping Ryan, Payton steals the ball and suddenly, Freddy and Roger are there. James moves up with Kai when their teammates get closer to the goal. Freddy kicks it back to Lucas, and Lucas zips past Fran with Martin sprinting closer. Stopping abruptly, Lucas passes the white and black ball halfway across the field to Freddy. Freddy pushes it back to James and he charges the ball across the half field, up towards Ryan. Payton and Dean block him, and the ball goes through their legs and to Freddy's feet. Damon smashes into James, pain shooting up his body as they both tumble to the ground. Ben paces backwards to the goal, ready to help block the shot for Lance.

With power, James lunges past Freddy as he pulls himself up and shoots the ball as fast and hard as he can towards the net. Lance stands in the goalie box and swerves to catch the ball, landing on his side. Mud splatters from the cleats digging into the sloppy grass. As James jogs back to his position, he watches as the soccer ball narrowly misses Lance's fingers and it bounces up and through the net when it lands.

From the far side of the field Kai, Ryan and Lucas cheer as Roger and Freddy go to high-five James. Curtis whoops and Richey holds up one finger on his right hand, and zero fingers on the other. "One to zero! Nice work, James!" he smiles.

"Keep it up!" Taylor shouts. James can hear Cole and Mitchell hollering from the crowd.

From the sidelines, a referee flips down a number card on the stand. Now the score is 1-0 Trojans. James, Kai, Richey, Curtis, Ryan and Roger, Lucas and Freddy walk back into position.

"Red ball!" Kevin calls. On the Roman's side, Damon, Dean, Martin, Payton, Fran and Cory and Sam line back up as well. Lucas and Roger go to face Dean and Payton in the center for another kickoff. Kevin blows the whistle as Wyatt follows the players. Cautiously, Dean moves forward and taps the ball behind him to Sam. Sam dribbles the ball a few feet as Roger lunges forward and Lucas motions for Ryan and Freddy to move back if necessary.

Roger whiffs the ball and Sam elbows past, Lucas in tow. Kai runs up to help Lucas and together they manage to take the ball and move it a quarter of the way down their field before Fran zooms by and skirts the ball away. Dean paces back as Damon toes the ball down the field. Sprinting to intercept it, James and Freddy crash into Damon.

The air is sucked from James' lungs as Damon's knee lands squarely on his gut. As he rolls away, James shoves him off and Freddy stumbles to his feet and up the trampled length of grass. The ball goes flying ten feet in the air and pops back to earth by Curtis. Seizing the moment, Curtis pushes past Sam and kicks the ball at Lucas. It ricocheted off his and Roger's shin guards like a pinball and flies to Ryan.

Maneuvering past Fran to the near center of the field, Freddy gets open as Ryan launches the ball across the field for him to headbutt it. Next, Roger jumps back to cover Freddy again. Meanwhile, Dean and Saml ball chase. Cory is standing by Curtis, giving each other dirty looks. Freddy runs up and dodges countless ankle kicks and jumps over Sam's foot as he slips and falls in the mud.

Arms pumping, Payton runs right next to Fred, arms flailing as he leans into him. Finally, Payton knocks the ball out toward the goal for Lance to throw out. Freddy manages to trip and come crashing down with Payton as Martin, on the opposite side, effortlessly captures the ball from Lance's throw.

Fran gets in front of Ryan to hold him off from Martin. Kai collides with Martin and Curtis blasts the ball down to the center line to Freddy, James, and Damon. James moves to intercept, kicking and grunting. Damon stares down James, his face scrunched up in concentration.

In an instant, Damon stomps on James's toes while in the process of getting the soccer ball, elbowing James' nose as he bends down to cup his foot. His head snaps back and within seconds, Damon leaves him bruised and bleeding on the hard ground. He rushes to Richey, ready to powerhouse him down with the leather sphere of death.

Blood starts gushing from James' throbbing nose before a whistle tweets. "Time out! Player down! Everyone, take a knee!" Wyatt shouts as Taylor rushes out to inspect James.

"Crap, crap, crap, crap." James mutters. His face and foot simultaneously throb. Coach Taylor hands him a few napkins as he tells him to pinch his nose to slow the bleeding.

"Let me check your foot out, I saw you got pretty rough out there." The referees walk over and Taylor holds James's leg out as Kevin slides off his socks and cleat. Grimacing, Taylor mumbles, "Either Damon has steel implants in the soles of his shoes or you really pissed him off."

"I know, but it wasn't—" James stops as Kevin interrupts.

"Well, I don't think it's broken. Possibly fractured, but that's a hella lot of swelling. Purple your favorite color? Because that's what it is now. We should get some ice on that." Turning to the benches, he calls for Trevor to bring over a bag of ice.

"Hold this on your foot until you can rest easy in the infirmary." Wyatt informs.

"In the meantime, Trevor and Lou can walk you down." Taylor says. Waving them over, Trevor slips under one arm while Lou takes the other. From the crowd, students, instructors, teachers, and friends cheer and clap as James is pulled to his feet and starts limping back to the main building. James mumbles his statement as he's pushed along. "It wasn't an accident." He whispers.

A breeze ruffles his dirty hair and he glances backwards. Damon narrows his eyes and makes a rude gesture with his hand when he notices him staring. Richey is silently having a conversation with Kai and the others while Taylor is choosing Chris to sub in for James. Suddenly, Cole and Mitchell are upon him like buzzing flies having pushed their way through the bleachers.

"Dude, you alright?"

"That was a nasty hit!"

"Why didn't you say something?"

"Can I see?"

Trevor chuckles. "Guys, I think you should hold off on the questions."

"Yeah, we'll talk in the infirmary where BelAnne will fix me up." James breathed, sore.

"You can join us." Lou said, holding the napkin up to James face with his other hand.

"Okay, fine." Cole trots along with Mitchell. "But later we'll plot our revenge against Damon Scott."

"Wait, do you think he hurt James on purpose?" Lou asks. Trevor gives his friend a droll stare.

245

"The man has a freaking hate list! He seems to wake up on the wrong side of the bed every single day. Are you blind? James is Damon's worst nemesis."

"Oh, sorry. Stupid question of the day." Lou responds. "Whatever, man. I'm just pissed because I didn't even get to play one half!" James grumbles. *Damn*, he thought, *why does Damon always have to ruin everything?*

"At least you made one goal." Mitchell says, adjusting his hat.

"Yeah, but we have another game afterwards and Damon is a lying, cheating', rough and tumble ass!" James chews his lip.

"Relax, Lou and I can still play and Damon will tire out eventually. At least we're ahead by one point." Trevor wipes sweat from his brow. "Anyway, I heard it's supposed to rain later tonight. Around seven-ish, I think."

"That'd be during the beginning of game two. We'd have to reschedule for tomorrow if it's storming real bad." Lou assumes.

Cole takes his sports glasses off and places them in his pocket as he talks. "Well, we could always rat out Damon to the coaches."

"They wouldn't listen. Besides, it's all done and over with. Once I'm healed, I'll find Damon and kick his ass." James grins.

"Sure. Hey, you two grab the doors." Trevor tells the guards at the entrance. The doors creak open as all five enter the hallways of Camp Wolf and stand at the top of the stairway.

Mitchell scratches his head. "Shoot, I forgot we have to go downstairs to get to the infirmary." They all groan, James the loudest. "Just scoot down on your butt. And remind me, why is the Camp designed this way?" Mitchell replies.

"Because if we were attacked from above, it'd be safer to care for the wounded in an underground bunker and easier to keep supplies safe in storage." Lou acknowledged, all history and battle strategy buff.

"Thanks nerd, but couldn't Halt have installed an elevator at least? It's the twenty-first century." he snorts.

246

"Because the Council folk are crabby old people in robes who can't ever make any decisions." Cole laughs.

"Hey, not all." Trevor says, a warning in his voice. James takes the stairs one step at a time, begging not to be seen. For all the world, it seemed as if he was a dog dragging his butt across the carpet.

"Almost there." Mitchell hops down the last flight. Holding the door open for Trevor, Lou, and James to pass through first, Mitchell and Cole enter last. Rows of hospital beds and dividers line the walls. Stands of medical equipment and silver trays stand in a corner by a water fountain. Laying James down on one of the closest beds, Cole grabs the phone off the wall and dials the number to the girl's private quarters.

It rings a few times before Arya answers. "Hello, Arya here. What's the problem?"

"Uh, it's Cole Burnett, Mitchell Garrett, Trevor Payne, Lou Dyke, and James Dawn. We think James's foot is broken, and his nose got whacked pretty hard, too. It's all swollen and gross." James could hear Arya whispering something to someone else. In the background, the the shuffle of papers and voices sound.

"I knew this would happen!" Natasha exclaims.

"Boys, always so troubled." Zoey sighs.

"Did you run into the goal posts again?" asks Elizabeth.

"Ooh, are Johnathen or Aaron there?" Meredith pipes up.

"Okay, we're coming down. Be there soon!" BelAnne squeaks into the phone. Cole hangs up.

Trevor and Lou sit down on a few of the nearby beds and relax their sore feet, sliding off stinky socks and sweaty shin guards. Mitchell turns on his phone and begins rapidly texting somebody. Cole moves over to sit by Mitchell.

Shifting into a more comfortable position, James punches the pillow on his bed. This was going to be one hell of a night.

☾

Nathaniel paced the den, staring daggers at Shadarr. The beast bares his teeth in a snarl. A large net was thrown over his body to prevent further movement after the paralysis spell wore off. After hours of searching the premises through and through, Nathaniel decided to pause the search. By now, Nekoda could be on a bus to Detroit. Or lost in a cave. Or taken by a pack of wild centaurs. Eaten by one of Gaea's minions. Attacked by a Cyclops. There were many options.

Down the halls and up the stairs Nathaniel had sent Tony, Bruce, Ezekial, and Luke to gather weapons and clothing and to turn on Nekoda's tracking device.

While she was unconscious on the way to his base, Nathaniel had implanted a chip the size of a bead into her wrist while the sleeping drug worked its way through her bloodstream. Nekoda, of course, could not see said chip.

When they powered on the chip, they would be able to look at a mapping device, like a Google Maps of sorts, and determine her location. Ezekial was the tech whiz; if anything, he was the one to work all the gadgets and didgeridoo. He was certain that she would be heading in one direction, and that was back home in Weedsport, New York. Nathaniel had to get the *Book of Spells* before anyone else, and the girl, too. They would travel to her house faster than she could on foot and ambush her there while gathering the talisman. It was like hitting two birds with one stone.

There was just one problem; her friends and her town can't know she's still alive.

It would ruin everything he's—*they've*—worked for.

Unless, somehow, they interfere on her journey to home and take her before she got to Weedsport. That way, two of his soldiers could search the backyard and dig up the Book—if it was still there. Meanwhile, Nathaniel could take Nekoda Jones down to pay his father a visit. But what would they do with Shadarr? Someone would have to fill up that hole he created before leaving. They couldn't risk being gone long, not while Shadarr was still breathing.

248

"Quid factures es modo?" What are you going to do now?
Shadarr asked. Nathaniel glanced down at his feet and pulled off
his sword belt. His blade shone in the dim torchlight.

"Quid dicam vobis?" He replied. Why should I tell you?
The Dragon narrowed his eyes. *"Quid est? Tu non vis effundet
Deus absconsa tua? Afraid I'll call it folly?"* What? You don't
want to spill your secrets? Afraid I'll call it folly?" he waited. *"Oh,
that's right. Et non est ulla affectus! Tu habent sensus ad motus
affectionum humanarum referuntur! Quod suus cur non dubitant,
et occidit David!"* Oh, that's right. You don't have any feelings!
You have no sense of the human emotions! That's why you didn't
hesitate to murder David!

Shadarr snorted, growing tired and furious.
"Can it, lizard breath! All I'll say is that you'll be seeing your old
friend very soon." Nathaniel hissed. And with that, he swept out of
the room, cloak and all.

☾

Tapping the screen, a red dot blinked to life. It was moving very
slowly, but it was *her* all right. Blinking in and out of existence.
Next to it was a green dot. Someone else was with her, and by his
luck, the Hellhound. Nathaniel had felt the slight change in the
atmosphere when Buddy was sent back to the overworld; his chest
tightened, and the hairs on the back of his neck rose. He knew
someone or something had been released past the gates of the
Underworld. But knowing his father's pet, Cerberus, he was great
friends with the Hellhound. Buddy had passed GO a long time ago
in the journey of life.

Ezekial was sitting in front of a wall of screens, pushing
buttons and sliding images on the glass. A green glow illuminated
his face. On one computer screen was a video of Mt. Saint Helens
in Washington. Another was of the streets of Nekoda's hometown.
Next to that was camera footage of the White House and the
Pentagon, and Area 51. The screen next to it flashed pictures of

Mt. Olympus, the sun shining above the invisible floating city above the clouds. And the screen at the far end came from a single hidden camera down in the Underworld. Hades' palace stood dark and gloomy behind the fields of Asphodel and between the River Styx and a treacherous cavern, spirits haunting to and fro, wandering. Lastly, there were satellite shots of the earth, storms raging around half the world.

"Tony, can you give me details on what I'm seeing here?" Nathaniel cleared his throat.

"Yes, sir. Recently, your father has received two messengers. One was a cloud nymph from Zeus and the other was one of Medusa's Gorgans, Kellum. Apparently, Kronos was rallying his armies up near Greece. He's camping on an island in the Mediterranean Sea. And as you can tell, your dad's siblings are growing anxious, waiting for Gaea and the other gods to strike back and unleash her Titan children." Tony shivered.

"Interesting. And what about our friend here, the gal who just recently ran away. Where is she?" he asked.

Bruce fidgeted beside Tony. Nathaniel stared him down. "Well, you see…we don't exactly know. The screen flashes and blacks out every once in a while, and her blip disappears to show up a minute later in a new position, farther away than last time."

"Oh?" Nathaniel raised his eyebrows. "How are we supposed to find her if her tracker won't even work properly? I thought we were going to find the talisman first?" Luke asked.

"We will, don't fret. I just have my doubts about Nekoda. She cannot go over to *them*." Nathaniel chewed his lip and glanced at Ezekial. "Can we tell if others interact with her?"

"Hmm, not really, sir. But supposedly she's around the area still. Somewhere, but *where*?"

"I wouldn't know. And Shadarr won't talk, nor do I want to bother with him anymore. Once we have Nekoda Jones in our hands again, we'll hold off on delivering her straight to my father. Maybe. No questions asked." He spoke.

250

"I suppose that's the best option, but what about the *Book of Spells*?" said Tony.

"Don't worry, my father won't get ahold of it, not before I get a peek. There's no way I'm handing him over one of the most powerful objects in the universe so quickly. Hades can deal with the girl if he wants. He raised and trained me to be who I am, why not Kody?" Nathaniel smirked.

From under his breath, Ezekial whispered, "What a nightmare that must've been."

"Because she's the most stubborn human being I've ever met." Luke answered.

"But she isn't human! She's a Skin-changer like the rest of us!" Tony stated.

"Yes, yes. We know that. But even against the might of a god, I doubt she'll listen. Nekoda has already been put through enough, there's absolutely no way it'll work," Luke responded.

"Still, it's worth a shot. And if he dares do anything to upset me again, he'll regret it." Nathaniel sneered. "So, let's get going. We should be in New York within a few days. Any of you who choose to stay behind with the dinosaur, fine by me. But listen close; any who want to cross my path again will end up like David."

Four heads glumly nodded.

Chapter XIII: Invisible Robber at Millennium Park

"Hey, Logan! What are you doing?" Anthony called down the hall. Logan's bedroom door was cracked open. Her voice carried down the hall back to her brother.

"I'm skyping Ashlyn from I.S.U. C'mere, she wants to see her baby bro!"

Ashlyn, now twenty, was spending her time at Indiana State University and studying to become a nurse like her mother. The last time Logan had seen her sister was early in the summer before she had to go back to school. Anthony came rushing in and flopped on her bed, a stick of beef jerky in hand. Logan wrinkled her nose.

"Eww, do you have to eat that stuff in *my* room?" She asked.

"Yesh," Anthony talked through a mouthful.

"He's a nimrod, always will be." Ashlyn spoke on the other side.

Logan laughed. "So, how're things with you and Danny boy?"

Ashlyn rolled her eyes. "Pfft, he spends most of his time looking at other girls than me. Last night I got a message from him saying 'Babe, I hate to break it to you. But I've been seeing other women. I'm sorry Mol. It's not you, it's me.' And then; "FWD: Yeah Jack, I know. Just dumped Molly, lmao. The plan is to date Ash until Kate returns from Rio de Janeiro. The night before the dance, I'll break up with Ash to go out with Kate. She's been getting on my nerves lately. I can't wait to get down with Kate.' Afterwards, I received another message; 'Sent to wrong number, oops.' Ugh! So selfish!" Ashlyn threw up her hands in despair, imitating a male's deep voice.

"Aww, I'm sorry Ash. I hope you broke his heart when you dumped his ass." Anthony chewed on a bit of jerky.

"Oh, I dumped him first and foremost. Earlier when we walked into the cafeteria I had went off to the bathroom and when I returned, he was sitting by some busty girl in a mini skirt. He rubbed her knee and continued to talk to her in a hushed tone. Mini Skirt looked past him and asked: 'Do you know her? That freshie keeps staring.' I picked up the nearest lunch tray and then…WHAM-O! Chucked it right in his face. 'Next time you decide to cheat on me, remember to keep your little plans quiet before sending the message to a Hendrix, you dick!" Ashlyn acted out.

Logan gasped. "What? Oh, he's such a—" She stopped herself. "Uh, never mind. I bet he's feeling pretty bad about himself now."

Anthony chuckled. "Yeah, cousin Ethel sent a video to me. It went viral! Moronic jock gets showed up by ex!"

"Bro, don't remind me. It was fun at first to see him dripping with garlic sauce on his head. Now, I'm single." Ashlyn sniffed. Her younger sister shot her older brother a look.

"It's okay, sis. There's plenty of fish in the sea." said Logan.

"I guess so. Anyway, I got to go soon. The new premiere of *Americans Vs Canadians* is on! Love y'all, bye!" Waving at the screen, Ashlyn logged off and powered down her tablet. Logan pushed Anthony off her bed and wiped the crumbs off the purple covers.

"Okay, out! Mom said to feed the cat before she gets home. Dad is at a conference, so you have to work the grill again if we want steak tonight."

Anthony crossed his arms. "And what do you have to do?"

"Sit here and be awesome," Logan snorted and shut the door as he grumbled away. Sliding open her phone, Logan noticed she had one missed called from Maggie Landrus. A crackling and buzzing sound emanated from the phone's speakers until Maggie's voice spoke on the other end.

"Hello?"

"Hey girl, what's up? I saw you tried calling."

"Yep, I did. I was wondering, are you free to hang tonight?"

Logan glanced around at her empty, messy room. "Sure. It's a Saturday night after all! And I have nothing better to do here aside from bugging Ant."

"Great! Pack your bags and head on over." Maggie said.

"I'll tell my parents, they won't care. Do I need to bring anything specific?"

She heard movement and the sound of a door shutting in the background. "Actually, yes. Bring a heavy-duty flashlight and a shovel. Wear some old shoes and bring a dark ski mask or hat."

"What are we doing, grave robbing my great-great-grandpa?"

"Eh, something like that..."

"You sound unsure."

"Just get over here, stat!"

"Fine, but we better not be doing anything illegal. I'm too young to go to a juvenile detention facility." Logan warned and ended the conversation.

Shuffling around in her dad's shed minutes later, Logan spotted an old shovel about three feet long with a wide scoop.

Strapping a chunky flashlight to her belt and her phone in her jean pocket, she shoved the shovel across her back in an old softball bag. Logan carried an extra change of clothes, her toothbrush, and hairbrush in a shopping bag. Anthony called their parents to let them know she was spending the night at the Landrus's before pushing her outside on the porch, bags in hand. Sending a text to Maggie, Logan stumbled to her bike parked outside the garage and slowly pedaled around the neighborhood.

Maggie was waiting for her when she reached the front door. Helping drag the bags inside, Maggie locked the door to her room when they entered, tossing the heavy bags onto the floor.

"So, what's this big plan of yours, exactly?" Logan questioned. Maggie twisted a lock of red hair between her fingers nervously. "Spit it out, girl."

"Okay, okay. But you cannot tell anybody! I mean it!" Maggie burst.

"Whatever, I won't. Just spill."

Maggie seemed to relax a bit. "At midnight, when the rest of household is asleep, we'll sneak out and head over to Nekoda's house."

"What?! Why do we need to visit a crime scene? We can't go to Kody's house, the whole place is under investigation! The police are trying to gather evidence for a possible homicide case!" Logan practically shouted.

"Shh! What I'm trying to say is, why kill—" Maggie slowed as her friend flinched. "Why take the lives of the parent's, if they're the ones who could pay the ransom? Most obvious reasons people kidnap: because they want moo-la. And lots of it. Kody was probably just one in a million of getting abducted in a small town. And whoever took her probably just wants the cash and nothing to do with the child. Am I getting through to you?"

"I understand that, but her abductees didn't leave a ransom note or notify the closest family, nothing of the sort. So how could we know if they'll make a trade? Besides, if you leave billions of dollars left in the spot they tell you to go, you won't find Kody. Only an empty wallet. It's happened before with other unsolved cases." Logan explained.

"Right, so Nekoda's godparents or aunts won't be able to figure out the reason why they kidnapped their niece. And so far the police department has absolutely no leads. I was thinking, why not have her best friends investigate themselves? Surely the cops missed something." Maggie stated nonchalantly.

"Hold up, hold up. You want us to go dig around the remains of the Jones' house and hopefully end up with a clue at the end of the night? Are you crazy? The area is blocked off by the NYPD; we aren't allowed access! What if we get caught, huh? I'll be in major trouble with my parents and worse, we still won't know what's happened to Nekoda!" Logan's vision blurred, tears threatening to spill over from the stress of the last week.

Maggie patted her friend's shoulder. "Hey, it'll be okay. We'll sneak past the ropes and just poke around for an hour. If nothing comes up, we'll go home for the night and try again tomorrow, and every day until Kody is back home with her two best friends. That way we'll have something to rub the police's faces' in. Both of us will be known as the world's youngest detectives!" Maggie wrapped her arm around Logan. She sniffled and stood.

Logan wiped her nose on her sleeve. "You know what, fine! We won't give up on Kody! She would've done the same if it were us. When do we head out?"

"At 1 a.m., after we watch a few movies and fall asleep," She made air quotes with her fingers. "And once my parents go to bed after checking on us, we'll sneak out the window and off the roof. It's only a small jump to the ground."

256

Logan walked over to her bags and pulled out the shovel.

"Okay, but I call carrying the flashlights while you dig. Don't just pinky-promise, cross your heart too, deal?" Logan extended her hand.

"Deal." The two girls shook on it and made the promise final.

☾

Beep, beep, beep, be—! The alarm clock tumbled off the dresser, ripping the cord free from the outlet. Maggie fumbled for her phone as Logan rubbed her eyes, focusing on the TV on the wall. The two girls actually had fallen asleep, despite their agreement not to. It was now 12:45 a.m. End credits for the movie *Titanic* rolled across the screen. Maggie stood up and brushed her hair into a low pony, searching through her closet for the shovels.

Shaking her friend awake, Maggie whisper-shouted, "Logan! Hey, wakey, wakey!"

Rubbing the sleep from her eyes, Logan rolled over and flopped onto the floor. "Oww," she moaned from below. Struggling to sit upright, Logan strapped the flashlights to her belt from the floor and quietly slipped on her shoes, grabbing a random black scarf from under the bed. "Ijustwannaslweep." Logan slurred, playing with the little strings on her scarf.

"C'mon, the faster we get there the faster you can go back to dreaming of Zac Efron." Maggie said.

"Okiewakemeupwhenyouhavebacon," Mumbling something incomprehensible, Logan crept to the bedroom door, her friend trailing behind her.

"Move it, slow poke. Oh, watch out for that first step. It creaks," Maggie spoke softly.

257

"Okie dokie." The softball bag rattled on Maggie's back, the shovels clanking together with each step. Logan almost fell down the stairway three times. Guided only by the moonlight, the two girls made their way to the back door where Maggie flicked the lock and pulled open the door. A slight breeze was blowing when they walked out onto the porch.

"This way." Maggie led her partner to the front of the house and by the garage. Their bikes were leaning against the side, waiting to be ridden. Hopping up on the pedals, the two girls biked through a quiet suburban neighborhood. Owls hooted and frogs croaked. Dead cicadas' shells lined the branch of a fallen tree. Leaves crunched under the tires as they whizzed by, holding their breath every time a car passed. A 2015 Honda Civic flashed its lights at Maggie and Logan, but it was only a middle-aged neighbor at the wheel, not anyone worth worrying about.

The two girls hide in the shadows after the last vehicle drove by, swiftly turning left and arriving on to Nekoda's road. With each quick turn of the semi-flat tires pushing her closer and closer, Logan's stomach flipped. She saw the news; she had heard the muffled sounds of her parent's crying, but she didn't want to actually come back. It was like waking up from a nightmare that stayed in your head for days and accepting that her best friend really *was* gone. Screeching to a halt, Maggie tied up her bike under a pine tree a few yards from the empty lot, making straight for the lines of yellow tape. Logan did the same and chased after her.

Logan shone a flashlight above her head for Maggie to pull out a shovel. The closest houses were nestled on the left side of the fence, across the street, and farther down in a cul-de-sac. Logan gathered her wits and sprinted under the police tape.

Only a few remaining pieces of tinder and brick still stood in crumbling piles, a light coating of ash and snow covering the rest of the remaining area. Logan chewed her lip and walked the perimeter, noting where the front door used to be, where her and Kody would play fetch with Buddy in the front yard. Though the poor dog was also assumed dead as well.

Grimacing, Maggie scuffled to the back area of the house, a line of trees and forests that stretched for miles. "What exactly are you hoping to find? Or want me to look for?" Logan wondered.

"Anything," Maggie responded.

Logan shined the flashlight beam left and right as her and Maggie scanned the area. She spotted something white wedged between a mound of wet, hard dirt and half of a brick. Squinting to get a better look at the object and silently cursing herself for not wearing her glasses, Logan crouched down on all fours and gripped the piece of paper between her fingers, tugging it out of its hiding spot.

It was a polaroid photograph. The tips were curled where flames had licked at them, burnt and stained with soot, but otherwise Logan could just make out four figures in the damaged image. Nekoda on the first day of fifth grade, her parents smiling behind her at the house as Buddy watched by the front porch, waiting for the bus to drive by. That had been a colossal day for the trio. Maggie proudly displaying her decorated locker and Nekoda laughing at all the glitter and additional piggy stickers Logan had stuck to the inside. That had been back in August seventeenth, five and a half years ago.

Logan called over Maggie. "Look at this," She handed the picture over.

"That's odd. Who do you think snapped this? How did it survive the fire?"

"I don't know, but it's sorta giving me the hibbie jeebies. Speaking of…" Logan glanced around the empty area.

"Here, hold onto it for now. Maybe it's a clue." Maggie folded it and passed the polaroid back to her friend.

259

"Maybe,"

Logan stuffed it in her coat pocket and sighed. Moving closer to the tree line, the two girls poked around, kicking up dirt and clumps of ash and burnt remains. Logan searched around for any tire tracks or unusual prints as Maggie prodded the honeysuckle bushes that had escaped the flames. The flashlight beamed landed on something other than rubble and leaves. A flowerbed. It bloomed in the darkness amidst the white ashes and mud, adding a sort of beauty to a scene of disaster. "Hey, Maggs. Take a peek at this. Clara's flower garden is still blooming." Logan murmured.

"Whoa, that's impressive. Mrs. J must've had a really green thumb…" The humor was plain, swept aside by a surge of madness. Logan stomped over to the flowers and kicked at the dirt, sending mulch flying and leaves spiraling in the air. "In what world do these—" Logan ripped out a rose, the thorns pricking her finger. "get to live when Nekoda—" Tears spilled and flower petals fluttered to the ground. "Doesn't!" Gripping the head of a single white rose, she yanked, not caring that blood was running down her palms and dripping onto the snow. The flower uprooted and Logan flung it behind her head.

"Wait, wait. Logan, stop! Stop! Maybe coming back here was a mistake!" Maggie reached for her friend's shoulder. Logan slapped it away and spat, "You think?!" and kicked at the ground once more. Her foot connected with something hard. Logan hopped backwards, gritting her teeth. "Ouch! Gosh da—" she stopped. Maggie was digging furiously with one of the shovels, dirt and grass flinging over her head.

"What are you doing?" Logan asked, astonished.

"I think you just discovered something," Creeping forward, Logan saw a small dark object jutting out of the ground. Grunting, Maggie threw the shovel aside and went on her hands and knees. Her friend bent down to help dig up the mysterious object. Finally,

260

with one last tug, the object came loose and was and now gripped in Logan's hands. "What is it?" Maggie furrowed her eyebrows.

"Umm, I don't know. A box, I imagine." And indeed it was. Carved out of white oak, it was intricately designed. It was about nine inches long and six inches wide. Gold and silver whirls and patterns spotted the lid, light bouncing off the box when the flashlight beam hit it. A line of text ran along one edge of the box, carved in a foreign language. A strangely-shaped keyhole was on the other side of the box. Maggie picked up the other flashlight for Logan to brush the dirt and dust off the top.

"I admit, this is a nice piece of woodwork. But why have it buried back here?" Maggie spoke aloud.

Logan shrugged in the darkness. "I don't have any answers. Nor would I be able to tell to you what it's for and why because we can't even open it. It could be one of those old time-travel boxes that you bury for people of the future to find."

"True. It is possible there's a key around here somewhere." Maggie dug doggie-style as Logan studied the box, angling it this way and that. A bead of blood swelled and rolled down off her finger as her hands worked at the hole. Maggie sat back on her heels. "Yeah, no such luck. I doubt the key would've been buried with the box too. That'd be too easy." She said, swiping snow and ash off her jeans.

"What do you mean it would be too easy?" Logan glanced up at her friend and huffed.

You know how in all those pirate movies the characters have to have a map that leads them to the key? And then that key leads them to the treasure? I feel that's the same way it is now. Nothing is ever so simple."

"But we don't even know what's in it. Maybe it's a time capsule for the next generation of Jones's, like you said."

"Or maybe it's full of gold."

261

"I doubt that very much," Logan giggled, her tears now drying.

"Hey, we weren't even here for half an hour and we already uncovered something that could possibly give us a clue about Kody. Or we're stealing private property."

"Technically, it was buried back here, hidden. So it didn't really belong to anyone anymore, did it?" Maggie explained.

"I guess not, but we should still be careful."

"No duh, and by the way, you can carry that on our way back to the house. I already got my hands full with our digging equipment. Plus, I don't have pockets."

"Whatever. I was going to suggest that," Logan sighed and went to unchain their bikes. A few minutes later, the teenagers had snuck back into the Landrus house, dirty and cold. Wiping off their mucky shoes, they quietly unlaced and set them by the back door. Maggie locked the door and clicked on another flashlight. Racing up the stairs without a care as to how much noise they made, the girls hid the shovels in the closet and stripped out of their gross clothes and into warm pajamas, relieved to be away from the crime scene. Logan slipped the photograph and the small box into her bag, waiting for her turn to shower off in Maggie's bathroom.

As soon as they were all washed off and dry, Logan brought the box out again. Holding her hand out, Logan motioned for Maggie to pluck a bobby pin from the dresser and place it in her palm.

"As a professional lock-picker, I vow I shall stop at nothing until this contraption opens and reveals its mysterious contents to us." Logan fidgeted with the lock hole and unfolded the pin. Wriggling the pin around in the disfigured keyhole, they strained their ears, hoping to hear a clicking sound from the box. Silence. More struggling. More tension.

"What if we try a house key or something?" Maggie tapped her foot.

262

"That won't work, it's an irregular shape. Could we have missed something at the site? We didn't look very hard." Logan the bobby pin tried again. Hit and miss.

"Really? Interesting. What do you think the key's shape's is?" Leaning over her shoulder, Maggie studied her friend's work.

"A crescent moon, maybe. Or something with a triangular shape?"

"Oh, that's unusual. Seems like something from *Twilight*."

"Any suggestions?" Logan questioned.

"In a couple hours, once my parent's wake up and go to my little brother's basketball game, we can sneak in the garage and blow torch the latches off."

"What? No, we can't do that! It'll ruin the wood on the box and burn it to cinders!" Maggie winced at her friend's raised voice. "Ack, sorry, I'm frustrated and tired. You know I get cranky without my beauty sleep."

Logan grinned a lopsided smile, lowering her voice to a whisper. "Yeah, well, we can figure this whole situation out later once we actually get some rest. Plus, we could go back out to the house again, 'cause we definitely missed some vital evidence."

"For sure. And I'll throw the dead flowers back in the woods and cover our prints." The two girls yawned and climbed back into bed, Logan resting her feet up by Maggie's head. They puffed up their pillows and drifted back off into sleep.

☾

Johnathen Dogo splashed along the riverbank, pebbles getting caught in his hiking boots. Aaron Smith was lagging behind, having to keep track of Pearl and Greyback this hour. The young wolves had a tendency to chase things off into the woods until they were lost, and more than once Aaron had to call them back. Greyback had startled him so much that when he crept up behind him and nipped his hand, Aaron yelled so loud that he startled Johnathen into whipped out his sword, pointing it directly under Greyback's chin. He whimpered and ducked down, frightened. Pearl had yanked the sword out of his grasp and gave a warning growl. After apologizing, the wolves and humans were forgiven and all four continued on their way, tensions high.

"How many miles is it from Yellowstone up to Niagara Falls, the New York side? It's just on the border, right?" asked Aaron, skipping a flat rock across the river.

"Right. But do you really want to know the answer?"

"Might as well hear it." Aaron moaned.

"It is about two thousand miles and thirty-three hours away by car." Pearl trotted happily along, walking in and out of Johnathen's legs as he ran. Greyback played tug-o-war with Aaron's backpack straps.

"Holy guacamole! There's no way in hell I can walk that far!"

Johnathen stopped dead in his tracks, nearly tripping over the young wolf. "I know that, but James said to stay on foot."

"But think about it! I'm pretty sure he was on something when he thought this through, because I am *not* walking all the way to *Canada*! No way, José! And who made the non-driver decide how best to travel?" Aaron threw his hands up, exasperated.

"We're just going to Nekoda's house, not Canada. And I *suppose* it would be faster by car, depending on how many rolling stops I can pull off. We can go to a dealership, there's one nearby. But you're helping pay for gas money. Jeez, man, you're right for once. I don't know *what* James was thinking!"

"Sure, whatever. And Pearl and Greyback can stick their heads out the window." giggled Aaron.

They made a U-turn and followed the Camp's supply routes down to the main highway. By sundown, the two boys had reached an Enterprise car rental company. "I've been here once before. When Alex and I went into the city, our loaned car from Halt had been in the repair shop so we came here to rent a vehicle for the night while at the movies." Johnathen explained.

"Wait, that was when you guys saw *Iron Man 2* without me!" Aaron gasped.

"Oh, yeah, I guess so." He shrugged and walked to the front desk.

"Excuse me, sir, but your dogs will have to wait outside. And preferably with leashes." The lady said when she saw the four of them come in.

"Oops, uh, sorry. Aaron, watch Pearl and Greyback while I fill out the paperwork." Johnathen addressed.

"Fine. Here girl, here boy!" Aaron patted his side and opened the door.

"Hello, I'm Jennifer. I will be your assistant today. What type of vehicle are you looking for, sir? Oh, and before I give you the keys, you'll have to fill out this—" She handed him a stack of paper and a pen, the glitter reflecting off her brightly painted manicure.

"Umm, is there perhaps an off-road truck around? Got any Ram's available?"

"Of course. We have various brands to offer such as Honda, Chrysler, Chevrolet and others. All cars you see here are all the ones we have that are currently rentable. Once you are finished with your vehicle, you may return to another business center of ours if you like. And if any damage comes to the property

265

while under you name, you are responsible. It says so and more in the packet."

"Okay, thanks for the info. And could you have one of your mechanics pull up the truck for us in a bit?" asked Johnathen.

"Of course, anytime." The lady replied.

"Thanks again," Johnathen went to take a seat in the lobby, ignoring the other patrons whispering around him. "Hmm, let's see…name—Johnathen Dogo and Aaron Smith. Brand—Ram. My age…twenty-four and twenty-three. Have I ever been in any accidents before? Once. Do I agree to these terms of policy…yes. Blah, blah, blah, check." He mumbled under his breath. After the papers were filled out, he walked back up to Jennifer and paid with one of Alpha Lockwood's debit cards. He waited outside with his friends in the chilly air until the red truck was pulled up around the corner of the building. The driver was a sour-looking man with a thin goatee and peach fuzz dotting his upper lip. When he coughed and handed the keys to Aaron after jumping down from the truck, his breath smelled strongly of cigarette smoke.

The boys threw open the back doors and had Greyback and Pearl hop in, tossing their bags in the trunk. Aaron took the passenger's seat and Johnathen climbed into the driver's side.

"See, that wasn't so hard now, was it?" Aaron said, fluttering his lashes in Dogo's direction.

"Shut up and let me focus on the road. Do me a favor and plug in the GPS." Johnathen rolled his eyes, veering into a new lane. Stuffing a granola bar in his mouth, Aaron unraveled the cord around his portable GPS and powered it on. Typing in the directions to Weedsport, the GPS spoke. "*Turn right in one-hundred feet, then continue northeast for six miles.*"

"It would be so much funnier if it spoke with an Australian accent." Joked Aaron.

"We could use Google Maps on your phone if you like."

266

"I'm not getting good signal now, plus I don't want to use up the battery if anyone tries calling."

"Who? Your non-existent girlfriend?" Johnathen snorted.

"Just keep driving before I punch your lights out," Smith warned, tapping a button on the GPS' screen. The older adult put his hands up in surrender before placing them back on the wheel.

"This is going to be a long drive." Johnathen yawned, cracking the windows open despite the freezing weather. Pearl stood up on her back legs and stuck her head out, the breeze blowing her ears back. Her partner, Greyback, curled up on the seat. Aaron buckled the seat belt around his furry body so he safely doze off. "Aww, how cute!" Johnathen cooed from the wheel.

"Thanks, I'm *soo* irresistible." Aaron winked.

"Oh, no, I was talking about Greyback." He laughed.

"I totally knew that." Brushing granola crumbs off his chin, Aaron adjusted the radio station and turned up the volume on the speakers. A remix of the song "Young Volcanoes" blasted through the stereo.

Two hours later, the sun began to set set on the horizon, an array of purples, oranges, and yellows illuminated the sky. Both boys hummed along to the song as Johnathen veered into a U-turn. Looking in the rear-view mirror, he saw Pearl sticking her tongue out. She happily attempted to eat the wind.

Johnathen suddenly perked up. "Hey, you hear that?" he began frantically checking his review and side mirrors.

"Erm, y-yeah." The hair on Aaron's arms rose, and he felt a tingling sensation in the back of his skull. He knew what that meant. The ground shook, and car horns beeped. Johnathen put the truck in park at the next stoplight and climbed out of the vehicle, and mortals were doing the same.

A large figure was tramping between the trees, heading straight into the traffic of the intersection.

"Uhh, dude—" Johnathen began, pointing straight ahead.

"WATCH OUT!" Aaron screamed just as a giant tree smashed into the front hood of the truck.

☾

My stomach growled so loud I feared the ceiling would come crashing down. I. Needed. Food. "David, how long have we been going for?" I asked. We were pooped, maybe not David's ghost, but Buddy and I sure were. I was exhausted, dirty, and sore, and I desperately wanted a double cheeseburger and a twelve-ounce Dr. Pepper.

"Hard to tell judging by how far down underground we are. Perhaps a hundred miles." He replied.

"A hundred miles! I doubt that, even though we seem to be walking for ages, there's no way we've made it a hundred miles. Not even twenty."

"That's the spirit," he scoffed.

"Unless you've mapped this place out in your head, I don't think we'll be out of here soon." I sighed.

"Oh, now *I* doubt *that*. Just stick with me for a few more hours and we'll be somewhere nice and full of life."

"Whatever you say. Are we under some city that I'm supposed to know of?" Stopping in my tracks, I leaned against the wall. Buddy slumped to the floor, tongue lolling out.

"Hmph, not yet."

"C'mon, you said you'd lead me home first and then to Camp Wolf. You promised. Look, I don't even know how far away from home I actually am. Just take us to the nearest bus stop and we'll do the rest."

"I know what I said. And you'll get to see for yourself what I did to you and what others *will* do. Our destination is only a few more hours away. And when we get there, act like everything's alright. Don't act suspicious. You might want to have Buddy Change into his mortal form."

"Fine, agreed. Let's just get there and get *home*." I snapped and walked ahead of him. My dog lazily stood up and followed.

The torch soon sputtered out, and I was tired of using my arm as a default. Taking another one off the walls, I exchanged torches and carried the new light source in front of me. David was urging Buddy on, about to collapse. After a couple more twists and turns over a small endless cavern leading into Neverland, our ghost told us to stop. We had hit a dead-end.

"Now what?" I had run out of patience a couple days ago.

"You see this circular line running across? I need you and Buddy to cross it at the same time. When I say so, press the outline of that carving on the wall and don't move. Things might get a little shaky."

"Shaky?" Giving him a questioning glare, I passed the line with the Hellhound and found the symbol carved into the rough wall. It was a circle, like a full moon. "Don't tell me I'm being zapped halfway across the world." Cautiously, I put two fingers against the symbol and pushed. The carving of the symbol sunk into the wall like a button, glowing a bright blue.

Abruptly, the ground began to move. David disappeared, and so did the hallway. Dropping the torch, I backed up, the floor beneath me spinning. The grinding of stone on stone came to a halt and I hurriedly crossed the line again. This time I was facing a different hallway, except I could hear *noises*. New noises. The honk of a taxi sounded from above, and shafts of light peeked in from somewhere along the ceiling.

David materialized in front of us. He smiled and motioned for me to grab a new torch. "Come here, Nekoda. Just a little farther." He glided away down the dank passage and I took one last glance at the moving trap wall before scrambling after him.

We soon stood before a door that had the same symbol etched into the dark wood. Buddy's tail was furiously wagging. Inching forward, I grasped the handle and pulled the door open. I stepped through and found myself inside a pub. Adults and university students alike were drinking, playing pool, or passed out at their tables, drinking glasses empty. Aside from seeming like just any ordinary bar, there were goat-legged men with horns poking through their hair serving appetizers and making margaritas at the back counter. Beautiful maidens wearing long silk togas and knee-high sandals walked around, singing and playing musical instruments.

Over in one corner, a man with the body of a horse was playing pool by himself, humming. Drunkards with animal-like features stumbled around the bar, and I watched as someone tripped right into a table.

Behind us on the door hung a sign in neon lights.

Welcome to the Blue Moon Bar & Grill

"Um, where are we? And why are their magical goats walking around serving food and a horseman playing pool? And how isn't anybody else noticing these people?"

David cast me a queer look. "Kody, by now you ought to know who these wonderful beings are! That horseman playing pool is a Centaur. Those lovely girls over there are Muses, and amongst them a few naiads and nymphs with the flowers and colorful skin. Our generous servers with the hooves are Satyrs. All

270

the other folks milling about are Skin-changers— your kind. And these half-mortals who are passed out at the moment are fellow demigods. In this large city, it's quite easy to blend in with everyone and anything."

"Oh. I guess I should've known that. But what if a human comes through here? Won't they be exposed for who they really are?" I gestured around at the mythical beings around me.

"No, they are hidden by glamours. It shields them from mortal eyes. Unless you were born with the Sight, any normal human would mistake you as one of his or her own. Nothing more." David looked around, waving at a nymph.

"Where are we?"

"In good ol' Chicago, Illinois!" He spread his arms out.

My jaw dropped. We had traveled all the way through an underground tunnel to Chicago? Damn! I've taken road trips up here before with my family to visit grandparents, but I never expected to be back in this city so soon. I have visited the Bean, the aquariums, the natural history museums, and Navy Pier many times before. Instead of replying, I spotted Buddy a few yards off lapping up the last of some poor sap's beverage. My dog was in his mortal form—a little fluffy poodle.

"Buddy, no! Bad dog!" The last thing I needed was a drunken Hellhound, if animals could even get drunk. I didn't want to find out. A server walked over and picked up the glass.

"Don't worry miss, it vas only root beer. No need to be alarmed. I had tricked him—" He pointed at the sleeping customer, "Into having soda so he vouldn't go out and valk in front of a car. He vas already as drunk as can be and highly unstable." The Satyr spoke with a thick foreign accent.

"Err, thank you?" I said meekly. His nametag read Ian.

"Vhy are you here? You seem a bit young, yes? Are you looking for someone?"

"No, my friend and I are just passing through," Nodding back at David, I turned to Ian. We just needed to use the restroom."

"Vee has a policy here. Your friend vill have to vait outside, and the vomen's restroom is down the short hall behind the pool table area." Ian pointed in the direction behind the lonely Centaur.

"Nekoda, he can't see me. Only you and other dead souls like myself, or people who have experienced death before can. That includes Buddy as well." David put a transparent hand on my shoulder, sending a chill went up my spine.

"Oops, my bad." I mumbled and walked to the bathroom.

On the way past the booths and customers, a hand reached out and grabbed my wrist. "Fetch me my chariot, peasant. I'm the queen of England now! Obey me or feel..." the lady lisped and fell unconscious, her face landing in her nachos, dark hair spilling across her shoulders. Shrugging my hand back, I limped to the restroom and passed the Centaur. He was humming "Twinkle, Twinkle, Little Star."

I almost didn't recognize myself in the mirror. A long purple bruise ran along my jaw, and various scratches criss-crossed across my forehead. Dried blood ran on my slit palm, sore from the knife Nathaniel had used. The cut on my cheek had faded to a white scar. There were bags under my eyes from lack of comfortable sleep, and my ankle had only gotten worse. It was still swollen as I rolled up my pant leg and untied my muddy shoe. Sighing, I splashed water onto my face and tried combing through my ratty hair with my fingers. Despite the chill of the season, I threw off my sweatshirt and tied it around my waist, my items safely tucked inside.

272

After thoroughly washing my hands and arms, I went back out to meet David. Carefully, Buddy, David, and I went up to the front counter and I asked for a first-aid kit. Surely the manager would keep one lying around?

"What's the problem, sweetie?" A purple haired nymph in fishnet leggings and tube top approached me.

"I, uh, tripped down a step and sprained my ankle. Perhaps there's a spare roll of gauze and an ice pack I could borrow?"

"Of course, but this is no place for someone your age to be. I'll let you clean up in the bathroom and then you and your company can exit. Did your older brother bring you here?" Scowling, she reached behind the bar and opened a cupboard. Apparently, she was one of the people who thought underage kids hanging out in a bar was inappropriate, even though she knew I wasn't of drinking age.

"Yes, he did. He was having a rough day at work so he picked me up from the…" I paused, going through the lie in my head. "Library. Obviously, he was only going to get one drink, but ya know boys." I shrugged my shoulders.

"Well, I hope your mother scolds him good when you two and your pet get home. Ah, here you go." I cringed at that. Winking, she handed me a red plastic box.

"Thanks. Oh, I didn't catch your name," I replied.

"No problem! And it's Daryl."

"I'm Kody, and thanks again!" As Buddy, David, and myself went off to the restrooms, she called back, "Have a lovely day, stay safe hon!"

Not likely, I thought. Closing the bathroom door behind me, I placed my foot up on the sink and rolled up the fabric of my jeans. I balanced the kit on the edge of the sink and unlocked it. Buddy, back to his original form, stood up on his hind legs and

273

handed me the band-aid box in his mouth after I rubbed cream over my cuts. Grinning at him, I rubbed Polysporin over the gash and covered it with a bandage. There was small bottle of Advil in the kit. I had to cup some sink water in my hands and swallow some down. For now, the medicine would help the pain. Biting off the end of a tape strip I carefully wrapped up my ankle, the athletic tape tight.

"So, what do we do? I'm starving and I smell and look like trash. Plus, we've got no money." Grumbling at David, I resealed the first-aid kit.

"We are in a very populated city, full of shops, cash, and fancy designer suits." Turning to face me, David had a gleeful look on his ghostly face.

"You have that weird, mischievous look on your face again." Folding my arms over my chest, I eyed my partners. One was immortal, the other was dead, and I was alive. Funny.

At last, David asked, "Kody, are you fond of pick-pocketing?"

☾

"This is a very, very bad idea! What if we get caught? How am I supposed to explain this to the cops? 'Sorry, my un-dead dog and my invisible somewhat-evil-ghosty friend told me to steal in order to survive. I was recently kidnapped and I'm trying to find my way back home and I need enough bus money though, so it's all good! By the way, I can also burn you to death if I summed up enough willpower!'" Rolling my eyes, we zigged and zagged between pedestrians and hot cocoa and taco stands. David had insisted I steal coins from a make-a-wish fountain or snatch a wallet from an innocent's purse, and where better than at Millennium Park in downtown Chicago!

274

Coming out of the shadow of a building, we jaywalked across the busy streets through Michigan Avenue and Madison Street. Into Millennium Park, the Bean shone bright in the sun before us. Constructed entirely of stainless-steel plates, it was a giant three-dimensional mirror and a giant tourist attraction shaped like...well, a bean. Behind the monument stood the fifty-foot glass-brick towers, spouting water through the mouths of Chicagoans flashing on the screens.

"How do you want me to do this?" I whispered to David, floating nearby.

"I think Buddy should be the bait. He'll cause the distraction. With him in his mortal form, Buddy will trot over to a group of young children. As soon as the parents see the cute little biscuit playing with their kiddies, they'll walk on by to see. Meanwhile, you will sneak behind and snatch their bag. Don't bother checking if anyone's looking, just grab and *go*."

"This is ridiculous!" I exclaimed.

"You want to go home, right? Then you need money. If you *want* money, you either get a job or snag some extra cash. In this case, you don't *want* anyone to notice us. So, you have to *take* what you want."

I wrapped my arms tighter around myself against the bitter cold. My breath blew out in a cloud of smoke. "Oh, fine!"

"Now choose a victim." David nodded at the nearby strangers.

"How about her?" Pointing at a middle-aged mother of three, the woman was studying her children splashing through the rain puddles. Crowds of university students and travelers walked around the freezing water-spitting towers despite it being fifty degrees in November. Off to the side on the concrete floor, the lady's picnic blankets were spread out and a over-the-shoulder bag lay by her feet. Taking her eyes off her two children, the mother

275

reached into the bag and produced a purple leather purse and answered her ringing phone.

David hovered nearby, watching as Buddy raced into the water, short tail wagging. The dark-haired twins giggled and clapped. Buddy nudged the little girl, and she shrieked in delight. "Puppy! Puppy!" She shouted. Her twin brother proceeded to jump up and down in his rain boots, soaking the dog.

"Yes, okay. The kids and I will meet you soon, honey. Uh-huh, yeah. Yup. Hey, hold on a minute, I'll get back to you." The mother threw her phone into her purse and set it on the blanket. Smiling, she kneeled down to her children and the unknown visitor. "Aww, is this your new friend, Sophie?" Chuckling, she ruffled her daughter's hair. Buddy rolled over and pawed at the air.

"Now! Hurry!" David shooed me away. As inconspicuous as possible, I strode to the bag. Keeping my eye on the small family, I rummaged around on the blanket until my hands made contact with something bulky and cool. Yanking out the purse, the chained strap glittered and clinked. David motioned me back, urgent.

I ran across to the Bean and crouched against the inside, heart pounding. I put two fingers in my mouth and whistled. A few seconds later, Buddy came running, cold water droplets drenching his fur. Both children and mother were walking back over to their spot, their new friend having run off. Unlatching the purse, I rummaged through the contents. Cherry red lipstick, makeup brush, elephant keychain, bedazzled car keys, touch-screen phone, and wallet—"Ah-ha!"

Facing so my back was to the few tourists under the reflective sculpture in the chill breeze, I studied the wallet. Credit cards were tucked into a pocket and a driver's license in another. The mother's name was Tessa, and she was thirty-six years old. In the middle pocket of the wallet was one hundred dollars in cash. I slipped four twenty-dollar bills into my sweatshirt pocket along

276

with my other belongings. Leaving the purse on the ground, I turned to my friends.

"Who in their right mind carries so much cash on them in one of the highest crime-rates cities of America?" I whispered to David.

"She does, apparently. 'Tis city life of the rich and famous."

"Riiight. Let's roll. Buddy, come."

We raced out as fast as we could, and I imagined the woman scurrying in panic, all her personal information gone along with her fancy purse. Until we reached the closest stairway down to the train station, I didn't stop running. During our brief escape, we decided it'd be faster and safer to take a train back home. It would take some time, sure, but it'd be far quicker than riding a bus.

Pushing my way through businessmen and shoppers, I arrived at the ticket stations. Cashing in a twenty through the machine, it produced two tickets. I had about sixty-four dollars left to spend.

Checking the train times, we had about eleven minutes left to spare. As we waited for the next rumbling, horn-blowing train to speed down the rusty tracks, I bought a pack of pretzels, one strawberry granola bar, and a large Dr. Pepper from a small shop. In total, I spent $4.97 and had $59.03 left in my pockets. I paced by the tracks, people bustling about around us. Buddy sat under a bench as I wolfed down my snacks and awaited the train. A few minutes later the train horn blew and travelers gathered closer to the yellow safety line, eager to get going.

The third door that flashed by opened, and we hopped on. Balancing up a few metal stairs to a second level of the train, we took our seats. David had disappeared but Buddy was sleeping on my lap in his mortal form. A conductor strode by and punched our tickets and handed me an extra leash to attach to my dog's collar since I wasn't carrying him in a crate. Buddy gave me such an angry look it was almost cute. Grinning, I slipped the leash on despite his grumpiness. "It's just for a little while until we switch trains. Besides, it's for the better. We ride, their rules."

A voice crackled to life over the speakers. "We will now be heading northeast through East Chicago. Passengers, please remain seated."

We would be traveling as far as Indianapolis, Indiana by train. From there we'd try our luck and hitchhike back home to Weedsport. I was pretty safe with a Hellhound bodyguard, so it didn't make a difference. All that I knew was that I wasn't going to this Camp Wolf, not yet anyway. I was going *home*. Or whatever was left of it.

This James I keep envisioning couldn't actually be trying to help me, could he? I had read the letters, David explained everything, and Buddy is helping bring me back. Obviously, I trusted Buddy, but there was still a part of me that was weary of David. Deep down he was still on the dark side, even *with* being granted a second chance. James and his friends seemed like the knights in shining armor that I needed to come to my rescue, but what if they were lying and they were really in line with Nathaniel? If so, then this trip would've all been for nothing, Shadarr would be safer if I hadn't escaped and maybe, just maybe, this was all a big hoax. But I've seen and done so much that I can't even explain myself! I knew I was lying to myself too, stalling. In truth, I had no idea who are the bad guys and who are the good guys.

If what Nathaniel said was true, and my parents were hiding something called the *Book of Spells*, it would be too dangerous for me to go back to New York. But if I don't go, how will I ever know the truth? It was just the mutant dog and myself.

My brain hurt from over-thinking the situation. I gazed out the train windows. About fifteen minutes later, I had made up my mind. In the reflection of the window, a university student was sketching on an art pad. Leaning out into the aisle, I poked her shoulder. "Um, excuse me, ma'am. May I have a sheet of paper?"

Her auburn curls bounced when she nodded. "Certainly." Flipping the page, she tore a clean sheet out. "Thanks." Mumbling, I sat back down in my seat and scratched Buddy's ears.

Pulling out my pencil, I braced the piece of paper against the glass of the window and covered it with one arm as I wrote:

To James at Camp Wolf,

I am coming. If you are who you say you are, then I have no other choice but to go to this mysterious place. At first, we (David's ghost, Buddy, myself) were planning on going back to my actual home in Weedsport, New York. Right now, as I write this, we're on a train in Chicago, Illinois. I've been thinking about all of it, and I've come to the conclusion that it would be best for me to stay at Camp Wolf instead, so says everyone else. Nathaniel and his gang I assume are searching for the Book of Spells as I write this. And I know this is supposedly a big issue, but do you yourself know more about me than I actually do? I'll be sending Buddy back to you soon, and I hope for a quick reply. I'm stubborn, so I won't change my mind again. Hopefully.

- Nekoda

Folding the note into a little square, I walked to the small bathroom on the train, Buddy trailing down the stairs with me. Locking the door behind us, I squatted on the bathroom floor and let Buddy deliver the letter. With the blink of an eye and the smell of burnt toast, he was gone.

☾

Cole saw him first. A black figure approached, big and red-eyed. A Hellhound. But it was a friendly, well-known animal named Buddy, meaning Cole had no need to pull his sword out. The boys were still in the infirmary when nurses had arrived.

BelAnne had established James' foot broken; at least a part of it. A small bone that connected his toes was shattered and the ridge of his foot was swollen, along with his nose. Meredith was occupied with wrapping his foot and ankle in a brace, and Natasha was sent away for some antibiotics for James' nose. Zoey and Arya were chatting away with Trevor and Lou; Elizabeth was getting a dog biscuit for Buddy.

"Dawn, you have a visitor."

Feigning surprise, James pushed himself up on his elbows and held a cold bag of ice up to his face. His fuzzy friend sat at the edge of the bed, paper in mouth.

"Oh, thanks Bud." He released his gentle grip on the note and jumped off the bed, striding over to Elizabeth who had found a Milk Bone treat.

As he read, James' eyes grew wide in surprise.

"Son of a biscuit!" He muttered and waved Cole over. Mitchell was currently preoccupied chatting with Trevor and didn't bother to glance up when his friend walked away. Leaning in so they could talk quieter, Cole braced his elbows on the bed and whispered, "What is it?"

Groaning, James whispered back, "It's Nekoda. She's coming here. Or at least is trying to. Read this." James handed the note over to his friend.

"Oh man, this is bad. We'll be questioned if Johnathen or any of the others are ordered back after suddenly disappearing. How far off do you think they are now?"

"Probably not too far, and they'll be punished for staying out late beyond the walls, but at least we'll have extra help getting Nekoda. I think Aaron and Johnathen should make a change of plans and travel to Chicago; they might be closest to Nekoda. I can call Alex, Jacob, and Will back to Camp."

"But what about—" Cole swallowed and inched closer. *The Book of Spells*? If anything, Nathaniel should not get his hands on that before we do. That'd be a major catastrophe."

"D-u-h." James spelled out.

"But how would we even know where to find the girl? Chicago is huge!"

"I'll send Buddy back with a reply and hopefully she can come up with a way to stay safe for the night. But what will we explain to Halt when he finds out?"

Cole sighed and rubbed his forehead. "I don't know. If and when it comes to that, we'll think of something."

BelAnne was through sorting through a medicine cabinet with Meredith and waltzed to the bed, cutting their conversation short.

"Listen up, Dawn, this is important. You will leave this cast on for about four weeks, no less. When you shower, be sure to cover your foot with a plastic bag or stick it out of the tub, away from the water. Each day you will take two pills of pain reliever for your foot and nose, and whatever you do, don't put too much pressure on your right leg. Your foot must be given time to heal properly before you're able to stand again. Also, your nose should

281

be back to normal within a few days. It's just going to be stuffy and red in the meantime. You got whacked pretty hard. Am I clear?" BelAnne instructed.

"Crystal,"

"Excellent, now I think you could use some rest. Mitchell, Cole, Trevor, Lou—you boys either stay and help, or leave. It's your choice, but my patients don't need to be bugged."

Before the fellow teammates and friends left out the door, James told Mitchell and Cole to contact his friends and let them know the crap-tastic change of plans. Soon thereafter he had Zoey search for a pad of paper. Furrowing his brow in concentration, James wrote.

☾

About five minutes after we had locked ourselves in the train bathroom and sent Buddy off, he returned. This time the script on the paper was much shorter:

Hello Nekoda,

I am glad to hear that, yet also very worried. My friends are in the middle of a search and rescue mission - for you. But all I can say is when they return; we'll be in deep trouble. Tell me your exact location whence you get off from the train & Chicago. My closest friends Johnathen Dogo, and Aaron Smith will come for you. (P.S. I know no more than you do, little one.)

Signed, James

I stuffed the note into my pocket and slipped out the door to our seats. Next stop at the station, I decided I'll call on David and travel down to Navy Pier. The plentiful restaurants and attractions would serve as a perfect coverup if someone were to notice a lone child wandering around unsupervised. But how would I know who and what Johnathen Dogo and Aaron Smith even look like? I guess it wouldn't hurt to ask around, although that may draw more attention to me than I need. Like the old saying goes, I'd just have to trust my gut.

Chapter XIV: Manhunt in Session

Johnathen cursed. Pearl thrashed around in the back seat, anxious at the smell of fear. This wasn't just some bizarre earthquake, but an unusual attack from a mountain Cyclops, too close to the city.

"Blood!" It roared, punching an oak tree in half as the ground shook beneath its lumbering steps. "I smell demigod blood! I want FOOD!"

Aaron's eyes grew wide.

"Crap! Why now? Of all times, he decides to take a nice trip to the city while we're on a mission. Seriously, can we not catch a break?!" Slamming the door open, he seized his pack and withdrew a small vial of Greek fire. The toxic liquid sloshed around in the bottle, warm.

"Dude, what the hell!" Shrieked Johnathen over the noise.

"Relax, I'm not throwing it yet! We've got to lure the monster as far from the city as possible. And since this is one huge Cyclops, he has one huge temper!" Aaron responded.

Greyback and Pearl stood with their human friends, fur bristling and teeth bared.

The Cyclops was well over fifteen feet tall, and its legs and arms thicker than a tree trunk. It was garbed in pieces of scrap metal; a tire swing was looped around his neck on a piece of rope and coils of wire wrapped about his wrists. Patched furs of his meals made for drab and smelly accessories; the putrid odor coming from him was enough to make Aaron faint.

All around them people were running and screaming as the monster trundled closer. Thankfully, glamours have been shielding the true forms of reality from all Sightless mortals for millennia. Only if you were born with the Sight would you see right through them and witness a childhood nightmare come alive. The men didn't know what the mortals saw—possibly a rampaging Kodiak bear, an animal rarely seen anywhere else but on the archipelago islands, or a feral mountain lion—but it was always hard to guess.

Without warning, Aaron scrambled closer to the Cyclops, waving his arms in the air. "Hey big, tall, and ugly! You want a nice, juicy flesh-bag like myself? Then come and get me!"

"What are you doing?!" Unsheathing his sword, Johnathen raced in the other direction, running out into the traffic. Cars screeched and attempted illegal U-turns, and the Cyclops smashed the back end of a semi before ripping out a fire hydrant from the sidewalk.

"I want food! Me HUNGRY!" the monster roared, lumbering after Aaron, who had jumped the rails and was now trying to lead the cyclops into the surrounding forest. Greyback was chasing away the humans, barking as he leapt onto the hood of a minivan.

A father and his son ran out of the car, yelling as the wolf chased them away to safety. Pearl followed suit with Aaron, splashing through puddles and jumping over potholes. By then there was a huge traffic jam in the intersection and those few mortals that remained were going back the way they came, or choosing to flee the scene.

Smart, real smart, Johnathen thought to himself.

The Cyclops had his full attention on his friend, so Johnathen took it upon himself to set up a trap. Racing ahead with Greyback at his side and his sword in hand, Johnathen had his pack ready. Pulling out his own walkie-talkie, he clicked it on and spoke into the mouthpiece. "J to A, come in. There's a creek up ahead behind the brook, lead the monster there." He waited for Aaron's voice to crackle on.

"Heading in your direction," Aaron's voice buzzed in and out as he crashed through trees. "Best hurry, and make it fast. I don't want to turn into actual bait." His friend clicked off and snapped the walkie-talkie to his belt loop.

About half a league away, Johnathen could hear a gurgling creek rushing by. With animal-like instincts, Skin-changers senses were twice as strong as any mortal's. A lone turkey vulture flew by overhead, wings arced.

From afar, Dogo could hear the monster growling after Aaron as he set out the trap. Strapping his sword to his back, he went to work tying a large net between two trees balanced on the bank's edge. Shooting out a spare flare, Johnathen hitched a grenade to a low branch, expertly tying a thin cord around the grenade's pin and connecting it with the makeshift tripwire.

Just as suspected, Aaron came rushing towards him, Pearl in front. With raised fists, the Cyclops tripped and fell over the tripwire. The pin came loose just as the demigods jumped behind the bushes. The device went off with a loud *BOOM!*

The monster roared and stumbled blindly. The brunt of the impact knocked the Cyclops into the water with a mighty splash; chunks of Cyclops flesh rained down as the explosion made contact with the creature. The net slung between the trees came loose and floated on top of the captured monster. Momentarily distracted by the net, Aaron yanked out his *gladius* and lunged at the monster's thigh, his sword sinking through flesh and bone.

Rushing to help, Johnathen prepared to attack, sword raised— but the Cyclops was faster. Swinging his hand as if swatting a measly fly, Aaron was thrown backwards into the water. The Cyclops ripped off the net and staggered to its warty feet.

Egging the foul-smelling Cyclops on, Aaron shot up and stumbled along in the current until he pulled himself up by a low-hanging vine.

The Cyclops stalked over to where Aaron hung and ripped him off the vine, shaking him around in his meaty hands like a child with a doll.

Johnathen leapt off the edge of the rise he was perched on and tumbled onto the Cyclops's back. Letting go of his hold on Aaron, the Cyclops focused on throwing Johnathen off. He slammed his small frame against the steep side of the creek, and Johnathen poked and slashed at pink flesh with his blade. Black blood spurted out from a puncture wound to the bicep, and the wet piece of sheepskin garb from the monster's makeshift gauntlet was ripped apart. Wrapping his arms around the beast's thick neck, Johnathen jabbed his sword through the monster's nape.

Gurgling in mid-step, the vile monster screamed and fell backwards into the embankment, trapping Johnathen underneath the waters.

Drowning under the weight of the body, Johnathen struggled to free his leg. From above, Aaron saw what was happening and began to shout at the monster to get up. When he saw that the pockets of bubbles floating out from underneath the Cyclops' back beginning to grow smaller and smaller, Aaron knew that his friend was running out of oxygen.

Pulling out his sword, Aaron ran the blade across his open palm, and let the first drop of blood splatter onto the ground.

A moment later, the Cyclops rolled to his massive feet, nostrils flaring at the smell of Aaron's blood. Aaron saw his best friend gasp for air as he resurfaced, shaking the water from his ears.

Dark blood oozed into the water from the various wounds on the Cyclops's body, but still it would not go down, not when it knew there was food close by.

The Skin-changers hopped back to land, covered in scratches and mud. Sprinting from behind and in front, the two warriors charged.

"*Now!*" Johnathen produced a small cylinder from his pocket and clicked the button. It morphed into a four-foot spear and whistled as it soared through the air. It plunged into the monster's thigh, cutting deep. As it bent to pluck the spear out, Aaron ran his *gladius* into the Cyclops's skull. With one last shaky breath, its eyes rolled up in its head, and the monster promptly collapsed. Splashing into the creek again, Johnathen pulled his beloved spear out of the body and gagged.

Aaron jumped off the dead body, wheezing. "Nice work, dude. If only I had one of those puppies," he pointed at Johnathen's cylinder weapon.

After drying themselves off, Pearl and Greyback were sent back toward the highway, a good distance away to patrol the area. Aaron uncorked the bottle of Greek fire and chucked it over the body, covering his mouth. In an instant, the body erupted in flames and was consumed whole by the blue fire. A thick cloud of smoke rose up above the treetops as Johnathen skirted out of the forest.

Unfortunately, the closest trees had collapsed on top of the wreck, the net tangled about, and soon there would be a raging inferno spreading throughout the forest if it wasn't put out fast enough. If the demigods had a child of Poseidon with them, the men would be able to go put the fire out themselves within a matter of minutes, but Aaron was a son of Aphrodite, and Johnathen was the son of Hermes.

Smith and Dogo raced back to their car abandoned in the middle of the road, tracking mud into the damaged truck. As they drove throughout the night, the walkie-talkie crackled to life, and a familiar voice echoed through.

☾

Alex Rayn was notified about the change of plans as soon as possible. Cole had contacted him through James' walkie-talkie. He was furious and confused as hell. Not even *two days* into their exciting mission, and there was no monster slaying, ass kicking, or celebrating yet. It was so freaking *unbelievable!*

Alongside him, Cherise and Joffrey nibbled away at their kill. Averting his eyes, Alex studied the path that would take him back to Camp and ran his fingers numbly through his hair. Leaning against a boulder, a single thought ran through his mind over and over and over…how were they supposed to explain to Alpha Lockwood and the Council about someone who supposedly does not exist?

☾

288

"Oh, shoot, really? No, no, I just rounded Horseshoe Bend. Wait, when did Buddy come? Oh, okay. Okay. Dang, we're screwed," Will finished his conversation with Mitchell after Alex had repeated the situation to him twice over the phone. One after the other, the boys were being sent back from a journey barely begun. The twins looked up at him with round eyes.

"It's going to be alright, Jaz. Izzy, drop the bird. Bad girl." scowling, Will Orchild unfolded his map and rubbed his forehead. So much for Dragon hunting.

☾

It had taken a long while to get Johnathen and Aaron to answer their walkies. But that personally wasn't their fault. One of the first monsters they'd seen in weeks had come out into a *city* and *attacked* them. The Cyclops, starving and alone, would have gladly roasted a human if the Skin-changers had not intervened. A once in a lifetime miracle had occurred—the Greek fire did not spread; instead, it was currently being put to out by a team of firefighters who had arrived at the scene after Smith and Dogo took off back to the mountains.

Everyone was being called back today, and if the questers traveled to Camp a day later it would mean more questions from Halt—something they were all dreading. As soon as Buddy Portaled back to James, he'd send one of his partners to gather Nekoda. Most likely it would be Johnathen and Aaron to the rescue. They were mission operatives of Camp Wolf, so technically those two had a valid reason to be out beyond the gates.

Mitchell was lounging next to Cole in their dorm while Trevor and Lou went down to the mess hall to grab lunch. They had left the infirmary a few hours earlier when the nurses were about doing their duty and James was busy cat-napping.

Now there only one person left to inform, and Cole was all too bitter to dial the number.

289

☾

Jacob was none too gleeful to hear the news, and his glum attitude put Orpha and Nike in a mood as well. Cupping his head in his hands, Jacob thought it over. He had *punched a guard* in the face; Orpha and Nike had both *attacked* two guards by *his* command; and he left Camp Wolf without Halt's permission. And all for the sake of some random girl had he disobeyed his Alpha's orders, and himself. The night before his friend had disappeared, Vincent had told Jacob to meet him by the Camp's library after his language class. Apparently, he was going to talk to Jacob about something important, and that it was imperative their conversation stay between them. Jacob knew just what he was to be asked, and would have happily said yes.

There were only two people left in all of Camp that were willing to give their lives for Vincent Ross Lockwood: Halt Lockwood and Jacob Vendéen. And they weren't giving up on him anytime soon.

"We can't go back, guys. Not yet. We'll be in so much trouble! I don't think I can handle that right now." Jacob spoke to his fuzzy friends, their ears perked and heads cocked, attention on their master.

Dripping with sweat even late in the fall, Jacob threw off his hoodie and tied it around his waist. Leaves blew around and crunched underfoot as a strong breeze rocked the trees from side to side. He had been running nonstop for hours, only stopping to check if anyone was following him. Now, Marco would be really peeved, as would the Council. But they'd just have to come to terms with what he was doing and accept it. James wanted to do something important, and he wasn't even allowed to really help; therefore, his friends were in his place and doing what they could.

"Mitchell, I need you to do me a favor. Yep. Yeah, check under your bed."

"What, why?" His voice buzzed through the speaker phone.

"Just do it."

A minute later he spoke into the walkie-talkie again. "Err, there's nothing under it, what's this about?"

Jacob swallowed. Took a deep breath. Said, "Exactly. *Nothing*." and waited for his friend's shocked response.

There was a moment of silence and the shuffling of footsteps in the background. Then— *"You took the sketchbook?!"* Mitchell's accusing tone stung, just like Jacob expected it would.

Jacob regretted saying what he said next, but continued on nonetheless. "Look, I had to, okay? You'll understand later. I promise. But there is something else you should know," He could practically feel Mitchell's anger radiating through the phone.

"And what's that?" Mitchell snapped.

Vendéen audibly gulped. "I have Camrice's journal."

☾

David, Buddy, and I got off at the second train stop and took a taxicab back to Navy Pier. Nighttime soon took over the city, but people were still out and about, partying and working night shifts, or enjoying the scenery of the lights playing out over the waters.

I sat on the cold metal seat of a bench overlooking the lake, my sweatshirt hugging my body as I squeezed next to Buddy. Earlier I had bought a soft pretzel, hamburger, and a water bottle from a lakeside grill to sooth the rumbling in my belly. Buddy finished the rest of my double patty hamburger as soon I was full.

We sat under the lamplight and watched the boats sail by for over an hour. Nobody had seemed to notice when I napped on the bench, my head resting against my arm for support. If anyone got too close to me, Buddy would heed a warning growl in his big bad wolf form. David was constantly talking to himself, about what I couldn't tell, since was too quiet. Oftentimes he would poof away for a couple minutes only to reappear feet away.

Receiving the letter from James had numbed my senses. I had hoped and hoped that *someone* would come and rescue me, but I had to solve that myself.

Now I was alone in the world, with a ghost and a Hellhound as my only companions. It would be incredibly easy to use a phone booth and contact my grandparents or aunts and uncles, but that option I had crossed out. I had had this conversation with myself many times over, if I were to run free from Nathaniel then I wasn't allowed to call my family and let them know I was okay. I couldn't risk putting them in danger, not if Nathaniel knew of their existence or not. And aside from that, the police investigators would ask me questions that I couldn't answer without sounding like a dumb kid.

I was pretty sure my friends back home were going crazy, wait with my parent's passing and the teensy tiny fact that I'm missing.

I'm not sure if I ever fell asleep in the first place, but the sun was just beginning to rise over the horizon as a soft voice drifted closer and closer.

Someone was singing. Flailing my arms, I jerked up in an upright position and looked around. No one was in sight. Odd. I frowned and lay back down, my aching body still sore from the rough nights.

"This is an anthem to the homesick, for the lost, the broke, the defeated. A song for the heartsick, for the standbys, living life in the shadow of a goodbye..." The soft voice drifted closer, sung to him or herself. "Do you remember when we learned how to fly, we'd play make believe and had time on our side. You're stuck on the ground. Got lost, can't be found. Just remember that you're still alive."

I stood up with my Buddy at my side and hummed along, gazing at the newfound stranger. She continued the song, repeating the second verse.

A girl around the age of twenty faced me, her hazel locks brushed back into a braid. She wore a floral shirt with a matching pair of riding boots and leggings, mascara smeared around her eyes.

To my utmost surprise, she continued the song, voicing the rap verse. There was no other way to describe her voice other than stunning. Her hands moved with the words, feet stomping out the rhythm, and her eyes lit up as she sang, voice as smooth as honey. It was a grand choice of lyrics for the song and its meaning. The girl soon came to the end of the rap. Her voice rose higher and higher, and I hummed the chorus. She then repeated the fifth verse over until the song was finished.

After a moment's silence, I spoke. "You have a wonderful voice."

Blushing, the girl shrugged. "Thanks. Are you a fan of Paradise Fears?" she asked.

"Not exactly, I've only heard of the one song, *Battle Scars*. Mostly I'm into pop rock kind of stuff, like Panic! At the Disco and One Republic. You?"

"Really? Cool, they're both *fantastic* groups! Fall Out Boy is my fave. And I didn't mean to intrude on your privacy either. I really just needed some fresh air."

"Oh, it's okay. Say, why are you out here so early?" I asked, wary, watching as her smudged makeup ran down her wind-bitten cheeks.

"I could ask you the same thing. But singing always seems to cheer me up. After my boyfriend ditched me and I was let go from my job, I've been singing all the songs from my playlist so much I fear my roommates will go mad." The stranger came over and sat down on the bench next to me, Buddy sniffing her hand.

"Well, sorry to hear that. Boys are so stupid. And I could use some cheering up right about now, too." That last part was an understatement. I flashed her a sheepish grin.

"Yeah, I guess so. But I think you need to explain why someone so young is out at Navy Pier by herself in the morning?"

I could feel my muscles tensing up. I had to think of a story, and fast. "Um, my dad works at..." Glancing behind, I read a few signs off the buildings. No, wouldn't do. If she ended up asking more questions about myself, I'd have to split. "The Blue

Moon Bar and Grill." Begging silently that she would believe my lie, I stared out at the lake. I could sense David hovering nearby.

She thought for a moment. "Oh, I've been there! One of my favorite pubs! But why would he let you walk halfway across the city by yourself?"

"Err, because he needed me to run a few errands, so I took a cab. But thanks, I'll be sure to tell my dad that. What's your name, by the way?"

"I'm Olivia." She extended her hand. We shook. "My name's Hannah." The lie stuck in my throat. David coughed behind me. Fortunately for us, Buddy nuzzled close for a scratch.

"Goodness, he's so sweet! What breed is he?" My dog was still in Hellhound form, but to mortals I suppose they look more like Rottweilers, since his immortal form was glamoured from Sightless people.

"Uh, he's a Great Dane and black Labrador Retriever mix," I answered.

"Well, he sure is a gentle giant. I better go, I have an audition soon. It is for a band," Olivia stood up to leave.

"Wonderful, and I'm positive you'll nail it!" Waving, my new friend gave the thumbs-up and walked away.

"That's odd." David said. I frowned as we paced the docks.

"What is?"

He gave me a queer look. "Her."

I raised an eyebrow in question. "Don't be rude. I just met Olivia."

"She isn't supposed to be able to see Buddy. Even in his immortal form, he'd still be shielded with a glamour." He responded.

"What does that mean?" Now I was the one confused. Then it clicked. "*Oh*, Olivia has the Sight! But how could she not know it?"

"She's probably a demigod in hiding. Or a Darkshadow not wanting to reveal her identity." David said.

294

I guess I could check that off my bucket list. Meeting an actual *normal* demigod. I wonder if that's how it was with my parents. Everything seemed perfectly fine in our life, as nothing major had ever gone wrong, and I had always seen Buddy as a little Toy Poodle.

At least until the night of my abduction, until he revealed his true self. And Nathaniel pulled out a green sword.

Before I could turn around and ask David if he knew of any good bakeries nearby, a large explosion sounded from deep within Chicago.

☾

"How do you explain this, son?" The god of the Underworld, keeper of souls, Grim Reaper, king of the dead, Pluto, sat upon his throne of bones, glowering.

Nathaniel watched as his father raised one hand and a swirling, misty scene like that of seeing through a crystal ball appeared in front of him. Persephone, Hades' wife, stood at his side, dressed in an elegant red V-neck gown. The River Styx rushed by behind them through a large glass window, souls of the damned wandering aimlessly in, trapped. The smell of death lingered in the air, and it most likely from staying too long in his father's kingdom had Nathaniel been able to grow used to it.

His minions, Bruce, Luke, Tony and Ezekial had already hurried and left for New York. They had gathered fake passports and forged money and licenses over the years so that they all could travel anywhere in the world with ease. In a few hours, the men would be on a flight to Syracuse, New York, and travel down to the Jones' house—or what was left of it—for the *Book of Spells*.

Meanwhile, Nathaniel had Portaled down to the Underworld to discuss matters with his grumpy dad in Tartarus.

Before him, flashes of scenes played like videos. Two girls around Nekoda's age were studying an old box. One was tall with strawberry red hair and purple-framed glasses. The other girl was

295

much shorter and sprightly, eyes bright with curiosity. The scene switched and showed them sneaking past a crime scene and digging up their prize, revealing a mystery item.

"Uh-huh. Father, how can I explain what I don't know? How about this: you tell me what's going on and I'll spill about how Kody, uhm, escaped." Nathaniel muttered meekly, ashamed that his cheeks were burning. Hades had already called his son every swear word in the book, throttled a Union soldier's walking skeleton, and smashed a hole in the palace wall.

"This box you see isn't merely a box! It holds one of the most powerful objects in the realm! And these *girls*—" spat Hades, "took it! They're human friends of Nekoda Jones and they stole what we've been seeking."

"You mean they uncovered the *Book of Spells* before I had? Impossible!" Sputtering, Nathaniel squeezed the pommel of his sword in its scabbard, knuckles turning white.

"The girl's names are Maggie and Logan. Two determined mortal friends wanting to *open* the box! Do you understand what I am saying now, boy?" Hades was garbed in a black cape and silver-plated armor, his two-pronged staff in hand and crown of invisibility upon his head. The faintest stubble of a beard covered his cheeks, and his beady black eyes matched his son's.

"Yes, my lord. But shall I propose an offer? If I catch the girl and the talisman, may I get my choosing of who or what I claim as my own?" He sneered.

"You failed me before. I entrusted you with capturing the girl and you let her slip away! Be thankful that Dragon didn't gobble you whole when he had the chance! Why should I trust you in keeping your side of the agreement? No, *I* shall make an offer: you rule by me as prince of Olympus, and like ordered, bring me back all four talismans and the prophecy child!" The god of darkness commanded a cup of wine be brought to him and Persephone by one of the enslaved butlers. His half-mother, Persephone, said not a word throughout the entire conversation.

In the back of his mind, Nathaniel cursed his father with every name he could come up with. "Fine," he relented. "But I get the honor of having my uncle's head on a pike once the Olympians are overthrown. Send for me when you want a *real* job done."

"We'll see when that happens." Hades grumbled as Nathaniel Portaled back to the surface. Before leaving his father's palace, Nathaniel had devised a new, cunning plan. His father wasn't getting anything but a kick up the arse once Nekoda was in his arms again. And of course, the talismans.

Because Nathaniel will soon be walking away with both the *Book of Spells*...and the girl.

☾

Four hours later, Ezekial, Luke, Tony and Bruce and their leader were all sitting on the plush seats at their gate, waiting for the next plane to arrive.

Bruce wore a raincoat with dark brown trousers; Tony had on a short sleeve tee and cargo pants; Ezekial was dressed in a plain white shirt and a leather jacket, combat boots laced. Luke had chosen something more fashionable to wear whilst on their travels: brown Doc Martins, denim jeans, a blue V-neck and a beanie hat paired with a dark vest. Girls gawked as they rolled by, no luggage in hand except for a heavy metal suitcase full of equipment. Nathaniel wore black on black on black, Aviator sunglasses to cover his unusual dark eyes, and his sword strapped on to his hip.

The x-ray machines didn't detect a single one of their weapons, nor did the TSA officers during the security pat-downs.

At the crack of dawn, they had taken their seats at gate B4. The plane would travel from Colorado to Michigan, and from Michigan to New York. Staring outside through the windows, the sky was a dark canvas of blues and greys with the approaching storm clouds.

Minutes prior to boarding the plane, the ticket checker announced that their flight was to be delayed because of severe weather warnings. "Damn you, Zeus!" Nathaniel mumbled under his breath. Time was power. Leaning in close, he spoke to Luke. "We shall try a different approach to speed up these accursed mortal transportation routes!"

Luke turned and hissed a plan to the others. About seventy passengers were to travel on the same flight as Nathaniel and his soldiers. He wanted to get to Weedsport as soon as possible, no delays, before anyone else could dig up the *Book of Spells*. Motioning for Bruce to move forward, Nathaniel walked up to the ramp's gate and stood idly by with Luke. Tony followed Bruce, waltzing up to one of the security guards. Clearing his throat, Bruce tapped the male officer on the shoulder, looking frantic.

"Help, help! Sir, there is a man having a heart attack in the facility! There's not a paramedic around. Please, come quick!" His deep voice echoed throughout the walls.

"What? Where is he?" The man in blue asked, clicking on his walkie-talkie, alert.

"Still on the floor, I believe. But I couldn't tell if he was breathing. Over there! I have a flight leaving, but I can't leave him like that!" Bruce pointed down the hall, a men's sign indicating the restrooms.

"Okay sir, thank you. Please calm down and take a seat, help is on the way." The officer spoke. "Calling in all units, this is officer Quinn. We need a stretcher and a paramedic over at gate B4, stat…what? Well, send the other team over!" A woman's voice said something back through the walkie-talkie. The man beside Quinn rushed down the halls, yelling, "Coming through, make way!"

Officer Quinn said one last thing to Bruce. "Thank you, sir. There's another team arriving, but there seems to be a mother delivering a baby on the other side of the airport." Quinn shook Bruce's hand and jogged after the deputy.

Whirling around, Bruce signaled to Tony.

Tony quietly ran up to a flight attendant with Ezekial, and Changed. "Excuse me, miss." He tapped her on the shoulder, revealing a hideous scar on his jaw and razor-sharp teeth, eyes changing from brown to yellow. Staring straight into Tony's ugly animalistic face, the flight attendant squealed and fainted. Whatever the glamour had made her see, it wasn't pretty. Ezekial quickly moved behind to catch her in his arms. A few spectators came over to see what had happened.

Nathaniel moved fast. Catching one of the plane's staff members, he gripped her arm and snatched off his glasses, looking her straight in the eye. She struggled as he held his grip. Her name tag read Rachel.

"Listen, Rachel. You are going to open that gate and tell your captain that he is to get this plane in gear. You are going to stand at your podium and check tickets, letting all passengers board the plane, regardless of the weather. If the captain asks you, your manager had ordered it be done since you're on a tight schedule." Nathaniel's pupils dilated as mumbled the order in Greek.

In a monotone, Rachel repeated the commands back to herself. "Good girl, now go." Nathaniel shoved her away. Waving his group over, he waited for the staff to announce the news.

Finally, a voice echoed through the loudspeakers around the lobby. "Attention all flyers, the 6:00 and 7:15 a.m. flights at gates A3, B1, B4, C7, will soon be leaving. If held up any longer by critical weather conditions, then we shall shutdown the runways. For now, please proceed to your destination."

Luke cupped Nathaniel on his shoulder. "That worked well, quick thinking."

Nathaniel glared at Luke and brushed him off. "Don't touch me."

"Oh, uh, sorry sir." Luke coughed and gathered the other's tickets, handing them to the people at the gate.

Trudging down the long ramp to the doors, Ezekial looked smug. "C'mon guys, we've got a plane to catch."

Finding their seats, Bruce and Ezekial sat diagonal from Tony, Luke, and Nathaniel. He slipped on his glasses once again and glanced out the small window. Studying his master, Luke noticed the smallest hint of a smile on Nathaniel's face. After relaxing back in his chair, Luke talked to Tony as the flight attendants and servers went over the safety guidelines of the plane.

At last, the seatbelt sign blinked on and the plane took to the skies.

☾

Halt was going crazy in his office. He kept re-reading the mysterious manuscript he had received over a day ago. In his last vision, he had seen the same scene he'd been imagining for the past couple of months.

Blood. Death. Destruction. A black Dragon. One girl.

It wasn't the most pleasant of memories, either. But whatever he's been seeing, it was for a purpose. Earlier that morning he had gone to the altar for about an hour. The pyre down in the courtyard, in an abandoned underground room, located the prayer temple. All students and faculty were granted access to the temple so that they could communicate with their deceased loved ones or godly parents about the going-ons of their lives. Like what Vincent used to do every morning before school.

Of late Halt had been praying to the Olympians— whichever ones that listened—about Damon Scott's report that his half-brother Michael Fells vanished along with a Dragon egg. He wished for the student's safety and the egg's survival, and prayed to keep more of his soldiers, students, and friends out of danger.

And now six of his best students had run off across the world.

Halt's warriors were bred and trained to be strong, resourceful, and brilliant people. But once in a while their true wild sides break through, and it affects them worse and worse with each full moon unless they learned to control it. Thirst for power and blood effects a new Skin-Changer after their Claiming Moon, which is horrific enough when experienced alone.

Halt was already flustered about Damon's father, Nickolas Scott, and his claims to rule the High Council to take over the institutes. He's been acting foolish enough as is, and demanding his own legion to pull back from the war between Greece and Italy was a damned move. Halt didn't think Nickolas still understood the extent of damage that was caused after the Roman empire collapsed and split into three different nations in A.D.476, because the same scenario was about to occur if Greece didn't drop out of the war.

Now, as the realm was prepping for a war they didn't know would come out of the aftermath between the Greek and Roman unions, Halt struggled with the conflicts at home.

For who, or what, or why, he knew only one thing was sure—

Something big is happening.

☾

"This is impossible! We've got to open this stupid box before I go nuts!" Logan paced around the room, visibly upset. The next day after she and Maggie met back up at the Landrus's house, they had tried all sorts of methods to break open the hatch—dropping the chest off the top of the stairs, picking it open with a knife, wedging it open with spacers, hammering the key hole to bits, smashing the box against a tree—but nothing worked. The beautifully carved gilded box had naught a single scratch on its surface.

Now Logan was keeping the box safely tucked away under her mattress. Every day, it taunted her. Anthony had left earlier, having gone off to Comic Con with his friends. Logan's parents were on call at the hospital, and she was left alone with her cat, Bangle, and her puppy, JJ, a one-year old Boxer.

The youngest Hendrix had already searched online for how to pick a lock in simple steps, easy-peasy lemon squeezy. But of

301

course, nothing would work. The box was being as stubborn as a mule, if inanimate objects could.

Whistling, she called for JJ. He rushed in, clipped tail shaking.

"What's up, bub? Oh, it's okay. The storm will pass soon!" Logan clicked on the TV in her room and watched the forecast. Their weatherman had called for scattered thunder and rain until the evening, and the sky was a grey overcast outside the large windows. Somewhere in the house, her cat was curled up, sleeping. Logan grabbed a can of Pringles from the kitchen and went back to her room, spotting JJ hiding under her pillows.

With nothing better to do, Logan's eyes closed.
A few minutes later, her phone rang, disturbing her afternoon nap. Hoping not to miss a call from her parents, Logan dashed to her dresser and answered.

"Hello, who's this?" She asked, unknown digits showing up on the screen.

"Who's this?" The caller replied.
"I asked you first, so state your business or I'm hanging up!" Wide-awake now, she leaned against her bedroom door.

A male's voice cackled. "You'll meet me very soon, honey, if you don't give me what I want." the caller said, stern. Logan rolled her eyes, ready to end the conversation.

"Oh, really? Because I doubt that, loser! Leave me alone!" She hung up. Irritated, JJ watched her yank out the box for the umpteenth time that day. Tapping the case, Logan worked her fingers around the smooth material, wondering if there was a secret little compartment for the key, like shown in spy movies. She scratched at the lock with her fingernails, light sparking off the golden lock. Leaning back on her elbows, she glared at the box, hoping lasers would shoot out her eyes and blast it apart.
Instead, the dumb thing sat on the comforter, looking ancient yet in tip-top condition.

Once again, the girl shoved it away and checked her messages. Emails from stores she shopped at, magazine coupons, restaurant deals, text messages from friends Maggie, Jillian, Elena and a group message from her rowing crew. Sighing, she scrolled farther down in her inbox until her phone's ringtone beeped twice. One new message from Unknown number.

"What the heck!" Logan exclaimed and breezed through it. The ominous message read: **Give me the book!**

Chewing her lip, she replied back: **What book? Are you some kind of secret librarian agent who checks for overdue articles? I dunno who u are! I returned "The Adventures of Huckleberry Finn" a week ago!**

Immediately, the stranger behind the screen responded. **No, stupid girl! Give me what I want! We're coming for you, so I'll get what I deserve either way.**

Logan sent one last text, and scrambled to her computer.

☾

Sneering, Nathaniel checked his temporary telephone again. A new message popped up on the screen: **What the fuck, dude! Go bother someone else, looney.**

He smiled; that's one victim suppressed. Throwing the phone away in the trash, his gang spanned out behind him to their next flight. Now in Lansing, Michigan, they would soon be at their final destination within hours— New York. He hoped Nekoda was ready, because he was rising.

☾

"James! James! Wake up! Great news!" A voice yelled in his ears. Startled, he made a fist and swung it in the air, connecting with someone.

"Oww! It's me, Richey!" The blurry figure came into focus as he sat up. Crowded around his bed, the Thundering Trojans team spread around him. Smiles lit up their faces, and Coach Taylor leaned closer.

"Hey bud! Glad you're awake!" he beamed.

"Wait, we won?" James wriggled his toes, still sore.

"Sure did! It was two to four, and the second match we ended with a tie. So that means we play the actual final game,against the Spiraling Spartans!"

"Whoo-hoo! And the Raving Romans and Greater Greeks are out of the competition!" Pumping a fist in the air, he high-fived and hugged his teammates. "And what about Damon? Were any more players injured because of his actions?" he scowled, crossing his arms.

"No, luckily Coach Billy put him on the bench for the rest of the game after your incident. And later he had gotten a yellow card in the second game." Chris, a competitive midfielder, explained.

"Oh my gods, that's amazing you guys! But what of me? I'll miss the final game! Crap." James pouted, sipping some nectar and ambrosia from a cup. All nineteen of his teammates and himself, frowned.

Taylor stepped in and patted his shoulder.
"Don't worry about it sport, we just want you to heal and relax. You could use a break. Oh, and the teams of the NSL tournament are throwing a big cookout to celebrate our big win next week!"

"Ah, I guess you're right. But I'm sorry I wasn't there for you all. I betcha kicked ass." James chuckled. After a few more minutes of chitchat, BelAnne and Arya ushered the sweaty, smelly boys out to their dorms.

Elizabeth wrinkled her nose. "Ew, why do men always sweat so much everywhere they go? It's gross."

James countered. "Hey, you don't get choked in a cloud of toxic perfume spray every time Zoey walks by." From across the room, she rolled her eyes and whispered something to Arya who was counting supplies in the medicine cabinet.

"Whatever," Elizabeth sauntered off. Natasha later came to check in on James and feed him more painkillers. As the lights in the halls dimmed, the nurses were heading to bed and gathering equipment.

Cole had arrived an hour after with Mitchell and brought their friend a few books. The Iliad and The Odyssey lay on James' tray table, open. The boys had also told him about Jacob, and he was grief-stricken.

Eyes wide as saucers, he whispered, "Are you absolutely serious? Please tell me this a joke, and you'll just laugh it off." But they didn't, instead they sat there in silence, not knowing what to do or say next.

Aaron Smith. Johnathen Dogo. Cole Burnett. Mitchell Pickering. Alex Rayn. Will Orchild. Jacob Vendéen. His best friends. Why? If it wasn't Vincent, it was Jacob. Everything started going haywire after Vincent disappeared. And soon, Jacob. He didn't have to follow in Vincent's footsteps; he shouldn't have been dragged into all of this, as it was only the Lockwoods problem.

As the boys went off to their rooms, James was left alone to dwell in his thoughts. James lay there, arms wrapped around himself, the soft comforter tousled at the end of his bed and his bad leg propped out on a chair. He let out a deep sigh, and tears began to burn at the back of his eyes. James knew another person in his life was gone, and there was a lot more to the story than Jacob was letting on.

☾

"Catch! Ack, JJ, down!" yelped Maggie. Logan caught the small tennis ball in her hands and threw it again. JJ was darting back and forth between the girls, the monkey in the middle, his tail wagging a mile a minute. Bangle was sitting atop the kitchen counter, purring.

After explaining the incident to her friend, the girls had decided to leave it be for now and forget about the mysterious box. Kelly Landrus (Maggie's mom) had agreed to drop her daughter off at the house to spend the night. Anthony was still gone and wouldn't be home until later that evening, past midnight. His buddies and him were going out to a party as soon as their first day of ComicCon was complete. Abigail and Justin Hendrix would both be working night shifts at their jobs, having caught an unlucky break. Fortunately for the two friends, they'd have the whole house to themselves.

Bouncing the tennis ball off the floor, it ricocheted against the wall and pin-balled between Logan's foot and JJ's mouth. His jaws snapped, and the ball evaded his slobbery mouth. Logan raced for it and wrestled it away from her dog, chucking it across the living room to Maggie . The weather outside was still dreary, rain pounding against the windows and thunder rumbling, ceasing any other investigations at the Jones' house until the next day.

Maggie stepped forward and reached for the ball as it flew her way, but not before Bangle leapt upwards and swiped it away with his paw.

"No, bad cat! JJ, get the ball!" Logan laughed. The puppy sprinted after the yowling cat and ran off down the hallway, hissing. JJ gripped his prize in his teeth and went to bury it under the mound of toys already piled in his doggie bed. Logan crossed her arms and glared at her pets.

"So stubborn, that one." She had changed out of her sopping wet clothes was dressed in a purple and navy flannel shirt, jeggings, and fuzzy socks. Maggie wore a long-sleeved tee and jeans, with a matching pair of boots.

The funeral for Clara and Kyle Jones was rescheduled for next weekend due to the weather. Almost everyone in town would be attending; neighbors would be stopping by the grandparent's house and giving eulogies, saying prayers or giving their condolences to the families. The morning of the funeral Logan and her siblings were to help arrange the flowers and chairs for the memorial service, and Maggie's dad was asked to help handle the catering services.

"What do you want to do now? I'm bored." Logan pouted.

306

"We could play a round of team deathmatch on the Xbox."

"Eh, I'd much rather play Call of Duty Transit. How's that sound?" She suggested.

"Fine by me, let's log on and see who else is playing." Maggie helped her friend gather some snacks before heading to the basement, a carpeted room with heaters, mini fridge, and the family's gaming systems. In one corner was Logan's Xbox 360, in another sat her older brother's PS4. Ashlyn had taken the old Wii with her to the new apartment a year ago, much to Anthony's protests.

Logan's setup was pretty rad. A plush swivel chair sat in front of the TV screen, a small laptop on a desk in front of it. Two controllers lay out on the TV stand atop a shelf of DVDs and game discs. Logan went over to the shelf and pulled out the C.O.D disc and set up the headset, turning the volume up on the speakers so Maggie could communicate with other online players.

"Nooo, Hellhounds! Crap, Kingzilla306, revive me! Okay, thanks. Yay! Yes, yes! I got pack-a-punch! Ha ha, nice shot, Maggs. Oh, great, we got three members down. I'm coming!" Logan's avatar moved around, buying new weapons in between rounds and helping fallen players surrounded by glowing blue-eyed computer-generated zombies.

"Drat!" Maggie was somehow the last one standing, everyone else having died prior. A horde of zombies jumped through the barricades and ambushed her character as she made one last feeble attempt to save herself. The gamers made it to round twenty-three.

Sometime around 5:30 p.m., the doorbell rang. Anthony was still out, as were her parents. Logan hurried to the door as Maggie kept JJ back by the collar. She handed the pizza guy the ten dollars her mom left behind for food and grabbed the sausage pizza out of his hands, quickly shutting the door. JJ bolted to the window, growling. As soon as he saw the car pull out of the driveway and head south, he circled on the couch and nuzzled up next to Bangle, who didn't bother to protest.

Clicking on the TV in the main room, the girls flopped out on the long couch, soda and greasy food in hand. Logan scrolled through the channels until she was satisfied with one, and cozied up on of the recliner chair, Bangle and JJ moving to curl up next to her.

Crying and laughing their way through the film *Marley & Me*, the girls still couldn't keep one thing out of their heads; it was like an itch that couldn't be scratched, withstanding chocolate while on a diet, or attempting to hold in a sneeze. Almost telepathically, the two friends ran to Logan's room after the credits and yanked out the special mystery prize from under the bed.

☾

Storms were fierce across the northeast regions of the states. Everyone from the east side of Michigan to Maine felt the skies' rage. Thunder crackled and lightning popped. Plane F-287 tipped and bobbed through the dark canvas of clouds; passengers groaned and children shrieked. A couple aisles up, an older woman stood and complained to their flight attendant, whom only responded with "Your flight will be over soon. I promise you it is safe enough to be airborne. We've had our manager and captains assure it, please ma'am, sit down."

Nathaniel listened to the mortal's snoring, eating, and whining. Pathetic. Utterly pathetic. Humans lived about a hundred years and wasted away their frail lives by stuffing their faces, partying too much, and constantly complaining about *everything*.

Irritated by the noise, Luke tapped Tony's shoulder and handed him a pair of headphones, slipping them on over his navy-blue beanie. Ezekial had fallen asleep by Bruce for a few minutes, but was awakened later by a loud clap of thunder. Surprised, he jerked and banged his knee on the open tray table. Glaring at his partner, Ezekial clutched his knee cap as Bruce roared with laughter. Tony chuckled, sounding very much like a choking hyena.

While serving snacks and drinks, Rachel tried her best to ignore Nathaniel. He noticed and winked at her from behind his aviators, unsmiling but bemused all the same. In a few seconds, their server was off again, carting the shelved trolley back into the cockpit.

Nathaniel smirked at the woman's reddening cheeks and wide eyes, and leaned his head back on his pillow.

He dreamed.

"Alessandra, come back, sweetheart!" She raced through the trees, hair flying, silk fabric flowing in the breeze.

"You have to catch me, Nathan!" For a split second, purple irises met his black eyes before she took off, giggling. She wore a soft knitted toga with trailing sleeves, a leather belt around her waist and flowers in her hair. Their sandals slapped the hard earth as the two ran along, the sun shining down on them. Growing irritated, Nathaniel pursued her, quickening his pace. They were entering dangerous territory far from their village.

"Aless, please don't take a step further! Wait!" Nathaniel called out. She brushed aside the low hanging tree branches and stumbled upon a burial ground. Unmarked graves sat before them, open holes filled with the deceased.

"We must get back before your parents find out!" His eyes darted around, checking for signs. There were a few bodies littered up in the trees, flies buzzing around the shredded soldier's dismembered limbs. Torn, bloodied cloaks covered the ground, and slain stallions lay where their riders had been cut down and thrown off, their guts hanging out of their soft bellies. Nearby, a spruce tree was snapped in half where claw marks were gashed into the soil. Someone had done this, and there was only one explanation. Before them, a deep rumbling came from within a dark cavern.

"My love, we must leave. This place is cursed!" Nathaniel said, a chill running up his spine. Suddenly, Alessandra kneeled over, clutching her skull. Whimpering, she feebly groped for

309

Nathaniel. He gripped her hand and held it, glancing behind her. "What do you see?" He asked, stroking her back. "I–I see…" Her back arched, and she cried out in pain. Rushing to help, he cradled her head in his hands. With their backs turned, they were vulnerable to any enemy that may still be near. In an instant, Nathaniel had his green sword out, blade shining. A rush of wind, and a rotting smell wafted his way. Covering his mouth with one hand, he inched towards the mouth's cave. Something was there, lurking in the shadows. A pair of bright, bloodthirsty eyes bloomed in the darkness.

It roared, and a spout of flames burst forth.

Chapter XV: An Unexpected Visitor

BOOM! Screams echoed within the city, and for an instant I wondered if some kind airstrike had occurred. The explosion sounded like it had come from somewhere near the Willis Tower or the Old St. Patrick's Church, about a block away.

Shuddering, David materialized by my side. I'd been wandering around Navy Pier all afternoon; gazing through the shop windows, watching folks make fools of themselves at the bars, and cheering on street performers.

Olivia had left a while ago for her audition, and I learned that before she wanted to get serious about her music career, she was a band and choir director. A normal job for a abnormal person.

Buddy's hackles raised, and he sniffed the air. Balling my hands into fists, I gave an order, "David, you stay here with me. Buddy, scout out the damage and make sure no one is harmed. Whatever's down there, it is trouble." Buddy took off like a bullet and disappeared down the street.

☾

Johnathen sped along the crowded roads, ignoring shouting pedestrians and red stoplights. "Woah, woah, slow down! Aaggh!" Aaron threw his hands in front of his face, preparing for a collision.

In the backseat, Pearl and Greyback were clawing at the seats, strapped in by the seatbelts. They were being thrown this way and that by Johnathen's spastic driving, whining. They'd been following the long, dark shadow the rest of the afternoon, into the night, and all through the next day. Startled at its sudden appearance the first time, it side swiped their vehicle and burst forward. The pair of wolves barked in delight, interested in this

311

new creature that had come upon them. Even with no idea of who or where it had come from, it was a clue. It was flying, yes, *flying*, in the same direction the Skin-changers were headed. Chicago.

After their conversation with James and hearing the shocking details, Dogo and Smith had sensed another disturbance about. Driving along on the highway, tunes blasting, they saw a huge figure gliding through the clouds.

The driver was so scared he almost crashed the car into the rails as the passenger looked on, bewildered. Aaron had pointed a finger, murmuring, "What in Aphrodite's name is *that*?"

"What?!" Johnathen had slowed the car a little, dropping down to sixty miles per hour on the freeway. Hardly anyone else was on the road that night, except for an RV and a few eighteen-wheelers.

The shadow had flown down and raced alongside their vehicle, one red eye staring through the window. It blinked and snorted and sped away, gaining altitude.

"The hell's up with that?!" Aaron cried out just as they crossed the state border.

"I don't know man, I don't know. Gods," Johnathen blanched, looking pale as a ghost. "Nekoda…she must have—dude, we have to call James! Or Will! Anybody!" Yanking the steering wheel left, the tires screeched as the car lurched around a corner.

Within hours, they'd make it.

☾

About twenty minutes had passed and Buddy had yet to return.

"C'mon!" I shouted and dashed forward with David on my heels. Bounding across the road and narrowly avoiding getting hit by an oncoming car, we edged our way through traffic. Some loud ruckus was the cause of the disaster smoking blocks away from our location. Heavy, choking smoke rose in the air, and police sirens blared to life down the busy roads.

I knew that whatever was by the Willis Tower had come for me, and me alone. I made to jaywalk across an intersection, and then I heard an all too familiar voice in my head.

☾

"Move, move, move!" Aaron's shield rattled against his back as he ran, Pearl leading the way. Johnathen was sprinting close behind, unsheathing his sword and unbuckling his cylinder weapon from his hip, all the while speaking into his walkie-talkie.

"James, you there? Cole, Mitchell, answer please! We've found the girl, I repeat, we've found the girl!" Frustrated at the silence from the other end, Johnathen zipped the device back into the bag.

"Over on the far west side of the road, by Starbucks. You see him?" A black streak darted towards them. Aaron waved. "It's Buddy! Oh my gods, it's Buddy!" Both Hellhound and wild wolf rejoiced, old friends together again after years had passed.

Greyback nipped Buddy's ear and perked his nose in the direction of the smoke. Apparently making a quiet entrance was too complicated for a lone creature of the skies.

If Dior, Cherise, Joffrey, Orpha and Nike, Jaz and Izzy were here, the men would have a whole team searching this city, and Kody would be safe in no time. For now, it was a two-man, four-beasts operation kind of deal.

Slowing to a trot, they devised a plan as they agreed on which direction the canines were going and calculated where, exactly, they were located in Chicago. Tall, glass buildings loomed above them. Skyscrapers seemed to touch the clouds with their needles, and old churches and structures were spotted here and everywhere within a certain district of Chicago. Cars honked as man and wolf dodged oncoming traffic.

313

Passing a drunkard stumbling along a place called the Blue Moon Bar & Grill, Aaron paused quickly to stare at the Satyrs and nymphs playing pool in the front windows. A small crew of demigods—or maybe Darkshadows?—wandered inside, black business suits crisp. "Hurry up, Smith!" His friend dragged him along. "Alright, Dogo!" He called back.

Buddy had Portaled in mid-step and reappeared someplace else, trying to keep the group together. He barked, and the misfit group of friends picked up their pace.

☾

"Nekoda! I know you're here, where are you? I can smell your blood!" Shadarr's voice thundered through my skull, crystal clear.

"Shadarr! Is that you making all the fuss? I'm heading towards the smoke cloud with David!" Fucking hell, Shadarr escaped? Where was Nathaniel now? Was he here, in Chicago? Had James finally arrived?

Lungs burning, I leaped over the hood of a yellow taxi, waving apologies at the driver. Growing closer to the explosion, I saw what the commotion was all about, and gasped.

Something large had smashed into the side of a building, something like a Dragon. Electrical wires had caught fire and were spitting sparks of red-hot flames around the remnants of the structure. Splintered wood and masonry caked the street, and people, coated in dust, ran away in horror.

Buddy reappeared at my side again, ears flopping. I rushed through the hole in the building and out the other side, careful to avoid stepping on nails and broken glass. Was this really Shadarr's doing; would he put innocent lives at risk for me? Why act so reckless? But there was a part of me that couldn't blame him; Shadarr couldn't even remember the last time he had seen the sun.

As soon as I made it out the other side, we turned down the closest road and cut through the traffic. I had to find Shadarr! He was probably halfway across the city, causing a major problem for civilians. Without warning, Buddy immediately Portaled again, popping up someplace else in the city.

What was I to do now?

☾

Aaron almost ran into a bus sign. Twice. The third time he did and tripped on the curb, skidding on his butt. Groaning, Johnathen pulled him to his feet as they watched the wolves continue on their way, sniffing out Nekoda.

High above, the first Dragon they'd ever lay eyes upon flew around, circling for the girl. He knew they were on the same side.

Black, scaly, and intimidating, it soared with a fifteen-foot wingspan. Small despite what the tales normally say: "Great beasts of many sizes and color, some grown to the width of ten men stacked abreast on top of one another; others as tiny as a steed, albeit built like war elephants. Muscular, strong, and hold a fearsome gaze."

Greyback threw his head back and howled before Buddy reappeared at his side. Pearl sped up, never tiring, never losing focus. The days of travel were weighing heavily on Johnathen in the cold; his face flushed, sweat dripping down his forehead.

But the Dragon took off again, and the sirens continued to sound; henceforth, he knew they had to keep moving. An officer tried to stop them as he directed the vehicles at the stoplights, but try as he might, a full-grown wolf was no match for a mortal. Both Hellhound and K9 barreled over him, whistle tweeting and limbs flailing.

"Wild animals on the loose! Two juvenile delinquencies cutting through traffic, contact the station!" The policeman shouted into his radio when they left him fuming in the middle of the street.

"That's bullcrap!" Aaron mouthed. Nearing the destruction, both boys stopped in their tracks, chests heaving. Running through the smoke, all three mammals were sprinting in a new direction, barking wildly.

☾

The baying of dogs alerted me that someone else was close by. Glancing to and fro, I spotted pedestrians screaming and panicking. David kept his eyes out for Buddy. My heart felt like it was about to explode out of my chest, and my bandaged ankle throbbed. Tears leaked from the corners of my eyes from the thick smoke, and my sore throat made it even more difficult to breathe. Flames licked at the walls of the building.

I searched for a fire hydrant on the sidewalk, spying a red one a good quarter-mile away. The firemen should be arriving soon and use it to douse the fire before it got out of control. Faint sirens echoed from a far corner of the city.

Bounding over to the hydrant, I focused all my attention on that one thing. If I can control fire, then just maybe, *maybe…*

I held my hands out in front of me, palms up. It was worth a shot. David supervised a few feet away, anxious as ever. As I began to concentrate, my stomach churned, and I felt a tightening in my chest.

Minutes later, we had no such luck. The fire was still blazing, consuming the rest of the structure. "C'mon, c'mon," muttering words of encouragement under my breath, sweat started to bead on the back of my neck. When I cracked open my eyes, two wolves stood before me with Buddy. One was a silvery gray color, the other a white and black dappled coat.

"Umm," David teleported back and forth, scanning the area. "Hey Nekoda, I think that's our clue to skedaddle!" the wolves appeared to frighten him.

"Just a moment…" I tried again, squeezing my eyes shut, concentrating on the swish of water underneath our feet in the sewers system and the quick pounding of my heart.

Soon, I was lost in the calmness of my mind and the depths of oblivion, lost to everything. I zoned everything out—the beeping vehicles spitting out their toxic fumes, the businessmen and tourists hurrying to a safe underhanging, the ringing of shop bells, and the clicking of heels—everything faded into the background.

For a brief second, my ears popped and my muscles ceased, emotions swirling around in my head like a blast of hot and cold air. Guilt, pain, sadness, anguish, love, and hope. Within an instant, my eyes snapped open and I thrust my hands upward, toward the sky.

With a gurgling roar, gallons upon gallons of water gushed out of the hydrant like a geyser, sprinkling down to soak the Chicagoans. Channeling my inner Avatar, I stamped my foot forward and *threw* the water upwards in a miniature tsunami. It roared down the rest of the street in waves, crashing into the buildings and soaking strangers. Steam rose and sparks crackled, but the backside of the building was drenched—as was the fire!

As I made a move to celebrate, I was overwhelmed with exhaustion, and pins and needles raced up my legs. I collapsed to my knees, sucking in a lungful of air. The rest of my energy was nearly spent. I think yoga would be extremely beneficial for me in this current situation. Or a fifteen-hour nap.
Buddy licked my face, egging me on. Struggling to rise, I looked up, scanning the crowd for David. Police sirens wailed closer, and my head was consumed by a massive headache.

That's when I heard the voices.

☾

Johnathen was exhilarated.

She was so tantalizingly close. Running halfway across the city, block after block, hadn't entirely drained him yet. Exhaustion was replaced with eagerness and joy. This was it; they had actually found her. After days of non-stop worry and a thirst for adventure,

317

they had discovered someone and something incredible. If anything would perk Alpha Lockwood out of his depression, it was *her*. Kody Jones. And more or less, the existence of an extinct species come back alive.

Alongside him, Aaron's face was flushed beet tomato. The stank smell of sweat drifted off of him. But even Johnathen could sense his true feelings. A slow smile crept across his face as they stumbled past the damage the frantic Dragon had caused. A mile off at the end of the street, four blurry figures stood.

Two wolves.

One Hellhound.

One somewhat translucent bloody spirit.

One girl.

☾

"Hey, hey you! Nekoda Jones!" My head whipped up at the sound of my name. Nathaniel and Tony immediately came to mind, but this voice sounded much lighter, friendlier, and Nathaniel would have opted to take me by surprise. A second voice called out, this one taking on a goofy tone.

"You're not dead, are you? Who's your ghostly friend?" He asked, footsteps growing closer. My vision was blurred around the edges, as if I was running through rain. Then they came into focus, two handsome, weapon wielding individuals. Eyes wide, I scrambled backwards. Was this...*them*? Johnathen and Aaron? Or some fools meant to recapture me? But no, no, Buddy would have warned us.

"David, how can they see you? I thought..." Scowling, I inched backwards and rose to my feet, movements slow.

"I guess some people can, others can't. But it does depend if you've experienced death, only those you have can see the dead."

"Hold on, stop, don't take another step. Stop," I coughed and held a hand up in warning. Both men continued to edge closer until they stopped a few yards from where the wolves and my companions and I were waiting.

"It's okay, we're not going to hurt you." The first man piped up. They looked no older than twenty-three. Ash and dust was caught in the dirty blonde hairs of the man who had spoken first, bright blue eyes studying my every move. A small, shiny cylinder was buckled to his belt. His company had sea-green, almost teel blue eyes and hair so blonde it reminded me of the sun. He kept fidgeting with the sword in his left hand.

I put up my defenses, double-checking if they really were on my side. "Right. And who are you supposed to be?" I snapped, stuffing my right hand into my pocket where James' crumpled note rest. Placing my other hand on Buddy's head, we put our backs to the wall. David stayed where he was, hovering over a manhole.

"Oh, uhm, I'm Johnathen. Johnathen Dogo." His eyes darted to his friend.

Clearing his throat, Johnathen fingered his sword. A double-edged blade, constructed of fresh Imperial gold, or maybe Celestial bronze. A celestial bronze and steel shield was wrapped around his wrist and a silver cylinder strapped to his belt. Both strangers carried loaded bags on their backs.

"Pleased to meet you, I'm Aaron Smith. These fellows here are our faithful friends, Pearl and Greyback." He pointed to the wolves; heads cocked at the sound of their names. "And who might you be?" Aaron gave a sly smile.

I took a deep, calming breath before deigning to respond. "Nekoda. Nekoda Jones. This is my Hellhound, Buddy, as you may or may not know him. And my friend, David." Tail wagging, my dog nuzzled up to me. "Also, I suppose I should present you with this." I handed him James' letter. Aaron eyed it before shoving it in his pocket. Sheathing their swords, they stepped forward. Johnathen gave me his hand, and I took it.

"Listen, you may not trust us at first. But we promise you'll be safe where we're going,"

319

I exhaled, "Camp Wolf." Both Aaron and Johnathen looked startled by my answer, and then loosed a relieved sigh.

Aaron beamed. "So, you know."

"I do. And James, William, Alex and Jacob? Are they real, too?" David grasped my shoulder, his hand floating through my collarbone.

"Yes, and they're the best friends I could ask for. We'd give our lives to protect one another."

Holding back joyous tears, I nodded. Johnathen gave me the small cylinder that was attached to his belt. "Click it," he instructed. I did. To my surprise, it extended into a four-foot, shining spear. The weapon felt light but not too heavy in my hands. I studied the material up close, and touched the sharp tip.

"Wow, thanks," Nervously we stepped closer until David could have floated through Aaron's chest. The animals sniffed one another, familiar.

"I figured our swords may be too heavy for you to lift because of your size." He paused at the face I made. "No offense, of course. You should have a weapon to protect yourself with, even with a creature as great as Bud." Johnathen winked. Aaron tapped him on the back.

"Hey, dude. We should get moving, and fast," he jerked a thumb behind him. "Because I do not want to explain the destruction done to the cops. Come Kody, let's hurry along." Aaron hefted his sword and shield, bouncing on the balls of his feet.

I tsked, scowling, "Don't call me that." Taken aback by my response, Aaron shrugged his shoulders and looked away.

"Sorry, *Nekoda*. I have a habit of shortening people's names straight away. We know you've been through quite a lot." Before I could reply, the ground shook with the force of an earthquake's tremor.

Johnathen froze, and a strange sound came from Aaron. Buddy, yipping happily, tore off again. Turning around, I recognized the black Dragon with the glittering scales and deep

320

ruby eyes. Finally, finally, I allowed the tears to fall. Wiping my cheek, I breathed in and spread my arms in welcome, gleeful.

"Ah, I guess I forgot to introduce you to my Dragon. Johnathen, Aaron, Pearl, Greyback. This is Shadarr," The men stood, open-mouthed. *"Hello, dear friend. Nice to see you again."* I spoke in my mind. With a snort, the Dragon flapped his powerful wings in greeting at the newcomers.

I genuinely smiled as Shadarr tossed his head back, and roared.

☾

"Maybe it was cursed by some old wizard or something," Maggie suggested. Logan laughed.

"It's probably one of the artifacts Gandalf never knew that little man had in his possession, unlike the ring, and they never got around to destroying it."

"Or it popped out of Narnia."

Logan rolled her eyes. "Yeah, if Gandalf was an actual being, and if wizards or evil demons or magical dimensions actually exist."

"Man, I'd love to see the day when scientists create a machine that zapped you out of reality and into a book. Because frankly, reality sucks!" Maggie sighed, looking glum.

"You're telling me, sis." It was a quarter till nine, and the house was quiet. The television was left on in the living room and the front porch light too, warding off any troublemakers that would take advantage of two teenage girls. The Hendrix's had an excellent guard dog and a feisty feline that would claw your face off if upset. And if anything went haywire, they could always run to the neighbor's house, the Collins.

The polished, wooden object sat before the two friends. The studded jewel on the top of the box sparkled, and the silver and gold linings on the box only added more to its beauty. "If this box is so invincible, then what could possibly be inside it that no one would want disturbed?" Logan mumbled, seeking suggestions from someone who knew as much as herself.

"I have no idea. But let's just think about the facts, and run through what we know so far. Let's see...the Jones' were like any other family," Maggie started, scratching her head.

"Clara Jones was a librarian, and Kyle was a police officer." Logan added, thinking hard.

"Their daughter was kidnapped and no one knows why," "Both parents were killed and for reasons unknown the captors did not opt to take hostages."

"Nobody has heard word from the intruders, and people don't expect to find a ransom note soon..." Maggie trailed off.

"So that means they don't want Kody to be found. Strangers broke into her house and murdered her parents, but left her alive. There's not a single clue as to why or where they'd take a child if it isn't for money, and police and fire departments can't figure out if there's actually some deeper explanation to this mystery. Possibly an old family feud or conflicts between certain people that grew overtime."

Maggie pouted. "At the crime scene there was but a single clue or sign of evidence. Plus, Nekoda never mentioned this item to us, did she?"

"I can't recall. But it's got to mean something if this was buried in the Jones' backyard for some time." She snapped her fingers. "What if—" Logan never got to finish before the lights flickered and popped, and the power went out.

Stumbling around the bedroom, Logan Hendrix relocated the mysterious box and slid it under her mattress. With one hand on the wall, she felt for Maggie's, and they guided each other out into the hallway.

"Hey, what happened?" Maggie asked.
"Power outage, seems like. Yet the storm died down an hour ago."

There was the sound of glass breaking and swearing as her friend cried out. "Crap! Oh my word, sorry Logan, but I think you may have to get a new lamp." Sighing, she tread around the broken pieces.

Logan picked her way forward until the moonlight shining through the kitchen windows made for enough light to head for the pantry. Fumbling, she grasped the handle of two flashlights. Handing one to Maggie, she clicked it on. "Follow me," Logan said, and wound through the kitchen and out into the main living room. JJ and Bangle were still asleep on the leather couch, dirty plates and cups sitting on the glass table.

As she banged her knee on the corner of the coffee table and swore, Maggie peered through the windows. "Hmm, seems like everyone else's power is out in the neighborhood." Chewing her lip, Logan pulled out her phone and sent a message to Anthony. He replied a minute later.

"Couldn't we just turn the cable box back on or something? It should be in the basement." suggested Maggie.

"I don't know. Besides, I've never known how to work it. Even if we could find it, my parents wouldn't want me jacking with it. And Anthony just contacted our electrician, so he'll be stopping by shortly."

"Oh, well..." Shining the flashlight so the beam illuminated her friend's face, Logan saw the wide-eyed look she gave her. "What is it?" She questioned, a tone of caution in her voice.

"L-look," Shaking, Maggie pointed a finger at the TV set. The screen was glowing blue. Running across the screen in bold letters, the message faded in and out. "Uh, i-is your house haunted?" She whispered, nerves rattled.

I TOLD YOU WE WERE COMING.

At a loss for words, Logan went to stand in front of the TV. She smacked the top of the box, making the screen jump and flicker. The message immediately disappeared, and a second later a more intimidating one than the first rolled across the screen.

Maggie froze. "You're not going to pull a *Poltergeist* scene on me and place your hands on the glass and tell me 'they're here', or something wacky?"

GIRLS LIKE YOU NEVER LISTEN, DO THEY, LOGAN?

"No, no. This is just all so... weird." Logan muttered, shocked, reading the same eight words over and over again. "The fact that your TV knows your name or the fact that someone's out to get us?" snorted Maggie.

"I don't know, you pick." She snapped, stern. Afraid of what would happen next, the girls jumped onto the couch and shook the animals awake. Hissing, Bangle jumped up and skittered down the hall. JJ yawned and growled, rolling over to stare at the TV. Shushing him, Logan tried the remote. She pressed the OFF button. The blue image still glowed. Frowning, she clicked the ON button. Nothing.

"Dammit, forget this! C'mon Maggie, let's head down to the basement."

"No way! We should go over to the Collins, see if they're home."

Worried, Logan eyed the TV. "What about Bangle and JJ?"

"They're animals, they will be fine. But us, on the other hand..." Maggie stuck her chin out in the direction of the TV.

"Fine, but—"

Behind her, the television made a loud buzzing sound, like that of a thousand bees, and a new message blinked to life.

MAGGIE AND LOGAN, IF YOU WANT ANSWERS ABOUT YOUR FRIEND, I SUGGEST YOU GIVE ME WHAT I WANT.

Screaming, the girls rushed to the front door, decision made. JJ barked and approached the plasma screen, tail tucked between his legs. "Fuck this demon shit, I'm out!" Logan yelped, frantically keeping pace with Maggie. The flashlight beams bobbed as the two teenagers made a mad dash for the door. Unbeknownst to them, someone was waiting. Feet from the painted escape hatch, the doorbell rang.

Logan tumbled backwards into Maggie, flailing her arms. The flashlights dropped to the ground and rolled away. From the other room, they heard the cat yowl and shriek as JJ frantically barked. Scrambling to her feet, Maggie put a finger to her lips. Logan nodded at the door and gulped. Realizing what she was about to do, she made signs with her hands and mouthed a few angry words.

Boldly, Logan shook her head and again pointed at the door. Her best friend scowled and inched closer. Hesitantly, Logan sucked in a breath and gripped the doorknob.

The door creaked open a few inches and the girls peeked out, tensed.

"Hello?" She squeaked. Standing before them, a large man was waiting on the front porch, inches from the door. In the moonlight, the girls could see every chiseled feature. He was intimidatingly tall and wore a long, dark coat that flapped in the breeze. His golden hair shone in the moonlight, and his hands were clenched at his sides, muscles taut. If he wanted, the man could have broken the door down, Logan had no doubt.

In the flash of lightning, the stranger's face morphed into a devilish smile.

"Good evening, girls. Going somewhere?" His voice came out silky smooth, yet sharp as glass. Flinching, Maggie and Logan both had the same idea. With a quick nod from her friend, Logan realized they were in silent agreement.

Instantly, the girls slammed the door closed in the man's face—but he was faster. Sticking a foot in the wedge of the door, he flung it open with his hand, nearly tearing it from its hinges.

Looking on in shock and absolute horror, Logan stole a glance into the living room where JJ was cowering under the table. Bangle had crept under, too, his green eyes glowing in the dark. A strangled hiss escaped his throat.

325

So much for a guard dog. Her pets had more sense than she ever did.

This man, who was clearly not the electrician Anthony had called, had a dangerous feel and definite look about him that made her shiver. Neither of them could stop him from stepping past the threshold and entering the house.

"So, tell me. Which one of you can give me what I want?" the frames on the walls shook with the force of the slamming door.

Voice quivering, Maggie took one step to the left. "W-what do you mean?" Next to her, Logan stiffly moved another small step away.

"Don't play stupid, I know you have it!" He barked. "Now give me the *book!*" Stepping forward, the girls tried to hide the fear that was plainly written on their faces.

Something isn't right here, Logan thought. A light bulb went off in her head, as clear as someone had just thrown one at her.

The box!
That stupid, frustrating box was the answer! For the most mysterious of reasons, that's what he was looking for! The object inside was what this man wanted, and that was why Nekoda was missing! Officer Mills had gotten that bizarre call from Kody for a reason; she had mentioned something about the intruders looking for a book, and somehow, this stranger knew that they were now holding the object he's been searching for.

The man flicked back the side of his long coat, revealing an object that flashed emerald green at his waist. At least, she thought it was green.

Were they about to experience the same fate Kody had? Was this the very man who hurt their friend, and the only family she ever had? Was it possible that Kody had been murdered, too, and her body disposed of in some wormy hole in the center of a corn field, having been pulled from the wreckage of the Jones' house fire? Or perhaps she was still alive, and was kicking and cursing and fighting for her life at this very moment in time?

Cold, paralyzing fear struck Logan's heart. Beside her, Maggie swallowed a scream.

As the man lunged forward to grab them, the she noticed something incredibly peculiar and wondered if Maggie noticed it as well.

His eyes.

They were black!

To Be Continued

ACKNOWLEDGMENTS

There is no better feeling than having finally completed something you've been crafting for the past five years. I've spent many nights stressing over this novel, and the day has come for my book baby to be in another's hands. As a seventeen-year-old junior in high school, it's very difficult to find time to read or write, as homework and extracurricular activities take up much of my free time. But over the course of five years, I have managed to complete the final draft of *The Hunted*, and the second draft of *The Camp* (sequel to book baby #1), and am currently in the midst of writing *The Dawn of War* (third book in the *All Powerful* series).

I have many people to thank for helping guide me along on this journey. First and foremost, my grandparents. Donald and Joy Goff were proud supporters of my work, from the very first sloppy manuscript a twelve-year-old girl wrote up on her mom's old laptop, up until the last time I was in their presence.

I also have my family, friends, and the wonderful people I've met through bookstagram to thank for their interest and support in my novels. Without their help and advice, or tolerating my constant questions of "Does this sound right?", "What do you think of this part?", and "Should I really shorten this fifty-page chapter?". I couldn't have done it. Thank you, guys.

And of course, my utmost gratitude to Evelyn Buress (dubbed the President of Awesome Art), the person who illustrated the cover for this book. You should totally check them out if you want your mind blown by some really cool art things! (That part definitely wasn't scripted by The Great Evelyn™ herself, ha ha.) You can find Evelyn via instagram at @the.nervous.artist., or email her at e.burr1030@gmail.com.

In the meantime, I will be editing book baby #2 and preparing for it to be out in the world! Stay tuned.

—Sarah

ABOUT THE AUTHOR

This is Sarah J. Simon's debut novel. In her spare time, she enjoys reading, writing, fawning over her pet guinea pig, shopping, fangirling over Supernatural and EXO, and watching endless BTS content while simultaneously jamming out to them. For more bookish updates, you can follow her on her bookstagram account at @thehuntednephilim.

ALL POWERFUL: THE HUNTED

Made in the USA
Lexington, KY
17 June 2019